THE LAND
BEYOND THE RAIN

Mary Male

particularly like the quotes @ beginning of chapters and how they relate to the story told in them

For Tina and Aoífe

"Believe that a further shore is reachable from here."
—Seamus Heaney

CHAPTER 1

ERIN

"We never know the love of a parent till we become parents ourselves."
—Henry Ward Beecher

Erin tucked a lock of her brunette hair streaked with the beginnings of gray behind one ear, looked up from the pile of her students' projects and sighed. "I don't know what to do about Axl. He just gives up—he writes a few words, draws a picture and scribbles "sorry.""

Katie rolled her eyes at her mom and pushed aside her own school project with relief, knocking over a stack of books with a clatter that made them both flinch. "If you worry about every single student like that, you'll never get done. And what kind of name *is* that, anyway? No wonder he's screwed up!"

Like many teen-agers, Katie's supply of empathy was limited. "Isn't it time for dinner yet? I'm starving!"

"Don't even start! You know how much it means to me to be a really good teacher the kind of teacher that students remember forever, the one who makes all the difference in a kid's life. I've worked too hard…"

"Oh, please, you think I don't know about that? You think I'm just another ungrateful teenager looking for attention—you just don't understand what *my* life is like. "Katie rolled her eyes and glanced down at her cell phone, which she knew would annoy her mom.

Something in Katie's pout got under Erin's skin, dragged her away from their comfortable San Francisco home, back to her own meager childhood in Northern Ireland in the midst of the Troubles between Catholics and Protestants, where food was often scarce and her mum closed herself off in her room, too depressed to get out of bed. Porridge was a feast, and… "No!" she screamed silently. "I don't have to go down that road anymore!"

Easier said than done. It seemed such a short time ago when Erin herself was a child, flowing auburn hair and brown eyes, bursting with energy and curiosity, a heart full of compassion for even the smallest creatures and a love for Harry Potter. While she shared her mum Tracey's devotion to the natural world, Erin looked nothing like her—her mum's darker skin and jet-black, straight hair was a contrast to her own wavy, lighter-than air reddish-brown locks that resisted scrunchies and braids. She must look more like her dad—but who was he?

Erin's earliest memories were full of highs and lows—the menagerie of pets, cats, dogs, birds, fish…taking the place of human family members. Her mum Tracey was a complicated mix of Texan by birth and Irish by desire and by heritage, daring and frightened; vulnerable and fearless, and fiercely devoted, scarily so, but with an eerie capacity to detach.

Although curious by nature, Erin had learned not to press too hard for family stories, Erin knew her family was different—just the two of them, after all, and shame attached. Her mum's funny American accent stuck out in the Irish Catholic neighborhood, as did the absent father. Already feeling different as a Catholic in Protestant-dominated Northern Ireland, she chafed under the bullying and teasing (and even worse, the silent shunning) of the neighborhood busybodies.

She hated moving from one squalid council flat to another. She felt suffocated by the dark, cramped, and airless spaces. Scrimping and pinching pennies to get by was normal in their world, but the sense of dread of something awful hanging over their heads was even worse.

But when Tracey's mood was up, they soared together— imagining a fairy tale world, playing dress up with the dogs and cats, who grudgingly went along. "Let's have a Pooh day," Tracey would proclaim, and their worries would disappear, replaced by a riot of tea parties and picnics, giggles and snorts, as the two made funny faces at passersby, filled poster paper with paintings and drawings, and pretended to be posh ladies or tie-dyed hippies.

Other days, a dark cloud would descend out of nowhere, and Tracey could barely get ou   d. They seemed to last forever, no food in the house, no reli   n the weight of the sadness that settled over the household   ense fog. Even the dogs and cats sank back into their hiding   knowing what was coming.

Erin did her best to car   he household, sharing her stale cheese sandwich with Come   black cat who slept at her feet, and Jazzbo, the Jack Russell,   knew better than to pester for treats or walks when the wall   d in.

Erin, who was sure she w   n knowing how to read (she couldn't remember a time whe   couldn't—just like her mum), pulled library books from the   and methodically arranged them from most to least favo   he read aloud in hopes of bringing her mum out of the de   Or sometimes she arranged the books by color, enjoying a bo   that looked like a rainbow. Sometimes she went by author's   me, as though each author was a personal friend (as indee   felt that way to her) or category; she learned that she ha   able to entertain herself. She got out her colored pencils an   e her own illustrations of favorite characters, waiting to show   to Tracey when the time was right, as hard as it was to gues   n that might be. And try as she might, Erin couldn't chase Tr   clouds away.

And now, here Erin was in anoth   t of the world, with her daughter Katie, who reminded her   self in so many ways, trying to make sense of the world she lived in

CHAPTER 2

JAMES

"I am opposing a social order in which it is possible for one man who does absolutely nothing that is useful to amass a fortune of hundreds of millions of dollars, while millions of men and women who work all the days of their lives secure barely enough for a wretched existence."
—Eugene Debs

The walls were closing in.

James, a strapping energetic twenty-two-year-old Ulsterman full of dreams and energy, was losing hope. The glens of Donegal, where he'd courted his beautiful Kathleen, seemed to have no future, but the snares and traps of the past. The family farm was going under. The whole country seemed to be going under. "An Gorta Mór," the Great Hunger, they called it.

In truth, "family farm" was not an accurate description of their home in Rathmullan. James' family had no ownership stake in it. Every family member worked for the benefit of the absentee landlord who lived in England, and most of what little income the farm could provide from its few dairy cows, chickens, and plot of land for potatoes, went to a local middleman, who made sure the English aristocrat received his money. The middleman, of course, was looking out for his own share, and had no interest in investing in the land or its people. The rent could be raised at a moment's notice, or the family could be turned out for the slightest infraction or whim. James' hatred the English beyond reason.

As a young boy, all James knew was that his family and all the other local Catholic families worked from dawn to dark, in the rain and the wind and never had enough bread to eat. He felt lucky, all things considered. His older brothers had either died of disease or hunger (the two went together) or moved away. Only his sister, remained, helping their mam with the house chores and wee ones. Although his mam was just over forty when James was born, she moved like a woman of 95.

That was what he'd thought—until that day he'd passed in front of the small market in town and suddenly, everything changed. His pa had sent him to try to sell a few eggs from the chickens that remained from a diminishing flock. Sometimes there wasn't even enough food to feed the chickens, and sometimes James had to sell one his beauties when they were especially desperate. James was reluctant, knowing the market owner was a staunch Protestant, but money was money.

A teen-aged girl several years younger than James was helping out at the counter. He noticed her sparkly eyes and beautiful complexion. He studied his worn shoes, cleared his throat, and mumbled, "we've a few eggs to sell, if you have a need."

To his surprise, she smiled warmly. "I'll see what we can do," she said. "Wait here." James could feel his heart beat strangely. Then he overheard a voice from the back of the store. "And what would I be wanting of those papist eggs and the eejits who gather them? Send that scum and his trash away."

When she returned, she took a few coins out of her apron and reaching for the eggs. "*He's* the eejit," she whispered, handing him the money. She winked, put the eggs in the box with others, and before disappearing around the corner to the rear of the store, waved good--bye.

He went back home, replaying in his thoughts the smile, the kind words, and the flirtatious wink.

After the next day's work was done, he went to the docks. The fishy ocean smells, the wind and the waves, and the energy of the fishermen after a successful haul of cod and mackerel fed his soul. As he crossed the last street before the wharf, he blinked--the red-headed girl from the market was pushing an empty cart, struggling a little to get it over the cobblestones and uneven pavement. He quickened his pace, approached from behind, and cleared his throat to get her attention.

"Beg pardon, miss, looks like you could use a bit of a hand with that wagon..."

She looked startled, as he approached.

"Why yes—that would be quite gallant of you, thanks! This old wagon gives me fits sometimes."

"Where are you bound? I'm surprised to see you out of the market," he inquired, hoping to find out more about her routines and habits.

"Our shop boy was sick today, so I'm bound for the boats to bring some cod back to the market. I hate being stuck behind the counter, anyway, so I was glad to get an excuse to leave," she responded. "It's hard work, but the market is so boring. Besides, you know what my pa is like, so I try to stay away as much as I can. What about you? What brings you down to the harbor?"

"If you think working in the market is boring, you should try mucking pigs and digging potatoes," he grumbled. He showed her his calloused hands. "I love it down by the docks, hearing the fishermen's stories and wondering about life on the sea. I come down here every chance I get."

James took the handle of the cart from Kathleen's hands, and they continued the bumpy walk along the streets leading to the wharf. James considered what he'd learned about her.

As they reached the dock, Kathleen took the cart back, getting back to her task at hand, and said gaily, "Maybe I'll see you down here again sometime!"

"Oh, I hope so!"

James trotted off home, a bounce in his step, whistling a folk tune.

CHAPTER 3

TRACEY

"There is no despair so absolute as that which comes with the first moments of our first great sorrow, when we have not yet known what it is to have suffered and be healed, to have despaired and have recovered hope."
—George Eliot

Tracey's grandmother, Oona, was frantic. She'd dropped in on her son and his wife Rita, and found their south Austin house unlocked and empty —except for two-year old Tracey, chewing on an empty pack of Marlboros and looking up wide-eyed at her grandmother. "Where's your mom? Where's your dad? Spit that nasty thing out!" she barked, sending the toddler into a torrent of tears. Temporarily chastened by the child's panic, Oona tried to calm herself. With no idea how long the child had been alone, and no idea where her parents might be, she needed a plan…and fast.

First things first: Oona picked the little girl up gently, comforting her as best she could, and trying not to gag as she felt the soggy, poopy diaper that had been on who knew how long. Looking around for a replacement diaper in the bedroom, she gasped as she saw a pile of used syringes on the dresser and a wastebasket of empty Lone Star beer bottles. She shook her head sadly, remembering her own long-ago battles with alcohol and her own sad marriage. She drifted momentarily into a tragic past, before being jerked back into the uncertain present.

"Diapers? Where are your diapers, little one? Show me!" Tracey stopped crying momentarily, looked up irresistibly at her grandma, and said "Di-po!"

"Yes, yes, yes—help me find a clean di-po!" Oona urged.

Tracey smiled and toddled unsteadily over to the closet, squishy diaper making her look a little bow-legged. She reached for the doorknob and struggled to pull the closet door open. "This is a child who's used to doing things for herself," Oona noted silently and a little sadly, as she pulled open the door. A single clean diaper remained in an empty bail of Pampers next to a pile of filthy clothes, smelling of urine, vomit, and sweat. Oona grabbed the clean diaper and quickly shut the door tight, her heart pounding, as the reality of this precious little girl's life began to sink in.

"Time for a clean diaper, Tracey, and then we'll get you something to eat." Oona wrapped Tracey up in a towel that was a little damp but at least clean—at least by comparison to what she'd seen in the closet. Placing her gently on the bed, Oona cleaned her off, relieved to find the little girl relatively free of diaper rash, so perhaps things were not as bad as she'd feared.

With Tracey in her arms, Oona went to the kitchen. She groaned as she saw the piles of dirty dishes in the sink. Her groans turned to gasps as she opened the door to the refrigerator. Half empty soda containers, left-over fast food boxes revealed husks of moldy food, and little else. No milk, nothing suitable for a toddler. Now what?

Oona shut the refrigerator door with disgust, put the little girl in some semi-clean clothes, and took a moment to leave a note for her troubled son and his wife. Grandma and granddaughter headed for the grocery.

Holding her in her lap, Oona carefully navigated to the nearest market to get some basics—cereal, bananas, applesauce, oatmeal, and some jars of baby food. Tracey punched the buttons on the radio until she found a station with Willie Nelson, and she grinned and sang along. Oona hadn't been in close touch with Tracey's parents—she herself had not been the best parent when her son was growing up, and sometimes it was just too painful to see history repeat itself in her son's family.

At the grocery, Tracey sat happily in the grocery cart, flirting shamelessly with every adult she encountered. With her dark curls, liquid brown eyes and long eyelashes, she could have been a model on a baby food container. "Peep-eye," she called out to the woman behind them in the checkout line, hiding her eyes then popping out with a giggle and a smile.

Oona was reminded of her own mother, Mamaw, whose father had emigrated from Ireland and had had nine children who'd adored her. How lucky she'd been to have such a loving and inspirational parent, who had managed the circus of kids and made sure each of them aimed for greatness and looked after each other. And how grateful her mother had seen her at her best and stood by her as she fought her way back from her worst, with her sister Ella's help.

Oona had her accomplishments—she'd been a beautiful model at Marshall Field's in Chicago and married a G-man in the Al Capone era of the 30s. Their lives were glamorous for a time, until too much glamour led to too much drinking, too much spending, and too much drama. At least she'd been able to turn her life around, with help from her baby sister, Ella, who'd dragged Oona back from the abyss after the suicide of her husband. Ella had gotten her to AA and a new life as an elementary school teacher.

Oona leaned down and hugged the little vamp, giving her a big kiss. "Sugars for Tracey" she cooed.

"Sugars!" cackled Tracey, as Oona bent down to kiss each of her granddaughter's ears.

The grocery checker grinned at Oona and Tracey as she rang up the purchases and put them in a bag. "That's the cutest baby I ever did see," she said. "And I see a ton of babies come into this store. You are one lucky grandma to have a movie star like that one!"

"Don't I know it," said Oona. Oona's heart melted to see the effect Tracey had on those around her. She knew she was going to have to take some drastic steps to save her granddaughter, fearing that there were no steps drastic enough to save her son and daughter-in-law.

Oona maneuvered the cart with the toddler to the car and unloaded the grocery bags, taking from one of the bags a small carton of animal crackers and some chocolate milk. "What a treat I've got for you, young lady, for being such a good sport in the store!"

Tracey held the container of chocolate milk in one hand and a cookie in the other, big smile on her cherubic face. Perhaps she was thinking "Now *this* is the way I want my life to be!"

Oona pulled into the driveway of the rented duplex where Tracey lived with her family. The place looked almost as neglected on the outside as it did on the inside, with paint peeling, a raggedy screen door, and a mostly dead lawn with remnants of flowers in pots Oona had given them to brighten up the outside.

Climbing up the steps, Oona looked sadly at the fireman's jacket, hanging on a hook forlornly in the entranceway. Jack, Tracey's dad, had been injured in a car wreck coming home late from a bar. Something about that wreck had sucked all the hope and ambition out of him, and he just never made it back to the firehouse. Nowadays, he worked odd jobs, mowing lawns or working in construction when he could find the energy. Rita, Jack's wife, worked part-time as a hairdresser. Between the two of them, they could barely afford their rent, much less food and the necessities for a little girl. Then once Jack started drinking, he and Rita spent more on beer and cigarettes than they did on food. They fell behind on the rent. And then came the drugs. Then came the fights—about money, about Tracey, about drugs, about everything.

Oona got little sleep; she felt so helpless as she watched the gradual slide of the little family go from one setback to another. Giving them money clearly didn't work, because the money often got used up before the rent, utilities, or food were even paid. Going to the grocery was a short-term band-aid, and Oona knew it. Hell, she had lived it in her own life, until Ella rescued her. But she was going to try to do something to help her little grandbaby; she just didn't know what it was.

As Oona and Tracey put the groceries in the refrigerator and on the shelves, the front door slammed, and Jack called out a cheery "Hey, Ma! Hey, baby girl!"

"Hey, yourself, Jack. Where in hell have you been, and where's Rita? Tracey was here all by herself when I stopped by. Anything could have happened! I've been worried sick, and there's no food or diapers in the house." Oona knew that yelling and blaming her son would lead nowhere, but she couldn't help it. Why couldn't he see what she saw—his life wasting away and his beautiful baby girl at such risk?

"You want to help out, Ma? Why don't *you* take the little girl? Rita's gone off with her no-good friends, and I'm left holding the bag. I'm in pain, I'm hurting, Ma, can't you see that? Can't you understand? You, of all people, should understand about pain! I'm in no shape to be a dad right now; I never even wanted to *be* a dad in the first place."

Jack's handsome face contorted with grief, and he began to cry. "I need help right now, Ma. I'll be getting some work soon, and things will change." Oona resisted the temptation to give him a hug, write him a check, or any of the other things she'd tried before. She knew better than to believe the addict's words, but her heart went out to him, and even more, to her beautiful granddaughter.

"I saw those needles, Jack. I know I won't be able to help you, because you won't help yourself. But I'm not going to let my granddaughter drown in your despair. She deserves so much better than that!"

"And what did *I* deserve? A mother who cared more about her looks and her career than her own kids? A father who went after the mob but got bought out by Capone? Coming home to find his blown-out brains all over the kitchen table, his gun and the pathetic note. "I did my best," the note said, "but I can't stand it anymore." Don't you dare judge me! You weren't there! You were never there!"

"Maybe I *will* take the little girl! I know I made plenty of mistakes in my life, but you have no right to judge me, any more than you don't want me to judge you. I'm sober now, a respected teacher living with my sister and doing fine. I'm here, and I want to help. If that means taking Tracey and finding a better life for her, I'll do it. Don't you dare leave her alone, do you hear me?

CHAPTER 4

JAMES

"Yes: I am a dreamer. For a dreamer is one who can only find his way by moonlight, and his punishment is that he sees the dawn before the rest of the world."
—Oscar Wilde

The chance encounter at the docks led to other encounters, less based luck, but more on creative ways to spend time together outside the eyes of Kathleen's protective father. Kathleen and James held hands as they walked in the glens among the shady trails and gurgling streams, humming Irish folk tunes. James woke earlier in the mornings and worked longer days to make time to meet this spirited, warm-hearted girl. Kathleen had fewer family responsibilities, but she was in school and then needed in the market. She told her family she was tutoring younger children after school, but instead, she would steal off to the quiet and beauty of the Donegal countryside.

He'd fallen under the spell of that red-haired beauty, and his tender heart opened itself to her gentle but determined spirit. Her family, Protestant through and through, had no use for the Catholic boy with no prospects except good looks and ambition, no family fortune, in a land where people, both Catholic and Protestant, were starving.

James worried about her mother's most recent attempt to match her with a suitable husband at a church social. Kathleen giggled.

"He didn't laugh at my jokes, and he hated my poetry," she explained. "He was a terrible dancer, and he had no interest in learning!" James knew She had no intention of getting stuck at home with too many children; she'd told him she wanted a life of her own, full of ideas, adventures, and time to write!

James could see that his mother had too many young ones at home and not enough land. What land there was produced so few potatoes and fewer cows, and not enough milk. Only a matter of time, it seemed to James, and that time was running out.

James missed his older brothers, two of whom had gone out with the boats and never returned in torrents and storms, two others who were on the way to drinking themselves to death after giving up their young dreams. James had felt protected from some family responsibilities, since he wasn't the eldest son, although he felt a huge responsibility for his mam and his sisters. James watched his dad grow old and sick before his time and wondered what he wanted for his remaining son.

James hated his father for his relentless belittling of his mother, whose weariness with child-bearing broke James's heart. The teachings of the Church about obedience and procreation left him cold. He had no use for the priests who primly taught the church's doctrine, paying no attention to the impact those doctrines had on his people. What did Father Michael know about children? What did he know about what it meant to be a mother over and over again?

James's disgust about life at home was tempered by his growing affection for Kathleen. He began to ignore the hopelessness his soul suffered at home; he threw himself into his work on the farm. His increased productivity earned him more time to himself…time to look for private places he and Kathleen could meet.

His favorite spot was the abandoned Carmelite Friary, built in 1516, later occupied by a Protestant bishop before falling into ruin. The irony of an oasis in a place of worship used by both Catholic and Protestant did not escape him; both he and Kathleen longed to find a place where their love could be in the open, and their relationship no longer a threat.

James explored every nook and cranny, looking for private places to call their own. Until they did, Kathleen and James contented themselves with a little cave beneath some boulders, where they'd brought a blanket or two, some candles, some of Kathleen's favorite books of poetry, which they read together. Sometimes they brought a picnic of bread and cheese to share, and they sang favorite folk songs. James grabbed her hand and twirled her around as she sang his favorite tune, lilting voice wafting over the ruins. James wanted to make sure Kathleen could see beyond his economic circumstances and could appreciate the strength of his character.

CHAPTER 5

MIMI

"It takes more courage to examine the dark corners of your own soul than it does for a soldier to fight on a battlefield."
—William Butler Yeats

Back at UT and living in the dorm, I grabbed for the phone when it rang. I hoped it was the guy I'd met at Barton Springs, but how realistic was that? Instead it was my Great-Aunt Oona, whom I usually saw when my mother dragged us all to the summer family reunions in Austin. I envied her glamorous fashion model past and marriage to a handsome G-Man working with Elliot Ness. Maybe she'd find the man of my dreams, my happily-ever-after Prince Charming who'd father my children and cherish me forever. Now she was a reformed alcoholic and pretty self-centered, currently a third-grade teacher living with another great aunt, Ella. How likely was it they'd be looking out for my social life? I shifted my attention to her call.

"Lovely to hear from you, Oona. What's up?" I knew better than to expect that the call was to check on my well-being, but I was curious.

"Well, dear, you know I have a beautiful two-year old granddaughter Tracey I'd love you to meet. Her parents are going through a rough patch, and I thought maybe you and your parents could help the family out by caring for her."

My mind flashed back to my own childhood and all the struggles I'd had trying to find a way to fit into my own family and what it might have been like to be plunked down as a toddler with a bunch of strangers.

I paused, getting back to the conversation at hand. I answered, "Sure, Oona, I bet my folks might be willing to help out. When? Next summer sometime?" My dream had always been to have a little sister or to start a family of my own. I needed more information.

"Well, actually, I had in mind something sooner. You see, if your parents don't take her in, she's going to have to go to an orphanage near Dallas. I've already asked everyone else in the family, and no one will help. I don't know what to do. I was hoping you might take her tonight!"

I turned down the radio, playing *"Help!"* by the Beatles, eerily a propos for the situation. *"Help! I need somebody, Help! Not just anybody; Help! You know I need somebody."*

I started coughing, choking on the coke I'd been drinking when she called. *"Tonight*?! Oona, I'm a *student*! I live in a *dorm*! I go to class, and I have a social life, even if it's pretty pathetic at the moment. Why did all the others turn you down? What are you not telling me? Why don't you and Ella take her?"

A longer pause. "Mimi, Ella and I are old and set in our ways. It's been decades since I've taken care of a toddler, and my own kids would say I'm a rotten choice. And Ella? She'd be great if Tracey was in second grade, but let's face it-- anyone younger than that is too little, and much older than that, and Ella would be completely lost. Your family—why your family is just like "Father Knows Best." What could be wrong with just giving it a try? It's almost Thanksgiving; you'll have a chance to try things out. Darling, don't you have friends in the dorm to help out?"

I flashed back to all the battles with my mom growing up, her battles with her own sister and their estrangement, and my dad's hands-off approach to the whole thing. My mom really knew how to pitch a fit, followed by shutting herself in her room for days, with psychic flames seeping out through the door jambs along with

"God damn it to hell, I never want to see you again. I'll stick my head in the oven and then maybe you'll see." Never sure what I'd see, worried at first about what I might find, and eventually hoping she'd do it. Stick her head in the oven. Get it over with. Guilt about wishing her dead.

Then I remembered when her only sister, my Aunt Clare, came to see us shortly after the death of my grandmother, whom I barely knew. My mother blamed Clare for her miscarriage, trying to do the heavy lifting for their mom, dying of a brain tumor. Clare, younger, married, no kids, finishing grad school. An epic shouting match, assigning blame, filled with bitterness about who was loved more, who had done more, who was hurt most by the loss. An old desktop radio in the top of a closet caught my aunt's eye. "Daddy's radio! I always wondered what happened to it. He would have wanted ME to have it. I loved it. How did *you* get it, you witch?"

"You *missed* this old radio? You *want* this old radio? I'll *give* you your precious radio!" My mom reached up and took the radio down from the shelf, held it over her head with both hands and heaved it as hard as she could on the paving brick floor of our family room, with tubes, knobs, and wood-grained plastic case crashing to the floor and flying across the room. Heart pounding, wondering what might happen next, I crouched behind the kitchen cabinets. When the shouting stopped, I finally got the courage to come out from my hiding place. I could see my aunt driving away in her 55 DeSoto sedan, and I could hear my mother in her bedroom hollering "If that worthless bitch ever shows up again, lock the door. If I ever see her again, it will be too soon! And I don't want *her* at my funeral!"

Oona cleared her throat, and my mind jerked back to the phone conversation.

"Oona, you know I'd love to help out, and you know I love kids. Who knows? It might work out just fine. I think I need to give them some warning. My mom made it pretty clear she was glad to be rid of me when I left for college; I have no idea how she might feel about taking on a project like this."

"It seemed like I should start with you. You'd be the first to meet her, and you'd be the best one to convince them that they'd be doing the right thing. I'll let you decide the best way to do it. Shall we say four o'clock? I'll bring her things."

I hung up, telling my roommate Betsy, "Holy shit, what have I just done? What am I thinking? Oona thinks my family should adopt her granddaughter—she thinks we're like 'Father Knows Best' but we're really more like 'The Addams Family.'" My roommate Betsy looked at me and asked "Are you out of your mind?" We'd been best friends for ten years, and she knew everything about me.

We'd grown up as faculty brats, living near the OU campus, 400 miles away. My mother felt suffocated by not having a career of her own after all the excitement and opportunity of the World War II years. She'd met my dad and married him after six weeks of a lively courtship filled with dancing, booze, and nights at the Officer's Club near her hometown, a lifetime marriage. She'd guided him toward a career as an English professor, and she was a housewife, in the 50s, in Oklahoma, which she loathed.

As an adolescent, I was conflicted. If she thought I was a shit kid, why didn't I try to live up to the title? A brief trial writing pornography was a good start. Sneaking out of the house in the wee hours of the morning rated fireworks and explosions. Drinking the dregs of cocktails in the background of grad student/faculty parties, feeling and acting silly, was an excellent choice. But all that got me was enrollment at a summer camp designed to clamp down on potential unruly teenagers—Kamp Kickeroonie, a summer camp run by Texas A&M sadists, who would have been at home leading training Army Rangers or Green Berets. Everything, including tooth brushing and shower taking was competitive, ranked by counselors with clip boards. I longed for "shit kid" status over feeling humiliated by the skills of my fellow campers, who seemed to have spent their entire lives training for the Olympics. Would I like another year at Camp Kickeroonie? I don't think so.

Released from the purgatory of Kamp Kickeroonie, I shifted and jibed into another tack. No more escapades. Most popular babysitter in the neighborhood? Check. Candystriper at the hospital? Of course. Vacation Bible School teacher? Duh! Ballet, tap, modern dance and of course, piano—She signed me up for everything, and I did my best, but I always fell short, confirming her expectations. My mom despised me, perhaps jealous of my closeness to my dad, resenting the freedom my life represented compared to hers, or just blue as a snake from forces beyond my understanding.

And then, just when I'd given up thinking we could ever be close, she'd come into my room singing *"I Am Woman Hear Me Roar, with numbers too great to ignore"* by Helen Reddy, and I'd feel like we were on the same team. Crazy!

I hung up the phone, and Betsy and I went off to pick up the basics for little Tracey. By the time we got back, we were both enthusiastic about the idea: it was totally preposterous, but more interesting than anything going on in class or in the dorm. I loved stirring things up, and this was a record-breaking opportunity! Betsy and I ran through the baby department at Scarbrough's, scooping up adorable toddler outfits, kiddie books and toys, helped by sales clerks who were fascinated by the idea of instant adoption of a toddler.

We were waiting at the dorm door when Oona arrived, struggling with a large diaper bag, Tracey in her arms. "Come on up, Oona, and let's get Tracey settled in."

Oona asked what my parents thought of the idea.

"They're thrilled," I lied. "I'm known for bringing home pets, people, or projects—besides, my mom remembers growing up with Jack when he was little. I bet you remember that, too! I figure once they meet Tracey and understand the situation, they'll want to help."

I'd actually called home to test the waters, and the reaction was lukewarm, beyond the notion of a stopgap Thanksgiving visit while Oona came up with another option.

Betsy and I took Oona and Tracey up to our room, put the diaper bag on a chair in the corner, and then invited them to come to the community kitchen down the hall, where we'd spread out brownie mix and baking pans. As we got Tracey interested in the mixer, the wooden spoons, and the brownie batter, Oona faded slowly back into the hall, hope against hope that she was doing the right thing.

Tracey was loving it! Her face covered with chocolate, she held a wooden spoon in each hand, stirring the batter and banging the spoons on the metal mixing bowl. Mimi was enchanted with Tracey's big brown eyes and long eyelashes, wavy dark hair, and beaming smile. Tracey chattered happily as the girls helped her bake her first batch of brownies! When we put the baking pans in the oven, the aroma of freshly baked brownies wafted down the hall, where girls began to drift away from the studies as if hypnotized, heading for the distraction of a tasty snack and the happy sounds coming from the kitchen. Maybe it was the first brownies they'd had in a while without marijuana in them!

"Well, who's this?" the chorus of dorm-mates chirped, as they trooped into the kitchen, where Tracey sat on the countertop cooing away at her new best friends.

"It's Tracey! I'm taking care of her until we go home for Thanksgiving. I'm hoping my parents will adopt her, because her own parents are scumbags and are giving her up. Will you help me? I still have to go to classes; my parents will kill me if my grades go down over this little darling."

"Of course, we'll help. God, she's cute. I'd like to take her home myself! Give me that sign-up sheet, and we'll make sure you're covered."

We quickly transformed our room from collegiate to nursery, while Tracey blossomed from all the attention, plenty of food, clean clothes, and things to do. It was an early bedtime. I curled up with Tracey in the twin bed. I didn't get much sleep, worried about how things would work out at home, how the next couple of days would go with Tracey spirited undercover in the dorm room, away from the nosy residential life staff. But what else was there to do? And who else was there to help?

When I woke up, Tracey was sitting next to me, big brown eyes and huge warm smile beaming. She clapped her hands and giggled, and my heart melted. "Okay, little one, time for some breakfast and then I've got to get to class."

The beautiful fall weather, with the leaves turning and the aroma of damp grass and cooler temperatures was my favorite. I had to get to class, show up for a big demonstration against the Viet Nam war and the UT Board of Regents who were under LBJ's thumb and clamping down on campus activists. My less politically active suitemates took Tracey to a park nearby. I bailed on distributing the latest edition of *The Rag*, the radical student newspaper, in favor of taking care of a toddler. Life was complicated, even though being loved by Tracey made everything worth it.

The next two days were a blur of doing the absolute minimum for class, and a maximum of playing with Tracey, finding out what she liked to eat (everything), and getting ready for the trip home for Thanksgiving. I couldn't let myself think too far ahead; I knew I just had to get this little girl to my family and let the rest take care of itself. I did my best to pack, but keeping up with tiny shoes and sox, baby food jars, and enough diapers (how do people even do that?) was hard work.

Betsy took us downtown to the bus station downtown to catch the bus to Temple, where we caught the train to Norman where my family lived, an eight-hour journey counting the bus to train transfer in Temple. I struggled with my own suitcase and a suitcase and diaper bag for Tracey. I wasn't sure I'd brought enough diapers; are there ever enough diapers? I worried about how she'd do sitting all day on a bus and a train. What if she had a temper tantrum? I began to have doubts about how strong I really was and if this was a great idea.

But if there was one thing I believed to be true, it was that my mother was loyal to her extended Irish roots, connections with aunts, uncles, and cousins we met in Austin reunion trips. So many memories and family stories of the nine brothers and sisters and their families, music and dancing, and helping each other through good times and bad. Each of us cousins learned to say all the first names of the nine siblings, in chronological order, just like learning the multiplication tables. When we got together as a group, we'd say them together, like reciting poetry, to smiles of approval from all the great aunts and uncles, the grandchildren of our ancestor James Lockhart. On reaching thirteen, we each received a lovingly crafted book of the family genealogy by Oona's sister Ella. Family *meant* something, I knew that, but what, exactly?

I'd made the trip from Austin north to Norman many times, but never with a toddler in tow. People looked at me funny, since I guess I seemed a little young to be a mom. "Oh, she's my new little sister," I explained. "Or at least, she's going to be. I'm taking her to meet her new parents."

The trip was nerve-wracking; Tracey was curious about how everything worked, and she wanted to walk up and down all the passenger cars, pushing the button to open the doors and flushing the toilet in the restroom, making a wonderful whooshing sound as liquid poured down on the tracks. I was terrified she'd mash her fingers in the doorway or get cranky. But the novelty of a darling baby to entertain made the hours of the trip fly by; Tracey was such a show-stopping Shirley Temple of a little girl, enchanting each passer-by, that I felt special, too, special in a way I often didn't feel with my own family.

The little train depot appeared on the horizon, and my heart started to pound. As we stepped off the train, my folks and younger brother were right there, with the hoped-for hugs and welcome. My dad smiled, swooping Tracey up in his arms and giving me the hug I'd waited for. My mother stood awkwardly off to the side.

"You're all going to love Tracey, Daddy; I just know it. Besides, what else could I do? Oona was desperate! Isn't she adorable?"

My dad gave me another hug. "I remember your taking in those little kitties when you were in first grade and then bringing home that tiny lost puppy Blondie when we moved to Norman. And all the kids you befriended, quirky, lost kids who had no one else. Then you moved on to old people and volunteered to do shampoos at the nursing home for old ladies. You're like a magnet for lost souls. But let's slow down a little bit so we can get to know Tracey and think carefully about what's best for her."

My stomach unclenched for the first time since Oona dropped Tracey off at my dorm. I looked up at my dad, and blinked my eyes to keep the tears from rolling down my cheeks.

"OK, I know it looks like a stretch, but once you're around Tracey, you'll understand. I promise to help!"

"Mimi, Oona took advantage of your big heart in her desperation to look after her grandchild. We're not making any commitments beyond Thanksgiving at the moment. Your only job is to get an education and *grow up*. Now let's go home, get Tracey settled, and talk about the visit."

An animated Tracey, excited by new people and another change of scene, chattered all the way home...*her new* home, I hoped, ignoring Daddy's cautionary words.

When we got home, my mom found it easy to fall under Tracey's show-stopping spell. She looked so happy sitting on the piano bench, Tracey in her lap, singing and putting Tracey's fingers on the keys. When I used to do that, she was full of comparisons about how clueless I was at playing by ear and how poorly I played. She loved showing me how easy it was for her to play anything— from Carole King to Chopin, and I could only nod, wistfully. I wished I could have been as cute and precocious as Tracey—maybe things would have felt different growing up.

I put Tracey down for the night on a special pallet next to my bed, although I bet that we would end up like spoons as we had in the dorm. I helped my mom put away the dishes; she slammed the cups and glasses into the cupboard with more force than necessary, finishing the performance off by ripping off her apron and throwing it at the washing machine. I was afraid to ask what was wrong; I guess I already knew.

"I don't know what you thought you were doing, but it's like so many of the rest of your hare-brained schemes," my mother started in. "You never think about how any of your decisions affect anyone else."

"I'm really tired, Mom. Can we talk about Tracey tomorrow?"

"You're goddamn right we'll talk about Tracey tomorrow, but first, we have to get through Thanksgiving dinner."

I slunk up the stairs to my bedroom, stopping in my dad's study to give him a goodnight kiss. I longed to ask him what to do about Mother's anger but decided against it. Maybe things would look better in the morning.

The crisp, fall Thanksgiving Day started early, with preparations for a family feast. A little subdued and saddened, I cared for Tracey. We took a walk around the neighborhood, passing fraternity houses and picking up pine cones while Mother busied herself with making pumpkin pie and turkey. My brother and Daddy shot baskets outside, and then came in for some ping pong. No one said a word about Tracey. After a while we came in, and I carefully tiptoed around the sensitive subject. The OU-OSU football game blared in the background on tv, with the band playing Boomer-Sooner at half-time and announcers making the game seem more important than it was, at least to me.

After the game, we all sat down for Thanksgiving dinner. Tracey sat in my lap, and she ate dressing, little bites of turkey with lots of gravy, and some green beans that I chopped up for her. She loved the pumpkin pie, especially with the large glob of whipped cream. Just a small family dinner this year, apparently, my family had no room to grow. I felt sad as I wondered what next Thanksgiving might be like and even more important, what Tracey's life might be.

After dinner, I helped my mom clean up, while my brother played with Tracey, building towers with blocks and then knocking them down, both of them giggling before the game started up again. "So what's going on, Mom?" I asked, fearing what might come next.

Finally, my mother spoke to me in a controlled voice, masking whatever anger or resentment she felt. "Honey, here's the thing. Oona called, and she reported that Tracey's other grandmother has gone ballistic finding her gone. The other grandmother's called the police, and if Tracey's not returned within forty-eight hours, they're charging you with kidnapping across state lines. That's serious business, Mimi, and there's nothing we can do. Oona was wrong about Tracey's family; they want her back, and they want her back *now*."

I watched Tracey in the next room, playing happily with my brother. "How can this be happening? What was Oona thinking? She never said a word about another grandmother. I was only trying to help! Can she really do this? Are you *sure* about this?"

"She *is* doing this, Mimi. Tracey's a beautiful child, honey, but she deserves to be with close family, not second and third cousins far away. I promised Oona we'd have Tracey back at her house by dinnertime Saturday. Your brother's going to a sleep-over at a friend's house. Your dad and I will drive the two of you back to Austin. You'll go to the dorm, and then your dad and I will take Tracey to Oona's, and we'll come back home on Sunday. Tomorrow we'll go shopping and make sure that Tracey's got plenty of new clothes and toys. We'll take her with us, so she can pick out some toys she likes. Don't upset Tracey by being sad; let's make this the happiest Thanksgiving she's ever had."

"The happiest Thanksgiving would be to give her the home she deserves, with a real family, where she already knows she's safe and cared for. You just don't care!"

I could see it was useless to argue further; what kind of alternative could I offer, anyway? My mother never backed down once she made up her mind, and all the cards were in her hand. I was still baffled by the kidnapping charge, but I didn't know what to do.

"Your dad and I will look after her tomorrow afternoon and evening so you can have some time with your friends. I suggest you get with the program. You have no other choice.

CHAPTER 6

JAMES

"But I, being poor, have only my dreams;
Tread softly because you tread on my dreams;
I have spread my dreams beneath your feet;
Tread softly because you tread on my dreams."
—William Butler Yeats

James tossed and turned, another sleepless night after another back-breaking day. He worried about his mam and cringed when he heard the creaky rhythm of his parents' bedsprings and the bang of the bed on the floor above his head. He knew exactly what that meant. He wanted to kill his father; he was sure he would have to kill his father if his mother was to have a chance at survival. Why didn't she smash his head in herself? His mother barely had a chance to get her health back after the last baby nursed the life out of her, before she had another one on the way. He hated his father with all his heart and couldn't wait to run away to a better life with his beautiful Kathleen.

He looked over at the sleeping forms of his three younger siblings, all lined up on one sleeping mat like a litter of puppies. His littlest sister was asleep in a dresser drawer in his parents' room, blissfully ignorant of the new life being created in the adjacent bed. Sickened by the very thought of it, James turned over and pulled the cover over his head to block out the sound.

The rooster crowed before the sun rose, and James, early bird himself, was out the door, taking care of the hens, mucking out the cages and looking for eggs, precious commodities these days, either to eat or to sell.

"Well, girls, how you be this beautiful morning? Who's got a gift for me family?" James picked up a couple of eggs, spread out fresh hay and feed, and made sure his hens were healthy and safe. But he hated the endless work in the garden, so much work for so little gain. His boots squished in the mud as he raked. The potatoes were meager and small; the weeds and grasses relentlessly tried to take over the tiny garden plot and choke out the few vegetables that were trying to grow.

He headed into the kitchen with the eggs, washed his hands, and had some bread and tea for breakfast, before helping his mam get the young ones ready for school. He worried that they would have to drop out soon, just as he had, because there was no money for what his pa called "useless clutter of the mind."

James was relieved to see his father leaving the house and setting off down the road, off to look for an odd job or two. James wanted no sight of him and wondered if the feeling were mutual.

James's mam smiled as she watched him make porridge for the young ones. She knew he wanted to be off at school himself, if circumstances were different. "You're working hard, James. You've got those chickens doing your will, son, and that garden—you've got the green thumb getting anything at all to grow amidst those weeds and that muddy soil." James could see the pride and joy she felt towards him by the warm glow in her eyes, her gentle words and compliments. He felt appreciated.

He took his hand in hers and looked at her with gratitude for her kind words. "Now I've got to help the little ones grow strong, so they can keep their mind on their schooling and not on a growling stomach. He doled out the porridge, his forehead creased with worry. He gave each one a pat on the shoulder or a tickle to let them know they were loved.

Then James headed out down the lane to the school with his siblings, with a bit of dry bread his mam had wrapped in paper for their lunches.

"I don't know why the good lord thought I needed another baby," she muttered to herself, "as I am not taking care of the ones I have properly. Surely this one will be the last. or it will kill me."

~~~

James returned from the school, worked all day without complaint, came indoors and stripped off his work clothes, covered with mud and soggy from the mist and fog. He washed up and set off for the meeting place that he and Kathleen now considered their home. The two of them had just enough time before dinner to enjoy each other's company, away from prying eyes, judgments and expectations of their families. James arrived first and spread the blanket out in their little hideaway, lit a candle, and gently placed some fragrant heather where he and Kathleen would lie together.

Moments later, she arrived, smiled shyly at the sight of the candle and the fresh flowers. She sat down next to him, put her hand on his shoulder, and the two embraced and touched each other with the exuberance of young love. Determined not to repeat the selfish and careless ways of his father, he withdrew from her before he came. "I've heard my parents at night, Kathleen, and my father forcing himself on my mam, when she's not even recovered from the last birth. I won't take a chance on that life for you, Kathleen."

"James, I know you're trying to protect me, and I know you hate what's happening to your mam. But you are not your father. I just want to love you without stopping."

Frustrating, but necessary. For her part, Kathleen tried to figure out when her "unsafe" days were, but it was not an exact science. She wished for more time, too, but knew that was impossible. Their limited time made their short visits all the more precious.

CHAPTER 7

TRACEY

"Where we love is home - home that our feet may leave, but not our hearts."
—Oliver Wendell Holmes, Sr.

A childhood lost—what was to have been a home with her maternal grandmother was a cruel joke on a helpless toddler. Instead of a stable home, Tracey found herself growing up in an orphanage, with the well-intentioned but businesslike Mrs. Reed. Farmed out periodically for brief respites with Oona, Ella, and other relatives, but not Mimi's family, even though Mimi kept asking where Tracey was, how she was doing. Tracey always was returned to "the buildin'." She refused to call the orphanage by its real name, the Scottish Rite Home. It was an institution, not a home, and no one explained how she came to live there. Was it something she'd done, she wondered? Tracey's only way of coping was to escape into books and school.

What had happened to that close-knit Irish-American family who took care of each other, no matter what, all for one and one for all? "We'd take her of course, but she's too darling and too smart— my own daughter couldn't compete!" one cousin noted wistfully. "We'd take her, but what about the baggage she'd bring? Those parents?" another said. "And what about when she became a teenager?" another worried. And Mimi, the cousin who'd loved her and tried to help? She was busy going to college, getting married, lost in her own struggle for identity and autonomy. Though she never forgot her darling Tracey, she was no different from any of the rest of them. Missing in action.

None of the backstories were spoken out loud, of course, but rather in sotto voce conversations among one or two, with fervent wishes that Tracey never be told the reasons why she remained in a sterile, impersonal orphanage, isolated and apart, with only her fellow residents for friends and family. Tracey hated her life, but she didn't hate the people who'd let her down. She knew she could count on no one but herself. She hated herself for whatever she'd done to deserve being sent away to live with strangers. With books as her best friends, her only friends, she kept the sadness shut away in her heart.

One day, after Tracey returned to the orphanage from school, her grandmother and great- aunt were waiting for her just outside the home. It wasn't a school holiday or occasion that Tracey knew of, but she was sure it must be bad news. If it were something good, surely she'd have been told. She approached slowly and cautiously, as if to protect herself from the next bad thing in her short life.

"Tracey, how you've grown since our last visit!"

Tracey thought, but didn't say, "If you came more often, you might not be surprised that I'm growing. What would you expect?" Instead, breathing carefully and managing her emotions, she responded "Lovely to see you two! What brings you up my way? Is something wrong? Are my parents dead yet?"

"Oh, my, no, dear. Let's not even think such a thing! We're here for a little chat and visit with you and Mrs. Reed. We think it might be time for a change."

Tracey's mind raced with the possibilities—most of them bad. Might they return her to her drug-addicted parents' care? Since her parents were no longer together, and neither of them had ever seemed to want her, how could that happen? Might the shrinking orphanage be closing and Tracey turned over to foster parents, who would be even worse than her biological ones, or even worse than the orphanage? Maybe she'd be adopted by strangers in a faraway place, with no connection to any of her family members or familiar surroundings? On the other hand, maybe her favorite teacher, Miss Donaldson, who'd taken Tracey under her wing when she started school in kindergarten, had finally stepped in as an angel to save the day. What were the chances? Zero, thought Tracey.

Tracey remembered the day Miss Donaldson had discovered her hiding in the coatroom when the other kids left for lunch. "Don't you want to go out and get some fresh air, Tracey? It's a beautiful day, and you can eat your lunch with the other kids." Tracey didn't want to admit she didn't have a lunch, and the last place she wanted to be was with the other kids, who teased her about living in the orphanage instead of with her family.

Tracey took a deep breath. "Miss Donaldson, I'm afraid I am just feeling a little…I mean, I'm not sick or anything like that, but it just seemed so nice and cozy in here, and I just didn't want to, there wasn't…" Miss Donaldson stopped her midway through the fumbled excuses.

"Tracey, I think you've just got a touch of the willies. I used to get those myself, when I started kindergarten. Why don't you keep me company, and we'll have a little lunch. Maybe you can help me erase the chalkboards for this afternoon's lessons?" Tracey smiled gratefully.

She reached for Tracey's little hand and guided her gently over to her desk, where she pulled out a bag lunch. "I made way too much lunch for myself," she said. "I wonder if you'd help me out by having the extra sandwich and apple?"

Tracey carefully considered the offer. She realized that Miss Donaldson always came prepared with extra lunch supplies. Tracey had been carefully taught not to accept charity, not to tell anyone about her so-called family or much of anything else. But she was so hungry, having not eaten since supper the previous evening, and Miss Donaldson was so kind. What could be the harm?

Tracey took the sandwich, white bread with the crusts cut off and spread thickly with peanut butter and honey; she wanted it to last forever. Before Miss Donaldson had even gotten the first bite of her sandwich chewed and swallowed, Tracey had devoured her sandwich and the apple in what seemed to the teacher like two bites. "Why, you're starving, Tracey! Did you forget to eat your breakfast?"

Tracey's smile disappeared. "Thank you for the sandwich, Miss Donaldson." She got up from her chair and went to the blackboards and started erasing.

From that first act of kindness until Tracey finished elementary school, Miss Donaldson, who had three children of her own at home and was a single parent, was Tracey's advocate, mentor, and friend. Miss Donaldson had seen from Tracey's first day in kindergarten how precocious she was; she could read and write; her art projects were creative, colorful, and plentiful. Tracey loved to draw, paint, work with clay (animals were her specialty), and she became a valued class member, thanks to Miss Donaldson's skill in placing her with other children who showed empathy and appreciation for Tracey's infectious giggle and schoolwork.

The lunchtime with Miss Donaldson was expanded to a group of 3 or 4 students, rotating throughout the class. Tracey was a standing member, quickly noticed by other kids in the class. When one of the students asked Miss Donaldson why Tracey was always in the little lunch group, suggesting that that wasn't fair, Miss Donaldson taught her a lesson about fairness.

"Do you sometimes like to eat your lunch outdoors and join in the playground games?" asked Miss Donaldson. "Yes," answered the girl. "Would it be fair if I made you stay indoors when you'd rather be outside?" "No," answered the girl. "Tracey prefers to stay indoors; she doesn't like the outdoor games and sometimes feels left out. Would it be fair to make her go outdoors when she's not happy there?" The girl shook her head no. "'Fair' doesn't mean that every person gets the same; it means that every child gets what is needed or preferred. You like to have lunch with our little lunch group sometimes and to play outside sometimes. So that's fair for you. Tracey prefers the little lunch group and dislikes outdoor games. That means staying indoors is fair for her." Satisfied by Miss Donaldson's explanation, the girl asked no further questions; the other students noted Miss Donaldson's explanation and moved on. Anyone who was unkind to Tracey was quickly corrected.

Although Miss Donaldson tried to break through Tracey's reserve and reluctance to share anything about her family or her life at "the buildin'" (as Tracey called it) her background remained a mystery. She knew that Tracey never came with a lunch like the other kids and that no money was ever provided for Tracey for class photos, field trips, or special programs. Although Miss Donaldson had little left over from her teacher's salary, she made sure that Tracey's world included the little extras that insured Tracey wouldn't be stigmatized by lack of support from home.

Tracey expected nothing, but she gave everything she had to success in school. She idolized Miss Donaldson and dreamed of being a teacher one day, just like Miss Donaldson and her elderly grandmother Oona and great-aunt, Ella. She daydreamed that Miss Donaldson took her home from school with her one day…and never returned her to the buildin'.

Tracey was jerked abruptly back to reality when Mrs. Reed said, "Tracey, dear, you look like you're about to faint! You're as white as a sheet! What can you be thinking about? Let's go inside and let's see what we have in mind."

The two elderly sisters and Tracey made their way inside the Home, where Mrs. Reed suggested "Why don't we go into my office? We have important things to talk about. Let's go inside and have a snack."

Now Tracey knew something truly awful was going to happen. No one ever got snacks between meals at the buildin'. In fact, the food was so terrible, who'd want more? But if you were hungry enough, even awful food, eaten in a hurry, was better than the alternative. That accounted for Tracey being overweight — whenever she got a chance to eat anything, anywhere, she was going to devour it.

Mrs. Reed got them all settled in her office and headed to the kitchen, where she got coffee for Oona and her sister and some milk and a couple of Oreos for Tracey. Tracey sat quietly, not knowing whether to ask about what was happening or to just sit and wait to see what the story was. She decided to wait, to put off the next horrible thing in her short life as long as possible.

Oona spoke first, not waiting for Mrs. Reed to return. "Tracey, Ella is retiring from teaching this year. Apparently, fifty years of second grade is enough for her, and ten years of third grade is certainly enough for me. We're ready for a change, and we'd like to invite you to make that change with us. Will you come live with us? We think living with family would be better than staying on here at the home. You'll be changing schools and going into junior high anyway, and for the first time, we'll be at home and can look after you properly."

Tracey did not wait a moment before responding, afraid that the opportunity might evaporate if she didn't jump on it, and not even caring if being with her old relatives would be worse than the home. It would be a home. It would be with family. That's all that mattered. "Yes! Can we go now?"

Oona cleared her throat and looked at Tracey, then at Mrs. Reed. "You know we've appreciated the care you've given our girl all these years. Although Ella and I loved Tracey, we both felt ill-suited for the job of filling in for her parents. You also know that we've never wanted to let her go—let her be adopted by anyone outside the family. But now things are different. We're retiring. We could use some looking after ourselves, a young person to liven up our lives." Oona smiled at Tracey. "I have no doubt that Tracey will do just that!"

"We've asked Tracey if she'd like to come live with us, and she's said yes."

Mrs. Reed looked at Tracey and then at the elegantly dressed, sedate ladies. "I've done my best to take care of this young lady, and I've hoped that this day would come, that she would return to her family." She paused, surprising herself by feeling choked up, emotion not being something she allowed herself, not healthy in her job as administrator of an orphanage. "Tracey, tell me yourself: do you want to leave us and go live with your grandma and your auntie? Will you behave yourself? You know you'll be a teen-ager soon, and that's a challenge for anyone. I wasn't looking forward to that part myself."

40

Tracey looked at Mrs. Reed, feeling nothing. Then she looked at her relatives, both loving and hating them at the same time, completely overloading her emotional circuits. She burst into tears, confusing the three women, and confusing herself. Did she not want to go live with Oona and Ella after all?

Once Tracey had regained her composure, she said calmly and strongly "I want to go live with my family. I've been waiting my entire life for a moment like this. I'll do my best, I really will."

Mrs. Reed, back to business as usual, explained "It will take a few days to get things sorted out, and you have another two weeks until school is out for the summer. That will give you a chance to say good-bye to your friends here at the Home and at school. And it will give Oona and Ella a chance to get settled in their new home, with a room for you to decorate as you like."

Now it was Oona and Ella's turn to become emotional, which started Tracey crying again. The three of them tearfully hugged each other a long, long time, as Mrs. Reed looked on, feeling happy and sad simultaneously.

CHAPTER 8

JAMES

"For he would be thinking of love
Till the stars had run away
And the shadows eaten the moon."
—William Butler Yeats

James arrived at their usual meeting place, surprised that Kathleen wasn't there. He'd brought a meager snack for them to share and a new candle that he'd taken from the village chapel, after making the expected donation. Who cared whether the candle stayed in the church or was used in celebration of love? After a few minutes, Kathleen arrived, out of breath.

"My mother has found out about us," she blurted out. "Someone in the village, I don't know who, has seen us. And James, I'm starting to show—I can't keep this baby a secret any longer. What will we do?"

James, pale as a ghost, was at a loss for both words and ideas of what to do next. If Kathleen's father and brothers didn't kill him, his own father would. He'd be expected to marry Kathleen, and the cycle of poverty he'd grown up in would continue. He couldn't bear that thought—not for himself, for Kathleen, or the unborn child they'd created.

After a long pause, he began to come up with a plan. "Let's run away to America, like so many others! We'll make a new life, where no one cares about whether you're Catholic or Protestant, where there's opportunity and food. I have almost no money, but I've heard you can sign a contract to pay your way if you agree to work on the other side. We're both hard workers; we'll see this through together."

Now it was Kathleen's turn to be silent, as she considered his proposal. She had a little money she'd hidden away, saving for something special for James' birthday. His family was so poor, no one would even think of presents when every shilling went for food. She was an adventurous girl, and the idea appealed to her, but she had to think of the baby now. What would it would be like to abandon everything she knew and loved for the unknown world across the sea? Her family would disown her; she was sure of that. She burst into tears, knowing that whether she eloped with James or stayed behind, her life would soon change forever. What would she do?

James became impatient, imagining Kathleen's father and brothers arriving at his house and confronting his parents. "Damn it, Kathleen, do you love me or not? Do you not know what our lives will be like if we stay here? Our two families at war with each other, us caught in the middle, and our child a victim of ancient hatreds we can't control? We need to go far away and get a fresh start. I have to get back home before your father turns up, and I have to let my own parents know what we're planning. I can't let them face your family alone."

"It's easy for you," she replied, tears streaming down her face. "You're not carrying a child. You're not a woman. You can run away and leave everything behind. I can't. I won't."

"I am going home to tell my family, and I know they will be afraid and angry. I've got to leave Rathmullan, Kathleen, and I want to take you with me. Think it over and meet me here before dawn if you change your mind. If you don't come with me tomorrow, I will send for you when I get to America." James desperately tried to seem confident, but he was terrified.

He ran all the way home. Kathleen's father had come to the house, demanded to know where James and Kathleen were, and told his parents about their relationship and the child to come.

James' mother dissolved in sobs, understanding for the first time why James had been sneaking out early and late each day and knowing the pressure he was under.

James' father, fortunately, was out of the house, at a pub, and would not know for at least a little while what was going on. Kathleen's father vowed to find James' father and give him a piece of his mind, if not bash his head in.

"Oh, James, what have you done?" his mother asked, sighing, not really looking for an answer.

"Mam, I've asked Kathleen to run away with me to America. I am so sorry to be such a disappointment to you. I was thinking of running away anyway, because there's no future for any of us kids here. But Kathleen—she's the heart of my heart. What else can I do?"

"You can stay here, stand up for your unborn child and marry Kathleen, if her parents will stand for it. They might kill you first though." His mam burst into tears again.

James' father returned from the pub drunk to a fare thee well, beaten badly by Kathleen's brothers and her father. James' mam cleaned up the blood, pulled off his clothes, and put him to bed.

"Go, then, if you must. Don't worry about us, but don't forget about us, either. You've always been my rock, young man, and you'll be in my heart, no matter where you are."

James' mam held him close, and James choked up, not knowing when he might see any of his family again.

The next morning, James gathered up a small knapsack of belongings for the long ocean voyage. His stomach was twisted in knots, and his brain was a cyclone of emotions. He was terrified of the risks of being at sea; so many of his friends who'd left had never made it to the land beyond the rain, or they'd made it but then perished once they'd arrived, not being able to find work or shelter, and having left everything important behind. He hoped and prayed Kathleen would be waiting at their hiding place, but he didn't expect it. He was wracked with guilt about leaving her, but he was full of determination and optimism for his new life. He saw a future beyond the misery of the past.

He hated leaving his mother and siblings behind, but what could he do? Staying here wouldn't help. Now that his mother knew about Kathleen's pregnancy, she'd insist that he do the "honorable" thing and marry the girl. He loved both these women, but he knew he had only one life, and it was not going to be spent knee deep in a pig sty, watching more little ones come into a merciless and soul-defeating world. He didn't care about leaving his pa; he'd be fine never to see his face again. Let *him* figure out the way forward the way he never had before.

He'd thought about his last visit with Kathleen. He had set aside a little money and a note in an envelope that he put in the post. He'd done the same for his ma and siblings. The rest he'd need for the journey.

Tomorrow he'd head for Derry and a new future.

CHAPTER 9

TRACEY

"You may not control all the events that happen to you, but you can decide not to be reduced by them."
—Maya Angelou

She was so weary of trying to find her way, growing up in an orphanage, then landing in the strange world of her elderly grandmother and great aunt. She began to fantasize about running away to Ireland, having heard so many stories about her great-great grandfather, who had immigrated to Boston from Rathmullan, in Donegal. The place names sounded so exotic, and the idea that she might have relatives there who might welcome her, where she could leave behind the burden of her drug-addicted parents, her elderly guardians, and her absent cousins.

Tracey had gone from being a polite and compliant middle schooler to an adolescent, testing her well-meaning relatives with minor conflicts about what clothes to wear, when she could begin shaving her legs like all the other girls, and when she could get her ears pierced.

Years in the orphanage where food was always scarce and mostly repulsive had led to food insecurity and binge eating and accompanying problems with weight. Tracey would wait for her granny and aunt to go to bed (since they went to bed shortly after dinner, she didn't have to wait very long), and then hit the cupboard, vacuuming up crackers, cookies, peanut butter sandwiches—all the comfort foods that were not available in the Home. She began to gain weight, and her appearance-conscious relatives clearly didn't approve. Tracey became secretive about what she was eating, and then secretive about what she was doing and who she was spending time with.

She tested Oona and Ella to their core by discovering boys and sex, as teenagers do. Since those things were not in the second-grade curriculum, Oona and Ella just denied that they existed. According to family lore, in fact, Ella had gotten married blissfully ignorant of the physical side of matrimony. She divorced her husband as soon after the so-called wedding night as she could, changing her name from his, back to her maiden name. To her surprise, a year later, when her ex was killed in an accident, she learned that he had never changed his will and had left her a very comfortable estate. She changed her name one more time in gratitude for his generosity. As a financially secure widow, she never again even considered romance (or horrors of horrors: marriage).

Oona and Ella enrolled Tracey in the elite private St. Stephen's Episcopal School, on a leafy green campus near Lake Austin in the posh Westlake Hills part of town. She loved the art classes and excelled in drawing and painting. She covered the walls of her room with her art. She imagined herself in Paris at the Jeu de Paume, copying Impressionist watercolors and then walking along the Seine, sketchbook in hand. She found academic success to be second nature (perhaps in her genes), and her beauty and charm set her up for success in the social arena as well, although the weirdness of her living situation was a hindrance. She loved her granny and auntie and was grateful that they had taken her in, but the idea of having friends over to her house sucked. No one else in her class lived with two old crones. She doubted they would have okayed it anyway.

Instead, she mastered the city bus system and UT's shuttle buses. After school, she met friends and acquaintances at Highland Mall and went anywhere she wanted to, the edgier the better. She discovered the UT campus and roamed throughout the buildings,

Student Union, and along the Drag, enjoying the attention she got from the confident frat boys looking for a good time. She sat by Littlefield Fountain and imagined she was a coed and on her own, finally able to do what she wanted.

Tracey was surprised one day to pick up the phone and hear her cousin Mimi's voice. Mimi called her Aunt Ella sometimes to find out how things were going, but she didn't remember ever meeting her. "Hi, Tracey, you're just the person I wanted to talk to. I'm taking this crazy class at UT to be an educational diagnostician, and I need a guinea pig to help with a school project. Could I bribe you into helping me out? Ice cream or dinner maybe?"

"You know what IQ is, right?" Mimi inquired.

"Sure, it's how smart you are," Tracey responded.

"Well, schools sometimes need to know how smart the kids are or which kids might need extra help. Some kids have learning disabilities and some are retarded, and schools need to figure out what's going on. It's sort of like being a detective, but about learning. I'm learning how to give IQ tests and write reports, and we have to have kids to help us learn. What do you think? Will you help me out?"

They came up with a date, and Mimi arranged to pick Tracey up after school, promising crepes, salads, and dessert as a reward. Tracey was a perfect candidate, being precocious, smart, and charming. Mimi's supervisor was immediately smitten, and given her performance on the tests, neither Mimi nor her supervisor was at all surprised that Tracey's IQ was in the gifted range. Mimi enjoyed this opportunity to reconnect even briefly with Tracey, even though Tracey did not remember that brief Thanksgiving when she was a toddler. Through her work with all kinds of kids, the quirkier the better, Mimi continued her quest to fill the empty hole inside her, left by her mother's hurtful words and actions.

~~~

On her 15th birthday, Tracey discovered she was pregnant. The reality of that fact sunk in as she listened to Tina Turner sing "What's Love Got to Do With It?" on her Walkman on her returned from one of her campus expeditions after school instead of coming straight home. She walked by a Walgreen's and then retraced her steps. She'd missed a couple of periods and, and she was terrified. She bought a pregnancy test with some of her birthday money and then stopped in the restroom at McDonald's to do the test. Her adolescent brain went into overdrive after she saw the results, blinking several times, in hopes of a different outcome. She considered the possibilities and scenarios, all of them bad. Would Oona and Ella throw her out? Would she have the baby? And if so, what then? Who could help her? What would she do?

As she sorted through the very short list of possibilities, she landed on Clare, her Aunt Ella's favorite niece. She was a therapist; she looked after Oona and Ella's affairs, and she was a generation younger. She seemed hip, even though she, too, was missing in action when Tracey had needed a home back in the bad old days. When Oona and Ella went out for lunch at the Frisco, their favorite Austin restaurant, Tracey used the time alone in the house to call Clare and ask for help.

"Tracey, how nice to hear from you. How are things going in Austin? What's it like at St. Stephens and living with Oona and Ella?" Putting on her therapist's hat, she probed gently, "I know it can't be easy, for you or for them. I'm here to help, but you have to tell me what's bothering you; you know you can trust me to keep it between us. I'm a therapist, remember?"

Tracey burst into tears. "Clare, I'm in trouble, big trouble. I went to a fraternity party at UT, and one thing led to another. I drank too much, and the next thing I knew, I'd been raped. Or I think I was raped. I passed out and don't know for sure what happened after that. I missed a couple of periods, and I don't know what to do. I hoped that it was something else, but the pregnancy test took care of that idea."

"I'm not going to ask what you were doing at a fraternity party at age fifteen, or drinking underage, or any of those ridiculous questions we grownups always ask. What do you think you want to do? What's your plan?"

"I don't *have* a plan; that's why I called *you!*" Tracey sobbed.

"Have you been to the doctor? Are you even sure you're pregnant? That seems like the first step."

"I'm afraid if I go to the doctor, he'll tell Ella and Oona why I was there. They would absolutely flip out, you know that."

"I can understand your worries. I think maybe you should come to Houston, and you can go to my doctor. I can set it up. Why don't you tell Oona and Ella that you'd like to come for a visit next weekend; I know my daughter would love to see you. You know you have a choice—you can keep the baby or you can get an abortion. Either choice will be with you the rest of your life, but at least you *have* a choice."

Tracey was relieved that she had the beginnings of plan and some support. She could get through this, she thought, with Clare's help.

"I couldn't possibly keep this baby; I'm fifteen! What do I know about babies? Besides, Oona and Ella would kill me or at least throw me out, and where would I go? Clare, I have to get an abortion; I've thought about it enough to see that's the only way. Will you help me?"

Relieved to hear Tracey declare what Clare believed was a rational decision, Clare remembered back when Tracey's mother Rita had gotten pregnant the first time; the choices were a back alley abortion or an unwed mother's home. Clare leaped into action, as Lockhart women were known to do. "Here's what we'll do—I'll make an appointment at the clinic, you'll come to visit me in Houston for a long weekend, and that will be the end of it."

"Oh, Clare, you've saved my life. I was truly thinking of just throwing myself in front of a bus. I'm so embarrassed and ashamed," Tracey sobbed.

Clare knew how the system worked from her career as a therapist in an adolescent psychiatric ward, and she knew the feelings of guilt and shame. She also knew the family history of alcoholism, drug abuse, suicide, and depression only too well. By the end of the day, she'd booked the medical appointments, spoken to Ella and Oona about the last-minute visit, and arranged transportation for Tracey to get to Houston the very next day. With the abortion behind her, Tracey could focus on finishing school and planning her escape.

CHAPTER 10

JAMES

"Twenty years from now you will be more disappointed by the things you didn't do than by the ones you did. So throw off the bowlines, sail away from the safe harbor, catch the trade winds in your sails. Explore. Dream. Discover."
—Mark Twain

James stood at the railing as the port of Boston appeared. The long journey was over, and he was ready for a new life. He put the memories of his family, both good and bad, out of his mind, and concentrated on what he would need for the road ahead.

His only belongings were the duffel he'd brought with clothes, a few mementos of Kathleen and his family, and the money he'd saved. He was among the first off the boat when it docked. The sights and sounds of Boston were overwhelming compared to what he was used to in Donegal and Derry, and he wondered how he would ever find his way around. He needed a place to stay and a job and had no idea where to begin.

He was surrounded by other young men just like him, searching for work and a place to stay. After several fruitless hours of wandering up and down the waterfront, exhausted, hungry, and frustrated, he felt he'd accomplished nothing. He found a flophouse to spend the night, hating to spend money to put a roof over his head without having found work to support himself.

He knew he wouldn't last long in the oppressive noise and crowds of the city. Having grown up on a farm in the rural beauty of the glens of Donegal, he had nothing but disgust for Boston. He'd walked up and down the streets and seen the signs in shop windows, "No Irish Need Apply." As a Catholic in Ireland, he'd become accustomed to the cruelty of the British, with their policies and attitudes that pushed the Irish to the breaking point. The famine had been the last straw.

He wandered up from the area around Boston Harbor and started asking questions. "I beg your pardon, sir, but do you know where a hard-working man can find work and a place to live? I'm aiming to move out of the city as quick as I can," he asked. Some people just ignored him completely; others shrugged and said, "Get in line, bub. We're all after what you're looking for." A strong, good-looking man with a firm handshake and a warm smile, James quickly learned a few things about his newly adopted country. Rail lines and expansion south and westward offered opportunity in the less settled regions of the country. He stopped in at the rail depot and learned a little about the geography of the country and where along the way he might find work—the railroad itself, or farms or small town businesses. Some people assured him he would find less discrimination against the Irish the further south and west he went. He figured he had nothing to lose; he bought a ticket and found a market where he could buy food for the journey.

He got off the train in Atlanta, weary of travel, and found work with the railroad, which was growing. Because of his size, strength, and willingness to work hard, James never found it difficult to get a job. He lived in a dormitory with other railroad men. The work was hard, and he hated being crowded in with men who smelled bad, snored, and would just as soon pick a fight as make a friend. He kept to himself, paid attention to the work, stayed out of bars, and he saved up enough money after a couple of years to continue traveling south and west, looking for a place he could buy some property and settle down.

~~~

He traveled mostly on horseback, preferring the company of his horse to the humans he encountered, and he kept looking for some land that reminded him of Donegal—green, hilly, with trees and grass. He crossed the border from Georgia into Alabama, and finally, in Perry County, he found a place that suited him. Midway between the larger communities of Birmingham and Montgomery, the rural pasture and farmland had a familiar look. He stopped in Brushy Creek to buy some food for his horse and himself and to inquire about work in the area as a farmhand.

A man about his age was buying hay and seeds, and he looked James up and down. "You're not from around here, are you?"

"I've come all the way from the glens of Donegal in Ireland, looking for a better life than the one I left behind. I can't abide the noise and crowds of the cities I've seen, and my gifts are working the land and taking care of the animals. I've been working for the railroad in Atlanta, saving money to buy my own homestead, but the city's no place for me."

"I came from Scotland myself a few years back, and I know just what you mean about city life. We could use a farmhand, if you've a mind to stay in the area, but I can't pay much, although I could put a roof over your head and some food in your stomach. You and your horse might be happy here. What's his name?"

"His name's Lucky, because he's the first good thing that's happened since I got off the boat. I won him in a card game in the railroad bunkhouse, and that meant I could tip my hat and be on my way," explained James.

"Hitch Lucky up to the wagon, and I'll take you home and introduce you to the wife and daughter."

James tied Lucky to the wagon and climbed up on the seat next to his benefactor. "My name's James Lockhart, and I'm pleased to make your acquaintance."

"I'm Oliver Abbott, my wife's Emma, and my daughter's Julia. We've lived here about five years. We've worked hard, but the life is good. The soil's fertile, and I can make a living."

The two men rode along in silence until they reached a small, plain farmhouse, made more welcoming by plantings of blooming roses, fragrant and plentiful. A young woman came out of the house to greet them. "Who've you brought home, Papa?" Julia was curious about the stranger and his horse.

James took off his hat and introduced himself to Julia and her mother, Emma, who'd followed her daughter out the door of the house to see what the commotion was about.

Oliver and James found a place for Lucky in the barn and gave him some oats and hay for his supper. "I don't really have a place for you in the house," Oliver said. James quickly interrupted him. "I have my bedroll and just a few belongings. I'd feel more comfortable out here with Lucky, to tell you the truth. I don't like being a burden."

"You're no burden at all," said Emma, "in fact, you're the answer to my prayers. We need your help, and Oliver's just too proud, and we're too poor to get it from others in the area. We have only a few neighbors nearby, and they're not much farther along than we are, although most families have sons to help. We have not been blessed in that way, though Julia does her best to help, and we're so grateful to have her."

Oliver, embarrassed by this conversation, gestured for James to follow him for a quick tour of the farm. James could see the potential, and he could see the labor it would take to work the soil and bring in enough crops to make the land pay for itself. With two strong men and three horses, James could visualize a living—at least for a while, until he could save up enough for his own place. He felt pangs of nostalgia as he saw the chicken coop and the small vegetable garden, and fought off feelings of guilt about his mam and brothers and sisters.

When the two men returned to the house to clean up for dinner, James found himself staring at Julia, who reminded him of a younger version of his beautiful Kathleen back in Ireland. "No, I

56

can't let myself think about her. That part of my life is over." Besides, Julia was obviously way too young for him; she looked to be barely a teenager, certainly not interested in an older man like himself, hardened by his time on the road, hands rough and calloused by the work along the way. Catching his glance, Julia looked at him with a smile, then blushed and looked away.

Emma motioned for everyone to come to the supper table, where she'd made a thick soup with potatoes and vegetables and hearty bread. James was grateful for the home-cooked meal and a family to share it with, in stark contrast to the bunkhouses often filled with boisterous, sometimes violent, often foul-smelling men. "I don't mean to pry, James, but I'd be interested to know where your people are and how long you've been on the road."

James had worked hard to forget his past, embarrassed by his abandonment of Kathleen and all he feared might have happened to his family, reluctant to open doors to memories he'd pushed aside for the years since he'd jumped on the ship in Derry headed for the States. He answered truthfully, but with little detail. "I'm just like all the other poor souls who left families behind rather than starve in Ireland. I've started over. I'm looking for a chance for a life, my own land, out from under the bloody English."

Emma sighed. "We know the stories, and our own's not so different. This new country's not easy by any means, but it's better than what we faced in the old. We're all longing for a better way of life, and if we can help each other along the way, maybe we'll get there."

"I've been fortunate, with help from folks like you, Mrs. Abbott, all along the way. I landed in Boston several years ago, lucky to survive the journey over the sea—a lot of people on the boat with me didn't. Boston and the city life were not for me, and neither was the hard feelings they had for the Irish. I didn't leave a country that treated its people so poorly only to come to the same kind of treatment in another. I prefer the country life, like that of Donegal, where I came from, so I've been working my way, saving a little, in order to find the place that feels like home. To tell you the truth, this is as close as I've come to finding that place, and I'm ever so grateful. I can't promise you I'll stay forever, and maybe you won't want me to, but I'll do my best while I'm here. I can see what Oliver's trying to do, and I know I can be of help."

He looked at Emma, and then at Julia, who smiled at him, before getting up to clear the table. "Thank you for the delicious meal. May I help you clear up the dishes?"

Emma looked at James in surprise. "Why, Julia and I usually take care of that kind of work. Oliver's always busy outside and by the time he comes inside, he's ready to rest."

"In my family, I was happy to help my mam. I'm not proud, Mrs. Abbott, and I hope you'll let me help wherever help is needed."

James went into the kitchen with the rest of the supper dishes, and Emma and Oliver could hear them making jokes and talking as they did the dishes together. "I like the young man, Oliver," Emma said. "He talks plain, he's eager to work, and he appreciates what he's given. What a stroke of fortune to come upon him in town."

Oliver shook his head in agreement. "I just hope he works as hard in the fields as he does in the house! We'll know more tomorrow."

After the dishes were done, James said goodnight to the family and went out to the barn, where he'd set up his bedroll and his few personal belongings. He checked on Lucky, making sure he had fresh water. He whistled an Irish folk tune and noted that he felt at peace with his life, a welcome feeling after being alone and on his own for such a very long time.

James slept very deeply that first night, awakened by the sound of roosters and chickens cackling. He awoke with a start, thinking he was somehow back in Rathmullan. He looked up, saw Lucky, and heaved a sigh of relief tinged with a bit of grief for all he'd left behind.

He put on his clothes and made his way out to the fields, where he found Oliver looking over his land. "Plowing these fields with two horses would be a damn sight easier than one old man and a horse, I think."

James nodded. "Lucky hasn't had any experience with a plow at all, but maybe your horse could teach him. I guess the first thing to do is to rig up the frame to do the work and then get the horses accustomed to each other and the plow." The two men went into the barn to see what lumber and parts were there and what they'd need to get a blacksmith to work up for them in town, turning a single plow into a double. They'd need a double harness for the horses, too.

Oliver could see that James was not only good with his hands, he was skillful at design, too. Even better, Oliver liked James' gentle but determined approach with the horses. James wondered what Oliver's plans were for the fields and the farm; clearly, he a vision, and James wanted very much to be a part of it.

"I've been able to add a little bit of land every year. Most of the farmers around here are putting their land into cotton and using slaves brought over from Africa to do the work. I don't want anything to do with that. This country's headed for war, James; cotton and slaves are at the heart of it. I want a peaceful life, with some cows to milk, some chickens to roost, and hay for grazing."

"I've learned plenty about slavery as I made my way down from Boston through the southern states. We didn't have 'slavery' in Ireland, but we might as well have called it what it was—and I watched people die from starvation and poor treatment at the hands of others. Like you, I want to work hard, but I don't want to earn a living by abusing other people," James explained, as they looked at the fields ready to be cleared and planted.

"I figure, we could plant grasses and wheat. I've got a bull and a milk cow, and they'll need food. The soil's rich, and we can take care of ourselves with the chickens and vegetables. I've been able to save a little money by selling off what we don't need and by renting grazing to other farmers nearby. With your help, I could do a lot more."

"Let's get to work," James replied. He shook hands with Oliver, and from that first conversation, both men marveled at the good fortune that had brought them together. James had the home he'd been seeking, and Oliver had help he couldn't afford to pay for, with no strong sons at home to help with the work. James worried that he might invest too much of himself in Oliver's farm, with nothing to show for it at the end, but he decided to take a chance and trust. He didn't feel like he had much of a choice.

Together, the two men started small, beginning with plowing the fields and planting grasses for dairy and cattle to graze. Realizing that the barn was not large enough to house the dairy cattle they imagined, Oliver reached out to his neighbors, asking for their help, as he'd given help to them over the years. Neighbors noticed the strong hired hand and the small steady changes they saw in the fields, vegetable gardens, and chicken coops. The renovated barn included a separate place for James to live, which made him feel even more like part of the family.

James showed Julia how to take better care of the chickens, resulting in more eggs and more chicks, and she now became part of the enterprise, taking eggs to market every week. She already was helping in the one-room school, teaching the youngest ones, while being watched over by a teacher hired by the small town. Barely fourteen, Julia felt deeply the responsibility of helping her small family, unusually small for the time. Emma had badly wanted to have more children, but miscarriage after miscarriage had thwarted that plan and had sapped her strength.

Although Oliver was not that much older than James, he treated him as the son he'd always wanted. The two worked easily together, dividing up tasks, solving problems as they arose, and enjoying each other's company. By the end of the third year, the farm had a dozen dairy cows, a thriving business of raising and selling chickens, and the grazing land continued to support not just Oliver's cows but others. They experimented with using chicken and cow manure as fertilizer for the hays and oats they were growing and with rotating the crops depending on what seemed to grow best.

~~~

Julia had her own horse that she rode to school, and her pony could pull her small wagon with the chicks and eggs she took to market. James still helped out in the kitchen and around the house, and the little family lived in harmony with the land and their neighbors, as Oliver had always dreamed. Neighbors became accustomed to seeing them at church on Sunday and in various gatherings around the small community. Julia, now sixteen and always mature for her age, began to fill out and attract attention from the boys of the nearby farms.

The only worrisome cloud on the horizon was Emma's health. She was a very private woman, greatly affected by her inability to bring more children into the world, and she had retreated even more since her last miscarriage, deferring to Julia the role of woman of the house. Thin as a string bean to begin with, Emma began to lose weight, and her energy level many days was not sufficient to warrant even getting out of bed. She hated being a burden, and she had no use at all for doctors, not that the doctor in town was much use. Julia made sure she ate breakfast and checked on her as often as she could during the day, but it was clear to all of them that Emma was declining…and rapidly.

The next winter, a long, cold, rainy cold ordeal, brought with it coughs, colds, and misery to the whole family, but Emma's symptoms persisted and worsened. Julia finally insisted that the doctor in the area be summoned, and he came out to the house, sniffling and coughing just like the rest of them. He listened to Emma's lungs and heart, and she told him how awful she had felt for such a long time. "I'm just too tired to keep going," she sighed. "I don't want to be a burden any longer, and I already know there's nothing you can do for me." As he was leaving, she began to cough, long, wracking coughs that broke Julia's heart.

The doctor took her aside, held her hand, and tried to reassure her. "Your mother has worked hard all her life, and she's only hanging on because she's worried about you and your pa. Let her know she can rest and that you'll all be fine. That's the only medicine I can recommend." Julia burst into tears with that prescription, even though she could see it was probably true.

Julia took her mother some herb tea and rubbed her back and hands with liniment, praying for a healing miracle. She leaned down and whispered, "I love you, mama, and I'm grateful to you for giving me life and teaching me everything I know. I'm grown now, and I promise you I'll take care of Pa and the farm. You don't need to worry; you just need to rest."

Emma smiled wanly at her beautiful, grown-up daughter, and thanked her for her words and for being so precious to her. "My time is almost up in this life, but I'm proud of the life we've made. Help your pa carry it on. You marry that James Lockhart and raise a family of your own, you hear? He's a good man, and you won't be sorry."

Julia blushed and spluttered and then became quiet. "James has been my best friend for a very long time, Mama, but more like a big brother than a beau. But the other boys in town seem so childish by comparison to James; I just don't seem to be able to take them seriously."

Emma's eyes began to close, and Julia brought the covers over her shoulders to make sure she was warm enough. "Just heed my words, girl, and you won't go wrong. Now let me sleep. I'm so very tired."

The next morning James took a breakfast tray in to Emma, as he often did, giving Julia time to check on her chickens and do a few chores before their own meal. She opened her eyes and smiled at him. "James, thank you for the breakfast, but I'm not hungry in the least. Pull up that chair, son; I have something to say to you."

James moved the tray away from the bedside and drew up a chair. He took her hand in his, and looked at her intently as she started to speak, her voice tired and weak. "I spoke to Julia last night, and now I'm going to speak to you. It's time for you and Julia to make a life together as a couple. I know you are close as brother and sister, but that's not what I'm talking about. I probably won't be around to see it, but I could sleep easier having told you my thoughts."

James wiped a tear from his eye and gave Emma's hand a squeeze. "She's a beautiful young lady, your Julia. I know, because

I've watched her grow up these last few years, keeping her at a distance to give some young man her own age the chance to sweep her off her feet. We've been good friends, you know, nothing more."

"Don't waste my time, James, I have neither energy nor patience to beat around the bush. The two of you were meant for each other, and any fool can see that."

James could see Emma's agitation affecting her ability to get her breath. "Emma, rest easy now. I'm not blind, and I'm no fool. I'm humbled that you'd consider my asking for her hand. Would you give me a chance to ask Julia myself?"

"Give me your word, James, let me go in peace." With those words, Emma closed her eyes and let go of James' hand. James got up slowly and left the room, breakfast tray in his hand. He passed Julia, who'd just come in from caring for her chickens, and he let her know her ma had not eaten anything and was declining.

By the end of the day, Oliver, Julia and James had gathered in the bedroom where Emma lay gasping for breath. They each gave her a kiss and let her know they loved her. They looked at each other helplessly until the end finally came in the middle of the night. They put the handmade quilt made by Emma's mother over her and closed her eyes.

"Time for bed, Papa," Julia importuned, tears streaming down her face.

"In a little while, my girl," said Oliver, "I haven't said good-bye yet."

James headed out to his shed, and Julia went up to her room.

Traditions of burial and funeral superseded the regular family routines; neighbors dropped by with platters of food and expressions of sadness at the loss of Emma. Friends shared stories of Emma's generosity and kindness. Over the next few months, Julia's relationship with James began to change, and they began to talk about those last conversations with Emma. James shared his concern about his age; Julia spoke of her lack of interest in the immature boys her own age in the area. They took long walks in the fields and woods nearby, glorying in the beginnings of new spring growth and the birth of calves.

Oliver's spirits had not recovered since the death of his wife, and he found himself no longer interested in new farming techniques (or even old farming techniques), farm animals, or any aspect of farm maintenance. James was taking on more and more of the chores and began feeling a little restless: he was putting his heart and soul into a farm in which he had no ownership interest, and he yearned to have a place of his own.

Julia bore the brunt of the responsibility of keeping the household on an even keel. She helped James wherever she could, tried to keep her pa engaged and connected to friends in town and busy around the farm, while she was grieving herself. She sensed James' restlessness, and perhaps she, too, was ready for a change. She grew weary of watching Oliver sitting listlessly on the porch, while James managed the lion's share of the chores.

One night, it all came to a head in the middle of a thunderstorm that made the cows moo and horses whinny with uneasiness; even the chickens were unsettled and clucked and crowed relentlessly. Julia had cooked a simple dinner, and her pa had been critical – the beef was too tough, the vegetables overcooked, the dessert dull and uninteresting. "Things just aren't the way they used to be when your ma was around," Oliver sighed and pushed his plate away.

"You're right, Pa, and no one knows it better than James and me, because we're the ones doing all the work. I'm sick and tired of your complaints and watching you sit on the porch doing nothing but feeling sorry for yourself." Julia felt outnumbered and outweighed by the two men, unvalued and unappreciated.

"You know, Julia, I've been thinking," said James, "maybe it is time for a change. I've been here just going on five years, and I'm not getting any younger. You're just coming in to your prime. Your pa's stuck in a rut, and we're just plowing the same old fields, year after year. I want my own home, my own land. I'm grateful for all I've been given here, but it's time I had a chance to follow that dream I came to America lusting for—that opportunity. If we sold this place, we could start a new life, in a new place. I like what I'm hearing about Texas, just barely become a state. I'd like you both to come with me."

"And what would you be using for money to buy this new place you're talking about, James?"

"We've farmed this land together since I arrived five years ago—all three of us have invested blood, sweat and tears, and you might recall, precious little in wages for all that work. What if the proceeds of the land sale were the basis of a new partnership, in a new land, with terms we'd agree on?" James took a deep breath, and another, wanting to avoid a confrontation about their financial relationship, never formalized more than a handshake on room and board for James' labor.

Oliver said very little, not really wanting to leave behind the world he'd created and loved all these years. But without Emma, he could see Julia and James' point: what was to be gained by staying, surrounded by memories of Emma, her belongings, her very soul which seemed to hang in the air all around them.

"I've been hearing about homesteading in Texas, under the Homestead Act, which would give us one hundred and sixty acres in exchange for farming the land for at least three years. Some of the people in town have been talking about it and thinking of leaving for greater opportunity. I'd be happy to have your help, financial and otherwise, but I'm not depending on it."

James looked with appreciation and affection at Julia, who'd shared her dissatisfaction about the status quo. He remembered his conversation with Emma and wondered if this was the right time to bring up the dream he'd kept buried in his heart since Emma's death. "I'm respectful of the opportunities I've been given her and the fact that you've treated me like family, and Julia's my trusted friend. The truth is, though, my feelings go beyond friendship for Julia, and I'd like your permission to court her, which is a little awkward since we live so close together."

Julia blushed, both embarrassed by the turn of the conversation, but delighted by the attention. "I was wondering when either of you was going to ask what *I'd* like," she teased, looking directly at James and then her father. "If the truth be told, I've been sweet on you ever since the day you came to the farm. Nothing's happened to change that, except that I've grown up, and I'm old enough to decide what I want for my own life."

CHAPTER 11

TRACEY

"Whatever you do, you need courage. Whatever course you decide upon, there is always someone to tell you that you are wrong. There are always difficulties arising that tempt you to believe your critics are right. To map out a course of action and follow it to an end requires some of the same courage that a soldier needs."
—Ralph Waldo Emerson

Tracey arrived at the airport in Shannon, Ireland, using the last of the trust funds that Oona and Ella had left her. There would have been so much more, but the trusting elderly sisters had turned over their financial affairs to a local attorney, feeling relieved that Tracey would be taken care of after they'd passed. Neither of them spent much of their pensions and were quite expert at scrimping and saving. It turned out, however, that they (and a number of other well-intentioned Austin senior citizens), had been taken in by the charm and confidence exuded by the lawyer, and in the end, the lawyer ended up with the bulk of the estate, and Tracey got very little.

At the airport, Tracey got a tourist visa valid for three months (even though she was quite sure she was never leaving.) As soon as she got off the plane, she heaved a sigh of relief. She'd arrived with the traditional leather-bound Family Genealogy book given to each of the children in the extended family of James Lockhart and a few personal belongings. She already felt like she was connected to family roots that could not be taken away, unlike the child she'd aborted.

She'd gotten on a bus at the airport and headed for Dublin, where she spent a week or two, doing some exploring at the Trinity College Library, looking at the Book of Kells, trying out traditional Irish dishes accompanied by fresh soda bread and tea, and surveying the people around her, all of whom seemed dedicated to making her feel at home. She checked out destinations from Dublin and found herself drawn to Cork, somewhat at random—she liked the way it felt on her tongue. "Why not?" she wondered. She checked out of the hostel and set off to the bus station. Four hours later, she climbed down from the bus and meandered to the university part of town.

Tracey went to the An Brog pub alone, having wandered up Oliver Plunkett Street, neither looking for someone nor wanting to be alone. She spent the first hour or so just wandering around all the nooks and crannies, studying the various posters on the walls. She felt at home here and could imagine making it her own "local"—if she stayed in Cork.

She was soaking up the ambiance, when a boisterous group at the next table caught her attention. She envied the easy banter (Tracey had learned about Irish "craic" from her travel guide) and imagined being part of the group. She glanced at the handsome young Irishman (judging by his hair color and accent), who smiled and gave her a tip of his cap. She looked away, then looked back, a little embarrassed, a little excited, wondering what might happen next. She finished her first beer, then ordered a second at the bar. As she was waiting, the young man got up from his chair and stood behind her.

Tracey ordered her beer, then turned around to face the Irishman. "You're not from around here, are you?" he asked. She rolled her eyes, "Is that what you say to all the girls? Can't you be a little more original than that?" He laughed. "I like a girl with spirit. Where are you from?"

"I'm Tracey Tompkins from Texas. Who are you?"

"I'm Brian Bailey from Ballinora. Welcome to Ireland! What are you doing here?"

"That's a really good question. My great-great grandfather immigrated to America from Donegal, and I'm doing something like that, in reverse. I landed in Shannon, spent some time in Dublin, then took the bus to Cork. I'm looking for a place to call home. I've actually been looking for a place to call home my whole life, but that's a long story. What's yours?"

Brian and Tracey picked up their beers, moved to a different table from the group of friends, and ended the evening in his hotel room, where they stayed for the next three days. Tracey was restless to explore more of Ireland, and Brian had to get back to the farm where he lived, back to the land he loved, the work he knew, and the routines he was comfortable with. Neither of them had any idea this weekend would change their lives forever.

Tracey walked to the bus and bought a one-way ticket to Belfast. After a weekend with Brian Bailey from Ballinora, choosing a city that started with a B seemed logical, somehow. Why not? she thought.

Tracey found the tourist office, and a kind woman pointed her in the direction of the Belfast International Youth Hostel, 22 Donegal Road. Tracey liked that her new home was on Donegal Road; she felt closer to her great-great-grandfather, as though she were one step closer to a forever home. She arrived, taken aback by its size and pleased that it was so well-situated in the center city. The staff greeted her warmly and gave her a quick tour, showing her the dorm and semi-private rooms. "I'll try the dorm," she said, "and I'd like to stay a week while I look for a place to live and a job." She was exhausted, physically and emotionally, and all she wanted was to stop feeling lost.

Without a work permit, she quickly learned that finding work would be a problem. She had enough money to survive a few months, assuming she could find a cheap place to live, but she had to count every penny. She was used to that; she'd made the inheritance from Oona and Ella last a very long time—long enough to make her way through UT with an art history degree, for whatever that might be worth.

She started each day passing by the news agent; she couldn't afford a *Herald Tribune,* but she did a speed read, and the man in the kiosk noticed her interest in what was going on in the world beyond Ireland. "You're not from around here, are you?" he queried.

"You know, I'm getting a little tired of the question, but I'm happy to tell you I'd *love* to be from around here, if I could just find a place to live and a job. I don't have a work permit, so it's not that easy," Tracey explained.

"You know, it's not that easy to find someone to work in the kiosk, if you want to know the truth, and I'm not getting any younger. Would you like to give it a try? With your looks, I bet you'd sell a lot more papers than I ever could!" the man joked.

"I'd be happy to give it a try. You have to admit, there aren't too many news agents from Texas in Belfast," Tracey said. "The novelty might well be good for business!"

"You're on," he said. "My name's James, news is my game, you'll be to blame—just kidding...we'll try it two days a week to start and see how it goes. My wife will be thrilled, after thirty years, to have weekends off."

Tracey knew she'd need a lot more than two days a week, but it was a start, and under the table worked fine for James, so it worked fine for Tracey.

"When do I start?" Tracey asked. "What's the pay?"

James shrugged and said, "Let's try 40 quid a week, eight hours a day. I'm open from 7 am – 7 pm, so I can catch people on the way to work or on the way home in the afternoon. How about you try 11 am – 7 pm?"

Tracey said, "I'm also looking for a place to live, really cheap, safe, and warm. Will you keep your eyes out for me? I have a little bit of money saved up for a deposit, and I'd be happy to work as a nanny or housekeeper to help pay the rent."

"I'll talk to the wife and we'll figure something out."

Tracey found her eyes filling with tears at the kindness of this almost total stranger. She was learning that in Ireland, people were much more apt to be helpful, generous, friendly, and kind than she ever had experienced in Texas, southern hospitality notwithstanding.

Tracey found it hard to imagine that something could be figured out, but she was willing to try. With one part time job and the possibility of a place to live, she was looking forward to being able to breathe without the crushing pressure of living on the edge, barely able to survive. "You've been so kind, James; is there anything I can do to show my gratitude?"

"I'm just doing what the good Lord put me on this earth to do, dearie. If you want to show your appreciation, pop into the chapel just down the street, light a candle, and say a prayer. Tell Jesus that James sent you."

Tracey had never been particularly religious; her family, as far as she knew, had been mainline Protestant. She had no idea what religion her ancestor might have brought with him. As she headed east up Castle Street from College Street and the university area, she saw the lovely chapel off to her left. She turned into Chapel Lane, and read a bit of the history of the beautiful church on the plaque outside. Apparently, in 1782, few Catholics lived in Belfast, and they were without a church. Local Presbyterians took up a collection to build the first Catholic Church in Belfast, completed in 1784. The Catholics had been disenfranchised from their religion, and although the Presbyterians were Protestants, they weren't part of the Church of England and felt excluded. The local militia formed a Guard of Honor on the opening day; most of the militia were Presbyterians, which showed that Belfast was a different place then compared to what happened later.

To the right of the church, Tracey noticed a peaceful small garden with a lovely grotto and stained-glass window, commemorating the church's role in sheltering evacuees from the 1956 Hungarian Revolution. "It seems like we humans are always running away from *something*," Tracey noted sadly. She returned to the door of the Chapel, saw that there was Mass at one o'clock tollowed by a prayer group. To honor James' request, Tracey decided to do both.

Tracey knelt in a pew and found herself praying—a prayer of gratitude for James and the opportunity to have a job and a place to live; a prayer of confession for so many things—the abortion, and all the ways she felt she'd let Oona and Ella down over the years, and a prayer of intercession, wishing for a miracle to give her the strength to build a new life in northern Ireland. With those prayers, Tracey found the burden of all her previous mistakes lifted. She'd never understood how prayer worked, the power of forgiveness whether given or received, and the blessing of giving herself over to a higher power, even temporarily.

After Mass was over, Tracey moved out into the aisle, where she saw a young man with a name tag indicating he was on the church staff. "I saw on the signboard that there was a prayer meeting after Mass," Tracey said. "Can you tell me where I might find it?"

"I can do better than that—I can take you to our Library downstairs myself; that's where the meeting will be held. My name is John Ross, and I'm a deacon here. Are you new to this area?"

"Yes, I am. I came to Ireland looking for connections with my family ancestors, and it looks like I may be putting down some roots for myself."

John led Tracey to a cozy room with a couple of small couches, a few chairs, and walls covered with books. A small table held an electric kettle, some cookies, and a selection of teas.

"Please help yourself to some tea and biscuits, and we'll wait just a few minutes to see if others will join us. I'm going to just run back up to the sanctuary to see if we've left anyone behind."

After John left, Tracey helped herself and looked around at the books on the shelves. She picked up some leaflets about programs and services the Church offered. After a few minutes, Joe returned by himself. "Some days are busy, but today we are on our own. I'm wondering if you have any special prayers you'd like to offer or if there are questions I can answer about our church. Did you grow up Roman Catholic?"

Tracey thought for a few minutes and then answered. "I grew up in an orphanage and then lived with my grandmother and her sister in Texas. I may have gone to a few church services on holidays and maybe to Sunday school a few times, but in Protestant churches, not Catholic. I only came here, because the newsagent down the street said I should come and tell Jesus that James sent me."

John smiled. "That's a better reason than most people have for walking through our doors. Tell me a little about yourself. It takes a lot of courage to move so far away from home."

Tracey snorted. "Home? I always think of the line from that Robert Frost poem-- 'Home is the place where, when you have to go there, they have to take you in.' But it sure wasn't the case with me. I guess I've been looking for that mythical place my whole life. But I'm all done looking for places to take me in; I've learned that if I want a home, I'm going to have to make it myself. Ireland's where my family came from in the first place, and I figure it's the place I'm going to call home from here on. It's here, or it's nowhere."

"Well, you've come to the right place, no question about that. Since you know your poetry, you're probably familiar with the Chinese proverb, 'A journey of a thousand miles begins with a single step.' You've certainly taken that step today, and I'm here to let you know you don't need to take any more steps alone."

John started to pull a prayer book off the bookshelf but changed his mind. "Sometimes a prayer from the heart is better than any prayer from the book," he said, with a warm smile. He asked Tracey for whom she'd like to pray, and after each of her prayers, he responded "Lord, hear our prayers." When she'd finished, he offered a closing prayer. "Hold your child Tracey in your arms and your heart as she makes a new life. Release her from any sins of the past and grant her strength and resilience for the challenges she'll face in the future. Walk with her, lift her up, and help her find the peace she is seeking. Amen."

Tracey stood up, shook John's hand, and thanked him for his support. "I expect you may be seeing me again," she said. "I should hope so," John responded. "By the way, what was the name of the newsagent who suggested that you come here?"

"His name is James," answered Tracey. "Why do you ask?"

"He's my brother," said John.

Tracey made her way up from the Library and out the door of the Church, her heart full from the encounter with the Deacon, preceded by her conversation with James, the newsagent. Was there something magical about Ireland, or was something changing inside her? She knew that something different was happening, and that she wasn't feeling so alone anymore.

She walked back to the Hostel on Donegal Road and checked in at Reception. She had three days left of her week's reservation, but she wanted the comfort and safety of knowing she had a place to stay until she found something more permanent. James had said he'd try to help, but she didn't want to rely on his generosity if she could find something on her own. To do that, she'd need more work. She walked back from her bunk to the reception desk and took a deep breath. The young woman at the desk looked up from her papers and smiled. "Was there something else you're needing?"

Tracey smiled back and gathered up her courage. "I was just wondering if you ever need someone to help out around here. I've just gotten a very part-time job at a newsagent's down the road, but I'm going to need a lot more than that if I'm going to stay in Ireland. And I *am* going to stay in Ireland, that part's for sure. If there's no work here at the Hostel, could you suggest some places I might try?"

"What kind of work are you thinking of?"

"I'm really open to anything. I mean, I've got a degree in Art History, but that's not too useful, obviously. I've been a nanny; I've worked in a library, and I've done all kinds of things to put myself through college, the usual waitress and clerk sorts of things. I have to be up front, though, I don't have a work visa yet, but I'm sure I can get one, and I'm a really hard worker, no matter what the job is."

"I wouldn't be too optimistic about the work visa. Have you already overstayed your tourist visa?" Sarah, the good-humored but business-like desk clerk at the Hostel, had seen it all in her years behind the counter.

"It expired last week. I guess I was afraid if I tried to renew it, they'd say no and deport me immediately, or something awful. All I know is, I have nothing to go back to, and every reason to stay here. My roots are in Ireland, and here I'll stay." Tracey's voice quavered a little, one tear rolled down her cheek.

"Oh, dear, it can't be all that bad where you've come from, was it? Here's a tissue, dry your eyes, and let's have a spot of tea and think about what to do." Sarah was struck by Tracey's determination and willingness to open up about her situation. The Hostel had emptied out for the day of the young people who were staying there, and Sarah felt comfortable taking some time to console her young visitor.

She put the electric kettle on and invited Tracey to come behind the counter and sit down. The two of them sat quietly with the rumble of the kettle as the water started to boil. Sarah took a deep breath and said, "Tell me a bit about where you've come from and what you're looking for."

"Sarah, you are so kind, but trust me, you don't have time to listen, and it's really hard for me to tell the long way. Here's the two-minute version: I was born to two heroin addicts and put in an orphanage when I was two. Eventually my grandmother and her sister, both pretty crazy, took me in until I was a teenager. I got pregnant and got an abortion. I inherited a little money when my elderly relatives died, but most of it was embezzled by the lawyer they'd hired to handle their estate. No relatives stepped up to keep me, although there were plenty of them who could have. I found a way to finish college and used the last of the inheritance to get on a plane and come here, because Ireland is where my great-great-grandfather came from, and it feels more like home than anyplace I've been so far."

Sarah wiped a tear from her own eye this time and put her hand on Tracey's. "That's quite a story!" She paused, giving herself a chance to think of a plan for this young woman. "Thanks for trusting me. Now let's get to work. We need room cleaners here every day, 7 days a week, starting at 8 am and ending at 2. Since you don't have papers, I can't pay you a salary, but we can put a roof over your head and feed you breakfast. Keep our little arrangement to yourself, so I don't get flooded with requests from others. You'll start tomorrow. I'll introduce you to our other cleaners and they can show you how the laundry works, where the cleaning supplies are, and what the job is. It's hard work."

"Sarah, I've already got work at the newsagent on Saturday and Sunday; I can pay you some rent to make up for the days I can't work."

"We'll worry about that later, after you get yourself settled and prove you're up to the work. Deal?"

Tracey smiled and nodded.

"Let's find a place to put your belongings and a bed you can call your own."

The two women found a small storeroom with a window, across from a bathroom used by Hostel staff. They put Tracey's backpack, her small collection of books, and toiletries on the shelves. Sarah found a spare cot, mattress, sheets, and towels for Tracey to use.

~~~

For a few weeks, Tracey settled into a much-needed sense of stability and calm. She had a place to stay, work to do, and she even had time to attend Mass and a few events at St. Mary's. She often stopped in to see Deacon John, who'd introduced her to the parish priest and a couple of women church leaders active in the parish. Pretty soon, Tracey became a fixture at the church, anytime she wasn't working.

She'd worked her heart out at the Hostel, doing the work of two cleaners if one or the other of the regular workers had to miss a day, happy to be busy and grateful for Sarah's generosity. She also made a point of greeting visitors and being helpful in all kinds of ways around the office, when her cleaning chores were done. She loved her little storeroom cubicle—it offered her privacy and a sense of safety.

She loved her work at the newsagent's as well, greeting by name the regulars who stopped by for the daily newspaper, lottery ticket, or magazine, or even just a candy bar. James was delighted that he'd gotten her connected at the nearby church, that she'd found a safe place to live, and seemed to be getting herself on her feet. The little bit of cash that James gave her each week was enough to buy food and pay Sarah a little bit of rent, important to Tracey's sense of fairness for the two days each week she didn't work for her keep. Tracey was proud of her ability to live on almost nothing and scrounge for everything she owned.

~~~

After a couple of months of hard work and new friends, she woke up with a familiar, sickening feeling. Nausea. She thought about what she might have eaten or where she might have picked up a stomach bug, but in her heart, she knew it was not so simple. As she heaved into the toilet across from her room, she knew what it was. Morning sickness.

She'd not been with a man, or even thought about being with a man since…that amazing weekend in Cork. She burst into tears, then threw up again. "Why am I so stupid? Why don't I learn from my mistakes? I've barely even started with my new life, and I just don't think I can deal. I just don't." Tracey sat on the floor by the toilet for a long time, head on her hands on the toilet seat, trying to make sense of how often she had sabotaged herself just as she was beginning to achieve something she'd wanted so badly. What did it mean? Now what?

She went to her cubicle and took the small stash of money from her bank, a marmalade jar with coins and small bills. First stop, Boots the Chemist to get a pregnancy test kit. She'd get two, just to make sure. She'd get some Pepto-Bismol to settle her stomach, in case it was some sort of stomach thing, and not the thing she feared most. She slipped out the back door of the Hostel, not wanting anyone to see her, afraid she'd lose it—tears or barfing, or both.

She made it to Boots in less than ten minutes, found what she was looking for, made her purchases, and asked if she could use the restroom. Once in the restroom, she felt nauseous again, threw up first, then sat down on the toilet to get the samples for the test kit. After waiting with her eyes closed for what seemed an interminable time for the results to show in the little test tubes, she opened her eyes. The tell-tale blue lines were undeniable.

She put the test kits in her purse, took a swig of Pepto-Bismol, and left the store in a daze. Instead of returning to the Hostel, she decided to go to the place where she'd placed her faith, the place where she felt her lifetime of bad luck and bad decisions had changed, at least temporarily: St Mary's Parish. Just a few minutes' walk from Boots, she took her time as she thought about who to talk to—Deacon John, who had been so kind, or Teresa, one of the women who'd taken her under her wing, inviting her to prayer meetings that had meant so much.

As she walked up the sidewalk to the church office, she felt faint and nauseous again, and the ground started to shift under her feet. She quickly sat down on a bench near a little garden, where the sound of water coming out of a fountain soothed her. She put her head between her knees and said a little prayer to St. Francis, whose small statue in the garden comforted her when she'd stopped there to pray on her daily visits to the church.

Once the dizziness had gone away, she stood up, feeling stronger, and ready to face her uncertain future. She opened the door to the office, and Teresa, welcomed her in. "My goodness, child, you're pale as a ghost. Come right on in and we'll have a cup of tea. You're not coming down with the flu, are you?"

"No, Teresa, it's not the flu. I've made a real mess of things, just as I've gotten started with a new life in Belfast. I have a place to live, two jobs, a church that's welcomed me in, and…"

Teresa interrupted her, "so it sounds like things are working out just as you'd planned?"

"That's just it, Teresa, my life doesn't seem to work according to any sort of plan. I'm just lost. And yes, things *did* seem to be working out, but there's ….a sort of complication."

Teresa, who had four daughters of her own, had been in church life for decades. She reminded herself to wait patiently to hear what was so troubling for Tracey and give her a chance to tell her story.

"I'm pregnant, Teresa. I just took two pregnancy tests, so there's no doubt. I'm not married; I barely know the guy I slept with. I'm thirty years old, I've already had one abortion. I've overstayed my tourist visa, and I don't want to go back to the US. My whole life seems like one giant lost cause, just like St. Jude." Tracey started to cry, and her tears turned into sobs, and Teresa took her into her arms, just as she had with her own daughters so many times over the years.

She got up to get a box of tissues and a glass of water for Tracey, before going to get the cups of tea and biscuits. "Knowing you, you've had nothing to eat, not much sleep, and you're probably dehydrated from all that crying. I've listened to you, and now it's your turn to listen to me, and listen hard. This child you're carrying is the child you'll keep. This is the child who will set your life on a proper course, and you will never want for a family again. This is the child you've been waiting for all your life. Instead of giving up hope, it's time for you to thank God for the blessing you've been given. We will all stand beside you in this journey; you will not do it alone. You have come into our lives, and we take care of our own. Now quit your crying, wipe those tears away, and look at me. You will have to have faith. You've lost your trust in others because of your rotten luck before. But your life has changed, starting right now. You will have to trust the good Lord and yourself to see this through. It won't be easy, but it will be worth it."

Tracey drank the glass of water that Teresa offered, then the cup of tea, and got up to leave. "You think I can do this?" she asked, a little tentatively.

"With God's help, you can do it. We'll be by your side."

Tracey walked back to the Hostel, thoughts like clouds drifting around in her mind. She decided not to tell Sarah at the Hostel what she'd learned but rather to keep her current life as normal as possible for the next few months. And the same with James, the newsagent. What was the AA slogan that her grandmother swore by? One day at a time.

The sun was shining, unusual in Belfast, known for its persistent grayness, and Tracey chose to see the sun as an omen. The leaves were starting to turn and float down in the fall breezes. As she considered Teresa's words, she felt her spirits start to lift. She dropped the bag with the used pregnancy tests in the trash. No looking back!

A new rhythm and routine dominated Tracey's life as work continued at the Hostel and the newsagent. She was a frequent participant in St Mary's women's prayer group, and she often stayed afterward to check in with Teresa, whom she regarded as her own personal saint. The fall days turned to winter; bare trees, fog, drizzly rain made for a bleak environment. "It's better than burning up in the Texas heat!" Tracey encouraged herself and just pushed through the short days, waking up in the dark, and walking home from church or the newsagent at dusk as afternoon turned to night. Tracey's bouts of morning sickness had diminished, and her spirits and energy had been buoyed by the arrival of the Christmas season.

That quickly changed, however, when she arrived back at the Hostel from the newsagent. Sarah handed her an official-looking letter with a return address of the Secretary of State, United Kingdom Home Department. "I'm not sure I want to open this," said Tracey grimly, handing it over to Sarah.

Sarah opened the notification, read it quickly, and said, "You'd better read it, and you'd better get some help. It says you've overstayed your visa, and you're to be deported."

Tracey's heart sank. She had been deluding herself that no one would find her. She knew that when she had checked into the Hostel, she'd had to provide her passport information, which presumably was passed along to the immigration authorities. What had she been thinking?

The next day after she finished her work at the Hostel, she took the official notice and went to the chapel first, hoping a prayer would be the right way to start. Then she headed to the office at St Mary's, looking for Teresa. The frightened look on Tracey's face concerned Teresa, who was as worried about Tracey's unborn child as she was about this young mother. "It looks like you need a cuppa, Tracey. Let's see what's going on with you and get you sorted." Teresa's business-like approach combined with compassion always relieved Tracey's worst fears and helped her feel less lost and alone.

"The Home Office is deporting me for overstaying my visa. That can't happen, can it? I've prayed and prayed about it, but that only goes so far, I guess."

Teresa gave her a hug and handed her a cup of tea with milk and sugar, just like Tracey always liked. She said, "Let me see the letter, and let's make a copy. We have people who can help us, and I've told you many times before, you're not alone here. You're not to give up! Now let's talk about something else. You need to be thinking ahead about housing for yourself and your baby-to-be. You're not going to be able to do two jobs and manage everything while you live in a closet at the Hostel, are you now? I've been making some contacts in Social Services and with Catholic Charities, and we've got some ideas."

Tracey handed over the deportation letter, and Teresa took it to the office copy machine and made a copy. She handed the original back to Tracey, who looked at it again and frowned. "Why should the Home Office of the United Kingdom want to deport me when I'm in Ireland, and my great-great-grandfather and my new baby are Irish?" Tracey queried.

Teresa replied, "You're asking questions about things that have kept people in knots for hundreds of years, my dear, so it's no wonder you're confused. You *do* remember that when you left Cork and came to Belfast by way of Derry that you crossed the border from the Republic of Ireland and entered Northern Ireland, which is part of the UK, right?"

"I guess I should have paid more attention. Teresa asked to see Tracey's passport and showed her the UK stamp and the expiration date for her entry. "Maybe one day there will be open borders and free entry back and forth, but for now, we are still separate countries, with different rules and bureaucracies."

Teresa instructed Tracey to go back to the Hostel and wait to hear from her. She would contact some immigration experts she knew and help Tracey take the next steps on that front and continue working on finding a place for Tracey to live.

Tracey put her teacup back on the counter and made her way slowly out to the street. She tried to accept Teresa at her word, but she had trusted so many people in her life before, and she had been disappointed each time. Why should this time be any different? She shook her head, knowing that that kind of thinking would get her nowhere except down in the dumps, and that's not where she needed to be.

Sarah met Tracey at the door when Tracey arrived back at the Hostel. "I was worried about you. Where did you go?" she asked.

"I've got a saint looking out for me at St. Mary's. She's helped me so much with everything that's happening, and I've never needed help more, that's for sure. She says there are people that can help with my immigration case and people who will help me find a more permanent place to live. She tells me to just put my faith in God and the rest will take care of itself. To tell you the truth, I don't have much experience trusting people or God, but I figure I've got nothing to lose. Trying to figure things out all by myself doesn't seem to be working, and people like you seem to be popping out everywhere I go in Ireland. Weird!"

Sarah heaved a sigh of relief. She'd just been told by her boss that Tracey would have to go. The last thing the Hostel needed was the Home Office hanging around and giving them grief about a guest; they did everything they could to avoid drama with their ever-changing roster of every sort of guest from every sort of place all over the world. Tracey was far from the first visitor who'd decided to call Ireland home once they landed at the Hostel, and the Home Office kept a close eye on things.

True to her word, the next day Teresa called Tracey at the Hostel and suggested that she come to the church office after finishing up her work at the Hostel and the newsagent. "I've been working with the North and West Belfast Health and Social Services Trust to find you a place to live and make sure you have pre-natal care leading up to your baby's arrival. We have an appointment with Mrs. Kincaid today at four. I think they will have found you a small flat to move into by Christmas. I'm still working on the immigration issue, but we're making some progress."

Teresa's call and mention of Christmas reminded Tracey of her hopes and dreams for her first Irish Christmas. "I just hope it won't be my last," she thought gloomily. She put that thought out of her mind and got busy with the laundry, floor-mopping, and dusting that went with the house-keeping job at the Hostel. She went on to the newsagent, where she relieved James of his chores and took over minding the small shop with its regular customers, an assortment of personalities and preferences, and the new people who turned up.

She left the newsagent just in time to meet Teresa at the church office to walk to the Social Services agency. They walked into the office, let the clerk know they had an appointment with Mrs. Kincaid, and then sat down in the waiting area, along with others also seeking government benefits. "I don't understand exactly how this works, Teresa. On the one hand, the government wants to throw me out of the country, and on the other, they want to help me find a place to live?"

Teresa shrugged. "The government, and Catholic Charities, for that matter, have the obligation to look after your unborn child. The agency that provides those services doesn't necessarily work with the Home Office that runs immigration. The same is true for your health care. The welfare of your baby is the responsibility of the government."

Mrs. Kincaid called out Tracey's name and ushered them into a small office cubicle. She looked over her glasses at Tracey, trying to determine from her looks what sort of person she was dealing with. "Mrs. Kelly has told me a little about your unusual circumstances, Miss Tompkins, and I'd like to hear your situation in your own words, too, if you don't mind."

Tracey knew how important this interview might be; she did her best to maintain a calm composure, trying not to get defensive about her situation, thinking instead of how she must stand up for the rights of her unborn baby, a prospective citizen of Ireland. "My baby has an Irish father, but we are not married. I am working very hard to support myself; I have a part-time job, and I'm looking for more work. I need a place to live, as the place where I was living has given me notice that I can't stay any longer."

"If you'll fill out these forms, Miss Tompkins, we'll see what we can do. You should hear from us by the end of the week." She stood up, signaling that the appointment had come to an end.

Tracey and Teresa left the office together for the short walk back to the Church. "Now about this baby's father. Have you tried to reach him to let him know what is happening?"

Tracey groaned. "I guess I knew I should try to get in touch, but I don't think he'll want to have anything to do with me. A one-night stand, well, I guess you'd call it a three-night stand, but still...he certainly never tried to get in touch with me."

"And how would he? I'd think it was a sight easier to find a pig farmer in Ballinora named Brian Bailey than it would be to find an American tourist in Belfast. I'll help you get an address, and you can write him a note. That might be easier than a phone call or a visit. And you can use the Church office as a point of contact until we get you a place to stay. We do have guest quarters, you know."

"I'll do it tomorrow, Teresa, if you insist. I guess you're right; he should know."

"You go on back to the Hostel and gather up your belongings and bring them back right here. Do you have money for cab fare?"

Tracey nodded, then gave Teresa a hug, suppressing an urge to collapse in a weeping heap at her feet. She walked to the Hostel, waved at Sarah, then went to her cubicle and began to put her belongings in her one suitcase and a black trash bag, a familiar means of moving possessions from her days at the orphanage, when kids came and went, taking their belongings in giant trash bags. Somehow if all your belongings were in a big trash bag, you sort of felt like trash, too, Tracey remembered.

Sarah came to find her and learn what had happened at the Social Services Agency and where Tracey would be going. She handed Tracey an envelope with some cash, donations from the other staff members of the Hostel who'd become Tracey's friends over the last few months. Tracey told Sarah she didn't want anyone to know where she was going, she didn't want to get anyone into trouble, and she wanted it to be as difficult as possible for the Home Office to find her. The two hugged each other and cried before saying goodbye. Tracey thanked Sarah and told her to thank the others who'd been so kind and generous to her.

She walked outside, dragging her suitcase and unwieldy trash bag, along with her sagging spirits, to the curb, where she hailed a taxi to St Mary's Church. Teresa was waiting for her at the door to the office. She picked up the trash bag and grabbed Tracey by the hand down a long hallway Tracey had never seen in her visits to the church. Teresa opened the door to a small, plain room furnished with a twin bed, a small desk and chair, a washbasin and a crucifix. "These guest quarters are sometimes used by visiting priests or nuns, or for a hosting guests at a retreat, or sometimes for situations like your own. There's a bathroom with a shower down the hall. We're lucky there's a space!"

"Don't I know it," said Tracey, looking at Teresa with gratitude and appreciation.

"Here's a sandwich and some fruit for your supper," said Teresa, pulling a small bag, some note paper, and a pen from her large purse. "Your homework for tonight is to write that letter to your baby's father. Mine is to find an address for him. Tomorrow we'll put it in the post and see what happens. Now it's time for me to get back to my family." Teresa gave Tracey a pat on the back and a quick hug goodbye, handing her the key to her room.

Tracey sat down on the bed, feeling weary and dreading the letter-writing assignment from Teresa. She washed her face and hands, ate the sandwich and apple, surprised by how hungry she was. She was reminded of the lunches long ago with Miss Donaldson, which brought a smile to her tear-streaked face. Heaving a big sigh, she left all her belongings packed away, feeling unsure how long she might be here and not wanting to take anything for granted. She got a glass of water, took out the paper and pen, and began to write.

Dear Brian,

It has been a few months since the weekend we met at An Brog in Cork. I don't know if you even remember Tracey Tompkins of Texas, and I guess I never imagined needing to get in touch with you. But I've learned recently that I'm pregnant, and you are the only man I have been with since I arrived in Ireland (actually, the only man I've been with in a very long time, since my younger days in Texas).

I didn't know where I would end up in Ireland, but it turns out that Belfast is my new home, and I don't plan to leave. I would like to talk with you about my situation, and I am asking for your help. I have no idea how you will respond to this letter.

I am currently staying in the guest quarters in St. Mary's Parish for the time being, so you can reach me here by mail or leave a message for me in the office. If I don't hear from you, I'll be calling in a few days.

Yours truly,

Tracey Tompkins
c/o St. Mary's Parish
Chapel Lane
Belfast BT1 1HH

CHAPTER 12

BRIAN

"By three methods we may learn wisdom: First, by reflection, which is noblest; Second, by imitation, which is easiest; and third by experience, which is the bitterest."
—Confucius

Brian came in from feeding the pigs, milking the cows, and checking on the chickens, and glanced at the mail. A handwritten envelope was unusual. Before going any farther, he went upstairs to take a shower and clean up, wondering who might be writing to him. His family members all lived in the area, so that seemed unlikely, and it didn't have the formal look of a wedding invitation.

Exhausted from a long day's work, he walked into the small, tidy kitchen, and took a bottle of Guinness from the fridge. He went into the den, put some coal in the stove, picked up the letter and sat down in his comfy chair. Brian was used to the damp, wintry weather; it was all he knew, really. He was not one to travel far from home, nor could he, with the responsibilities of running a farm on his shoulders.

He looked first at the return address—St Mary's Church, Belfast. It didn't ring any bells. Then he opened the letter and quickly scanned its contents. He felt his heart rate increase, and his mind quickly went into denial. He remembered the American girl and the weekend he'd spent with her, but the thought had never occurred to him to use protection. Most women took care of that on their end, he thought. He hadn't brought any condoms with him to Cork, for the simple reason that he'd never been one to fool around. The weekend with Tracey had been a one-off fling for sure, and how was it even possible that one weekend could lead to a pregnancy?

Now that he thought about it, he wondered if Tracey had set him up. She'd seemed so whimsical, so natural, so unconcerned about anything except enjoying their time together. Maybe she was a nut case? What had he been thinking? He'd never come close to a situation like this one before. He'd lived a simple, straightforward life, with a weekend or two in Cork to get a bit of relief from the sameness of his daily life, or when he had a doctor's appointment or errand to run in the City. What was he going to do?

He was too embarrassed to tell anyone, especially anyone in his family, and certainly not any of his friends. Ballinora was a tiny town, and his family would be mortified with the gossip and titters about his little escapade. A few of his friends had kidded him when they saw him leave the pub with Tracey, but what he'd done was so out of character that no one imagined that he'd had a three-day orgy of sorts. Where had that come from?

The last thing in the world he was going to do was to answer Tracey's letter. Maybe she'd have the good sense to know that he would have nothing to do with her request for further contact, much less support for the unplanned baby, if she were even pregnant. Maybe she figured him for an ignorant bogger, a country boy who'd give her money to make sure word didn't get out about their fling, and she might not even be pregnant. That was probably what was going on. He wasn't going to fall for it, either.

His mind raced, as he became more and more agitated about being taken advantage of. He went over every detail of their meeting in the pub; how could she have picked him out of the group of mates? How much beer had he drunk that he became so easily attracted to her? And when they'd parted, she'd not expressed any interest in keeping in touch or seeing him again.

How had she found him, anyway? What was she doing in a church in Belfast?

The more he thought about it, the more trapped he felt, and the more uneasy he felt about what might come next. He wanted a plan, but a plan for what? She couldn't prove anything, and she might not even be pregnant. He wanted to stop worrying, but he couldn't get the letter out of his mind. He folded it up into a tiny square and put it in the back of the middle drawer in his desk, where it would stay. Out of sight, out of mind.

He fixed himself a simple supper, cheese, home-cured sausage, and some bread that his sister had baked for him. Since he'd never married, and his parents and siblings lived in towns nearby, his family tried to make sure he knew they cared about him and felt looked after. They couldn't understand why he'd never been interested in a family of his own; he was quite devoted to his nieces and nephews and extended family.

He'd told them he had all the family he needed, with the pigs, horses, cows, and chickens; who had time to take care of anything else? And he had his faithful border collie Brady, now getting on in years, but good company nevertheless. The two of them trudged up the stairs and settled in for the night. Tomorrow would be another long day of work, as every day was, but it was what he knew and what he loved.

A week went by, and Brian felt relieved that no further contact had been received from Tracey. Maybe without a reply, she had given up her useless attempt to deceive him into providing support for her alleged baby. At least during the day, his chores and routines kept the matter out of his mind. But at night, he was plagued with doubts and dreams.

The next Sunday night, after a day of visiting with his family, he arrived home and greeted Brady with some special doggie treats baked by his favorite niece. The phone rang, he picked it up, and the call he'd been dreading had finally happened.

He heard Tracey's voice, not as animated as when they'd been together in Cork, start out a little haltingly. She didn't blame him for not answering her note, and she seemed almost apologetic for the call. She took the initiative by expressing what he'd suspected — that she was just trying to take advantage of him with a baby that might or might not be real. He was taken aback by her honesty; she didn't sound crazy or out of control.

"I can't help you, Tracey. I'm married with a family of my own, small children and all the rest. I didn't tell you that when we were together, and I'm not proud of that. But what you're saying would destroy them, and I don't think you're the kind of woman who would do that. Please leave me alone and don't ever contact me again."

Brian heard a click on the line, and was relieved that the connection had been terminated without any further discussion or dispute. He wasn't proud of his lie, and he wasn't proud of his behavior that weekend in Cork. But he was relieved, and he hoped that would be the end of it.

Brian's life before he met Tracey was not much to be proud of, either. He'd not been a particularly good student, and he'd had a hard time making friends. He'd been bullied by other students, and as he grew larger and stronger, he took to bullying others in self-defense or out of revenge. In those days, not much was done about it. He had a terrible temper, out of control many times, and his desperate parents had sought counseling for him after the number of referrals for bad behavior began to pile up. His parents had never had any illusions about higher education for any of their children (but some had surprised them), and when Brian decided to go into farming, his parents thought it was a sensible choice.

After Brian met Tracey, and he ignored her note and rebuffed her phone call, he became even more short-tempered and difficult. He had some financial problems, which he solved, at least temporarily, by stealing cows from his neighbors. He'd hoped to sell the cows, until the thefts were reported to the Gardaí, and DNA technology showed the ownership. He folded quickly under prosecution and restored all the calves to their owners; the settlement of the charges required some community service, but nothing more, given than he'd not had any criminal record before.

The local newspaper, the *Corkman*, reported the incident this way:

> *Judge Patterson asked for a full Court Welfare Officer's report on a 38 year old Ballinora man who pleaded guilty at Mallow District Court, to stealing 10 calves from both private properties and Kilmallock mart between the beginning of April and the end of May.*

> *Brian Bailey pleaded guilty to stealing a Semmental bull calf, value £265 and, an Angus bull calf, value £185, from the property of John O'Flynn at Rossa, Buttevant, and and to stealing a pedigree Friesian heifer, value £300 and property of Michael Haynes, at Kilcolman West, Buttevant on May 28. Bailey further pleaded guilty to stealing a Limousin bull calf, value £250, the property of Denis McNamara, and a Belgian blue calf, value of £287 and property of the mart; and to stealing a whitehead Hereford bull calf, value £200 and property of John Shinnick at Kilcolman West, Buttevant on May 27. There were also pleas to stealing an Angus bull calf at Newtown, Doneraile on 15/16 Apri , the property of Michael Cotter and valued at £100; and a pedigree Charolois heifer calf, value £1,000 the property of Daniel Lucey, at Kilcolman, Buttevant, on 15/16 April 2000.*

> *Finally, Bailey pleaded guilty to stealing a Belgian blue heifer calf at Ballytarsa, Cashel, Co Tipperary between April 1 and May 29, the property of John P O'Dwyer and valued at £175; and to stealing a Hereford bull calf, valued at £200, from Kilmallock mart on May 1.*

> *Inspector Michael Keogh told the court that a search warrant was obtained in respect of the defendant's premises when Gardai became suspicious that a number of stolen animals were being detained there.*

Inspector Keogh added that the defendant made a statement after caution admitting taking 10 animals, and: "He went further and admitted that he had transported two to his brother's farm in Athy, Co Kildare."

Solicitor David Waters stressed that his client fully co-operated with Gardaí at all times and 'arranged for all of the calves that were stolen to be returned immediately.'

Noting that his client is a man with no previous convictions, Mr. Waters said: 'For some number of years prior to this he has been treated by a consultant psychiatrist.' Mr. Waters also said that the fact that, very shortly before these incidents, Mr. Bailey was involved in civil proceedings where a considerable cash order was made against him, might have a bearing on the case. Adjourning the matter for a report from the Court Welfare Officer including suitability for community service, Judge Patterson indicated that he would hear Mr. Water's full submissions in relation to his client on that date.

As if cattle rustling were not enough, Brian had gotten involved in petty disputes with his neighbor. How it all started was not too clear, but they followed the same patterns that had characterized his school days.

The *Corkman* reported it this way:

"Two feuding neighbours spilled into a court room as one accused the other of holding a breadknife to his throat. However, after a contentious case before Christmas, Judge Brian Sheridan dismissed the case against James O'Leary of Brough Cross, Doneraile. Mr. O'Leary was charged with assault on Brian Bailey at Ballinora on November 10. Mr. Bailey told Mallow District court that he was sitting in his jeep and on his mobile phone when Mr. O'Leary 'put a big long breadknife' up to his neck. Mr. Bailey claimed that he

cut his fingers as he moved the knife away. He also claimed that he now has no feelings on the tops of his fingers.

Solicitor David O'Meara, representing Mr. O'Leary, said that Mr. Bailey was furnishing the court with 'selective evidence.' Mr. O'Meara said in Mr. Bailey's statement to Gardai he had stated that Mr. O'Leary's son had 'got compensation' from him. 'He [Mr. O'Leary] knew I hated him,' stated Mr. Bailey's statement, which was read out by Mr. O'Meara. Mr. O'Meara said a cow belonging to Mr. Bailey had knocked Mr. O'Leary into a ditch. Mr. O'Meara said that his client never did anything to Mr. Bailey. Mr. O'Meara said as a direct result of Mr. Bailey's behaviour, Mr. O'Leary made a statement to Gardai.

He also said that Mr. Bailey had 'driven his jeep' towards his client in an intimidating fashion. He also said rubbish had also been dumped on Mr. O'Leary's property. Mr. O'Meara said: 'Years ago there was no problem between the two but then Mr. O'Leary's son took a claim and then things got sour.' Mr. O'Meara said there was no bread knife.

Mr. O'Meara also said that when the court broke for lunch that Mr. Bailey had approached his client in the toilet at Dunnes Stores in Mallow and said to him: 'I will get €30,000 off you, you pauper.' He also said Mr. Bailey had called Mr. O'Leary "a scum bag". Mr. O'Meara said his client was 'not a man who would put his health at risk' as he had donated a kidney to a brother. 'The last thing he wants is to look for any sort of trouble from the likes of Mr. Bailey,' said Mr. O'Meara.

He said the entire allegation of assault was 'entirely made up' by Mr. Bailey.

'This entire thing is a total figment of Mr. Bailey's imagination, said Mr. O'Meara.'

Garda James Hosford told the court that, on the day in question, there was a cut on Mr. Bailey's finger and some dried blood on his head. He said that Mr. O'Leary had admitted to him that he had caught Mr. Bailey by the neck and had threatened him, but he had had absolutely denied having a knife.

Mr. O'Leary told the court that he had sued Mr. Bailey on behalf of his son, David, who had sustained a broken collarbone in an incident. He said his son, who was 13 at the time of the accident, had stepped off the step of Mr. Bailey's jeep and he had fallen and broken his collarbone.

He said Mr. Bailey then drove off and a neighbour came to his son's rescue.

'My son got €22,000 and that started the animosity,' said Mr. O'Leary. He said Mr. Bailey has driven in a 'very intimidating way' towards him. 'If there was a pool of water he would just smash into it. But I copped on to that and I would run past the water. It's his aim to intimidate and harass me on a continuous basis,' said Mr. O'Leary. He said he was 'just fed up with Mr. Bailey's capers.'

Mr. O'Leary did admit that he did catch Mr. Bailey up by the neck and said he would kill him if he did not leave him alone. He said that he wanted to 'put an end to the harassment.' However, after listening to the lengthy debate from both sides, Judge Sheridan dismissed the case as he said he had a 'serious doubt' about the evidence regarding the bread knife.

After Brian had put these incidents behind him, along with the phone call from Tracey, his life had returned to the solitary habits and routines of a farmer. He had done a better job of managing his money and his temper. Brian's nephews and nieces found him avuncular, generous, and funny, in his own quirky way.

The years passed as years do; his nieces and nephews grew up; his parents grew older, and Brian thought only occasionally about Tracey's whereabouts and the phone call. Years of raising livestock and caring for the farm went by uneventfully, with no further issues from his neighbors. He went to Cork as he always did, but more often than not it was for a doctor's appointment, not a romantic adventure as he'd had with Tracey. He never returned to An Brog; his weekends in the city were fewer and were mostly limited to a few beers with his mates and some local music and craic.

He no longer dreaded the ring of the telephone and the delivery of mail, although he sometimes dreamed of a child knocking on his door, seeking the identity of a biological parent. He woke with a start those nights, wondering if he'd ever be free of the weight of his careless behavior and the lies he'd told Tracey.

CHAPTER 13

TRACEY

"Our greatest glory is not in never failing, but in rising up every time we fail."
—Ralph Waldo Emerson

Tracey shrugged and hung up the phone from her call with Brian, feeling fortunate that she that Teresa had listened in on an extension across the room. "I can't say I was surprised by what Brian had to say," she sighed. "He's just as useless as any other man I've had in my life.

"Keep your eye on what's important, dear, and be proud that you've taken steps on your own behalf and your unborn child, even if Brian denied that he could be the father. We could get a solicitor, compel Brian to take a paternity test (or at least threaten him with one), and see about child support," Teresa suggested supportively.

"You know, Teresa, I'm all done with trying to make people be part of my family. Do you have any idea what it's like to grow up with parents who don't want you, family who don't want you, men who want to have sex with you but then don't want anything to do with you? I'm all done with that. I've proven to myself that I can find a job and a place to live, and take care of myself. I'll just keep doing that when my child is born. Do you think we could just call it a day? I'm exhausted."

Teresa was sympathetic up to a point, but she wanted to be sure Tracey was tough enough for the challenges she could see up ahead. Not only was Tracey an unwed mother in a conservative and religious country, but she also faced significant challenges to staying in the country. She was going to have to be willing to file endless petitions, appeals, respond to requests for depositions and interviews, all while trying to be a good mother, hold a job, and keep a roof over their heads.

Teresa would see to it that the Church stood by them, and that Tracey received all the social services that she was eligible for, but Tracey had to be strong and be willing to endure more than a single negative phone call and ignored personal letter. Teresa remembered Tracey's stories of her rocky childhood and even rougher adolescence; did she really have what she needed to get through what were certain to be very tough times ahead?

Luckily for Tracey, Teresa was an experienced and capable resource, who had networks of contacts in social services, the legal establishment, and the Catholic Church that she'd cultivated over years of working behind the scenes in the parish. She had the courage of a lion, the compassion of a saint, and the determination of a bulldog, all wrapped into her tiny frame. When she took on a cause, she would not let it go until every possible avenue had been tapped out. She would hold Tracey's feet to the fire, if not for her own benefit, for her baby's welfare

CHAPTER 14

MIMI

"You can have the other words--chance, luck, coincidence, serendipity. I'll take grace. I don't know what it is exactly, but I'll take it."

—Mary Oliver

I had packed my bag for my first ever trip to Ireland and reviewed the itinerary. Only one detail was missing: how to find Tracey. I called my Aunt Clare.

"I know you don't know where she is, but you're the only hope I have. I have let Tracey slip through my life and done so little to help. I'm not trying to make trouble; I'm not blaming you for anything that went wrong in trying to help her. I just know that I can't carry this weight in my heart the rest of my life without finally doing something."

I tried my best to explain my plan to Aunt Clare, who'd been the executrix for Oona and Ella's estates and had tried to help Tracey find her way. My aunt had looked after the two elderly sisters more than anyone else, but she had her own family. She was weary of doing her best and feeling blamed and shamed for everything she did, especially by her older sister, my mother. She listened to my plea for help and responded in her best counseling mode, knowing that when it came to her own family, a therapy license often was of no use.

"You've carried this hurt for a long time, I know. We all have. I don't want to say it's a lost cause, but don't let your big heart get in the way of moving on with your life. Here's the mailing address where I sent the last of the money from Oona's and Ella's estates. When the money was gone, that was the end of the contact. The address is in Belfast. I think she had a child."

"Belfast is our last stop," I explained. "I'm going to that address, and I'm going to search until I find her. First, I'm going to learn all I can about Ireland—the potato famine and what drove James to immigrate to the US. I want to learn about the religious issues; are our family roots Catholic or Protestant or both? And I'm going to find the Lockharts in Donegal who might be connected to our ancestor."

"If you find Tracey, please give her my love. It sounds like an amazing trip. Be careful!"

Clutching the scrap of paper with Tracey's last known address in Belfast, I returned home with fantasies of what I might learn on my first visit to my homeland, Ireland. In Dublin, my husband Matthew and I visited Kilmainham Gaol. James Lockhart immigrated to the US before many of the wars for Irish independence. But I knew so little about the Irish republic, the "Troubles" and the violence that separated those Irish people who wanted to stay in the United Kingdom and those who wanted out. Irish Catholics (and Tracey had become one, according to Aunt Clare) wanted the freedom to practice their religion, but the exact sequence of events and cast of characters were hazy in my mind.

The trip we planned took us clockwise around the coast. Dingle was an important stop. I was struck by seeing so many people who looked like me. People were so friendly; the food was so tasty, and I found myself feeling at home, embracing my Irish identity. In the pubs with their informal folk music and dancing, I remembered how important singing and dancing had been to my mom and to all the cousins of her generation. The gift of "craic" (wisecracks, jokes, humor of all kinds), willingness to sing or dance or both on demand at family get-togethers, which I found excruciatingly embarrassing, made more sense when experienced on Irish soil. I felt sad to have missed so much by resisting the call to perform or by being embarrassed (or absent) for family celebrations.

The bars! So many bars and so much drinking! I understood why alcohol was an issue in my family, remembered overhearing hushed conversations about family members' addictions and mental health issues passed down through generations. I could see it first hand in Ireland—up close and personal!

In Dingle, I rented a bicycle in a hardware store (half hardware store, half bar, of course) to ride out to the tiny dock where the Great Blasket ferry called at Dunquín. I carried the heavy bike down a long flight of stairs and blanched when I saw the tiny boat bobbing up and down in the waves. The boat heaved in the waves one way, while the dock bobbed up and down another. The water looked cold and gray, and the wind blew in gusts that made the transfer from bucking dock to rolling boat terrifying. "Put yourself in the mind of an Irish farmer out in the islands—the only way to get your sheep to market or your sick child to the doctor was to load them on a boat just this size, and back then, there were no motors; it was all done with oars," the boat captain explained.

No one has lived on the islands since 1953, but the journey out there in that boat, listening to lively stories told by the boat captain, gave me a heart-wrenching sense of what life was like in mid-19th century Ireland. Isolated and poverty-stricken, Great Blasket Island was a taste of what James Lockhart might have experienced before deciding to immigrate.

Once back on solid ground, I pedaled back to the warmth and steadiness of the hotel, where Matthew had made the rational choice to stay warm and dry while I went exploring. We set off by car to the Blasket Centre, a museum full of photographs and stories of Blasket island life, subsistence fishing and farming, hard work and home lives, housing, and entertainment. James Lockhart's choice to immigrate to the US made more sense, although I could feel the pull of my ancestors, the power of roots here in this beautiful country.

After a night of dreams through time and space, I continued my journey to find James Lockhart. We made our way up through

Donegal, along the beautiful bay to Rathmullan, where the family history from my treasured leather book, done in my great aunt Ella's own handwriting, began.

The emerald green countryside of the glens and forest gave way to the striking coastline of Lough Swilly, a bay off the North Sea. The scenery took my breath away, as I allowed myself to be in two places at once—the Donegal I was seeing for the first time, and the Donegal of my ancestor James, as he left home for the last time, knowing he might never to see his family again.

We drove slowly down the narrow lane that led to the end of the road at Rathmullan. The mid-afternoon sun shimmered on the water; no boats were out, but a few grizzled men stood around the small store, the only evidence of commercial activity at the waterside. Matthew hung back, as I approached each of the old-timers. "I'm looking for the Lockharts," I said. "My great-great grandfather came from around here, and I'm wondering if I have any relatives nearby."

"Can't say that there are any Lockharts in Rathmullan...but I can't say there aren't, either. Are you sure it's Rathmullan you're after, and not Ramelton?" I was pretty certain that Ella's genealogy was accurate, but I didn't want to overlook any opportunity to find my roots. "I'm going to try the postmaster next," I said. I'm thinking that if there are any Lockharts, they'll be known there." Somehow my fantasy had us bumping into Lockharts standing around the shore, just in time for our visit. Since that hadn't happened, I would need to call upon my inner detective, determined to turn up Lockharts or else.

"Next stop: the post office," I directed, and we pulled away from the coast to head inland a mile or two to find the post office, a lone tiny building with no other signs of life. I walked in and smiled at the postmaster, who was doling out mail and stamps to a customer. "And how might I help you, young lady. You're not from around here, are you?"

"I've come all the way from California to learn more about my family history. I'm traveling to Belfast to find a cousin, but I'm starting in Donegal to find out if I have any relatives left here.

Rathmullan is where my great-great grandfather emigrated from. Do you know if any Lockharts live around here?" The postmaster scratched his head. I could tell he didn't want to disappoint me.

The woman buying stamps thought for a moment, and then piped up, "I don't think there are Lockharts in Rathmullan, but there's the dairy farm in Ramelton. Those are Lockharts, I think, don't you?"

"You're right, as always. You'll be taking my job away, if I'm not careful."

The woman smiled and walked outside with Matthew and me and pointed the way to Ramelton. "You'll see the sign on the left just after the second turn on your right. You can't miss it—there's a cow, big as life, on the sign. Good luck finding your family!" she said cheerily as she set off on foot down the lane.

As promised, the large cow on a sign showed the way to the Lockharts' dairy farm. I clutched my leather-bound family tree and headed up to the front door. An older woman answered the door and looked quizzically at us. I explained "My name's Mimi, I'm from America, and I'm looking for information about my ancestors and for cousins who might be living nearby. My great-great grandfather, James Lockhart, emigrated from Rathmullan and ended up in Texas. One of my great-uncles was in the dairy business. I'm wondering if we might be related?"

The woman was unfazed by my question and immediately invited us in for tea. Matthew whispered, "Any chance of that happening in the US?" "None," I whispered back.

"How'd you find us, dear?"

I explained about the postmaster and the woman in the post office. "I have a family tree with me, and I've come a long way to learn about my family. Do you think we might be cousins?"

"Of course we're cousins! I don't need your Family Tree to tell me that. But let's have a nice cup of tea and I'll get our family Bible and let's take a look."

After settling Matthew and me in the living room, Mrs. Lockhart brought in a tea tray with china teacups, a teapot, and some biscuits. Then she went to the bookcase and brought out an enormous family Bible, the size of a picnic basket, and the weight of a bowling ball. She opened it to a family tree that went back two hundred years; she and I looked over each other's shoulders, hoping to find a match in all those generations over all those years.

I was disappointed not to find an ancestor in common, but Mrs. Lockhart's warm welcome was undiminished. "You're a Lockhart, I'm a Lockhart, we're cousins! Now tell me about yourselves and your lives in America." A couple of hours passed quickly as my new cousin and I swapped stories about lives in California and in Donegal. A new friendship was born.

"Oh, my," I said, looking at my watch. "We must be off to Derry, where we're spending the night. Tomorrow is the last day of our trip, the day I'm going to find my cousin Tracey in Belfast, who's been lost to me for so many years."

"My son lives in Derry, and he's the genealogy buff in our family. Tell me where you're staying, and I'll see if he can add anything to what I've shown you. If there's a connection anywhere, he'll help you find it."

I unfolded the trip itinerary, gave her the name of the hotel and Mrs. Lockhart copied down the address and phone number. The three of us exchanged hugs and said good-bye. "Slán's the Irish way to say it," instructed Mrs. Lockhart, as she accompanied us down the drive.

I was quiet as they drove away. I felt the closeness of my connection to Lockharts who may or may not have been actual cousins. And what does "actual" really mean? If people believe they are cousins, isn't that enough? Or why is being a cousin even important? What makes it matter? Matthew and I began to talk about their amazement at showing up at a stranger's door, in Ireland, and being treated as family, when no "real" relationship seemed documented. Ireland felt so very different from the United States, in such a magical, wonderful way.

We drove into Derry, parked near the ancient walls, looked out over the River Foyle, and absorbed as much history as we could, trying to understand "the Troubles," the Potato Famine (which most Irish people viewed as genocide on the part of the British, regardless of Protestant or Catholic religions), and hatreds based on colonialism and religious prejudice. I kept thinking to myself "Why can't we just get along?" the question left over from the Los Angeles riots and arrest of Rodney King.

Walking the walls of Derry brought history to life, and I learned that the bloodshed reflected in the powerful murals in the Bogside area commemorating the deaths of 14 civil rights protestors on "Bloody Sunday" by British soldiers were really part of battles that had been going on since the city was laid siege in 1688 by the Earl of Antrim and the Catholic forces of James II, the English king deposed in favor of the Protestant James of Orange.

Because the boundaries of Northern Ireland and the Irish republic were so close together in Derry (or Londonderry depending on which side you were on) the bitterness and violence was just below the boiling point at any given moment in time, and had been for almost 400 years. I thought to myself, "Is this how it will be with Afghanistan in four hundred years? It sure feels like it!" The difference was that the US had not been at war with anyone on our immediate border and except for the Civil War, we had not experienced war on our own soil. I had a hard time getting my mind around what it might be like to live under the shadow of bombings, terror, and the weight of so many years of conflict.

We settled into our Derry hotel room and started to think about our plans for the next day. Weary after a full day of walking the walls of Derry, we decided to go to bed early. Just as we turned out the light, the room phone rang, and we looked at each other, hoping the call was not a disaster from home, but we had no idea who it might be. "Hello?" I fielded the call with some dread.

"Hello, Mimi, you don't know me, but my mum gave me your number and told me about your visit and your interest in our family history. I live not far from your hotel, and I've got much more detailed information than what's in the family Bible. Might you be interested in seeing it?"

"I'd definitely be interested, but tomorrow I'm tied up trying to find my long-lost cousin and the next day we head back to the States. Where are you calling from?"

"Actually, I'm down in the lobby. I have to work tomorrow, and my mum said you didn't have much time left on your trip. My name's Frank, by the way, Frank Lockhart."

Without a moment's hesitation, I said, "We'll be right down. Let's meet in the bar. It'll take us a minute or two to jump into our clothes, but we're delighted to have a chance to meet."

I shook my head in wonder and amazement as I explained to Matthew what was happening next. We jumped out of our pajamas and into street clothes and headed for the elevator. "I didn't ask what he looked like, or what he was wearing, or anything..." I worried about not finding him. "Don't worry, dear, he'll be able to recognize us; we stick out like a sore thumb, much as we'd like to shake the tourist stereotype."

As we entered the bar, we saw a tall, young man poring over a sheaf of documents, clearly family trees. Finding each other was not going to be difficult after all! Matthew and I greeted Frank, still nonplused by the care and friendliness of Mrs. Lockhart that had brought this latest reunion of so-called cousins together. I had brought my leather family history down from the room.

Just as we had at the Lockhart dairy farm, the three of us searched in vain in these new materials for names and dates on Frank's documents that might correspond to my book of Family History. Once again, we came up empty-handed. "I'm so sorry you took time to round up these papers and come to see us, and we didn't learn we are cousins after all," I apologized. "Let us buy you a beer at least..."

Frank smiled kindly and demurred. "I'd best not be getting on the road after time in a bar," he said. "But I'd take a cup of coffee and would so much like to hear the story of finding your cousin and your life in the States, and how your trip in Ireland has gone. Just because the genealogy doesn't line up perfectly, *we* know we're cousins, and that's what matters."

"That's just what your mother said when we had tea. We'll get you some coffee then, and *we'll* have a beer, since we're not going anywhere."

A couple of hours later, after the newfound cousins had swapped stories of life in the US and in Ireland, sharing the importance of family and finding missing cousins, and what their trip to Ireland had been like so far, Frank glanced up at the clock and groaned. "I had no idea it was so late; you must be exhausted! I hate to end this very pleasant evening, but it's an early day for me tomorrow."

We gave Frank a warm hug and headed back up to our room, incredulous at the warmth, generosity, and openness of their new Lockhart cousin. My mind was buzzing with all I had experienced that day and in anticipation of what I hoped would be the discovery of my cousin, Tracey, tomorrow.

Over an early breakfast in Belfast on the last day of our trip to Ireland, Matthew and I talked about our plans. I was eager to get started with my detective work, while Matthew was interested in the area around the old port. We split up, and I set off to get acquainted with the town, but most importantly, finding Tracey.

Clutching my leather Family History and a map of Belfast, I checked in with the hotel desk. "What's the best way to get to this address? I'm looking for my cousin, and I don't want to get lost or into trouble."

"You'll be wanting to get in one of the black taxis that go up and down the Falls Road. You'll also learn a bit of history that way. Do you know anything about the history of the taxis?"

"I've studied some in the guidebooks, but I'd appreciate anything to prepare me for the neighborhoods I'll be exploring," I said.

"Things are pretty calm these days, but forty years ago it was a different story. Belfast was in turmoil. The conflict was at its height, barricades and riots were commonplace. The main roads were regularly blocked and bus services were often suspended especially in West Belfast. A couple of local people had the bright idea of going to London, to buy some old black taxis and to set up an alternative service. It caught on and soon hundreds of these, sometimes very old and dilapidated black hacks, were travelling up and down the Falls, Andytown and the Whiterock.

Frequently up to eight people would cram into the vehicle – six in the back and two in the front. If roads were blocked, they drove down side roads, over the rubble of riots, along footpaths. Nothing stopped them. Not even the British Army checkpoints. It was a unique solution to a unique problem – providing transport for citizens of this area in the midst of major conflict."

"The taxis ferried people to and from work and kept families in contact with each other. But it has been at a high cost. Their success meant that they became a major target for the British and unionist state, and an element of the media. The taxi association and the taxi drivers were demonized, and targeted by unionist death squads. As a direct consequence, eight drivers were killed in sectarian attacks and scores more were assaulted, arrested and harassed. And today there are battles still to be fought against discrimination and bias."

I got on a city bus to West Belfast, near the Falls Road. I took a deep breath, held out my hand and flagged down a black cab, already filled with people. I showed the driver the address I was looking for, and the driver nodded, motioning for me to get in. I hoped my anxiety was not too apparent. After letting out passengers and taking on new ones at almost every street corner, the driver said "This is where I let you out. Cross the street and follow that road to the end. You'll probably need to ask for directions along the way. Good luck."

I crossed the street, carefully paying attention to the street directions being reversed in the UK. "I'm *not* going to get flattened just before I find Tracey," I muttered to myself. As I got into the residential neighborhood, the streets got smaller, and the signs of history became more vivid and real. Bullet holes dotted the sides of buildings, and many plaques were posted on street corners in memory of a child or innocent victim of gunfire by the British army. "We're not in Kansas anymore," I noted grimly to myself.

After what seemed like a long time of walking up and down streets, I found the right street, and the right street number. I spent a few minutes calming myself down; I had been waiting for this moment for a very long time. I looked around at the place Tracey had been living, a council flat, attached to other flats just like it that lined the street. Small, plain, non-descript, but not scary. I walked up to the front porch and knocked loudly on the door. No answer. I knocked again. Since there'd been no response, I peered in the large picture window, covered by ancient-looking curtains, very hard to see in.

I slowly walked back down the stairs and around the back, where a locked gate kept her from looking further. I walked back up to the front porch and sat down on the steps, disappointed and confused about what to do next. I could not imagine leaving without finding Tracey, and I wouldn't let myself imagine the possibility that Tracey didn't even live here anymore. But I couldn't waste time on this porch if I needed to be looking somewhere else.

I put my head in my hands, gazed down at my feet, waited for some sign from the universe about what to do. When I looked up, I saw an older woman standing in front of me, looking me up and down. "Is there something you're wanting, dear?"

"I'm looking for my cousin Tracey Tompkins from Texas. I've come from California, this is my last day in Ireland, and I'm not leaving until I find her. I got this address from my aunt. It was the last address she had, but there's nobody home." I returned my gaze to the pavement, feeling hopeless.

"I *know* Tracey Tompkins from Texas, and her little girl, Erin! They *did* live in this house until just a couple of months ago, but they moved away."

"But where did they go? Why did I wait so long? What am I going to do?" I was about to burst into tears, but I kept my composure, focused on solving the problem, not getting written off as a crazy person.

"I know just what you can do. Erin was a student at St. Patrick's School, not too far from here. I bet you can find her if you go there. Long-lost cousin, eh? You know, I think those two could really use some family right about now. It was just the two of them, you know, they kept to themselves, and I never saw anyone else come around much."

"You've been so helpful! Thank you so very much! Can you tell me how to find the school? Can I walk from here?"

"Oh, dear, no, it's much too far to walk. Do you know the black taxis on the Falls Road? You'll need to get a taxi and just tell the cabbie you want to go to St. Patrick's School. He'll get you close by."

I stood up, gave the woman a big hug, realizing immediately that hugs were a California custom as she stood somewhat awkwardly, with her arms barely touching mine. I set off back to the Falls Road, feeling a little more confident having had my first successful Falls Road taxi experience. I was able to flag a taxi almost immediately, and in a few minutes, he let me off and gave me a set of complicated instructions to find the school. "Never mind," I said, "I'll just ask for directions along the way. Thanks!"

After another bit of wandering through another residential area, a little grittier than the first, I was able to find the school, having stopped several times to ask for help. I kept reminding myself to just keep breathing, that it was all part of the adventure. I was a little nervous, because it was now mid-afternoon. Would anyone still be around?

I approached the school, followed signs to the office, and could see the school principal sitting behind her desk. Sister Marie saw me looking around hesitantly. "May I help you with something? School is out for the day."

"I'm from America, and I'm looking for a cousin I haven't seen for many years. I went to her last address, but a neighbor said she'd moved. She told me that her daughter went to school here and suggested that you might be able to help me. My cousin's name is Tracey Tompkins from Texas, and my name is Mimi Lockhart from California. I'm a teacher myself, so I know you probably won't be able to share information with me, but this is my last day in Ireland. If you could help me, I'd be ever so grateful. You have no idea how much this means to me."

Sister Marie took her time in responding, as she looked her visitor over carefully to ascertain if this was some sort of crazy person, or someone who had a cause worth pursuing. Sister Marie was a no-nonsense sort of person, it seemed, but maybe she might be the miracle Mimi was praying for.

"Would you like to see the school, dear? You might be interested in seeing where your cousin Tracey's daughter Erin was in school."

I understood that Sister Marie would use the school tour as an opportunity to get better acquainted with this mysterious stranger who'd shown up at her doorstep, curious about one of her students. After a lively conversation about the students at the school, curriculum, and extracurriculars, Sister Marie and I returned to her office.

"I'm glad you understand about our privacy rules. I can tell you that I know Tracey Tompkins and her daughter very well. If you'd like, you can write a note to Tracey, and I'll deliver it. If she would like to contact you, she can reach you at your hotel." Sister Marie handed me a pad of paper and a pen and showed me to a chair just outside her office where I could quickly compose the note.

"Dear Tracey,

I am your cousin who knew you when you were a little girl. Your grandma Oona was my great aunt, and your Great-Aunt Ella was my Great Aunt. You don't remember me, but I worked very hard to get my family to adopt you when you were a toddler, because I loved you so much. I met you again when you were in junior high and you helped me with a testing project for one of my graduate classes. You have been in my heart ever since then, and I've tried to find you, but until this trip to Ireland, I just couldn't figure out how. Every time I saw my aunt, I asked her where you were and how you were doing, but she kept putting me off. When my husband and I decided to come to Ireland, I asked my aunt to give me your last address, and I went there looking for you this morning. Your neighbor let me know you'd moved, and she told me the name of your daughter's school and suggested I come here to find out where you live now.

I hope you'll call me at my hotel if you'd like to meet...Benedict's of Belfast—I'm staying there with my husband. We're in room 510. Here's the number: 28 9059 1999.

Love,

Mimi"

I handed Sister Marie the note, choking up as I said "You have no idea how long I've waited. I'm sure I told you that I'm only staying in Belfast one night. I have no idea how you'll get this note to her, but I know you'll do your best." Sister Marie read the note, took my hand, and said "You must have faith. I *will* take care of it." Then she stood up, the interview clearly over, and showed me out the door of the school.

I set off one more time to the Falls Road, for my third ride in a black taxi, trying not to give up hope, trying to be realistic about the possibility that I might have to leave Ireland without accomplishing the most important goal for my trip—finding Tracey.

Matthew met me as I came in the door of the hotel. "I want to hear all about it! Let's have a beer in the bar, and I'll tell you about the Titanic, and you can tell me about Tracey!" Worried that she might miss Tracey's call, if it came in, I stopped by the front desk. "What can I do for you?" inquired the clerk.

"It's a long story," I said, but I've come to Ireland to find my cousin, and there's a chance that she might call me. I'm going to have a beer in the bar with my husband, if you can promise me you'll find me if the call comes in."

"I promise—and if I leave the front desk for any reason, I'll be sure whoever is here finds you in the bar. I promise!"

A few beers later, and the call still had not come in. I began to get more and more discouraged. Just then, I looked up and saw the desk clerk making wild gestures and motioning for me to come to the house phone. I leaped out of my chair, raced across the lobby, nearly colliding with a baggage cart and a group of elderly tourists just checking in.

"Mimi, this is Tracey. I understand you've been trying to reach me?"

"Tracey! You *called*! I was so afraid you wouldn't get my note! I was so afraid if you got my note, you'd decide *not* to call. Thank you! Thank you! Thank you!"

"Your note said you'd like to get together. Would you like to come over to our house? We don't have an easy way to get downtown."

I gave Matthew a quick hug and raced back to the hotel front desk to ask the clerk to call a taxi. The taxi pulled up in front of Tracey's house, and I paused, finding it hard to believe that I was really here. Tracey didn't wait for me to knock, opening the door and welcoming me in with a warm hug. The house was chilly, so I left my coat on.

"Well, this is it -- home, sweet home," Tracey said, perhaps embarrassed by the tiny worn-out looking dwelling. I could see Tracey's daughter in the background, a little behind her mom, in the kitchen. "Come on in and sit down; I'm really curious, as you might guess, about your note and your trip to Ireland. By the way, this is my daughter, Erin."

I smiled at Erin and said, "I'd guess that you are about the same age that your mom was the last time I saw her. I imagine it seems kind of strange to have someone show up on your doorstep and introduce herself as your long-lost cousin from America!"

Erin nodded shyly, but said nothing.

Tracey and her daughter sat on the small well-worn couch, and I sat on a chair a few feet away. "I'm not sure exactly where to begin, because when I first met you, you were a toddler, and I was eighteen years old. I thought you were the cutest, smartest, funniest little kid I'd ever seen, and everyone who saw you agreed. I wanted my parents to adopt you in the worst way. I was in college, living in the dorm, and your grandma, my Great-Aunt Oona, dropped you off, hoping that I could take you back home with me for Thanksgiving and then just move right in."

I paused, letting the first part of her story sink in. I looked around at the walls covered with art, water colors and drawings by Tracey and her daughter. "You are both talented artists, I see." "Mostly my mum," Erin smiled, holding her mother's hand.

"So what happened next?" asked Tracey.

"After a few days in the dorm, with my suitemates helping babysit while I went to class, we caught the bus and then the train home. I'd bought you some books, clothes, and diapers, and you just came right along. I thought everything was going to work out; I just knew our family wouldn't let you go to an orphanage. And then, the next day, my mom told me that your maternal grandmother wanted you, and we had to rush back to Austin. It was awful! And I just let you go; how could I have even done that?"

Tracey smiled, wistfully, "You weren't the only one, Mimi. A lot of people let me down along the way. Wait a minute—you said my maternal grandmother wanted me? I never even *met* my maternal grandmother; she wasn't in the picture at all."

I gasped, shell-shocked, trying to get my mind around the betrayal. Several minutes went by as we both processed this long-kept secret. "My mother said your grandma had gone to the police to have me arrested for kidnapping you—that she wanted you and I had to give you back." I slumped down in my chair, my mind reeling with this new piece of information that destroyed the story I'd believed for decades. I was speechless, angry, and validated all at the same time.

"It all makes sense now! My folks didn't want to take on a two-year old with a sketchy family, and they also didn't want me to go ballistic or do something crazy like run away with you. So they made up a plausible scenario, and I bought it, with barely a whimper."

Tracey was subdued and quiet as she took in the magnitude of the impact of my mother's lie. "It makes for a good story, I guess, but I lived in the orphanage until I was twelve, and Oona and Ella took me in."

We looked deep into each other's eyes, realizing how improbable our reunion was, the sheer magic of a meeting after all these years, the magnitude of cousins, across the ocean, finding each other. Magic? Luck? Force of will?

"Yes, you were living with Oona and Ella the next time I saw you, and I used you as a subject for my IQ testing class. You were off the charts, by the way, and just as precocious as you were as a toddler."

As Tracey and I swapped stories of the previous decades of their lives, Erin sat watching the conversation go back and forth, with eyes like dinner plates. My world turned upside down with the revelation about Tracey's alleged maternal grandmother.

Erin was face to face with the reality that she had a *relative!* A *cousin!* In her whole lifetime, she'd always believed her family consisted of just her mum, and no one else, making her a real oddity in the Irish culture of huge extended families. Worse still, without a father, Erin had faced the stigma of being the child of an unwed mother, mercilessly shamed by the kids in the neighborhood and the school.

I could see the future just as clearly as if I had a crystal ball in my lap, the road to America set off like beacons on each side of an airport runway. "It's not just me, you know, Erin. You have a whole world of cousins in America—seven of us in California, and too many to count in Texas. You'll see! I'm thinking next summer we'll have a reunion in San Francisco, and you'll get to meet us all!"

My plan didn't stop with a reunion, though. I could imagine Erin coming to live in the States—maybe as an exchange student in high school, or college. It was a sure thing, as I saw it, that Erin had a future in America. What I didn't know at that moment was that Erin had had that same plan since she was a little girl, the third secret that was revealed that evening; Erin just didn't know how it was going to work, but she was sure it *would* work.

My plan for a reunion of the Lockhart clan appeared fully formed in my mind, and I knew I'd need to do a major sales job to make it happen before I left Tracey and Erin. "I know a really cute little hotel in San Francisco, and we can all stay there together on the same floor. Two of the cousins live near Golden Gate Park with their families in the same house; we'll spend some time with them.

We can go to Chinatown, have lunch at The Rotunda at Neiman-Marcus, ride the cable cars, and so much more! Please say you'll come! And after San Francisco, I'll take you to Yosemite, and we can hike, and raft, and swim. Don't worry about a thing—all you have to do is say 'Yes!' and I'll take care of everything else."

If I had to guess, Tracey's inclination would have been to say a vehement "No." She hadn't traveled at all since the trip that had brought her to Ireland. She hated crowds, airplanes, the pressure of rushing from place to place; just thinking about such a trip made her anxious. And then there were the cousins, whom she hadn't seen since she was a child, and mostly barely remembered. She hated the idea of being judged. At least the two of them could travel on their US passports (Tracey had wisely obtained a US passport for Erin from the US Consulate in Belfast when she was born), so clearing border controls for them was not an issue.

But I watched Tracey look at her beloved daughter, who was clearly spell-bound, with the biggest smile. How could she say no? Did they believe I was for real? Could I be trusted not to break Erin's heart with another disappointment? I tried to put myself in Tracey's place, with so many disappointments in her life. How hard would it be to trust one more person, one more time?

I could see the fear in Tracey's eyes, contrasted with the excitement and joy on Erin's face. "Tracey, I know I let you down when you were a child. I've carried that weight in my heart for so many years, and I promise you, I won't let you down again. We'll have plenty of time before you come to the States for us to learn to trust each other. We have the chance we didn't have before. Will you at least think it over?"

I watched Erin's face fall. I could see that she was sure her mother would retreat back into the safety of their little world, and her chances to see another world across the ocean would fade as the visit came to a close without a definite commitment. I was surprised that Erin blurted out "Well, I'm going, that's for sure. Won't you come with me, Mummy? We've never been anywhere together, and now that I know I have American cousins, I want to meet them. Please say yes, please." She looked at Tracey and me with pleading eyes, clinched and unclenched her fists with nervousness, and wriggled in her chair with impatience.

I stood up, gave each of my cousins a big hug, and said "Next year in San Francisco!" My heart was bursting, and I couldn't wait to get back to the hotel to tell Matthew about the visit...and to start planning the San Francisco reunion for real.

CHAPTER 15

ERIN

"When I look back on my childhood I wonder how I survived at all. It was, of course, a miserable childhood: the happy childhood is hardly worth your while. Worse than the ordinary miserable childhood is the miserable Irish childhood, and worse yet is the miserable Irish Catholic childhood."
—Frank McCourt

From a very young age, Erin knew that she was the only real-life, human attachment Tracey had. She knew that without Erin and without the Catholic Church, her mother would very likely have killed herself. Erin bore the double burden of being an "Out of Wedlock" child, or as the kids in the neighborhood called her "the little bastard." She believed that her mother's very survival depended on her relationship with her. They were very, very close.

It was always just the two of them. Well, really, the three of them, if you count the Church. Tracey had little to say about her family, just that her parents had died, and her other relatives couldn't take care of her, so she ended up in an orphanage for most of her childhood, or on her own. She said Erin didn't really have a dad; it was just a one-night stand, after meeting him in a bar. She didn't say much about that story, either. Bottom line, it was just like the Helen Reddy song she always used to sing as a lullaby when Erin was going to sleep...

"You And Me Against The World
You and me against the world
Sometimes it feels like you and me against the world
When all the others turn their backs and walk away
You can count on me to stay
And when one of us is gone
And one of us is left to carry on
Then remembering will have to do.
Our memories alone will get us through
Think about the days of me and you
You and me against the world."

Erin loved to write poetry, and one of her early poems expressed her devotion to her mum:

"A Poem to the Best Mum Ever
by Erin Tompkins

Some people might say you're not a big success
But you give me so much love it's impossible not to express.
People might think I'm very very wrong
But we've gone through so much and we're still standing
    strong.
You've cared for me always without any rest.
So I think I've strongly proven that you simply are the best.
You've helped me when I'm sick or when I have a bad bug,
Or I need to cry and I need a loving hug.
You help me with my schoolwork and you pay the rent—
You really are like an angel that God has sent.
If there was a competition you would come first,
Because you give me so much love my heart is going to
    burst."

Erin grew up with total confidence in herself and trust in her faith. Like her mum, she found her strength and salvation in the Catholic Church. She didn't just go to catechism class, she lived and breathed the Church's teaching. She built a strong relationship with

God and wrapped her religion around it like a blanket. That faith, plus her success at school, gave her everything she needed to deal with the hard stuff. She could weather the bullying about her lack of a father and about being the girl who rode a bicycle in the rain when everyone else got to school a different way. She felt a sense of pride in her individuality built on the pillars of school and church.

She made a best friend for the first time called Deirdre. The two of them were inseparable. They were together at school; they talked on the phone when they were at home. They shared everything. Erin had never imagined having a closer friend than her mum until Deirdre came along, and it was sweeter than anything she could imagine.

Then one day, her world exploded. The sweetness of the platonic friendship they'd had for years morphed into something more. They were walking home from school, and Deirdre reached out and took Erin's hand. Erin was a little startled, but it felt just right, as though it was obvious their friendship was meant to be this way. They let go of each other's hands quickly, but something inside Erin just knew that a seismic shift had just happened in her life.

They got to Erin's house, and Tracey was at work. They usually did homework together at Erin's house, because Deirdre's house was full of her siblings, noise, chaos, and bickering. Erin's house was quiet and private.

Erin opened the door, they put down their books, and before they knew it, they were gently, sweetly, hugging each other, and then kissing each other, and then looking intently into each other's eyes in an entirely new way. Erin had always heard about "love at first sight," but this was not their first sight. They'd known each other for years, then became best friends. But this feeling was different from friendship. Butterflies in your stomach, irrepressible giggles of joy, private winks, notes passed--this was love, for sure.

Erin felt the purest, most beautiful kind of love, indescribable in its intensity and its sweetness. Her every thought was of Deirdre, and Erin went mad thinking about the next time she could dare to hold Deirdre's hand under their adjacent desks, or reach out and touch Deirdre as they moved from class to class, or when the next opportunity might come to be alone with her.

The joys of Erin's first love were accompanied by a heart heavy with the secrets that love required. She dared not tell her mum anything about the friendship that had become a passionate love affair. Even more frightening was the impact of this love on her relationship with God and the Catholic Church. Her whole life, at home, at school, at church, was entwined with the Church and its teachings. At long last, she'd discovered a love that transcended everything she'd been taught and experienced, and it was clear to her that she couldn't have both.

One day, Deirdre and Erin were discovered kissing behind a classroom doorway after school was out, by a teacher who entered the classroom unexpectedly. The teacher's reaction was one of revulsion and anger. She yanked Erin's arm practically out of its socket, and she slapped Deirdre across the face. "Don't you ever, ever let me or anyone else ever catch you acting against God's teaching in this holy place," the teacher snarled. "You can bet your parents will be notified, and it's likely you'll be suspended. I've been watching the two of you. I've had my suspicions, but I kept them to myself. That was a mistake, I can see that now."

Erin burst into tears, but Deirdre just got very, very quiet and small. "If you tell my parents, I will kill myself. I may kill myself even if you don't. I can't go on living in this way, hating myself, loving Erin, set apart from a God who thinks I'm the devil. What is the point?"

Frightened by Deirdre's threats but clear about what she saw as her responsibilities, the teacher responded, "I have no choice here. I must inform your parents and the school administration, and I don't know what will happen to your status as students. I've been a teacher here for a very long time, and I can tell you that at your age, students are often confused, and it's a phase that passes, if one trusts in God and follows his teachings. I've heard more about these things happening in boys' schools, and I'd hoped I'd never have to take action here at St. Patrick's. I suggest that you go home and tell your parents, because you will not want them to hear about it fir from Sister Janet. Now promise me you will never violate the rules of conduct here and you will not tell any other students what we've discussed."

Both girls nodded solemnly, wishing they could just disappear into the floorboards and never be seen again. Erin had never felt so ashamed of something she'd found so beautiful, and she had never felt such feelings of hatred for the Church that had meant so much to her. She was confused, devastated, tormented, embarrassed, angry, and lost, all at the same time. She wanted only to hold Deirdre's hand to let her know they were still friends, even though the rest of their relationship was probably over.

Erin tried to imagine what she was going to tell her mother. Tracey, probably the most religious person Erin knew, also had a few sins under her belt. Erin, for one. If Erin were thrown out of St. Patrick's, she didn't think her mother would ever forgive her. Erin would not be able to forgive herself, because her mother had worked so hard to get her into the school and to make sure she did well. Erin knew that her very future rested on her academic success. That's certainly what everyone told her, and she believed them!

Erin went out to her bike for the long ride home, with the drizzle soaking through her rain jacket. She wasn't sure if the condensation on her glasses was from the mist or from her tears, but her sorrow blanketed her soul like a shroud. She pedaled home at a glacial pace, and it was after dark when she arrived. The porch light was on, and Erin's dog Jazzbo was waiting for her in the window, her usual spot, her tail wagging in anticipation.

She walked in the house, took off her damp jacket and called out to let her mum know she was home, as she always did. Tracey was in the kitchen making dinner. Erin dropped her heavy backpack and walked in to sit on the kitchen stool, instead of starting in immediately on her homework. Tracey looked up from the soup cooking on the hob, and said, "You look like you're carrying the world on your shoulders, and your eyes are swollen and red. What's up?"

"Deirdre and I are in trouble at school, Mummy. A teacher caught us snogging in a classroom, and she's going to report us to the principal, and you're going to get a phone call, and I'll probably be thrown out of school, and my life is ruined, and God hates me. Other than that, I guess everything is ok." Erin bent down to give Jazzbo a scratch to avoid looking at her mum.

For once in her life, Tracey was speechless. She put down the wooden spoon she was holding, turned the fire off on the hob, and put her arms around Erin, whose shoulders were heaving with sobs. They stayed in that hug for a good long time, before Tracey cupped Erin's chin in her hand and said, "Why didn't you tell me about your feelings for Deirdre long before you became secret girlfriends?"

"What does that have to do with anything? What a weird question, Mummy! I'm losing everything that is important to me — my lover, my school, my church, my future. I'm lost! You don't understand, that's why. You'll never understand," she shouted. "I'm gay. I'm in love with Deirdre. If that means that God doesn't want me in his church, then I'll leave the church. But what does that mean for you, for us? What about my school? What about my future?"

Tracey looked at Erin with her eyes full of tears. She said nothing for a while, waiting for Erin to say more. Finally, she did her best to speak calmly and without a lot of extra words. "Erin, you know how important the Church is to me and how important I think school is for you. I know they are important to you, too. But you must also know that you are more important to me than anything else in the world. When I hear from the school, we will figure out what to do. But I can only imagine that if you choose to stay at St. Patrick's (and I think the chances are good that they will let you), you will have to discontinue your relationship with Deirdre."

"I had already decided that I had to end the relationship with Deirdre. I don't know about the friendship. It seems like the two are inseparable. But giving up my physical relationship with Deirdre also means that I will give up my relationship with God.

124

Yes, I want to stay at St. Patrick's, and I know that means at least acting like I'm a good Catholic. But you need to know that staying there means that I will be wearing a mask at all times."

Not another word was spoken between Tracey and Erin about the situation with Deirdre. Erin went to school the next day and discovered that Deirdre had been moved to other classes, without explanation. Erin noticed that a buzz of conversation would stop as she approached, but she chose to ignore it. After all, she'd never had any friends at St Patrick's besides Deirdre anyway, and she had borne the brunt of bullying, shunning, and teasing her entire life. The only thing that was different now was that she didn't see Deirdre. She and Deirdre talked on the phone during those times when parents on both sides were away or busy, and that contact was almost more miserable than no contact at all. Erin felt helpless to stop the calls.

After a week, the school principal asked Tracey and Erin to come in to the office to discuss an important matter. During the meeting, Sister Marie explained what she had been told by the teacher who had caught Erin and Deirdre "in a compromising situation." She asked Erin if the teacher had been telling the truth, and Erin said yes without any further explanation. Sister Marie said she had considered expelling both girls, but had decided to pray for a week for guidance, knowing that both girls were excellent students, both were on scholarships and were from families from extremely limited means. Expulsion would effectively mean the end of any sort of quality education. Sister Marie's decision, which she had implemented by separating the girls into different classes was to wait and see whether the girls would try to resume their contact with each other, or would be so mortified by what had happened that they would be "scared straight" as the saying went. That appeared to be what was happening. After all, if the girls were expelled, there would be questions from other students and their parents, and the gossip would be potentially more damaging than the girls' presence at the school, assuming appropriate behaviors were maintained.

"As you could see, my decision was to separate you into different classes and to observe whether you would comply with the rules and norms of our school. You appear to have done that. If you wish to stay at St. Patrick's, you will have no contact at school with Deirdre, and you will be under close scrutiny. Do you understand? These are not just the school rules, these are God's rules and the rules of the Catholic Church as well. Since your behavior and scholarship have been exemplary since you entered St. Patrick's, I'm going to offer you one chance, and one chance only. Do you accept?"

Tracey looked at Erin, with a pleading look in her eyes but saying nothing. Erin looked at the floor, studying her shoes, and almost inaudibly said "Yes."

Sister Janet nodded. "That's what I'd hoped you'd say. We will not say one more word about this episode, and you both must agree that you will discuss it with no one from this day forward. Is that understood? If I hear one whiff of a suggestion that you are not obeying these agreements, you will be expelled immediately without further recourse."

Tracey and Erin both nodded. They left the office and went home without saying a word to each other. Erin went straight to her room and started on her homework as if nothing about her daily routine had changed. She could feel her chest tighten, feeling like a vise was squeezing the life out of her, and she could hardly breathe. But her determination to pursue the path to her future was strong, and schoolwork was her salvation.

Erin went back to school and buried herself in classwork; after school, she devoted herself to ju-jitsu. In the evenings, after Tracey had gone to bed, she and Deirdre commiserated about the loss of their intimacy but were determined to preserve the friendship, even though they knew they couldn't see each other, in school or out. From the outside, Erin looked like a well-adjusted, hard-working student, quiet but attentive in class, as always, and volunteering to help the teachers she liked best, working with students who were struggling to keep up. On the inside, though, Erin was miserable. She shut herself off from her mother, refusing to go to mass on Sundays, and spent more and more time closed up in her room. Jazzbo, Erin's Jack Russell terrier, and Comet, the cat, were her only friends, besides her now-secret friend, Deirdre. She refused to have anything to do with anyone in school or out, except for the most superficial exchanges.

She tried to describe to Deirdre what had happened with her faith this way: "I couldn't just give up my love and my friendship with you and not have intense anger toward God, ruining my relationship with Him anyway. Even if I gave up my relationship with you, it's not like doing so would mean I could just go back to the way things were before."

CHAPTER 16

TRACEY

"May the roots of your family tree grow deep and strong."
—Irish blessing

The whole thing was too far-fetched to believe, really. Out of nowhere, a mysterious third cousin from America shows up, goes to Erin's school, meets Sister Marie, the grammar school principal, who turns up on the doorstep with a poignant note about knowing Tracey when she was a toddler. When the doorbell rang, Tracey and Erin were surprised by seeing Erin's former school principal and even more confounded by the note itself.

Tracey read the note, and she and Erin wondered whether they should make the call to the cousin or not. Sister Marie came in for tea and described the person she'd just met. "She seemed quite nice, interested in the school, and interested in the two of you. I'd worried that this might be some sort of scam or prank, but she seemed so serious and determined to find you. Her story was clearly heartfelt."

Tracey was curious, of course, and Erin was adamant. After all, she was the one who had no other living family members, as far as she could tell. What could it hurt to just make the phone call? So Sister Marie went on her way, and Tracey called the number on the note and made the arrangements for the visit.

The whole experience of reuniting with this cousin was so preposterous that she couldn't get it out of her mind. That a complete stranger would show up and offer to bring Tracey and Erin to San Francisco blew Tracey's mind and consumed her imagination. She kept feeling that she had to follow through with the reunion invitation just to prove to herself that it was a not a mirage, a hoax, another cruel joke. If it were a real possibility, however, she realized that perhaps getting Erin away from Belfast, away from Deirdre, and away from all their usual routines and habits might be just what Erin needed to distract her from the despair over her lost faith and her lost love.

That thought took on a life of its own as she began to receive a stream of emails not just from Mimi, but from other Lockhart cousins who would be attending the event, urging Tracey to accept Mimi's invitation. Erin's spirits perked up measurably as Tracey shared with her the plans, photos of the people they'd be meeting, places they'd go, and details of the activities that Mimi had planned.

~~~

Tracey returned from home from work and scanned the usually meager stack of mail, mostly ads and some bills. At the bottom, however, was a very thick packet addressed to her with the return address of the barrister who had been assisting with her case to remain in the UK. She was accustomed to getting packets of papers; she'd lost count of how many appeals and reviews had been filed on her behalf, how many affidavits, depositions, hearings, assessments, and how many people had worked to help her stay in the UK with her Irish daughter.

Somehow, she'd been able to stay one step ahead of the final order to deport. Thanks to the hard work of Teresa and all the network of social service people of the government agencies and the Catholic charities, she'd made it one day at a time, low wage jobs, crap housing, no money, but she was still here.

She sat down at the table and opened the latest documents, jumping to the end to see what the final judgment had to say. She felt sure she had post-traumatic stress syndrome from re-reading so many times the sordid story of her life before and after arriving in Ireland, but she felt sure this was the last time she would have to read such a document. One way or another, a final decision was about to be delivered.

COGC 1111

IN THE HIGH COURT OF JUSTICE IN NORTHERN IRELAND

QUEEN'S BENCH DIVISION (CROWN SIDE)

IN THE MATTER OF AN APPLICATION BY TRACEY LEE TOMPKINS

FOR JUDICIAL REVIEW

In this case the applicant, Tracey Lee Tompkins, seeks judicial review of a decision, by the Secretary of State for the Home Department ("Secretary of State") to deport the applicant from the United Kingdom.

The applicant is a national of the United States of America, having been born in Texas, and, in the course of an affidavit, she furnished details of her childhood and adolescence. She stated that her parents, both drug addicts, divorced when she was very young, and subsequently overdosed and died. She spent approximately ten years at an orphanage before going to live with her grandmother when she was eleven years of age. She has described her adolescent life as being "extremely chaotic and unhappy" and, from time to time, she received counseling and therapy for depression. The applicant has stated that, upon one occasion, she attempted suicide. The applicant attended the University of Texas and, ultimately, successfully completed a degree in Art History. Thereafter she worked "from time to time" supporting herself with the assistance of a small inheritance.

Miss Burden, a Social Worker employed by the North and West Belfast Health and Social Services Trust ("the Trust") recorded in her report that:

"During this period Ms. Tompkins' apparent self-destructive lifestyle and erratic employment history reflected significantly the lack of family stability she experienced in childhood and adolescence. As a consequence Ms. Tompkins stated she suffered from depression. Ms Tompkins has also alluded to several episodes of therapy and one self-referral to hospital for mental health difficulties." The applicant became pregnant at the age of fifteen and subsequently underwent an abortion. At all times she has been acutely aware of her lack of a stable family background and she has expressed herself as being deeply frustrated by American "values."

At various paragraphs of her affidavit she stated that she decided to move to Ireland because she believed that she could find a "better, more nurturing, way of life" although she told Miss Burden that she had decided to come to Ireland "for a holiday." Miss Burden recorded that the plaintiff told her:

"She had recently converted to Catholicism and states that she had a great-great grandfather from Donegal. As an isolated and rootless adult who seemed to feel keenly a sense of isolation in the USA she had a, perhaps, romanticized notion of gaining a sense of belonging and connecting this in a small Irish community, also states she has an interest in Irish history and politics and this brought her to Belfast."

The applicant left America and arrived at Shannon Airport. At the airport her passport was stamped with a three-month entry permit although it seems that she subsequently lost her passport. The applicant travelled from the Republic of Ireland into Northern Ireland, thereby acquiring leave to enter the United Kingdom for three months in accordance with the Immigration (Control of Entry through Republic of Ireland) Order. Thus, her three months leave to enter the United Kingdom expired and thereafter she has remained unlawfully within the United Kingdom.

It appears that the applicant became pregnant within a fairly short time of her arrival in Northern Ireland; she gave birth to a female child named Erin Frances Tompkins at the Royal Maternity Hospital in Belfast. The applicant had booked in for ante-natal care at the Royal Maternity Hospital and it appears that she was hospitalised on three occasions during her pregnancy.

During the course of compiling the report for the Trust, the applicant told Miss Burden that she had contacted the Catholic Welfare Care Association Adoption Agency stating that, in the event of being deported, it would be preferable for her to arrange to have her baby adopted in Ireland and that she would then commit suicide.

During the course of the hospital admissions she was assessed by a Psychiatrist as being in need of emotional support and she presented to Night Staff at the Royal as very distressed and expressing suicidal thoughts. She was then assessed by a Clinical Psychologist who recommended referral to the Community Psychiatric Service. After the birth of Erin, staff on the ward requested a further psychiatric assessment after becoming increasingly concerned at the applicant's level of distress.

The applicant has stated in her affidavit that she has been in contact with the father of her child who is "an Irish citizen," but it seems that he has at all times refused to acknowledge paternity.

The applicant first came to the attention of Social Services when she applied for financial assistance and, at a case conference prior to the birth of the child, the Trust decided that, in view of the applicant's history of mental health problems, suicidal thoughts and history of disruption, the baby's name should be placed on the Child Protection Register and the applicant should be asked to consider a placement in a hostel for assessment of her parenting skills. The applicant consented and, in due course, arrangements were made for her admission to Thorndale. The outcome of this assessment was very positive and Miss Burden noted that a strong bond existed between mother and daughter with the mother displaying good management skills and insight into the needs of the child. The child's name was subsequently removed from the Child Protection Register.

The applicant wrote to the Immigration Office informing them of her continued presence in Northern Ireland and she subsequently consulted the Law Centre to pursue an application for leave to remain in the United Kingdom.

The Irish authorities confirmed that the applicant's Declaration of Irish Citizenship on behalf of her daughter Erin had been noted in the records of the department, and Erin's Irish citizenship confirmed.

The applicant was interviewed by Bernard Langan at the United Kingdom Immigration Office in Belfast, and a decision was made that day that she should be deported from the United Kingdom in accordance with Section 3(5) of the Immigration Act. The circumstances under which that decision came to be taken have been set out in detail by John Hill Waddell of the Home Office Immigration and Nationality Directorate in his affidavit.

The applicant lodged an appeal under Section 15(1) of the Immigration Act. As a matter of course, this appeal prompted a reconsideration of the decision, but the conclusion reached was that the previous determination had been properly made.

The Order 53 statement in support of the application for judicial review was lodged and, in the light of that application, the impugned determination was reviewed for a second time on behalf of the Secretary of State. The matter was reconsidered generally by Mr. Stephen Still of the Home Department Immigration and Nationality Directorate, and this reconsideration included an assessment of the applicant's grounds for judicial review together with the affidavits and exhibits thereto. The circumstances of this further review of the applicant's case have been set out in detail by Mr. Still in his affidavit.

Dr. Philip McGarry, Consultant Psychiatrist, lodged an affidavit on behalf of the applicant to which he exhibited a report on the applicant. Miss Burden, Social Worker, lodged a brief affidavit to which she exhibited an up-to-date report from the Trust relating to the applicant. Miss Ann Grimes from the Law Centre lodged an affidavit exhibiting a report from "Legal Aid of Central Texas" relating to financial and psychological support that would be available for the applicant and her child in Austin, Texas.

These materials were all considered by Mr. Still who lodged a further affidavit indicating that these up-to-date developments had been taken into account and that, having done so, the original decision taken by Mr. Langan had been confirmed.

The relevant domestic legislation Part 1 of the Immigration Act created the concept of "the right of abode in the United Kingdom" and, as a general rule, those possessing this right are: (i) British citizens, and (ii) Commonwealth citizens.

Tracey put the documents down and rubbed her eyes. So far, it was all the same story she'd heard over and over. She had no rights, she overstayed, and that was the end of it.

> In relation to the applicant's circumstance the Commission noted, at page 8:

> "In the present case, the applicant, 3 years old, is likely to follow her mother on removal. As a result, she may have to leave the society where she was born and face the hardship of living in a society where, due to family, socio-religious factors her mother risks having difficulties in integrating into any community there. With reference to the applicant's links with her father, it does not appear from the material before the Commission that the removal would disrupt the relationship, there being no apparent established bond between them."

> The one factor which might be argued to be of particular significance in this case in relation to a potential breach of Article 8 is the potential for the applicant to commit suicide and I propose to consider this aspect of the case in further detail later in the judgment.

> Article 8(a), paragraph 1 of the Treaty on European Union as amended provides that:

> "Every citizen of the Union shall have the right to move and reside freely within the territory of the Member States, subject to the limitations and conditions laid down in this Treaty and by the measures adopted to give it effect."

> Mr. Larkin, counsel for appellant, submitted that Article 8(a) created an autonomous substantive right to move and reside freely in community territory and that the impugned decision to remove the applicant would have the inevitable consequence of precluding her child, Erin, from freely exercising her rights in accordance with Article 8(a).

Mr. Larkin accepted the significance of the UK reservation to the Convention, but submitted that the proper way for this to be dealt with was for the decision-maker first to consider the interests of the child and then to determine whether, in the circumstances of a particular case, it was right to apply the domestic legislation, ie. the Immigration Act and Rules. He argued that the respondent's affidavits did not disclose any material to indicate that the interests of the child had been properly considered. In my view this submission simply does not do justice to paragraphs 5-10 of Mr. Still's affidavit. I consider that any legitimate expectation enjoyed by the applicant would have been limited to an expectation that the provisions of the Convention, including the reservation, as interpreted by domestic law would be taken into account by the decision-maker in relation to her child. I am satisfied on the basis of Mr. Still's affidavit that this expectation has been fulfilled in this case.

While I accept the cautionary words of Laws LJ in Begbie's case that the categories are not "hermetically sealed," if it was necessary for me to do so, I would be quite satisfied that the facts of this case place any legitimate expectation which the applicant might enjoy in relation to the provisions of the Convention firmly in the first of the three categories identified by Lord Woolf MR at page 645 of the judgment in Coughlan's case, and that, consequently, the court is confined to reviewing Mr. Still's decision upon Wednesbury grounds. It will be clear from my previous remarks that I am quite satisfied that such grounds have not been established in this case. Accordingly, I reject Mr. Larkin's submissions in relation to this aspect of the case.

Irrationality and the Convention.

As he had in relation to Article 8 of the ECHR, Mr. Larkin also argued that it was Wednesbury irrational to merely "have regard to" rather than to apply the provisions of the

Convention. I reject this argument also for the reasons set out in the previous section relating to "Irrationality and Article 8 ECHR".Paragraph 5 – mis-direction in relation to the risk to the applicant's life.

Tracey's eyes rolled back in her head with all the paragraphs delineating the complexities of both UK law, since Tracey was living in Belfast, Northern Ireland, as well as European Union laws because they applied to the Republic of Ireland, where Erin was a citizen and where her biological father lived. All the case law from other cases, which didn't seem that similar to her case, but seemed at the same time to apply, made the whole matter even less comprehensible. She made herself continue reading.

During the course of setting out the applicant's history I have already referred to an alleged suicide attempt together with subsequent threats to commit suicide. During the course of her hospital admissions she was psychiatrically assessed by both a psychiatrist and a clinical psychologist with the latter recommending referral to the Community Psychiatric Service. As I have already noted, she presented to the Night Staff at the Royal Victoria Hospital in a very distressed condition expressing suicidal thoughts. After the birth of her child, staff on the ward requested further assessment after becoming increasingly concerned at the applicant's level of distress, although I have also noted that, ultimately, the child's name was removed from the Child Protection Register.

In the course of his report, Dr. Philip Megarry, Consultant Psychiatrist, recorded that he had been involved in the applicant's treatment during her stay in the Royal Maternity Hospital and that he had seen her again on for the purpose of carrying out a medical examination and recording a full personal, social and medical history. Dr. Megarry noted that, upon that occasion, he found no evidence of psychotic symptoms, current suicidal thinking or clinical depression.

The applicant told him that she could not face the possibility of being returned to America and that, if this happened, she thought that the best thing might be for her to give up the baby for adoption and commit suicide. Dr. Megarry advised the applicant to continue on her anti-depressant medication and concluded his report in the following terms:

"Ms. Tompkins has indicated very clearly that not only would she be very unhappy about returning to the United States but she has stated openly to me that she would be likely to take her own life. She has clearly given serious thought to this and it is clearly a major concern if she is to be deported."

Stephen Still lodged a further affidavit dealing with his consideration of the Report of Legal Aid of Central Texas, as well as the affidavits sworn by Janique Burden and Dr Megarry. Mr Still referred to Dr Megarry's negative findings on examination and, in relation to the applicant's suicide threat, he said, at paragraph 4:

"I note that the applicant expressed this in terms of a possibility and there is no firm evidence to suggest that it would in fact occur. Dr. Megarry has not analysed or discussed in any detail the motivation or genuineness of this threat nor has he analysed in detail the prospect of the threat materialising on the basis of the concluding paragraph in Dr. Megarry's report, I accept that there is a risk of the applicant committing suicide in the event of deportation to the USA and this is one of the factors which I have taken fully into account."

At paragraph 7 of the same affidavit Mr. Still confirmed that the determination to deport the applicant remained unchanged stating, specifically in relation to the suicide threat:

"The Secretary of State is not persuaded that, in all the circumstances, the applicant's statement of threatened suicide whether in isolation or in conjunction with other factors on which she relies is sufficient to displace the considerations highlighted in my first affidavit and, in particular, the normal course prescribed in paragraph 364 of the Immigration Rules."

Mr. Larkin submitted that the content of paragraphs 4 and 7 of his second affidavit indicated that Mr. Still had mis-directed himself with respect to the nature and gravity of the risk to the applicant's life in the event of deportation as detailed in Dr. Megarry's report.

By way of response, Mr. McCloskey refuted the suggestion on any mis-direction and reminded the court that Mr. Still had indicated that he had taken into account the risk and Dr. Megarry's report. In such circumstances, according to Mr McCloskey, the relevant test was that of Wednesbury unreasonableness with weight being a matter for the decision-maker. However, the right to life is recognised as fundamental not only by Article 2 of the ECHR but, I venture to suggest, in common with a number of other Convention rights, and also at common law. In practice, the applicant in these proceedings is a "single mother" and consequently the risk of her suicide also has devastating implications for her child.

In Austin's application NI Report 327 I respectfully adopted the approach of Sir Thomas Bingham MR, as he then was, in R v Ministry of Defence ex parte Smith QB 517 when he approved the test of irrationality in this type of circumstance in the following terms:

"The court may not interfere with the exercise of an administrative discretion on substantive grounds save where the court is satisfied that the decision is unreasonable in the

sense that it is beyond the range of responses open to a reasonable decision-maker. But in judging whether the decision-maker has exceeded this margin of appreciation the human rights context is important. The more substantial the interference with human rights, the more the court will require by way of justification before being satisfied that the decision is reasonable in the sense outlined above."

I would also refer to the judgment of Lord Woolf MR in R – v- Lord Saville ex parte A [1999] 4 All ER 860 at 870g-872e and 881f to 882c. In this context I note that Dr Megarry's report was exhibited to his affidavit subsequent to three considerations of the issue each of which was determined against the applicant.

Taking into account the fundamental nature of the right concerned and subjecting the decision to anxious and rigorous scrutiny in accordance with the decisions of the Court of Appeal in Smith and Turgut, I have come to conclusion that the Secretary of State has misdirected himself in relation to the risk of the applicant's suicide. It is clear from paragraph 4 of Mr. Still's second affidavit that he did depreciate the evidence of this risk by reason of the fact the applicant expressed it only in terms of a possibility, that Dr. Megarry did not analyse in detail the prospect of the threat materialising, and that he did not analyse or discuss in any detail the motivation or genuineness of the threat.

Tracey looked up and threw up her hands. She thought, here we go again. It was just the same as all the other legal mumbo jumbo.

In my view this simply does not reflect a proper or balanced assessment of the opinion expressed by an eminent Consultant Psychiatrist who, after taking into account his personal knowledge of the applicant, together with a detailed personal, social and medical history, came to the clear conclusion in relation to the risk of suicide that it was "clearly a major concern if she is to be deported." In my view this opinion in itself was quite capable of providing firm evidence that the risk would occur.

Accordingly, I will make an order of certiorari quashing the decision upon this ground.

The decision to deport is hereby annulled, and the Secretary ordered to grant applicant indefinite leave to remain.

IN THE HIGH COURT OF JUSTICE IN NORTHERN IRELAND

QUEEN'S BENCH DIVISION (CROWN SIDE)

IN THE MATTER OF AN APPLICATION BY TRACEY LEE TOMPKINS

FOR JUDICIAL REVIEW

JUDGMENT OF COGHLIN J

Tracey read and re-read the opinion, which made her head spin. She gave up all hope with one paragraph, then grasped at the straws of the next paragraph which appeared to contradict what had been said before. She was so grateful for all the support she'd had from her barrister, Mr. Larkin, and Teresa's friends who'd helped her find him. When she got to the last sentence, she gasped.

~~~

Her barrister had sent her some additional materials explaining exactly how her residency status would be affected: she would have legal status to reside in Northern Ireland although she would not be a UK citizen, but legal status meant that she could now work and live…and breathe, free from the crushing burden of worrying whether she would be deported. As she went back through all the appeals, focusing on her mental health, she was as certain now as she was when the case was opened that if she'd been deported, she would have given Erin up for adoption in Northern Ireland and gone back to the US to kill herself, as she'd threatened. The relief that came from being freed of those two awful courses of action was huge, and waves of emotion spread over her, as she cried tears of joy and gratitude.

Finally, she could clear some space in her mind to think about a trip to the US. And she could begin to plan a career beyond marginal temp assignments for work. A future that had seemed completely out of reach for herself and her daughter just a few weeks ago was taking shape before her very eyes, represented by the sheaf of legal documents. She had decided not to burden Erin with the details of her immigration status long ago and had kept all the legal wrangles out of their daily lives. She'd continue to protect her worry-oriented daughter from matters that needn't occupy her mind.

When Erin returned from school, Tracey greeted her with news of her decision. "Dear heart, I've made up my mind. We're going to the States for the reunion. It's time we started thinking about our plans." Erin did a split-jump and squealed with joy. After the initial conversation when Mimi's life-changing visit, her mum had been non-committal. Erin knew better than to push. Something felt different about this decision, about her mum, and about herself, too. She felt her horizons opening up and she began to sense her childhood slipping behind her.

At work the next day, Tracey fired off a quick email during her break to Mimi with her decision. She included the amazing news about her court case and the lengthy court deliberations, which she felt might go a long way to explaining what her life had been like since arriving in Belfast and having Erin.

Mimi responded quickly with suggested round trip flights for the summer reunion from Belfast to San Francisco. Mimi didn't mention the cost of the flights, so Tracey hoped that what she had promised was going to come true. She still wasn't sure what to make of it all; she had the sensation of being on a roller coaster lift hill, strapped in, with no choice but to close her eyes and enjoy the ride, even while feeling terrified.

~~~

The days, weeks, and months flew by, as Tracey and Erin prepared for their trip. True to her word, Mimi took care of every detail for their flights, hotel, and all the amazing things they did on the trip.

The reunion included three nights in a small, quaint, European-style hotel in downtown San Francisco, where twelve of the cousins gathered as a group for sightseeing in Chinatown. Erin and several of the little girls tried on silk kimonos and found just the one to suit each of them. Erin was so beautiful in hers, and all of the girls had fun showing off at an impromptu fashion show at a cousin's home where they had dinner, after a walking tour of Golden Gate Park, which was nearby. The next day they had lunch in the very posh Rotunda of Neiman-Marcus, a Dallas, Texas, landmark that had a branch at the center of Union Square.

They rode the cable cars from Union Square to Ghirardelli. The husband of one of the cousins managed a very swanky restaurant on Sutter Street, and he arranged their dinner one night. Rather than staying in rooms by family grouping, the cousins rearranged themselves to put the kids together, and the whole visit felt very much like a combination summer camp and dormitory, with late night stories, jokes and much laughter. Erin had never felt so happy, surrounded by a variety of ages, sizes, and shapes of cousins. She had trouble understanding why Tracey had kept this amazing family such a secret for so long.

CHAPTER 17

ERIN

"Doing all the little tricky things it takes to grow up, step by step, into an anxious and unsettling world."
—Sylvia Plath

When Erin contemplated her summer plans, she wondered if her friend Deirdre, who'd attempted suicide several times, actually had the right idea. She and Deirdre were still friends, as close as friends could be who couldn't see each other. Erin felt that even though she no longer believed in God--what sort of God would accept a world where two people in love were not welcomed by the Church? She was still living in Purgatory. Is it possible to believe in Purgatory if you don't believe in God, she wondered?

Her mind wandered back to her long-ago plan to come to the States for college, made real by her time at the cousins' reunion in California. Her cousin Mimi, trying to be helpful, had taken her to her own church, an "open and affirming" progressive congregation, full of rainbow flags, inclusive language, and a revisionist version of Scripture that left Erin confused and isolated.

Mimi had also taken Erin and her mom to mass, perhaps in hopes of demonstrating how hopelessly backward, sexist, and unacceptably rigid Catholicism was. Mimi did her best to restrain her enthusiasm for her own church and minimize the eye-rolling in the Catholic liturgy, but noted that Erin tuned out both of them.

As the school year wound down, Erin felt more and more hopeless as another summer loomed. Deirdre always visited her father's family in Germany in the summers, so contact was even more limited then. She thought of calling Mimi and angling for some sort of invitation to California, but she wasn't sure she was ready for a summer with people she didn't really know, in a place that was appealing but scary. She was sure her mum would feel abandoned if she left. Besides, Mimi probably had no interest in having her come anyway. What was she thinking?

Tracey had written to Mimi about her concerns about Erin—her loneliness and isolation had led Tracey to believe that Erin was facing battles with depression similar to her own. Erin knew that Mimi had hoped that she would come to the States for another summer holiday after the successful reunion experience; Erin seemed to thrive when surrounded by family. She was especially happy around her younger cousins, and the young ones were enchanted by their cousin with the exotic accent. Erin was reluctant to come back by herself; she worried about how her mom would do without her.

Mimi made up her mind to not let a summer go by without Erin in it. She and Matthew already had arranged a home exchange in the Netherlands for the summer. Mimi created an itinerary that would be so irresistible that Erin would not be able to say no: Paris, the French countryside, and Holland.

Erin and Tracey read Mimi's email with the invitation for a summer trip to the Continent with excitement. Erin didn't detect any concern or worry from her mum, just joy for the wonderful opportunity. After all, Erin was studying French in school; what a perfect opportunity to try it out!

~~~

A few weeks later, Mimi met Erin at Charles de Gaulle airport, and they navigated the RoissyRail train into Paris and onto the Metro until they reached the stop closest to Notre Dame Cathedral, where Mimi and Matthew had rented a little apartment just steps away. They climbed the 94 steps to the fifth floor and got Erin settled. They began with a long walk along the Seine, passing the bouquinistes along the banks, where second hand booksellers plied their wares to passing tourists and locals alike. On the other side of the Seine, at the Pont Neuf dock, they boarded a Vedettes de Paris boat and cruised up and down the river at sunset. Erin's face lit up with excitement as they passed the famous monuments and buildings she'd learned about in her French class.

Mimi remembered wistfully her own first trip to Paris long ago with her father, when she was not much older than Erin. As the sunset turned into evening, the lit-up buildings were glowed with life and history. They passed the Ile de la Cité, couples with picnics in the little greenspace at its tip.

"It's even more beautiful than I imagined!" exclaimed Erin.

"I know," replied Mimi, "and it's every bit as good no matter how many times you've seen it."

After the sunset boat ride, they meandered down the little streets of Ile St Louis, ending up at Mimi's favorite bistro, Auberge de la Reine Blanche, where they celebrated Erin's birthday in style. Mimi was getting used to Erin deferring any decision about what to order (decisions about anything, really), and Mimi hoped to help Erin find her own voice. "I think I'll order Coquilles St. Jacques," said Mimi. "How about if you try something different, Erin, and we can share tastes?"

The waiter approached the table, and Mimi explained in French that it was Erin's birthday, and they were celebrating her first trip to France. The waiter was delighted that these tourists were speaking French, and of course, he was taken with Erin's naiveté and youthful charm.

"Tres bien, madame. Un peu de champagne?" he smiled broadly at Erin.

"Biensûr, monsieur. Et des escargots, s'il vous plaît?"

The three of them ordered several courses of the delicious cuisine of the tiny restaurant and took their time with the festive meal. Erin was clearly dazzled by her first French dining experience. "I haven't been to very many French restaurants," she said. Mimi knew that Erin hadn't been to *any* French restaurants, or many restaurants at all in her short life, but that was about to change.

After dinner, they wandered back to their little apartment, up the 94 stairs, and looked out at the stars from their tiny balcony. "We should probably go to bed early tonight," Mimi said, "because tomorrow we want to be first in line to get into the Louvre, and from there…"

Matthew rolled his eyes. "Get ready for the Mimi travel experience, Erin. She'll run you ragged if you're not careful. Be sure to say, "Enough already! Feet up time!""

Mimi, who liked to pack each day full of experiences, and Matthew, who preferred a very few activities combined with time in cafés, parks, or in their apartment to put his feet up and just enjoy life, had found perfect balance in their relationship: enough things to do for Mimi with enough time to reflect and enjoy for Matthew — they both got what they wanted and best of all, could enjoy it together!

Erin remembered all the things crammed into the San Francisco reunion, and she had no doubt that Mimi would not waste a moment of this visit either. With all she had on her mind and in her heart (i.e., Deirdre), she was more than fine to stay busy.

Mimi sent Erin across the street to the small patisserie to buy croissants early the next morning, so she could practice her French. Erin was very skeptical that she was up to the challenge, but so excited that she ran up all 94 stairs and burst in to the apartment with her bag of fragrant, freshly baked delights, which they enjoyed with café au lait. Then they set off for the Louvre, as Mimi had promised, standing in line for over an hour waiting for opening time. Mimi pointed out some of the major favorites, but they also made time to wander around, just enjoying the variety and vastness of the museum.

When their feet gave out, they stopped in the café near the I.M. Pei pyramid for chocolat chaud and got ready for their next stop:

the Luxembourg Gardens, where they met Matthew. They had a picnic, watching the children play with their boats in the small ponds and a Punch and Judy show (in French, of course) in a tiny theatre.

On the way back to their apartment, they went in to Notre Dame to gaze at all the stained glass windows, changing colors as the afternoon turned to dusk. Mimi showed Erin the statue of Jeanne d'Arc, her personal favorite. They visited the Mémorial des Martyrs de la Déportation, tucked away behind the Cathedral, and thought sadly of the 200,000 lost in the Nazi death camps in World War II and what it might have been like when Paris was occupied by Nazis.

They stopped in a patisserie for a baguette and then on to a boulangerie for some cheese and meats for dinner. Mimi made sure that Erin conducted the transactions with the proprietor in her halting schoolgirl French. Her confidence was still minimal, but Mimi was determined to see that Erin got as much practice as possible. Too tired to take another step, they ate their dinner while they talked about what they'd explore the next day.

Earlier than most tourists, they hopped the Métro to the Eiffel Tower and bought tickets to climb the staircase. After going up and down 94 stairs to their apartment several times a day, climbing the Eiffel Tower seemed like a natural next step. They made it to the top of the stairs and were treated to the panoramic views of the city. Erin kept pinching herself to prove it was all real, so far from the life she'd known in Belfast.

The next day, Mimi and Erin shopped for a beret, finding a purple one, Erin's favorite color. She put it on and wore it every day; it went well with her purple t-shirt that said "MERCI BEAUCOUP" purchased by her mom for the trip. They took a long walk through the market streets of the Left Bank near the St. Germain des Pres church, Mimi's favorite part of town. They sampled fruits, cheeses, pastries, and bought some picnic supplies to take to the little triangular park, Square du Vert-Galant at the end of the Ile de la Cité.. After their picnic, they crossed the Seine and headed for the Musée d'Orsay, the smaller modern art museum, installed in what had been a train station. On their way from the Musee d'Orsay, they walked through the Tuileries Gardens and along the Seine. Watching the people pass by, speaking hundreds of different languages and dialects, reminded them that Paris was truly a world capital.

"Now *this* is something few tourists think about putting on their list of Paris attractions," Mimi commented with pride. For something completely different, Mimi took Erin to the Islamic Center of Paris, where they tried out the hammam, the Turkish baths where women were sponged, scrubbed within an inch of their lives, and then massaged, before relaxing on the heated stone benches. Mimi had had the experience in Turkey and loved it . She was curious to see how Erin would handle it. She hadn't given her a choice nor much information about their afternoon destination.

Erin was completely unprepared for the vast catacomb of naked women of every size, shape, and age, and surrendered herself to the experienced hands of the female bath wardens. She felt proud of herself for showing Mimi how open she was to any opportunity being offered to her.

~~~

Another tiny bistro on the Ile St. Louis was their destination for the last night in Paris. When the waiter approached, Mimi nudged Erin, who still tended to freeze up when put on the spot. Often when asked what she wanted, she'd respond "I don't mind" meaning "give me anything, I can't make up my mind," which drove Mimi crazy.

"Mademoiselle?" the waiter asked. "What are you having, Mimi?" Erin asked. Mimi responded, "Je ne parle pas anglais. Qu'est-ce vous voulez a manger?" Erin giggled, and Mimi winked at her approvingly. "Coq au vin," Erin responded, turning bright red with embarrassment. "Tres bien," noted the waiter, who then turned to Mimi and Matthew for their orders. After the waiter had left to get their drinks and bread, Mimi gave Erin a high-five, and they celebrated Erin's progress—not just with the French, but the confidence!

Early the next day, they said good-bye to their home of the past week and set off for Chartres, where they would stay with Mimi's ex-pat friends in their restored chateau in Yméray, just a few kilometers away. Hal and Mary Ann met their train and took them to the Chartres Cathedral, with its history and beauty. Now Erin had two cathedrals to compare! The indoor and outdoor labyrinths, the size and scale, the gardens all blew Erin's mind. Hal and Mary Ann had visited the cathedral many times, but they never got tired of introducing it to someone for the first time, and Erin was clearly making the most of it.

The little restaurant nearby, Le Pichet, was a treat; Mary Ann and Hal were "regulars," so the proprietors treated them like family, making suggestions about what to order, which wines to taste, and treating them to "amuses bouches" between courses, a new concept for Erin. So many new things danced in Erin's imagination as she enjoyed this over-the-top holiday with her cousin.

After lunch, they drove to Yméray, where Mary Ann introduced Erin to her horse, Quincaina, and showed all three of them around the estate, which they had lovingly restored from a ruined shell. "And tonight—a special surprise," Mary Ann announced. "We've been invited to celebrate Bastille Day in a villa nearby, complete with fireworks, music, dancing, and wonderful food. You've chosen the perfect day to visit!"

Erin's eyes lit up at the prospect of her first Bastille Day celebration (this was truly a trip packed full of "firsts," and she busily wrote in her journal at the end of each day all she'd learned and experienced). "I feel like I'm in a movie," she said, "and it doesn't seem to have an end."

After dusk, Mimi, Matthew, and Erin walked to the villa where the July 14 celebration was to be held. A lively crowd was celebrating with champagne and tables full of delicious hors d'oeuvres with music in the background. Mary Ann and Hal were clearly well-known in the community, and they made sure to introduce their American friends and their Irish cousin. When the sky was completely black, the fireworks show began, and everyone was dazzled by the display. Erin had experienced St. Patrick's Day and the July 12 Orangemen's Day in Northern Ireland, but found those holidays quite different from Bastille Day or July 4 in the States. The spectacle of light and sound together was amazing.

The next day, they gave affectionate adieux to their hosts and returned to Chartres to catch the train to Paris and onward to Leiden, Holland, Rembrandt's home town, where the home exchange had been arranged. They changed trains in Rotterdam and arrived at the train station in Leiden, absolutely amazed by the hundreds of bicycles as far as the eye could see—parked at the station and on the move in the specially designed bike lanes separate from the roadways.

They took a taxi to their home exchange residence and settled in, delighted to find bicycles for their use in a small shed in the garden. The home exchange offered Erin her own room; in Paris, she'd been on a fold-out couch in their little Paris apartment.

Matthew and Mimi were happy to offer her some privacy, but they could see the downside; once Erin disappeared into her bedroom, they saw her only when they called her to meals or set out on expeditions. Mimi thought about emailing Tracey for guidance but was afraid she'd worry, and afraid of going behind Erin's back for advice. She decided to leave it alone and instead keep Erin occupied every minute.

Except for getting groceries, they rode bicycles, walked, or took the train. Amsterdam was a short train ride away. Mimi and Erin visited the Anne Frank Museum one day; another day they took a canal boat ride past picturesque homes and gardens and tried the traditional Indonesian feast rijstaffel. The weather was beautiful, so several days they took long bicycle rides to the beach at Wassenaar and the quaint little town of Delft, full of interesting little shops. Mimi engaged Erin in a search for antique Delft tiles and souvenirs.

Erin was a willing participant, but she was clearly preoccupied. One day they went to Utrecht where Matthew had friends with kids around Erin's age, and she clearly held herself apart, clinging to her cell phone and barely interacting with their hosts. Erin and the teenagers from the host family had their own pedal boat in the canals, but that didn't seem to break the ice, either.

Although they'd explored Leiden extensively, Erin was extremely reluctant to set off by herself, afraid she'd get lost. She knew that Mimi specialized in getting lost, believing that getting lost was at the heart of every good trip—having to stop locals and get help or directions, or both. Erin reluctantly headed out the door when Mimi suggested "Find something interesting to you, take some photos, and come back with a story!" Erin set off hesitantly and returned a short time later, feeling buoyed by her success in getting around—at least in the immediate neighborhood. She'd ridden her bike to the nearby grocery and bought some snacks to share.

~~~

The summer holiday visit to France and Holland came to an end. Mimi and Matthew took the train to Amsterdam with Erin to put her on the plane back to Belfast. Erin was so grateful for the time away from her usual life and for the freedom to talk to Deirdre on the phone as long as she wanted, even though it was bittersweet, since nothing could be resolved with their relationship. But she'd missed her mum and her pets. Matthew and Mimi gave her an affectionate hug; Erin was still not used to that kind of physical contact, which was neither part of her cultural experience nor her psychological comfort zone. After growing up without any family besides her mum, feeling completely at ease with her new cousins was not going to happen in a couple of visits.

Tracey was at the airport to meet Erin when she returned from her European adventure. She was hungry for details of the trip and hoping a break from the summer routine in Belfast would boost Erin's spirits and help detach her further from the disastrous love affair with Deirdre. Tracey had kept in touch with Deirdre's mother, disturbed to learn that Deirdre had had to be hospitalized after a suicide attempt. Tracey wanted to make sure that contact between the two girls had ceased, but she cared for her daughter's friend and her mother, and hoped to avoid similar mental health crises for Erin.

One of Tracey's goals for Erin for the rest of the summer was some therapy. Tracey wanted to help Erin over the loss of her first love, her sense of loneliness and isolation. She felt she needed a boost as she started high school and faced the significant increased academic pressure to compete for high scores on the UK's version of Advanced Placement classes, the GCSEs leading to a place in a good college.

Erin was not enthusiastic about therapy, but she was not satisfied with her life as it was, either. She was terrified of Deirdre's despair and threats of suicide, and she felt helpless to intervene, especially since, as far as her mum knew, there was no contact between the two girls. She wanted to earn some money to help out with expenses at home, and she knew she needed to stay busy or she really would go around the bend with boredom and anxiety. The idyllic Europe trip was a pleasant but fading memory as she faced the reality of her life.

She got on her bike and headed for downtown Belfast to see about a job for the remainder of the summer. She parked and locked her bike and walked up and down the business district looking for "help wanted" signs, which were few, the economy in a slump. Her heart sank as she passed the Burger King, with its sign soliciting job applicants. Erin sighed, took a deep breath, opened the door, greeted by the blast of noise, fast food aromas, and the depressing low-end clientele.

She inquired at the counter for an application and when she might be able to speak to a manager about summer employment. The manager, a gruff, all-business type man, handed her the form and said, "You're here now, right? No time like the present! Just fill out the paperwork, and I can talk to you as soon as you're done."

Erin could imagine what the rest of her summer would be like; she accepted her fate with a determined grimness.

The manager reviewed her application and her resumé, glanced at her up and down, and said, "I think you'll do. I'll just check your recommendations, and we'll start you on Saturday. You use a bicycle to get around, do you? And you're not one of those flighty teenagers who take the job and then disappear, or show up late and leave early?"

Erin had to work hard not to take his negative attitude personally. "No, sir, you'll see I'm a hard worker, steady and reliable. I'm hoping to save up enough money for a computer for high school."

"All right then. We'll see you at eight am on Saturday, training on the job."

With Erin's goal of getting a job accomplished, she pedaled back home. Tracey wasn't home from work yet, so Erin had a chance to call Deirdre and let her know about her job. No one answered the phone; Erin wondered if she'd already left for Germany where she went every summer to visit relatives.

Saturday morning, Erin pedaled off to Burger King, feeling nauseous and anxious about the summer ahead. She arrived, parked and locked her bike to a bike rack behind the eatery, and went in. Her boss was waiting for her, with an apron, hairnet and Burger King cap and latex gloves, the tools of her new trade. Erin hated it already.

Most customers at this hour were buying take-out coffee for work, so it was a good time for her boss and another employee to show her the ropes—how everything worked, the safety and health rules, and how to work the till. A couple of hours later, and everything was different, with everyone in a hurry, rushing in with their orders.

Erin hated the pressure of taking orders, prepping the to-go bags, wiping down tables, and bussing trash. She found herself getting confused as customers changed their mind; she had a hard time remembering a whole order, and she was aware that her boss was watching her closely. It felt like he was just waiting for her to make a mistake so he could yell at her, which he did frequently.

"Why is this so hard?" she wondered. "I'm not stupid, but I can't seem to get the orders straight, and being watched and yelled at doesn't help!" The only good thing about the noontime rush was that the time passed very quickly, followed by a slow slog through the afternoon when there wasn't enough to do, and she was bored out of her mind.

She did her best to keep an eye on things that needed to be done, but she could already tell this was going to be the longest summer of her life. She tried to focus on how happy she'd be to have her own computer, which she would buy with the money she made, after she had given her mum some money for expenses.

She swore to herself that next summer she would find some sort of work that she was good at, where people liked what she did, and where she could learn something. The next time that Mimi offered to sponsor some sort of summer activities, she was not going to turn her down.

After her shift, Erin hopped on her bike for the long ride home, delighted to be out the fast food grind. She usually got home from work before her mum, and she enjoyed the chance to walk Jazzbo and see what might work for dinner, although after spending the day at Burger King, she didn't have much of an appetite.

Tracey walked in the door and made the mistake of asking how her day had been. "I reek of burger grease, my uniform is covered with stains, my feet are killing me, and I hate my job. The manager yells at me, the customers are cranky, and the people I work with are all creeps," Erin ranted. "I know I'm working to get a computer, but I'm not sure it's worth it. It's so gross, Mummy!"

Tracey sympathized, remembering all the soul-killing jobs she'd had to take to support the two of them. Still, she thought it was important for Erin to learn about hard work and what it took to survive in a tough world. "It's not forever, it's just a few weeks of summer, and it's a good reminder of what life would be like if you lose sight of how important your schoolwork is." She didn't burden Erin with what life had been like for her childhood, having to grow up way too fast.

"I know you're set on me seeing how hard life is, but I already know that. I've seen how hard you've had to work, and I'm grateful. I'm doing this job partly for you, and partly for the computer I need for school. But I want *you* to think about doing something for *me*. I think it's about time you stood up for us with my father. I've talked to kids at school, and I know that the law makes dads provide support for their kids. You've let my dad off the hook without a fight. So here's the deal: I'll keep working at Burger King, and you go to court and fight for the support that we deserve. It's only fair!"

Tracey said nothing. She had wanted nothing to do with the father of her beautiful daughter since the awful humiliation of the phone call and unanswered letters when she discovered she was pregnant. In her view, there wasn't enough money in all the world to compel her to go through another round of rejection. She didn't want her daughter to experience that rejection, but maybe it was time for her to see what the real world was all about. She knew Erin had dreams of her father coming in to her life, even after all these years, and making up for all that lost time and opportunity.

"Mummy, did you hear me? I'll keep going to work at Burger King, but you have to promise to get what's coming to me from my father. It's not fair for him to get off doing nothing when the law says he has to provide support. I've done the research!"

Tracey could see that resistance was useless. Her daughter was every bit as stubborn and determined as Tracey had been, and Tracey knew Erin would relentlessly nag her until the request for support was filed.

CHAPTER 18

JAMES

"Only those who will risk going too far can possibly find out how far it is possible to go."
—T.S. Eliot

James looked at his beautiful bride as she came down the aisle on Oliver's arm, wearing her mother's wedding dress. Oliver gazed at her, and kept blinking as he saw Emma in his mind's eye. The whole community had turned out for the wedding in the little church in the center of town. After the ceremony, Oliver had invited everyone to the farm for the wedding celebration, complete with music, dancing, and a banquet produced by all the friends who'd watched Julia grow up in their community and then blossom in the friendship that had turned to love under their very eyes.

They had not waited long to announce their engagement, wanting to avoid the gossip of the local busybodies once their romantic relationship became public. Julia dismissed that notion. "Who cares about the old biddies in the town and their gossip; we're simply ready to get married; why wait?"

A few tongues wagged about the difference in their ages and the fact that James had been a hired hand, but Julia was a beloved part of their community, a teacher in their school, always on the spot when a family needed a helping hand. The young men her age were a little disappointed that she hadn't chosen one of them, but they'd watched how hard James had worked on the farm and how he'd always pitched in when anyone needed help with their animals or crops.

After the wedding service was over, and they were in the receiving line at the back of the church, Julia said tearfully, "I just wish my mum could have been here." James held her close, and said, "She's here in spirit. You know, she told me her last wish was for us to wed; she knew I always kept my word."

"Are you saying the only reason you're marrying me is because my mama told you to?" Julia teased.

"It's just one of the many reasons, dear one, and I think you know that."

"Well, perhaps you didn't know that my mama told me the same thing, the night she died. She knew how I felt about you, even though we never talked about it."

After the last person had given their congratulations and best wishes to the couple and to Oliver, a caravan of partygoers headed out to the farm, where the music and a feast awaited, set up by womenfolk in the community. Julia and James welcomed the crowd, and Oliver offered a toast to the newly-weds. In honor of James' Irish roots, he gave the traditional Irish blessing:

> May the road rise to meet you.
> May the wind be always at your back
> May the sun shine warm upon your face,
> the rain fall soft upon your fields.
> And until we meet again,
> May God hold you in the palm of his hand.

James, touched by the thoughtful gesture of his new father-in-law, toasted his new family, who had taken him in and given him a new American life. Others added their own tributes, made more boisterous by the free-flowing beer and whisky in honor of the occasion. One of the guests piped up with a typical wedding reception question, "So James, where will you be taking your bride for your honeymoon?"

The crowd quieted as the soft-spoken James said, "This seems as good a time as any to share our news. Julia and I will be honeymooning in Montgomery County, Texas, where we will be making our new home. Oliver will be joining us as soon as he can sell the farm here." One little girl, who'd been one of Julia's students, piped up with the question on everyone's mind. "Why do you have to leave? Why don't you just stay here?" Oliver stepped up to answer. "Too many memories of my Emma. Too much opportunity in Texas for a young upstart like James, who needs to farm his own land and build his own life with Julia."

A buzz started up in the crowd, and small groups formed around the bride and groom and Oliver for more information. Everyone wanted to express both best wishes for life ahead, but also sadness for the loss of one of the community's strongest and most faithful families.

Looking back, Oliver mused about how fortuitous it was to have made the announcement about the move at the wedding reception. Once he had made peace with the idea of leaving the farm and his memories behind in favor of supporting James and Julia's new life, he was ready to throw himself into the enterprise of selling the farm and moving on. The farmhouse and fields had never been as beautiful as they were for the occasion of the wedding, and anyone who could conceivably have been interested in buying the place had been on hand that evening for the presentation of the plan.

James and Julia spent their wedding night in the farmhouse, in Julia's room. Oliver had insisted on spending the night in the little cottage James had built for himself next to the barn. After all those furtive encounters with Kathleen (and Julia knew nothing about any of that), pleasurable though they were, thanks to Kathleen's coaching, James was at last able to take time and care with his young bride, wanting their first night of intimacy to be filled with gentleness and pleasure.

He was haunted by the sounds of his parents' brutal marital relations from his childhood and was determined that his married life was going to be different. Julia was eager and impatient, but

James calmed her with slow, steady, moves that only made her want him more. He whispered to her and caressed her until she was sure she would lose her mind. As they came together, nestling afterwards in each other's arms they sighed in satisfaction and dreamed of their shared future.

Julia spent the next few days going through her belongings as well as her mother's. Her father had said he wanted a fresh start and hoped Julia would not think of trying to move all her mother's things. Julia could understand his feelings, but she wanted a few of her favorite things from her childhood to come with her, a few reminders of her mother's love. She loved the grandfather clock, which had come down from her mother's parents, and she wanted a few of the quilts that her mother had made with such care, including a baby quilt called "sunbonnet sue" that had been on her bed as a child.

Julia and James agreed to take the larger wagon drawn by Lucky and Julia's horse, Charlie. Oliver would take the smaller wagon and one horse and some of his favorite tools. Everything else would be sold or given away when the farm went on the market. Oliver had spent a great deal of time with an attorney in town and the local banker to take care of the legal and financial aspects of the sale, wanting everything to go smoothly…and quickly.

He also spent quite a bit of time talking individually with the farmers who grazed their cows on his land, to make sure their interests were protected and to see if they might be interested in some sort of cooperative purchase, so that what had worked these past few years could continue, but in an ownership arrangement, not as tenants. He was determined that the farm he and James had worked so hard to protect would not fall into the hands of someone from outside the area, but would stay in the hands of those who'd helped him along the way.

James was eager to set off for Texas. He'd received the papers documenting his homestead in Montgomery County; he had Oliver's blessing to take Julia and start the long journey and begin the work of turning empty land into a productive farm and building a home.

James knew that Julia, who had grown up as an only child, was eager to start a family. James, with his experience of too many children without enough food, preferred to establish their livelihood first. He wanted Julia to have the freedom that he knew his mam had longed for, the chance to become a person on her own, before getting locked into the responsibilities of motherhood. He was not inclined to press his opinions, since he was asking Julia to leave everything that was familiar behind, to take her chances with him and this new land.

Montgomery County, the third county established in Texas, was founded around the first settlement, Montgomery, that was named for Lemuel Montgomery. Montgomery was situated on the stagecoach line that ran from Huntsville to Houston, was made the first county seat and became the focal point for new immigrants to the area.

By the time James, Julia, and Oliver moved there, the first courthouse, a two-room log structure built in 1838, was replaced in 1855 by a large Greek Revival-style brick courthouse. The population grew quickly during the 1840s and 1850s, as large numbers of settlers, lured by the abundant land, moved to the area. In 1850 the population was 2,384, and by 1860 it reached 5,479. The vast majority of the new immigrants came from the Old South, many of them bringing their slaves with them. James, Oliver, and Julia had been an anomaly in Perry County, Alabama, by refusing to follow the trend of moving from dairy and grass farming to the production of cotton, which brought with it the increasing use of slave labor, which Oliver and James abhorred. They didn't plan to change when they arrived in Texas, even though in 1850 there were 1,448 slaves in the county, and by 1860 their number increased to 2,416, or nearly half of the entire population.

They were weary when they arrived in Montgomery after their long trip from Alabama. They'd stopped a few times along the way, camping out in the wagon under the stars. Julia had never camped out before, and she found sleeping outside exotic and romantic.

James, who'd slept outdoors probably as much as he'd slept indoors in his life, was amused by Julia's romanticized version of the outdoors and appreciated her excitement about something that was second nature for him. The soft, warm breezes and the feeling that they had the whole world to themselves released all their inhibitions. James never imagined that he could feel so happy and satisfied, with everything he'd dreamed of in his life coming true.

Julia and James went into the general store to see about finding a place to stay while they settled on the piece of land to homestead. They introduced themselves to the proprietor, who encouraged them to stay at the hotel. After the long, dusty trip from Alabama, they were both ready to sleep in a real bed and have a bath. But James was firm about wanting to find a place where they could settle in while they waited for Oliver to arrive and while they were breaking ground on their home. On their journey, Julia and James had already begun to plan their first home and make lists of all the things they'd need to buy to get their start.

James didn't know that Julia had been drawing pictures of her dream house ever since they started to plan their move. James hadn't told Julia that he had been corresponding with a local landowner and several business owners to get the lay of the land in Montgomery. He had received several maps of the area and had his eye on a particular piece of land that looked like a perfect choice: close enough to town that would make it easy to transport goods back and forth and close enough that Julia and their children would be able to participate in the local school. He had recommendations of suppliers for materials he'd need.

He imagined a farmhouse with a wraparound porch. Oliver had already expressed interest in a small cottage for himself near the main house; he hated the idea of getting in the way, and he knew that Julia had plans to have lots of children. He wanted to be close enough to be able to be helpful to the family, but not so close that the noises of droves of small children would drive him crazy.

They walked around the town and were pleased to be welcomed by their prospective neighbors and tradespeople. Everyone was curious about where they'd come from and how they'd ended up in Montgomery. They loved that James and Julia were newlyweds ready to start a family; they were curious about Oliver and when he might arrive.

James and Julia were equally curious about the town. Julia wanted to know about the school and how many children were around. They were relieved that no one asked about their slaves; perhaps they thought that Oliver would be bringing them. They certainly didn't want to get on anyone's wrong side before they'd even built their house and farm.

They'd walked up and down the main streets of town, deciding that they'd give themselves one week in the town's hotel to give James a chance to survey the countryside and give both of them a chance to get better acquainted with their neighbors. They circled back to the hotel, as the shopkeeper had recommended, and got settled into a room, after making sure their horses were cared for and the wagon secured.

No sooner had they lain down than they fell into the deepest sleep they'd had since leaving Alabama, protected from the elements, under the soft, warm down comforter on a bed that welcomed their tired bodies and weary souls. They didn't wake up until the next morning, hungry, refreshed, ready to get cleaned up and start the serious business of finding their homestead.

They went down to the hotel's dining room for breakfast, enjoying the luxury of a meal prepared and served by someone else, after their long road trip's diet of canned provisions and whatever fruits and vegetables they could find along the way. While they were finishing up their coffee, a man approached their table and introduced himself. "Please excuse the interruption of your breakfast, but my name's Simon Hollister, and I've been awaiting your arrival. We've been corresponding about land and homesteading in these parts. Word travels fast in a small town, and both the storekeeper and the hotel owner let me know the two of you were just in from your journey."

James introduced himself and Julia and invited the gentleman to join them for coffee. Although it was customary to let the menfolk take care of the business, Julia was not about to miss out on any information or decisions that might affect her family's future home. Mr. Hollister wasted no time in getting to the point. "From your letters, I think I know what you're looking for, and I think you'd both enjoy seeing a bit of the land around our little town before you get serious about a single section of land. I'd be honored to show you around and introduce you to some families. We take a lot of pride in our community, and I think you'll like what you see."

He unrolled a map of Montgomery County, showing the layout of the homesteads that had already been claimed and pointing to various pieces of land that might be appealing to James and Julia. James wondered about the characteristics of the soil and what might grow best; Julia wanted a place with a creek or spring nearby, with an accessible year-round water supply.

"I appreciate your help, Mr. Hollister," James said. "We're ready to go whenever you are."

Mr. Hollister smiled. "Please, call me Simon. We're all friends in this town."

By the end of the day, James and Julia felt much better acquainted with the territory around Montgomery and the plots of land they felt would be best suited to the dairy farming and pasture of their experience. Julia didn't want to be too far from town; James didn't want to be too close.

James didn't want to have to clear too many trees and preferred the flatter plots of land; Julia loved the tree-covered rolling hills. Simon's head spun, as the two of them engaged in lively discussions about which piece of land best suited them. He was a little surprised that James listened so closely to what Julia wanted, and even more surprised by how knowledgeable and opinionated Julia was about what made a farm work well, not knowing that James and Julia had run their farm in Alabama as a team, with Oliver as their guide.

As the sun began to set, the three of them headed back to town, having marked on the map their favored choices for a farm of their own. Julia went back to the hotel to rest before dinner, and the two men headed for the saloon, getting down to the business of how a transaction might be made. Julia had hoped her father might arrive before a final decision was made, but she understood and accepted that James was eager to make the decision without relying on her father's opinions.

James and Julia awakened early the next morning, and they enjoyed another breakfast in the bustling dining room, a gathering place for the little town. After another solid night's sleep, James was ready to commit to a particular piece of land that Simon had shown him. He went to the courthouse to apply for the homestead and pay the fees required to establish his title to the land. James had brought with him a supply of cash that Julia's father had given him, a generous wedding gift and unpaid wages due to him for his work, which he wanted to deposit in an account at the local bank.

Julia went to check on the horses and to talk to the owner of the feed and seed store, where they would likely become customers. She visited the general store again and made a point of introducing herself to anyone who came in, wanting to make friends and learn as much as she could about the community.

She was eager to see the schoolhouse, and she sat on the steps, waiting for the teacher and students to come out when it was time for recess. She could hardly wait until she had her own little ones who would go to school here, and she was happy that the teacher seemed so pleased she'd come to visit. "I was assistant teacher back in Brushy Creek, Alabama, where we've come from. I guess I've always wanted to be a teacher ever since I was small. I didn't have brothers or sisters, so I just pretended my dolls were my students. I taught them all to read and do their numbers," Julia laughed as she shared a little about herself with Miss Mason, the teacher in the one-room schoolhouse. "I expect you won't have much time while you and your husband settle in," said the teacher, "but if you get bored, you're always welcome here, right, boys and girls?" A chorus of voices rang out with a welcoming "Yes, ma'am!" Julia excused herself after being given a little tour of the classroom, each student enjoying attention from the newcomer and excited to share their work.

She walked back to the hotel, where she found James and Simon, looking over the papers from the title office and beginning to sketch out where on the property to put the barn, the main house, and Oliver's little cottage. Julia's heart swelled to see her dreams become real, as she saw her new home beginning to take shape on the paper, just as she'd described it to James. "My daddy will be so pleased," Julia exclaimed. "It's ever so much nicer than our old farm in Alabama; it looks bigger, too!"

Within a few days, James had completed all the legal and financial arrangements, and the land was theirs. They worked with Simon to find a crew to help them build, and they ordered logs, lumber and building supplies. Julia bought provisions for keeping the work crew fed, starting with only an outdoor fire pit and buckets of water from the nearby stream. She'd made sure to bring her dishes, pots, pans, and utensils with her, and she was delighted to be able to start using them. They'd moved out of the hotel, and they'd been using the back of the wagon as their bedroom—not as comfortable as the hotel's bed, but with her mama's homemade quilt, on their own land, her heart burst with pride each day as she awakened, wrapped up in James' arms.

After a month, word arrived from Oliver that all the transactions related to the sale of the Brushy Creek farm had been completed, all the belongings that he wanted to bring with him sorted from those he'd sold or given away, and all the farewells bade to his lifetime friends, most of whom he was sure he'd never see again, and he was ready to set off for Texas. A couple of his best friends had insisted on coming with him, bringing two wagonloads of supplies for the new homestead. "Who knows," Oliver mused, "maybe they'll find the promised land there and bring their families out, too."

With winter on the way, Oliver wasted no time on the road; he hadn't seen Julia in months, and he was eager to see the homestead Julia and James had written so much about. He was weary of living on his own; he still missed Emma, and he hated to admit it, but he was tired. The beautiful autumn weather boosted his spirits, though, with leaves turning as they reached the piney woods of east Texas, with live oaks and elms on rolling hills under blue skies and balmy fall temperatures. By the time they reached Montgomery County, he was renewed and ready for the new life ahead.

The three wagonloads of possessions and the road-weary travelers arrived in Montgomery mid-day. They briefly considered staying in the hotel, but Oliver couldn't wait to get out to the homestead and see with his own eyes what James and Julia had described in their letters. He stopped in at the general store, figuring that Julia and James would have established themselves as customers there, and he was greeted warmly by the proprietor, who was happy to give them directions to the Lockhart homestead, two miles outside of town. Oliver thanked him, and the small procession of wagons set off again.

Julia rushed out to greet them, and Oliver gave her a long hug and looked around with admiration at how much had been accomplished in the months since his daughter and her husband had left Alabama. A crew had finished the barn and was now working on the framing for the farmhouse. Oliver had arrived expecting to sleep outdoors, but now it looked like the barn was ready for occupants, and he and his friends could unload the wagons and keep them out of the weather. Oliver walked around the property, surveying the meadow, the stand of pines and oaks on rolling hills just on the other side of the spring. Oliver wondered where he might want to put his cottage. "We waited until you arrived so that you could make sure it was exactly as you wanted," James explained.

"James, I knew you were a hard worker, but I never imagined you'd have so much done before I even picked up a hammer and a saw. You've picked a beautiful piece of land, and before long, we'll have the place full of cows, sheep, chickens…and…"

Julia interrupted, "Children," Julia interrupted. Lots and lots of children." All three of them laughed. Julia gave them both a look, and said "You think I'm joking. But the first one is on his way." Julia saw them look at her with awe, and she felt more confident and happier than she had ever been.

Oliver looked at James. "You HAVE been busy." Julia blushed as she grasped hands with her father and James. "Time for lunch!"

she announced as workers, friends, and family gathered around the outdoor table for a hearty lunch of stew and corn bread, baked in Julia's outdoor oven.

CHAPTER 19

MIMI

"Education is not preparation for life; it is life itself."
—John Dewey

Each summer, I invited Erin to come to the US to work, study, or travel. I sent Christmas and birthday presents, which she acknowledged with appreciation. Her address changed periodically; Tracey's employment continued to improve slightly from short term temp work in several businesses to stable temp work in a single organization. Tracey felt the pressure of never having enough money; any unexpected expense sent her little family budget into crisis.

I received frantic emails from Tracey about how stressed, lonely, and anxious Erin was, and how worried she was about Erin's fragile mental health. I muttered to Matthew, "Erin's dealing with all that Catholic bullshit in school, and her mother's a religious fanatic; how can I spring her loose?"

In desperation, I emailed Erin in the middle of summer before her senior year:

> *"Hi, Erin,*
>
> *I haven't spoken to your mom about this idea; I thought I'd pitch it to you first. Would you consider coming to California for your senior year? The last time we messaged on FB you were planning a busy summer working, and that was two years ago...it seems to me like you must have had*

three summers of work since then and might be ready for a change.

I know a high school that builds its program around its students' gifts and interests, and you would graduate with a California high school diploma, which might help if you decide at some point on college (Residency gives you a big break on college tuition.) If the answer is yes, write me back. Or write me back anyway. I always think about you in July, your birthday month; would the idea be a good birthday present?"

About thirty seconds later, Erin emailed a response.

Hi, Mimi,

I've considered your proposal and actually think it may be something I'd like to do. I realise that it's a very short time until then, but if you think it could work then that's pretty cool. I feel you may not understand that I may not be as good as you would hope in some respects; you may find coping with me difficult since I may not be going for what you would consider 'the right reasons.' I do have some issues that I consider pretty irresolvable, but your offer is one that I am seriously considering. I am quite on board and I don't see that changing. You, on the other hand, are free to retract your offer in the near future.

Many thanks, Erin"

I gasped when I read Erin's email, partly because I hadn't clued Matthew in on my latest plan to get Erin to the States. The way I saw it, both of us are retired, our kids grown and off on their own — why not make a miracle happen for this young girl?

I quickly typed back,

"I was blown away by the speed and the content of your response! I realize that you may have second thoughts, that your mom may have opinions, and that Matthew may have

opinions, too. If it's ok with you, I'm not going to say anything to your mom until you get back from camp and have time to think things over. It's a huge step for both of us, and I'm honored by your trust. I assure you that I may not be as good as you would hope in some respects, and you may find coping with me difficult as well.

Perhaps some time away will give you a chance to reflect on your irresolvable issues in a new context. I often find that a change of scene leads to new perspectives on things that seemed impossible previously. So we have each given the other the option of changing our minds, but we have also affirmed our current intention for you to come to the US for the school year and for me to do all I can to support your figuring things out. Xoxo Mimi"

I knew that the email negotiations were delicate, crucial, and so very personal. I tried to listen with my whole heart as Erin responded:

"I still would like to go to California for my senior year, but I don't feel really sure about anything in my life. I have a really hard time thinking about the future and find it practically impossible to carry out the steps necessary to bring it to fruition.

My school has been putting a lot of pressure on getting ready for university—they are very intense about it. One of my issues was that they were unable to help me plan or get ready for American universities and it was difficult being pressured to do things that didn't apply to me, while knowing I should probably be doing something equivalent for America, but not knowing what that was exactly. They don't have anything like guidance counselors over here and preach to the masses, expecting everyone to fit into the same prescribed box.

I used to be really focused and sure of my academic future, despite it being different, and I wasn't necessarily opposed to them pressuring me because I know it's important to be on the ball and I love planning and being sure of things.

I am now in a state where I can't try like I used to. I've recently sort of had to let go of my grand ambitions for myself because I am paralysed at the prospect of things like university applications, especially to competitive universities. Thinks like essay questions on the applications really threw me because I can't talk about myself or my ambitions because I have severe identity issues that are too complicated to explain.

Anyway, I just think we should both be clear with each other our intentions for all of this — a list of expectations, if you will. You may remember that I was set on going to East Coast universities, and it's not that there's anything inferior about the west coast, but me going to a California university instead is me sort of relinquishing control over who I was supposed to be (according to myself).

The reason your proposal is something that appeals to me is because, in the state I am in, I don't see myself being able to go to America at all. I just see myself getting a menial job and staying at home and withering. That is why your help, and just biting the bullet and going (because I have nothing else to lose) would be a good thing, otherwise I will never move at all. My mother can't help me.

I realize that all of this has probably put you off, and understandably so, but life's too short not be honest. I won't obfuscate things, since that's more complicated in the long run and not fair to you. I will allow you some time to ponder things. Many thanks for your patience and your offer,

Erin"

I was relieved that Matthew signed on immediately. We talked for hours and crafted a response that we hoped would engage both Erin and her mom, without scaring them to death.

"Hi, Erin,

Matthew and I have had a chance to talk in some detail about what might be the benefits and joys as well as the potential pitfalls and difficulties of welcoming you into our family for the next year. We are honored by your trust in us and yourself to take on this adventure, and we are excited about offering you opportunity. Here are some ideas of how the year might go, what we would expect of you, and what we would offer:

We will do our best to connect you with experiences, opportunities, and people who can help you think about and perhaps resolve some of the many questions you have about your identity and your future. Some of these may be helpful, some may not, and some may at least challenge your thinking. We'd ask that you come with an open mind and heart, ready to try things out—and to engage with us about what works or doesn't. You may want to keep a journal. We remember how much fun it was to be with you in Europe, as you explored with us...and we remember long periods in Leiden when you were closed up in your room and we had no idea of your state of mind. We'll expect you to be an active part of our household.

You'll want to complete the requirements for a US high school diploma while you're here. I'm sure your own high school transcript will more than fulfill our US requirements. (I need a copy of your latest transcript, your social security number, and any other documents that you think would be helpful –immunization record, medication records, health issues—ASAP.)

We will not be your parents. We will not be imposing discipline or bossing you around. We will make sure you are safe and help you think about what you are doing, but we will not be providing answers—the idea is for you to figure out the best answers for your own life. You can count on us to be good listeners and to ask hard questions, as appropriate to the situation.

I will buy you a round trip ticket from Belfast. I'd like you to commit to stay for the academic year, but if that becomes unworkable, you can return home.

I would like to engage your Lockhart cousins in this adventure, making it possible to visit them (San Francisco, Berkeley, Houston, Austin, Dallas) as part of your US experience. I will let them know that you're spending this year with us and let them know you might be interested in coming to visit.

Xoxo Mimi and Matthew"

The emails continued to fly back and forth; my heart stopped each time one popped into my inbox.

"Hi, Mimi,

Thanks so much for your detailed reply. It sounds like I won't be able to meet your expectations, especially the first two paragraphs of number 1. I care about not disappointing people, so I could force myself to carry out explicit requests, but it seems you want more of an emotional engagement, which I would likely be unable to give since I've been that way for a while now, such as being in my room in any of my spare time and being in solitude.

Me being so open, as I am in these messages, is unusual for me and no doubt easier because it's not face-to-face. I doubt it will become a regular thing. I don't have a very open mind or heart for what I feel are people's useless endeavours, and feel they are incapable of understanding. I also know society is big into things only working when the person wants to help themselves. I don't think I can be 'saved' from myself.

Sorry for the negativity—but this is me being honest. I had therapy with one person for over a year (as well as antidepressants) and by the end of it he was still saying things that showed he didn't understand my basic conflict at all. And several other mental health professionals made similar incorrect conclusions about me. It's always the same limited understanding no matter how well-intentioned the people are. I still want to go to California but more because I have nothing to lose, rather than something to gain.

It seems you only want me if I am willing to improve myself and understandably so. My mother finds my surety that my identity conflict is unsolvable very upsetting. My mother is on board with all the practical things you mentioned, but I realise it is me as a person that is incongruous with your expectations.

It is with a heavy heart that I say these things, knowing I am losing an important opportunity. Many thanks for your time and patience.

Erin"

My heart sank as I forwarded Erin's email to Matthew. Once again, we put together a reply.

"Hi, Erin,

You have written painfully honest, detailed, and articulate emails about your situation. Your reaching out to us, without using your mom as a go-between, and expressing your desire to make a change in your life, shows a remarkable amount of personal growth, self-awareness, and determination to run your own life, from the young person we traveled with in Paris and in Holland several years ago.

In that way, you have already met the requirement for emotional engagement with us. It may be that our best means of communication for the more personal, introspective reflections will be in writing. In that way, you are likely to feel you are right at home in this household, because both Matthew and I value our time alone, and we often feel more comfortable expressing our deepest thoughts to each other and to others in writing. (Of course, not all situations lend themselves to this type of communication, but sometimes writing down one's thoughts help put them in an order or perspective that can then be shared out loud—in part or in whole). Your explicit denial of being able to emotionally engage (Paragraph #1) shows that you, in fact, ARE ready to engage and are doing so.

In other words, writing IS a valid communication, and in the place you're in at the moment, it may be a way to begin. You feel you want to come to California because you have nothing to lose. I think, in your heart of hearts, you want to come to California because you believe you may learn something or see some things differently from the way they look to you at the moment. In truth, you have a lot to lose by coming to California, because if you refuse to try new things and imagine things differently, you will return home even more hopeless than you are at this moment. California holds at least a hint of possibility. You know exactly what your life will become if you continue on the course you have chosen so far.

You have no idea what might happen if you make your way out to the end of the diving board and jump into the pool—it might be good! By taking yourself prematurely out of consideration of coming, you ensure that things will stay exactly the same. By affirming that you're willing to try new things, you keep the California possibility open. ('If you always do what you've always done, you'll always get what you've always gotten.') On our end, Matthew and I have much to gain by your coming, and we will be disappointed if you opt out so easily.

For example, we loved seeing Paris through the eyes of a youthful first-timer, and we loved stumbling our way through unfamiliar territory together in the Netherlands. Remember when the washing machine overflowed and sent rivers of water down two flights of stairs in the flat where we stayed? Getting lost on our bikes on the way to Delft? Eating rijstaffel in Amsterdam?) We also have much to lose if you come and then refuse to sample the variety of people and experiences that will be new to you. We will be investing

money, time, space in our home and, most importantly, in
our hearts, for your well-being and happiness.

We have raised three boys who are now young men,
through the throes of adolescence and into adulthood. We
know what we are getting ourselves into: life well-lived is a
roller coaster, with highs and lows. If you are determined to
say no, we will accept your decision, with sadness. Instead of
dwelling on your lack of capacity for engagement, you might
consider all the ways you have shown the exact opposite
already, in your emails. If you'd like to come and are willing
to work through the issues as they come up with us, we're
still happy to have you. Please let us know what you choose
to do.

Mimi and Matthew"

I couldn't leave the keyboard as I waited for the next email. My
heart pounded, and my head burst with all I wanted to say. I felt
like a hostage negotiator!

~~~

"Hi, Mimi,

Wow, I didn't expect you to still be onboard after all that
honesty, but I am grateful. YES, I want to come and stay with
you in Santa Cruz. I'm willing to try my best with things
that you want me to do, as long as you are aware that I can
seem to be having enriching experiences (and no doubt these
things are better than rotting here in Ireland) but having a
good time with you doesn't mean that the underlying
problem is fixed.

Since I have affirmed my decision, my mother will try
and get the documents to you ASAP. It's all very exciting
since it's only three weeks away.

Two queries I have include:

You have implied I will be going back to Ireland after my stay with you. While I understand I will be leaving your residence after the year, I am still planning on going to university in America.

You have implied that I wouldn't be attending high school, as in the usual 9-5 way. I always imagined that I would be doing the usual high school experience. Now I'm not necessarily opposed to your ideas about this, but I feel it's something we should discuss. Your help with the university application thing is indescribably invaluable to me, but on the other hand, I'm not sure how much pressure or expectations you want to place on me to strive for the academically elite. Due to my inability to think about the future, I have postponed studying for the SAT subject test (necessary for many of the good universities I was looking at, but maybe I should set my sights lower considering my 'issues'). It's just something to think about. Many thanks for your acceptance and kindness.

Erin"

I heaved a sigh of relief and gave Matthew a big hug.

"Hi, Erin,

I'm glad you were surprised and grateful. We're surprised and grateful that you want to come! That means we're all starting out in the same place! Here are some answers to your queries.

When I checked for fares, going round trip was not much more expensive than one-way. I also was not clear that you were certain that you are going to university in the US. I will look more carefully at one-ways now that we have a plan.

We thought you might be ready to get off the hamster wheel of high stakes high school/college prep and give yourself some space to consider alternatives. It might well be better to come earlier so that you yourself could visit a variety of options and see for yourself. We have some excellent schools in Santa Cruz and there are pros and cons to all of them.

One of the things we'd like you to do when you come is meet with my dear friend who is a private college counselor, working with students just like yourself (honestly!!!) to figure out what's best. We can say without any hesitation that your choice of type of high school will not make any difference in the universities you find yourself wanting to go to. Any school you would want to go to would be impressed by your taking time to consider who you are and where you are going. The bigger question is how to pay for it. That will depend on your mom completing the income tax returns and the FAFSA in a timely way.

We are not going to put any pressure on you whatsoever to go immediately to an academically elite university or any university for that matter. Until you begin to feel comfortable in your own skin, you are not likely to be able to make good decisions about where to go and for what reasons. We are determined to help you explore the dimensions of yourself that are troubling and to look for schools and programs that engage seekers like yourself. It will be a grand adventure!

I have a built-in bias for travel, service, and work exploration as well as the need to try out LOTS of things across social, recreational, spiritual, psychological, vocational arenas, etc, so that you can be confident when you say 'tried that, don't like it' or 'tried that—am passionate about it.' Saying either without enough experience for comparison is not that helpful. Stay tuned!

It's a huge step for both of us, and I'm honored by your trust.

Xoxo, Mimi"

Erin continued the correspondence, exceeding my expectations about her ability to engage and be honest about her feelings and experiences.

~~~

Three weeks until Erin's arrival! I threw myself into the kind of planning that an ordinary senior in high school would have done during her junior year. The first step was to ascertain where Erin would go to high school: a traditional high school with AP and honors classes, requiring a warp speed transition not only academically but also socially with extra-curriculars and college planning crammed into two months, or an alternative high school, with much greater flexibility and much less pressure. I was pretty sure I knew what she would choose, but I wanted Erin to be the one making the choice, and I wanted her to have the experience of each setting before making up her mind.

I stayed up late every night making lists and plans, my specialty. I bought a used bicycle, helmet, and lock, and Matthew equipped it with a crate on the back to carry books, ju-jitsu gear, tennis racquet, and all the other essentials.

I emailed the counseling department at the highly regarded local high school to find out exactly how to go about getting Erin enrolled, if that was the course of action she wanted to take. I was taken aback that even with Erin's spectacular UK high school record (11 GCSE's with A's– unheard of!), the gatekeeper for the counseling department didn't even want to make an appointment.

"We don't admit new students to our high school if they are already 18," she snipped. "Perhaps Adult Education might be an option." After decades as a teacher educator and advocate for students and my own children, I wasn't about to accept *that* answer!

"Please show me in the Education Code where it says that students cannot be admitted to high school when they are 18." I tried not to snarl, but I wanted to scream! I knew that I'd be dealing with this dragon for the whole year, if this was any indication how she treated students and families. I drew on my lifetime network of colleagues and connections in the education world to work my way all the way to the school principal and district superintendent to win the crucial first battle—eligibility not just to enroll, but to enroll in AP and honors classes.

Next I contacted Alternative Family Education, where one of my sons had gone, and, as expected, I was welcomed warmly and encouraged to bring Erin in for a visit to check it out. "After 11 years in an all-girls Catholic high school, I can't imagine that she would feel at all comfortable here, even if our program might be just what she needs. The lack of structure, the need to take the initiative in designing a program, trying to fit into a new family and a new culture all at the same time—I'd be betting she'd take the more familiar path at Santa Cruz High," the head teacher responded to my questions. "But we'd love to meet her, and I could be entirely wrong! It certainly wouldn't be the first time." I was grateful for the warm welcome, the empathy, and the support we received in trying to find the very best start for my young cousin in her new life.

With the high school options lined up, I went to work on the college application process. I had a contact in the Admissions Department at UCSC, who kindly agreed to compare and evaluate Erin's Irish high school transcript, so that she could get credit on her US transcript for all the work she'd done. She also provided explanations of the UK GCSEs for both the high school counseling staff and prospective colleges. Fortunately, Erin had taken the SAT in her junior year, and her scores were impressive.

Then I had lunch with my friend, the private educational consultant who helped families and students navigate the college application process. I hoped she might be willing to help Erin. I shared the whole story. "I feel like I'm getting on board a freight train roaring down the track, in danger of going off the rails," she responded. "I usually have two or three years to do this work with a student and the family. You're asking me to do it in two months! And I'm not even sure, given what you've told me, that Erin should even consider going directly to college. She's likely to get the bends, just like scuba divers who come to the surface too fast. These decisions are expensive, Mimi, and I'd hate to see Erin crash and burn."

My eyes filled with tears. "After how hard she's worked all these years to get to America and to launch the dream she never really thought she'd have, I'm not going to tell her to just take a year off. *You* can suggest that possibility, but I think when you meet her, you'll understand what I'm talking about. Will you meet with her? Will you help us?"

"Of course, I'll help you, up to a point, for the next two months. But you have to know you and Matthew will be working full-time on this project, and I don't want you to be disappointed if it doesn't go the way you want it to.

CHAPTER 20

ERIN

"I think she is growing up, and so begins to dream dreams, and have hopes and fears and fidgets, without knowing why or being able to explain them."
—Louisa May Alcott

Three weeks later, Erin arrived, full of wonder and amazement at the world she was entering, a world she'd imagined since she was quite small, alternately believing and not believing it could ever happen.

She settled into her new room, put up some photos, posters, and a wall calendar to keep track of all her activities. She floated between appointments that Mimi had set up. As predicted, she was alternately horrified and curious about the alternative high school and opted for the traditional high school (to Erin, it looked and felt just like a Hollywood movie set). Once she and Mimi had made their way past the dreaded counseling secretary, they were able to set up her year's schedule—an Advanced Placement English class, honors US History, PE, and electives.

The AP English class, taught by the legendary Mr. Griswold, was a stunner. Unlike the classes at her Catholic girls' high school, US classes were much more interactive. Mr. Griswold was an imposing, stimulating teacher who didn't care much about grades, while imposing very high standards on the work he'd accept. The novels he'd selected for the class to study were thought-provoking, and Erin loved the way the students felt free to express their opinions. In fact, Mr. Griswold insisted on students having a point of view, well-supported by what they'd read.

The small group of students, mostly girls, bonded over their adoration of Mr. Griswold, and he let them stay in his classroom to have lunch, which was just the social glue that Erin needed to get through the year. The large, diverse high school was noisy, chaotic, and bewildering to Erin, but she desperately wanted to have the most complete American high school experience possible, and then move directly on to her goal of a small liberal arts co-ed college on the east coast once this year was over. She jumped on every opportunity Mimi encouraged her to try – the tennis team, the mock trial team, and a membership at a ju-jitsu martial arts academy, all the while gearing up for the college admissions process.

Mimi's college consultant friend, Susan, was true to her word, providing Erin with a compressed admissions process unlike anything the consultant had tried before. Mimi was adamant that Erin not limit herself to east coast small liberal arts schools, so the search included large state schools and small private northwest schools, to give Erin a sense of the variety of experiences that might fit. Not only did Susan have personal experience at these schools, her services included software that analyzed every conceivable variable that students (and their parents) might consider in the decision-making process. Mimi and Matthew (who, along with most of their friends of a certain generation) had only applied to one or two schools and not really given much thought to the decision, compared to today's students, who frequently applied to fifteen or twenty. Matthew took on the job of helping Erin with the financial aid part of the search, and Mimi helped plan the trips to visit colleges.

Amidst all the frenzied activity of maintaining her spectacular academic record and extra-curriculars, Erin was learning to live in an American household, with Mimi and Matthew as de facto parents. Mimi was taken aback at their first family dinner when

Erin inquired meekly, "Do you think it might be all right if I had seconds of peas?"

Erin was not just using her good manners but was reflecting a childhood growing up in poverty. She was scrupulous about asking before she took anything from the refrigerator or cupboard, as if helping herself might be construed as greedy or inappropriate. Mimi and Matthew repeatedly encouraged her to just help herself to anything she needed in the household, as she was to consider the household hers. Erin seemed to find this concept very hard to accept, and obviously quite different from the way she operated at home with her mom.

One morning, Erin came down for breakfast and found Mimi cutting out an article in the local paper about a free all-day workshop led by local writers for high school students preparing for college applications! When Mimi asked if she'd be interested, she didn't hesitate.

~~~

Erin stayed up late each night doing the next day's homework and staying ahead on big projects. One of those nights, she worked on a first draft of her personal statement, to give herself confidence when she went to the workshop.

Mimi and Erin got up early on Saturday and rode bikes together to find the workshop location. Erin had very little sense of direction, was desperately afraid of having to ask someone for directions, and was often so lost in her own thoughts as she was riding along, she paid little attention to where she was. A newcomer to town, most things were unfamiliar, including riding on the right side of the road, instead of the left.

Mimi spotted the sign and stopped in front, while Erin continued to pedal down the street, until she realized she was riding alone. Mimi waited for her a half block away, and Erin turned back, embarrassed. Mimi congratulated her on discovering her mistake and gave her a hug.

"Good luck, Erin—most of all, have fun with the day. See if you can make a friend," Mimi encouraged. Her greatest challenges with Erin were to get her to relax, let down her guard a little, and find time for friends and fun. Mimi pushed her to just get on her bike and ride sometimes, without a destination, and find her way back to her new home. Mimi didn't know what it was like growing up in Belfast and feeling so alone on her bike. Certainly no one would have suggested riding without a destination; straying off the Falls Road could be a death sentence in a non-Catholic neighborhood, an invitation to Protestant bullies to taunt her, harass her, or worse.

Just before noon, Mimi looked up from the book she was reading, surprised to see Erin cruising into the driveway with a big smile on her face.

"You're home early. Is everything ok? How was the workshop? I thought it lasted all day. I want to hear everything! You're smiling, so something interesting must have happened."

Erin locked her bike, took her backpack into the house, and drew out a sheaf of papers. "I didn't tell you, but I did a first draft just to make sure I had something to start with. Sometimes when I get stressed out, my mind goes blank, and I can't think of a thing to write. I didn't want that to happen today—it's just too important!"

"So you had a draft to share when the workshop started. I bet the writers were impressed! How many other kids came prepared with a first draft?"

"I wasn't the only one. But the writing coaches were so nice. The first one took a look at my first draft, and then she called over another writing coach and then another. They all looked at each other and said "You've done it! Your first draft is better than almost all the final drafts we've ever seen."

Erin blushed as she told the story. "It wasn't really my first draft. I must have re-written it twenty times. I didn't sleep at all last night. I was so excited to think about this essay—this is actually the first step to getting me where I want to go."

"No, Erin, you've taken so many steps before this one. But you're right, it *does* seem important. Anyway, what happened after that?"

"Each of the writers sat down with me and asked me questions about what I'd written. Each one had a few suggestions, but they were minor. After our individual conversations, they all agreed that I didn't need any more help from them. They were sure my essay would stand out and even better, that I'd get into a small liberal arts east coast college.

"Would you be willing to share it with Matthew and me? I realize that it's a very personal story, so feel free to say no if sharing with us makes you feel uncomfortable. Will you share it with your mom?"

"I'm fine to share it with you two. But please don't share it with my mom. There are parts in there that would hurt her, and there's no need for that."

Erin handed over the essay, notable in its absence of critical comments or edits from the writing coaches, and Mimi began to read.

College Essay for Common Application – Erin Tompkins

Just one step. I repeat this, trying to block out all the other things this is and could become. I could repeat this phrase forever, paralyzed by all the ramifications, sacrifices and possible regrets of following through. But indecision is not what drove my American mother across the Atlantic, fired up having watched Braveheart fifteen times. Their fierce battle cry was channeled by my mother every time things seemed insurmountable and every time she had to get out of bed – my mother, the daughter of a nameless heroin addict. The daughter who belonged to a hundred care-workers and blurry-faced relatives, and who belonged to no one at all. I take one step across the threshold of her dark room that would seem empty except for the recognizable mound of blankets and the oppressive Saturday afternoon silence in our cramped, dirty house.

I may not remember when I first hear the "B word", or when I fully understand what it meant, but I felt its weight every time I was asked to talk about my family at school and was the only one who had no family to speak of, no father or anyone else, except for my American mother. My heart pounded twice each second before my turn to speak came and their heads turned in unison with the expectation of a response I wish I could give.

I didn't grow up fully understanding what it meant that my mother was dependent on her anti-depressants, but I felt the immense burden and beauty of her dependence on me — her first real attachment. Not with a mature portfolio of facts did I understand her euphoria at being finally granted legal residency in Northern Ireland when I was nine, preceded by the fear of deportation and of never having a stable home. But I felt her stress each time we moved and rented a new house, and I felt the desperation in her fanciful notions of moving back to America. America — that elusive land beyond the rain that explained my hybrid accent and might be big enough to help me find others who didn't fit into a box, or fit into too many boxes — a place where my raging dichotomies could be seen as complementary and not negating.

What do you think when you hear of a single mother who had a one-night stand? Perhaps not of a devoutly religious Christian woman. Or of her daughter.

*I am the girl who didn't just passively accept the Catholic dogma; I studied, questioned, and built it around a close relationship with God. I faced the slew of amused smirks and condescending mockery from my classmates for actually **caring** about God as more than a canned recital of the Hail Mary. So much more.*

I am also the girl who fell in love with her best friend, which was absolutely unacceptable, but terrifyingly beautiful to me. In my hometown of Belfast, students didn't use bicycles for transportation; I became known as 'that girl who rides her bike to school every day,' drenched, out in the open pouring rain. But did they know that girl who furtively held her best friend's hand underneath the table? Would they guess it was the same child who came alive when teaching her friends from her mini whiteboard, who gazed down as she passed the crucifix on the wall and swallowed her daily Prozac pill?

*But I am not my mother. I knew from the age of 5 that I was born to be a teacher, and that I would move to the United States, and there I would find my people. When my distant cousin from America (who I didn't know existed until I was 11) asked if I wanted to move to California in a **month** for my senior year of high school, I knew it was time to stop feeling paralyzed by all the risks of living. I took that one step onto the plane, and every day I become more ready to take that next step for college.*

Mimi clutched the essay to her heart. "You are so ready for the next step, Erin, and you know we'll do everything in our power to help."

While Erin was determined to do as much of the college search on her own, she quickly realized that without Matthew and Mimi's help, she was not going to be able to accomplish her goals. Her mum had not ever submitted a US tax return since she'd been in the UK. Since she wasn't working in the US, she had figured there was no point in dealing with it.

And to make matters even more complicated, Tracey reported that Brian, the father that Erin had never met and who had never provided any support, had submitted to the requirement of the Irish court that he provide some minimal support to Erin as long as she was in school. While the amount of the support was small, the fact that he was in the picture at all made the financial aid picture murky. What would he be expected to contribute, according to the federal financial aid rules? How would they go about proving that Brian had never been a part of Erin's life?

Matthew gritted his teeth, as he imagined donning a green eyeshade to do all the calculations and voluminous paperwork required for a successful financial aid package to be awarded, crucial to Erin's college future. When Tracey failed to send Matthew the completed income tax forms, Mimi just filled them out herself and signed them with the information Tracey had provided, just to move things along.

Tracey's contribution to the process was to send along a list of 100 colleges that Erin should consider attending—all of them Catholic. When Erin saw the list, she made a face. Mimi suggested that they visit one or two Catholic schools just to show her mom that they were not ruling Catholic schools out completely. Erin shrugged and rolled her eyes. Mimi didn't want Tracey to feel like she was working to push Erin farther from her Catholic roots. Erin was delighted that Mimi understood her lack of interest in a Catholic university, no matter how good, and no matter how much financial aid support might be offered.

Kicking off the college tour experience were the local California schools—UCSC, UC Berkeley, and yes, the University of San Francisco, a Catholic school. These were day trips, where Mimi and Erin stopped random students walking around to ask what going to school there was like (although they'd also done their homework with Susan's amazing software and each school's websites.) Erin was really reluctant to engage with strangers (to tell the truth, she wasn't crazy about engaging deeply with anyone!)

A dear friend with a daughter in Portland offered to take Erin for the northwest college visits, where Erin had her first tastes of staying in the dorm at Reed and Lewis & Clark Colleges. Erin found the climate very similar to Belfast, and she loved the small school environment and the quirky kids who went there. But in the end, she secretly held on to her dream of the small co-ed liberal arts college on the east coast.

Erin was overjoyed at the prospect of a weeklong east coast college tour, giving her the chance to experience actually having her feet on the ground of several colleges, plus spending some nights in the dorm. Negotiating a week of absence at the high school was not easy or pleasant, but Erin had perfect grades in all her classes, and had already proven herself as a capable, cooperative student in all respects.

Erin's eyes grew wide at Mimi's assertiveness with the school. "We are *going* to take the trip, because it's the only chance Erin will have to experience the kinds of schools she wants to apply to. The question is, will the absences be excused or unexcused?" The school principal finally agreed, and Mimi got busy with the arrangements.

Erin kept pinching herself to prove that she was really on the college trip she'd fantasized all during high school. They started in Boston, visiting Wesleyan, Smith, Hamilton, and Williams. They stayed with Mimi's lifetime friends, Julie and her husband Max, who lived nearby, and used their home as headquarters for the trip. Erin chattered with excitement at the people she was meeting and noting the similarities and differences among the schools. She vibrated with anticipation at the thought of being a part of that scene herself.

Erin especially loved the experience at Hamilton, where Mimi's beloved dad had gone to school Mimi had never visited. Erin noticed that Mimi choked up as she explained to the admissions welcome staff how special this visit was. One particularly nice woman showed her pictures of her dad from the 1939 yearbook on the shelf. Hamilton was also where their middle son Craig was on the faculty, which gave them a chance to attend his classes and dig deeper into campus culture, as well as staying in his home and enjoying some sightseeing around the town.

They were due to visit Boston College on their last day, a token visit to a Catholic university. At the last minute, Mimi suggested, "How about we skip Boston College and do some sightseeing in Boston instead?" Erin gave her a big smile and a wink and off they went for a walking tour with a historical character guide; they connected with their roots in an Irish cemetery with immigrants who had fled the potato famine and not made it any farther than Boston, unlike their ancestor James Lockhart, who'd made it all the way from Boston to Texas.

A harbor tour gave them the experience of what it might have been like to arrive in his shoes, ready for a new life. Erin dipped her toes in the water, feeling her new life beginning just like his. They stopped in at Legal Seafood for Erin's first experience with a steamed lobster dinner. As they took the return flight to California, Mimi was deep in thoughts of the past, about her dad, feeling as though she'd had a visit with his spirit. Erin was lost in thoughts of the future, imagining herself in one of the places she'd visited.

Back home in California, Erin was up until two am most nights, and she got up at six, rushing out the door on her bicycle, prepared for another day. Mimi nagged her gently to take some time to hang out with her fellow students and develop some friendships. Erin countered with evidence of her social opportunities through tennis and mock trial. Mimi and Matthew hosted a tennis party for the team as the season ended, and Matthew drove a carload of students to the state mock trial competition in Sacramento, in hopes of getting a glimpse into Erin's social connections and challenges. In interactions and conversations overheard, they could see that Erin's private self rarely, if ever, was revealed.

One day Erin surprised both Matthew and Mimi by announcing that she had been invited on her very first date, a boy in one of her classes. A year behind her in school, he was too young to drive, so he and his father picked Erin up and dropped off the two of them downtown for a movie. Afterwards, the young man invited her to his house nearby to meet his family, but Erin hadn't invited him in to meet Matthew and Mimi. They waited for her return, waited for her to share any tidbits about the encounter.

"He was very nice, and his family was friendly, too. He walked me up to the door, and I shook his hand and said thank you. He gave me a kiss. I'm pretty sure he'll want to go out with me again, but I'm saying no."

"Your first date! Good for you for giving it a try. I guess it wasn't love at first sight, huh?"

"Hardly," Erin replied. "The kiss was sort of like licking my own arm. But I did want to see what it felt like. The girls in Mr. Griswold's class thought I was crazy for going out with a younger guy, but it didn't matter to me. Well, that's about all the report; I need to get back to my homework."

Mimi knew better than to press for more than Erin was willing to offer. All things considered, Erin was extending herself socially more than Mimi had expected.

The next big life challenge was for Erin to decide which colleges would get her applications and make sure all of the essays, transcripts, financial aid information, were in order and sent in on time. With those in the mail, the nail-biting would begin until the acceptances (hopefully) started to roll in.

After Christmas, Mimi and Matthew invited the entire extended family for a trip to Todos Santos, Baja California, for snorkeling, boogie boarding, and hanging out at the beach and the cute artist colony. Erin was delighted to be able to add one more foreign country to her passport and was very curious about what traveling with nine other cousins would be like, ranging in ages from 5-65. She was especially thrilled to have her own room with a view of the ocean and a chance to experience another language and culture. As with every other new experience, Erin commented "I haven't been snorkeling very often," which meant, of course, that she'd *never* been snorkeling.

Having grown up with no family at all except her mom and never having gone on a family vacation, Erin had no idea what to expect. Erin's impeccable manners, appreciation for every new activity, and participation with every member of the group won their hearts—she played video games with Mimi's five year old grandson, snorkeled with Mimi's son and his girlfriend, watched the turtle hatchling releases on the beach at sunset with awe, and joined in her first cooking class with Chef Iker at the small family resort where they stayed.

She weathered the bickering and banter that went with a blended family retreat. "I haven't been on very many family vacations," Erin noted. Mimi loved experiencing the trip through her eyes, which helped her overlook the difficulties in moving a large group through their days.

After the family holiday, Erin sailed through first semester finals, straight A's, and a new set of classes. Mr. Griswold's was a year-long class, so Erin had some continuity with her small group of friends. Mimi was delighted that a few invitations for sleepovers and parties trickled in, leading up to the end of the year. As Erin had predicted, the young man she'd gone out with had invited her out a couple of times, but she told him she only wanted to be friends. He was understandably disappointed.

With Mimi's encouragement, Erin applied for a job at the Santa Cruz Boardwalk, a historic amusement park where so many of the town's teenagers (as well as teenagers from all over the world) came for their first job. Like Mimi's son, Erin applied to be a ride operator, proudly wearing her turquoise t-shirt with the roller coaster logo and khaki slacks. She was looking forward to earning money to help her with the expected family contribution to her financial aid package at whichever college she decided to attend, to pay for her airfare back to Ireland and transportation on to college at the end of the summer.

She had to step up her assertiveness skills, as she was appalled to learn that many parents would harass her for not letting their too-small children get on a more advanced ride. "It's for your child's safety, sir!" she was taught to say, and after several instances of having to push the button for a supervisor to assist her, she learned to say "I'm going to have to ask you to step aside, sir" in a firm, no-nonsense way. She wanted to yell *"Back off!"* but it just wasn't in her to be rude, nor was it recommended in the employee manual. The contact with unpleasant, pushy parents reminded her of the unpleasant times with her boss back at Burger King in Belfast, but most of the time, she just enjoyed being outdoors, soaking up the California sunshine, and listening to the happy squeals of kids on holiday.

~~~

As spring progressed, the fat and skinny college letters and emails started arriving. Erin was thrilled with the acceptances. The state schools, however, offered little or no financial aid to an international student, as she was considered, and she was discouraged by the wait-list letters from some of her preferred east coast schools.

Finally, she received a fat envelope from the University of San Francisco, the only Catholic college to which she'd applied, and even then only with encouragement from her mother, with a full ride financial aid package. She grimaced. The suspense continued.

Then the letter from Hamilton College arrived: acceptance, with an even stronger financial aid package than USF. Privately, Matthew was strongly in favor of Hamilton; Mimi was selfishly hoping for USF, since it would mean Erin would be close by.

They scheduled a special family dinner for Erin to reveal her decision, with champagne to acknowledge all that had been accomplished since Erin had arrived in August. "It really shouldn't be any surprise to you at all," Erin noted, "since I came with the dream of a small liberal arts co-ed east coast college. I've chosen Hamilton." Although disappointed to know that Erin would not be nearby, Mimi was thrilled that Erin's dreams were now a reality.

The frenzy that had occupied them the entire school year could be put aside, traded for the new excitement of planning for Erin's transition and celebration of her high school graduation. Erin called her mom, who had prepared herself for the fact that a Catholic university decision was unlikely, and was thrilled that Erin's dream was coming true. Tracey was comforted to know that Erin would be a few hours closer to Ireland.

Erin rushed off to school the next day, eager to share with her AP English buddies the outcome of her college decision, and returned with exciting news: they had decided they would all go to Prom together. Mimi clapped her hands with excitement. "I've always wanted to buy a prom dress, but with three boys, that opportunity was just not offered up to me until now. Let's go shopping right now!"

Mimi and Erin headed off to shop, and the next hour flew by as they swept dresses off racks and went back and forth to the dressing room and the mirrors. Erin found the dress that suited her perfectly: purple, her favorite color, covered in sequins and sparkles, and a big slit up the side. It took Mimi's breath away, as she looked at Erin becoming a young woman before her very eyes, her auburn hair cascading over her creamy shoulders. "What a perfect choice!" Mimi exclaimed. "Now let's find the perfect shoes!" When they got home, Erin modeled the dress and shoes for Matthew. She kept the dress hanging on the outside of the closet door for weeks so she could see it.

Plans for the prom hit a slight speed bump, however, when Erin went to her next ju-jitsu competition at the kendo where she trained. In the last moment of the match, she felt a crack, her knee gave way, and she turned white as a sheet. The sensei rushed over to her, and he called for an assistant to get an ice pack. Her teeth began to chatter with the pain. One of the parents who was waiting to pick up her son offered to take Erin home, but Matthew and Mimi were already on their way to pick her up and head to urgent care.

Once there, they were all reassured that nothing was broken, although the ACL had been badly damaged and would need months of rehabilitation and care before she'd be back in competition. She'd be going to the prom on crutches! Pain medication and ice packs on the knee would get her through the night, and she'd need to keep the leg up to reduce the swelling for the next couple of days. Erin usually had no use for pills or medication, but she could see no reason to argue in this situation.

Wearing a wrist corsage with pink roses intertwined with purple and pink ribbons, Erin gamely headed off to the prom with her gang of girlfriends. "Dancing with crutches is a challenge!" she reported. She sailed through final exams and joyfully tossed her decorated mortarboard in the air at graduation, along with her classmates, US style. Matthew and Mimi looked on with pride, reflecting on all that had transpired since that fateful exploratory trip to Ireland.

CHAPTER 21

BRIAN

"We are made wise not by the recollection of our past, but by the responsibility for our future."
—George Bernard Shaw

Years had passed since Tracey's phone call about her pregnancy. Brian had shut it out of his mind as best he could, but the niggling doubt had continued to plague his dreams. He'd not made good choices after that phone call. He'd had few friends in school, had been targeted by bullies, and had no interest in school anyway. He found himself with limited options as an adult. His family pressured him to find a wife, to make a real life for himself, but his anger and resentments crowded out his judgment. He drank too much; then feeling guilty, he drank even more. He developed a reputation as a hothead, the life of the party in a bar, but volatile. Gradually, friends from the village dropped away as they grew up and started their own families.

After the altercations with his neighbors and encounters with the police over stolen cattle, Brian's life began to fall apart. The court required him to take anger management classes as a part of settling the cattle rustling charges against him, and his mother encouraged him to get some counseling. The whole family was worried.

He liked his therapist, a young woman who seemed to understand his demons. What did he want in his life? What seemed to be missing? When was the last time he was happy? He hung his head, at a loss for words.

Then he looked up. "The last time I felt truly loved was with this young American girl. We spent a weekend together in Cork, and I don't think I've ever been happier. But we knew we had no future. She was looking for something I was sure I didn't have, and I was too stupid and didn't even know what I was missing. She had no plan or destination, and I didn't even try to keep in touch. Then a few months later, I had a letter from her and then a phone call saying she was pregnant. I thought it was a scam, and I was embarrassed and scared. But I haven't stopped thinking of her and wondered if I was wrong. What if she was telling the truth, and I have a child I've abandoned? It's haunted me ever since."

The therapist just listened, not saying anything at first. Then she said, "That's a heavy burden to bear." She waited awhile for those words to sink in. "So what's your plan? What do you want to be different?"

"I want to stop being so angry. I want to be a decent uncle to my sisters' kids and to stop bringing shame to my parents. I'd like to have a friend or two."

The therapist smiled and said, "Those sound like reasonable goals. What needs to change?"

"I guess you're going to tell me to stop drinking," Brian said, looking glumly at his well-worn shoes.

"I'm not going to *tell* you to do anything. I'm wondering what *you* think you need to do to get what you want," the therapist responded.

"I guess I could try that for a while and see what happens," Brian said. "I'm not making any promises."

"And what about your family? What might you do differently there?" the therapist kept putting the responsibility for change back on Brian.

"Honestly, I don't do much. I wait to let the family take care of me, and I don't do much about reaching out to them. I guess a phone call or two once in a while wouldn't kill me."

"You could try it and see what happens. If you get the results you want, then it's working. If not, then we could see what else might work."

"That means you think I ought to come in to see you again?" Brian questioned.

"That's up to you, too. If you think it helps you to be accountable or if you feel differently after we talk, maybe it would be a good idea. What do you think?"

"I really thought you'd tell me what to do and then I'd do it. At least for a while," said Brian.

"You still seem really hesitant. I suggest you think it over, try a few of the things we've talked about and then make an appointment to come back and check in."

Brian had thought about the therapist's questions, and he'd given up drinking for the most part, except for special family occasions. He'd reached out to his family, apologized for not doing more and expressed his appreciation for their reaching out to him.

He'd returned to the therapist, dutifully, for several months, expressing some surprise that yes, he *did* think things were changing. He felt less isolated, and his family commented on the changes he'd made. He hadn't found a serious relationship, or any relationship, really, but he did feel a greater sense of ease and connection. Years later, he was grateful to the therapist for helping him find his way to a less combative, more connected life.

He was reflecting on his progress as he went out to the postbox to check for mail. An old habit, since he received so little mail he didn't even bother to check much of the time. Today, however, there was an ominous-looking, thick envelope with an official-looking return address, with what looked to be legal papers. "Now what?" he thought to himself. "Just when I was thinking my life was my own and things were going well."

He went inside, tore open the envelope, considered having a Guinness to dampen whatever bad news he felt sure was inside. He sat down on the couch, trying to make sense of the information he'd received. Apparently, Tracey had had a baby seventeen years ago, and that child was now ready to go off to college. Tracey was once again asking for support. "Well, at least this time, I know there *is* an actual child," he thought, with all the feelings from years ago flooding back into his mind.

The legal papers requested information about his income, expenses, and debt. He was given the option of taking a paternity test to confirm (or contest) his status, and was given information about how to do that.

He could accept Tracey's claim that he was the father of her child, or he could contest it, using the results of the paternity test to support his denial (if they were negative). He looked at the papers a long time before figuring out what he was going to do. He wondered if he should talk to his family. "Hell, no," he thought. He thought about talking to his therapist.

He replayed his conversations with his therapist in his mind. She kept asking what he wanted for his life. He wanted to stop being angry; he wanted connections with family, and he wanted greater ease.

Demanding a paternity test, challenging Tracey's assertion that he was the father, and denying any responsibility for his behavior led to anger and confrontation, and probably a lot of expensive legal fees. He was not going to choose that path. He could see that clearly.

He was going to accept responsibility, and he was going to pay whatever was required. But he was also going to insist on meeting his alleged daughter. He felt sure he would be able to tell if she were his. He wasn't even going to consider another alternative.

Once he reached that conclusion, the clench in his stomach started to relax. He signed the documents, put stamps on the envelope, and walked it out to the postbox. He wondered what would happen next.

CHAPTER 22

JAMES

*"I know why families were created with all their imperfections.
They humanize you. They are made to make you forget yourself
occasionally, so that the beautiful balance of life is not destroyed."*
—Anais Nin

James and Julia held their baby son in their arms, both beaming with pride and happiness. Their new home was finished, and Oliver's small cottage nearby was nearing completion. Crops were coming in, and the dairy farm was flourishing. The couple's devotion to each other was evident to all in the community, and their new little family reflected all the happiness they'd found in Texas.

When James looked at his new baby son, he couldn't help but flash back on the child he'd left behind. He'd had little time to think about Kathleen and his life back in Rathmullan, except during the nighttime, when his sleep was interrupted by nightmares and restless thoughts about what might have happened. James had told Julia about Kathleen and the unborn child even before they were married, and now that they had their own first child, she insisted that he try to find out what had happened. "It's time," she said firmly, "to make things right and to visit with your family."

James grew quiet. He knew that Julia was right. For all of the many blessings in their lives—the prospering farm, the beautiful baby son, the supportive community in Montgomery County, and

Oliver's presence in the life of their family — James was still plagued with nightmares and guilt about the family he'd left behind. Hardest of all, he just didn't know what might have happened, so there could be no closure to his worries.

"But how will you manage while I'm gone?" James said, knowing when he said it that Julia was the guiding spirit and energy on the farm, with her father's reassuring support close at hand. They had hired help, and having been generous supporters of their neighbors and friends in the area, Julia would be well taken care of.

Julia gave him a long look, and then both of them burst out laughing. "Make the necessary arrangements, James, and leave the rest to me."

James had protected himself from knowing what he expected to be bad news from Ireland since he'd arrived in the States years before. He'd not written to his family, and they had no idea how to write to him, even if they'd wanted to, which he expected they didn't. He knew only that the disastrous economic situation in Ireland had consumed so many lives, and the hatred between Catholics and Protestants consumed many others. He didn't really want to go back, but he knew Julia was right. He could never be free of the burden that weighed on his spirit, particularly in his dreams.

With Julia's support and urging, James began the preparations for his transatlantic journey to Ireland, his former home. James decided it would be faster and easier to take the train from Houston to New York, a trip of about a week, rather than the much longer and more unpredictable journey by sea from Galveston. James studied ocean liners between New York and Ireland and settled on the RMS *Oceanic*, the first ocean liner for the White Star Line.

He spent the next few days with Oliver and visiting with his neighbors, wanting his mind to be at ease about the welfare of Julia and his son during his absence. He took time off from farm chores to hold his baby son and to enjoy time with Julia. He packed a bag, including small gifts that Julia had made for his family members and friends. "It can't hurt to be thoughtful, James, even though you did not leave your home in the way you might have wanted." James appreciated Julia's quiet, thoughtful way of being generous—not showy, just genuine and caring for others.

With his affairs in order, he set off for New York, where he sailed on the *Oceanic* as a first-class passenger, which seemed like an extravagance to him, but Julia was adamant. He did not argue very vigorously, since he was not eager to repeat his experience in steerage on his initial journey to Boston from his home in Ireland.

Arriving in Rathmullan after more than two weeks at sea was a sobering experience. James hardly recognized the little town; so many people had fled or died in the Famine. He, too, felt different. He took his time, looking for familiar landmarks, studying the faces of everyone he encountered to see if he recognized anyone, or if anyone recognized him. He dreaded both.

He made his way first to the tiny farm where he'd grown up. A young girl met him at the gate and gave him a puzzled look, as he took off his cap, put down his bag, and stared at his old home. He was amazed that it was still here, which struck him as ridiculous. Just because he'd left did not necessarily mean his whole previous world had ceased to exist!

The young girl spoke first. "And who might you be?" she wondered. "I guess I was wondering the same thing about you," he replied, with a wry smile. "My family and I used to live here, about ten years ago…"

The young girl burst into tears, unexpectedly, and ran into the house. James was not sure if it was his looks or what he'd said that had produced such emotions. He stood there awkwardly, waiting for her to return or for someone else to come outside.

After what seemed like a long time, an older woman emerged slowly from the house, accompanied by a boy a few years younger than James had been when he left home. The two of them approached the gate, eyeing each other, not believing what they were seeing. James' mother reached out her hand and touched James' face, as if he were perhaps a ghost. "James," she said, and her voice broke as tears streamed down her face, "you've come home at last."

Now it was James' turn to be dumbstruck. "Mam, you're alive! I was so afraid...I mean, I'm so glad to see you and to see that you're still here. I know I left under the worst circumstances, but I just couldn't wait any longer. It's eaten me up inside..."

A strangled sob choked off his words, and James' mom took him in her arms, as the two other children watched the scene, not sure what this strange reunion was all about.

James' mom patted her grown up son and stroked his hair, looking him up and down. "I've had you in my heart all these years, and I know you did what you had to do. I worried that you'd not survived the voyage, or that something terrible had happened once you arrived in the States. Why didn't you let us know, James? Why did you have us worry so?"

"Mam, I was a disgrace to the family. I let you all down; I let Kathleen down. I left an unborn child with no father. Why would you ever want to hear from me again?"

"I don't know quite where to begin, son, but first, come inside. You've people to meet, and you look quite worn down by the long journey you've had. Let's get you something to eat and some time to clean up before we go any further. Sean, carry your brother's bag for him now; get him some clean linens to wash himself."

While James got cleaned up, his mam made tea and brought out some cakes. James was astonished at his mother's improved health, the changes in the home without so many little kids about, and with repairs and upgrades to the house itself. No mention had been made of James' father, and there was no sign of him anywhere in the house.

James made his way into the kitchen, where his mam had a fire in a new woodstove, and pots and pans were polished and arranged on shelves, unlike anything he'd seen when he lived here. James' mam poured tea and served cakes and they all sat down around the kitchen table.

"After you left, James, we were in shock, and your father went mad with rage. He couldn't face Kathleen's father, with his superior airs and his threats to have us thrown off the land we'd cared for so long. One night he went off to the pub, and he didn't return the next day. The priest came to break the news that he'd fallen off his horse and broken his neck, died instantly."

James stared at his mother intently. "I hated him, you know. I hated how he treated you and all of us. I wouldn't have been sorry," he said quietly.

"He was a difficult man, James, in a difficult time. So much suffering and poverty everywhere, and…" his mother tried to soften James' lingering bitterness.

"Please, Mam, don't stand up for him. He never stood up for us. He was a pig, and a lazy pig at that."

"You were always my pride and joy, James. Your father was jealous of how clever you were, how you could make things out of nothing, and how your hard work always helped us get by. He felt shamed by you. I think he was relieved when you left, and left under a cloud. I knew you had to leave, and though I missed you in every fiber of my being, I was so glad to see you choosing a different future than the one you'd face here."

"Mam, when I left, you were literally dying, day by day, before my very eyes. I almost didn't recognize you when you came out the door. You're still too thin, of course, but you're alive! What happened?"

"When your pa died, I knew what would happen to my babies if anything happened to me. It didn't hurt that after he left, I could devote myself to helping the young ones growing up, instead of making new ones every year. While you were growing up, I starved myself so that you children would have a little more in your stomachs each day. And you remember Anson Kirkpatrick, who lived down the lane? His wife Jane died of influenza, and I helped out with him and his family until he got his feet back on the ground. We became friends, and then more than friends. He's been a second father to the young ones. Now he's my husband. I'm happy, James. He's not like your father; he's a gentle man, kind, hard-working, and generous."

James stared at his mother, who had looked increasingly like a ghost for most of his years growing up, pale, stoop-shouldered, skinny as a rail. Now she stood up straight, with color in her cheeks, and hope in her eyes.

"Now it's your turn to tell us where you've been the last few years, James." James had the rapt attention of his mother, as three young children gathered around the table to hear stories from this handsome gentleman who'd come from the land beyond the rain.

James described the ocean voyage in steerage after he'd left the Rathmullan farm, arriving after a frightening time at sea, braving storms, hunger, sickness and death around him, and finally, miraculously making landfall in Boston harbor. He told stories of the kindness of the people he'd met, as well as the prejudices he'd faced as an Irishman in a city with the same anti-Catholic and Irish prejudices he'd known in Ireland. He'd had adventures working many different kinds of jobs, in cities, on railroad crews, and on farms, as he worked his way down from Boston to Alabama, always looking for some land in the country to remind him of his roots in Rathmullan.

When he spoke of arriving in Brushy Creek, Alabama, his eyes glinted with tears as he remembered his wife Julia and his young baby son, who waited for him now at their farm in Texas. "When I arrived in Brushy Creek, my life changed for the better for the first time. A very kind family took me in to their family farm, giving me a place to live in exchange for helping out with chores. There was just the three of them, Oliver, Emma, and their young daughter, Julia."

"We worked together, and we built a successful farm, before Emma passed away. Julia and I had become best friends over those years, even though I was quite a few years older than she was. And then with her mother gone, her father tired and lonely, we decided to move to Texas, where there was more opportunity and a chance to build our own lives. I wanted my own farm, Mam, and I wanted a family."

"Julia and I married, and we packed up everything and everyone, and moved to Montgomery County, Texas, where there was good land, hills and trees, and a feeling that it was home. Now we have our first baby, a son. The only thing that was missing was my first family—I wanted to know what had happened and do my best to make things right. Julia pushed me to come, and I'm so glad she did."

James' mom beamed with smiles with the news of his family and success in Texas. She drew the little girl who had greeted him at the gate close to her, and she held James' hand. "Since we're talking about the family, with the sadness of loss and the happiness of good fortune, I'd like to introduce you to Frances. James, a few months after you left, your beloved Kathleen gave her life to bear this beautiful, healthy baby girl. That baby girl is Frances, and she is your daughter. She came to live with us soon after Kathleen's death."

Frances looked up at her pa shyly. James could see his beautiful Kathleen in her smile and in her eyes. He was overwhelmed with the news—the loss of Kathleen, the tragedy for her family, but the blessing of the birth of a daughter—his daughter, now eight years old.

Frances reacted a little stiffly, as James took her in his arms. He looked with affection at the other youngsters, his brothers and sisters, and his beloved mam, who'd not only raised her own children but had taken on his daughter at birth. They looked at him, wondering what to make of this unexpected, strange, and beautiful family reunion.

"You've been the baby of this family, Frances, and now you've learned you have a father and a baby brother, who live across the sea. I loved your beautiful mother very much, you know, and I begged her to come with me to America, but she couldn't leave her family. I feel so very, very lucky to meet my wonderful daughter, after all these years apart."

James' mam was relieved that he didn't suggest what might happen—unlikely he would abandon his American family, but so painful to imagine his taking her granddaughter and going so far away. One look in his eyes let her know that was exactly his intention, but he would not be so heartless to do so without taking the time to earn Frances' love and trust, healing the hurts of the past as best he could.

Frances had an adventurous spirit and an open heart, just like her father's, and before long she was talking with excitement about the voyage across the sea, to a land where she would live with the father who had come so far to find her. She loved her grandma, who had taken her in, but she could see the longing in her papa's eyes, and she wanted to meet her new mam and her half-brother. James promised to bring her back for visits. She began thinking about what to take with her on the journey.

When the preparations were complete, James said good-bye to his first family, feeling whole and complete for the first time he could remember. He longed to be back with Julia and his baby son, and he knew this time he would be a faithful correspondent with his family in Rathmullan.

~~~

James and Frances left Ireland together for a journey she'd never forget. A few weeks later, they were back in Montgomery County, where Julia had prepared a big welcome celebration to welcome them. Julia and James made a promise not to be separated anymore, as the time apart had been so hard on both of them. James was so grateful for all he'd learned on the momentous journey, and for the addition of Frances to his family.

The next year, James and Julia prepared to welcome another family member, which was to be repeated six more times in the next twelve years. The last cherished arrival was Katie, more spirited than the rest of the children put together, Julia claimed, but perhaps it was because she and James were older now and settling into a new phase of life, their family complete.

CHAPTER 23

ERIN

"If you cannot get rid of the family skeleton, you may as well make it dance."
—George Bernard Shaw

Erin was determined to go home for the summer, even though she knew that Mimi hoped she would decide to stay in California. Erin was equally determined to have a long visit with Jazzbo and Comet, so the matter was settled, which suited Tracey just fine. Erin had already earned enough from working at the Boardwalk to satisfy the family's expected contribution for her financial aid package; she could find some meaningful volunteer work in Belfast (no more Burger King, she was sure of that!) and then head for Hamilton at summer's end.

Not long after she'd gotten her feet on the ground in Belfast, the phone rang. Erin jumped at it, hoping it might be Deirdre and not wanting her mum to get to the phone first. Erin still felt incomplete from the break in their relationship, and she still worried about Deirdre's mental health. To her surprise, a man's voice said, "Is this Erin Tompkins?"

"Why yes, it is. And who might this be?"

"I'm Brian Bailey. We've never met, and I know it sounds a little strange to say, but I believe I'm your father. I'd heard from your mam you'd be returning from the States for the summer, and I'd like to meet you."

Erin was at a loss for words; she didn't know where to begin. She didn't know whether to be polite, or angry, or curious, or any of a thousand different emotions she felt.

"Are you there, Erin? Please don't hang up. I know it may be hard for you to hear from me after all this time, but I've been sending money to your mam for your education. I think it's about time we met. Would you be willing to do that?" Brian was just as nervous as Erin, but he'd been practicing what he'd say in this phone call. In fact, he'd written it all down, so he wouldn't get tongue-tied and make a fool of himself.

Erin took a deep breath to calm herself and spoke carefully and slowly, to give herself time to think. "Yes, my mum told me you'd had a change of heart after all this time, and I've been wondering if we might ever meet."

"What are your plans for the summer? Do you think you and your mam might be willing to come to Cork for our first meeting? I've done a little research on the bus schedule. If you came on a Saturday, we could have dinner. I'd put you both up in a hotel, and then you could return home on Sunday. Of course, I'd be paying your expenses."

"I can't make any commitments without talking to my mum first. You'll understand that. She doesn't like to travel, and she hates to miss mass on Sunday. But I think she might make an exception in this case. I'll have to talk to her and see."

"But what about you? Do you have any interest in meeting me?" Brian was afraid Erin would say no, fearing the worst. Erin paused, composing herself. After a lifetime of wanting a father and pushing her mother to press the lawsuit compelling Brian's financial support, she felt surprisingly detached. She wanted to protect herself, and also her mum from further hurt and disappointment. Part of her wanted to scream at him, and part of her longed for this meeting more than words could say.

"I think it would be nice to meet you. I'll talk to my mum, and we'll call or email with a plan. I'm sure my mum has your phone number, but what about text or email?"

Brian answered, "I'm not much into technology. I don't have a computer, so it will have to be by phone or regular mail. The number's 353-555-3231."

Erin wrote the number down, thinking to herself "What sort of troglodyte doesn't have a computer? Does he not have a cell phone, either?"

"Fine. I promise you'll hear from us within a few days. So long for now." Erin hung up the phone, hoping to sort out her thoughts and her emotions before her mother got home from work. She took Jazzbo for a walk to kill some time and get some exercise. The fog was drifting in after an unusually warm summer's day, and she found it comforting somehow to be back in Belfast, her home, with her pets and her mum, after a year of being away.

Erin put Jazzbo's leash away and fed him and the cat. She heard her mum pedal up on her bike from work and opened the door, eager to start the conversation about Brian. "Let me help you put your bike away. Guess who called?" Erin blurted out.

"Let's see," replied Tracey. "Was it a scammer from Russia? A bill I forgot to pay? Or maybe we won the Lotto?"

They chained the bicycle to the fence and walked up the back steps together.

"No to all three. It was Brian Bailey. Remember him?" Erin tried to keep her tone and manner light, even though she was vibrating with her tangle of emotions.

"Indeed I do. And what might be on his mind?"

"He's thinking we ought to meet. He's offering to pay for the bus and an overnight at a hotel in Cork for the two of us, maybe on a Saturday and Sunday, so you don't have to miss work," Erin explained. "What do you think?"

"Well, I can't say it'd be at the top of my list," responded Tracey. "You know I hate to travel, and then there's the animals, and mass that I'd be missing. I don't have much to say to the man after all these years, after all."

"That's exactly what I told him you'd say. But I think *I'd* like to meet him, and I won't go without you. So the decision is really in your hands." Erin's voice cracked. "He *is* my father, and he is contributing to my education, at least in a small way."

Tracey looked in Erin's eyes and saw the hurt, and the longing, and the confusion, all mixed up together.

"Let's make some dinner together and talk about it, shall we? I'm dead on my feet, as usual, and I don't think straight until I've had a bit of supper and time to decompress from work. It's been a busy day."

Erin gave her mum a hug, and the two of them decided what to make for dinner—a piece of broiled fish, some potatoes and a veg. Simple, healthy, and filling, and quick to prepare. As they sat down at the table, Erin described her conversation with her father. It seemed weird to her to even say the word, but she now felt entitled to use it.

Tracey did her best to conceal her concerns and reservations about the visit, knowing how important it was to Erin to meet her father. She would do it, and do it with grace. It was long past time. Tracey and Erin agreed on a date for the trip to Cork, and Tracey called Brian to confirm the details.

~~~

They took the bus, riding mostly in silence for the long five hours of the bus ride. As promised Brian was there to meet them, and when they descended from the bus, Erin and Brian looked each other up and down. A paternity suit seemed clearly irrelevant since the two looked so much alike.

Brian stepped forward and extended his hand first to Erin, then to Tracey. Erin was relieved that he didn't try to hug her before remembering that hugging was the California custom, not the Irish. Then he took Tracey's hand in his and said, "It's been a long time, Tracey."

Erin watched her two parents carefully as they used their best manners for an uncomfortable situation. Brian loaded their small bags in his car and drove them to the Premier Inn nearby, where he'd reserved a room for them. "I'll get you checked in, and give you some time to get settled. I'll come back and pick you up for dinner in an hour. Nothing fancy, but a quiet little place where we can talk."

Neither Tracey nor Erin knew what to say or do; nothing had prepared them for the awkwardness of the moment. Erin surprised herself by breaking the ice and speaking first. "I think that would be quite nice."

After Brian had gotten them checked in, Tracey and Erin went to their room and sat facing each other on the two beds. "He's being quite polite, don't you think?" Erin asked her mum, as they both tried to make sense of the situation.

"Yes, I think so. I can't say I ever expected anything like this to happen, and I certainly didn't know what to expect. What on earth do you think we'll talk about over dinner?" Tracey wondered out loud.

Erin tried to reassure her mum, all the while wondering the same thing. "I'm sure it will be quite interesting."

"No kidding," said Tracey, wishing she were anywhere on earth besides where she was.

Brian returned as promised and drove them to a plain-looking restaurant, nothing fancy, as he said. Tracey was relieved he hadn't taken them to the bar where they'd met; why would she even think he would, she wondered. They went in, and Brian asked for a quiet table for three. They sat down, all three of them silent at first. Brian started the conversation by asking Erin why on earth she'd wanted to leave Ireland to go to school—first high school and now college. Since Brian had never ventured much beyond his farm and the nearby homes of family members, he clearly had no understanding of what Erin had longed for her whole life—a life beyond the familiar world in which she'd grown up.

"My Irish friends ask me the same thing, but my American friends understand completely. I have always been curious about the world outside Ireland; I want to see as much of it as I can," she explained.

"Now that I've met you, I hope you won't mind if I try to convince you to come back to Ireland, to stay closer to your roots," Brian entreated.

"You can try all you want to, but I'm set on my plans for now. I will come back to Ireland for vacations and visits, of course, but I feel drawn to my American roots, too," she said, a little defensively. "Tell me a little about your life in Ireland, how you became a farmer, and what your family is like."

Erin did her best to listen with an open mind, but the world he described was not a world she found attractive at all, especially after traveling in America and her brief travels to France and Holland. Her extensive reading had already transported her to so many worlds beyond the confines of Ireland, and her curiosity had no boundaries, although that curiosity also included the world of a farmer, surrounded by animals and the natural beauty Brian found on the farm.

"I've already bought you a calf," Brian exclaimed. "After you meet her, you can name her. You can meet all the animals; I hope you'll like it there. I'd like to invite you to come for a visit when you're home for the Christmas holidays from your college. I'd be glad to buy your plane ticket."

"Whoa!" Erin thought. She felt very uneasy at Brian's clear bias and energy towards convincing her that a life in Ireland was in her future. At the same time, she was fascinated by his obvious love for his life on the farm, and the family of nine brothers and sisters, all of whom lived nearby with families of their own. What a coincidence that his family was the same size as James Lockhart's — that Irish ancestor who seemed to connect them all.

Tracey watched Brian and Erin interact without saying much. She felt oddly disconnected from him and very protective of her daughter. After all, where was he when they needed him most? Now that Tracey had her legal resident status, a stable job, a fairly tolerable home at least for the time being, and Erin was ready to launch her life in America, who did Brian think he was to come barging back into their lives?

They finished their dinners; Brian drove them back to their hotel, and they said good-bye. He offered a formal handshake, and he drove away, promising to be in touch about the plane ticket and the Christmas visit. He talked about getting a computer and hoped that Erin might teach him how to use it.

Tracey thought, "I'll believe that when I see it," but then reminded herself that she wouldn't have believed that the last two days would ever have happened either, much less the small but regular on-going financial support for Erin's education.

Erin would have been happy to put the whole matter out of her mind, but Brian continued to write and call every few days during the rest of her Irish holiday. She didn't care for the pressure, but she felt guilty turning him away, since she was the one who had motivated contact in the first place. The internal conflict left her feeling stressed and incomplete: all these years she hadn't had a father, and she'd really wanted one, and now she had a father, and she wasn't at all sure what to do with him.

Finally, she wrote him a letter asking him, in so many words, to back off. She told him of her conflicted feelings and let him know that she wasn't at all sure she wanted the relationship to continue. After putting it in the post and hoping she'd feel some relief at bringing things to a close, she found that she felt even worse. She worried that he would cease the little support he was offering, and she felt selfish for turning him away so abruptly after his initiatives to achieve some sort of connection. She wrote him again, apologizing for the abruptness of her previous letter. She let him know she would be taking things slowly, step by step, without any pre-conceived ideas of where the relationship might go…or not. That felt better. She didn't want to talk with her mother about Brian, or much of anything. She just wanted to finish up her volunteer work in Belfast and get on that plane back to Hamilton.

~~~

Erin blinked her eyes, flashing back to the series of miracles that had transported her from her Irish home in Belfast to an American high school graduation, a whirlwind college application process, and now, as she stepped onto the Hamilton campus for the first time as a student, she was really here, the place she'd dreamed of since she was a little girl.

All around her, she observed the sea of families dropping off their sons and daughters, lugging large suitcases, finding their way to assigned dorms and settling in. She felt that familiar sense of being different, from all her growing up years, which passed quickly as she recognized how lucky she was that Mimi and Matthew's son Craig, a visiting professor at Hamilton, was right by her side as they joined the throngs of other students. How different this experience would be if she had no one, and she noticed that there were a few bewildered students standing around looking like lost sheep waiting for a shepherd to lead them.

Craig gently guided her towards her dorm. "I bet you're feeling a little overwhelmed, not to mention jet-lagged. I remember feeling both scared and excited at the same time, circuits over-loading, and it was nice having my dad at my side. It's really satisfying to be on the other side now, and I'm having fun playing the dad role."

Erin smiled appreciatively. "You have no idea! I've never had a dad before, and I was just thinking how lucky I was not to be one of the poor souls wandering around lost. That's just what I'd be right now, but thanks to you, I'm not!"

"Let's have a look at your dorm room and see if your roommate's arrived yet. Then we'll go shopping and get everything you need to make your room your home. I know you're exhausted from the travel, but don't even think of going to sleep until it's bedtime tonight. That will really help you with jet lag and give you a good start in the morning."

"I don't need very much, really, and I know you're really busy..." Erin demurred.

Craig interrupted. "Mimi told me you'd say that, and she made me promise not to listen. Her instructions were to make sure you had everything you needed, things you didn't know you needed but would be handy to have, and some things just for fun. Don't worry about money."

"That sounds just like Mimi, but really, Craig, I couldn't possibly…"

"It's settled then," Craig said with a smile. "You might be able to say no to Mimi, but I've got my instructions, and your job is to enjoy the ride. Please say yes."

They paused outside McLaren Hall, an ivy-covered, older building that looked just like what Erin imagined her dorm would be, at the small east coast liberal arts co-ed college she'd set her heart on. They looked at the welcome letter from Residential Life, checked the room number and walked upstairs to the second floor.

Erin took a deep breath as she opened the door. She was a little startled to see three girls already there, chattering away as if they'd lived there all their lives, even though they were all incoming first-year students. She could feel her confidence leaking out through her toes, but she pushed through.

The girls stopped talking and looked up at Erin and Craig. "You must be Erin. But who are you?" one girl asked, looking at the handsome young man who was with her.

"Yes, I'm Erin, and this is my cousin Craig. He also happens to be a professor here. He's helping me get settled."

The girls looked Craig up and down approvingly, and then Ellen introduced herself and the other two girls.

"Sylvia and Nancy already knew each other before they came. I'm your official roommate, but as you can see, the rooms are arranged with bunks in one room and desks in the other, with a bathroom in between. I think it's kinda weird myself, but I guess we'll get used to it."

Erin put her suitcases on the remaining bottom bunk and stood awkwardly as the girls looked at her and Craig, as though waiting for them to take the next conversational step. After several long seconds, Craig stepped in.

"Well, Erin, we've seen the layout. Shall we head out and do some shopping?"

Relieved at the opportunity to escape, Erin replied, "Yes, I'd like that very much."

Craig made another attempt to engage the three roommates. "Is there anything we need to get that isn't obvious?"

Sylvia quickly responded, "Chocolate. A desk lamp. A mini-fridge. A small fan. A large screen TV and a game system, and maybe an Oriental rug." She paused, looking at Erin's face, which had gone pale, and then laughed. "Just kidding."

"Pay no attention to her, Erin. She's crazy, but in a good way. You'll get used to her sense of humor, or maybe you won't," warned Ellen.

"All right then," said Erin, as she edged toward the door.

"Nice to meet you all," said Craig. "I'll drop Erin off after while; I probably won't see you until classes start. Anybody taking psychology?"

"I will if *you're* teaching it," cracked Nancy.

Erin and Craig shut the door as they set off down the hall and on to shopping, hearing the girls chatter and cackle as they left.

They drove to the Walmart in Utica, the next town over from tiny Clinton, and began going up and down the aisles. Craig had a good sense of what Erin might need, based on his own not-too-distant experience going off to school, although he had to prod Erin with each addition to the shopping cart.

"Do I really need a desk lamp?" Erin wondered.

"Those rooms are dark," Craig noted. "And the overhead lights are glaring; you might not want to use them if you're staying up late studying. Mimi says you're prone to doing that," he teased.

After all the essentials were in the cart, Craig stopped in the candy aisle. "Chocolate was mentioned. Let's get a bunch."

Erin sputtered. "Chocolate's not essential. It's not even healthy."

"The roommates requested chocolate. It's a good gambit to let them know you're one of them. Besides, it's cheaper than an oriental rug!" he laughed.

"Well, you're the psychologist, I guess, so I'll trust your judgment." She grinned and tossed a bag of Hersheys with almonds in the cart.

After they'd checked out with their purchases and made their way to the parking lot, Craig gently probed. "How are you feeling about your roommates and your new home?"

"The dorm is beautiful, and the rooms are a little different from what I expected, but they'll be fine. I like having a whole room to study in. It's much too early to tell about my roommates, but I'm sure it will work out."

"Keep in mind that everyone is finding their sea legs and is in the same boat, so to speak. Some people find new social situations exhilarating and some don't."

"Yes, believe me, I'm used to feeling the odd person out. That won't get in the way of why I'm here, though."

"Don't forget, you have family here—that means me—and if you hit a rough patch or just want some company, I'll show you where my office is, and you can find me."

When they got back to campus, Craig helped Erin carry her purchases up to her room but didn't come in. He figured it was time for her to settle in. Now he knew what it felt like to be a parent—wanting to help ease the way, but also wanting Erin to use her wings.

Erin lovingly unpacked the shopping bags—new towels, sheets, a down comforter, the desk lamp, some posters for decoration, school supplies, laundry detergent...and chocolate. Her roommates looked with approval at her purchases, especially the chocolate, and Erin heaved a sigh of relief.

She wondered what the dining hall would be like, and she noticed that she'd been too anxious and too busy to realize how hungry she was. She hoped the other girls would invite her go to eat with them, knowing she would not take the initiative herself. Sylvia and Nancy disappeared without a backward glance, and finally, Ellen looked up from her book and said, "Are you hungry? Let's go grab some grub!"

The two of them walked to the dining hall. From her earlier visit to campus the year before, Erin knew what to expect, but she was overcome with all the choices. Stations with different kinds of food from pizza to salads and vegetarian main dishes, and a machine that dispensed soft serve ice cream – all you could eat. Even after a year of living with Mimi with home-cooked meals every night could not compare to the bonanza of eating options in the dining hall. She flashed back to Belfast and her childhood briefly, where lack of money limited the food choices to a bare minimum and extras were out of the question. Ellen said, "Well, are you going to get something to eat or just wander around all night?"

"I've never been good at making decisions, Ellen, but you're right! It's time to eat." Erin settled on lasagne and salad, with ice cream for dessert, and Ellen went for the pizza. They sat by themselves at a booth and ate in silence, before Ellen asked, "I know you're from Ireland, and you have a little bit of an accent, but it's not as Irish as I would expect."

"You're right, I'm a bit of a hybrid. My mum's American, but I grew up in Belfast, so I have a little of her American accent mixed up with an Irish accent. I grew up speaking Gaelic in school, so that's another ingredient. Last year I lived in America and graduated from an American high school. I think I absorbed a lot of American slang and lost some of my Irish," Erin explained. "Where are you from?"

"I'm from all over," replied Ellen. I'm an Army brat, but I went to high school in Germany, with other Army brats. But I've lived in Korea, Japan, and the Philippines. I've never been to Ireland, though."

"I *love* Japan. You're so lucky! I've always loved everything about Japan. I've taken ju- jitsu for years; I love animé, and the Japanese tea ceremony and kimonos and origami…just everything! I'm going to take Japanese and hope to do my junior year abroad in Japan."

Ellen responded, "I was really little when we lived in Japan, so I'm afraid I didn't catch the Japanese bug like you did. I guess all I really wanted was to stay in one place. I hated moving and saying good-bye, and I didn't really appreciate the opportunities I had. Making new friends all the time was a real pain."

"We never went anywhere when I was growing up, although I did come to New Jersey a couple of times in the summer, and my cousin Mimi has taken me a few places. But I didn't find it easy to make friends either, even staying in just one place," Erin confided.

They both went quiet again, aware of their different experiences but also their similarities of temperament. When that became awkward, they took their trays to the bussing station and trudged back to the dorm. Erin was struggling mightily to stay awake.

When they got to their room, Nancy and Sylvia were still out. Erin shared with Ellen what her trip from Belfast to Clinton had been like, the overnight flight to JFK airport, the cancelled flight to Syracuse, the night in the departure lounge in the airport waiting for the flight the next morning, getting picked up by Craig. Thirty-six hours with little sleep. "I'm taking a shower and crashing," she said; "I just can't stay awake any longer."

Erin awoke refreshed, eager to get started with orientation and preparations for the school year to begin. Each student had to choose from three types of adventures for a multi-day team-building trip planned by the school to help the incoming class make friends and get accustomed to Hamilton's culture and traditions. She'd been given a choice of orientation options, ranging from the "Exploration Adventure," trips to museums, plays, and performances around the area to "Adirondack Adventure," which featured camping out and a selection of kayaking, canoeing, hiking, and rock climbing. The third option was "Outreach Adventure," a series of service projects and community volunteering.

Erin didn't hesitate before selecting "Adirondack Adventure." Erin was surprised to learn that Ellen had chosen Exploration Adventure, which had a minimum of outdoor, physical activities. Each type of adventure offered three levels, from "spicy" to "medium" and "mild." Erin had chosen rock-climbing and kayaking, from the "spicy" category, wanting to stand out from the others as someone who was willing to take some risks and try new things.

Of course, for Erin, the physical challenges were nothing compared to the interpersonal ones. Erin's lifetime of holding herself apart, keeping her private life unexposed, putting all of her energy into schoolwork rather than making friends, was the biggest challenge she'd face, and she knew it. But knowing it and doing something about it were two different things; she could see that.

That meant Erin would be heading out with a bunch of kids she didn't know. She'd hoped that she could go with at least one familiar person. Sylvia and Nancy were like Siamese twins and worse still had already connected up with friends in another dorm. Hopeless!

Erin packed up her duffel and headed out in a 12-person van. Student leaders engaged the newbies with getting-acquainted activities and ice-breakers along the way, and Erin started to relax a little. She loved the contrast of the lush green trees and hills, dotted with ponds and lakes of the upstate New York landscape and the amazing stars at night, so very different from gritty urban Belfast, so often covered in clouds, fog and drizzle.

Each student was given a sleeping bag and tent and allowed to pick a spot to set them up, with help as needed. Erin appreciated that everyone had an individual spot, so that her feeling alone and isolated wouldn't be noticed. Each morning began with yoga and stretching exercises, to get everyone limbered up for the physical challenges of the day. Erin was grateful that she already had some kayaking experience from her Baja trip at Christmas, and her ju-jitsu discipline made the hiking and rock-climbing well within her reach.

Her confidence level increased as the days went quickly by, and Erin loved being outdoors in the beautiful mountain setting, surrounded by trees and the rippling water of the stream nearby. She was starting to feel at ease with the other students.

The morning of the last day, though, she tripped on a rock and twisted her ankle, sending a lightning bolt of pain through her ACL. Not good! Erin grimaced, and Anna, the student leader rushed over to see what had happened. "It's my stupid knee. I've hurt the ACL tendon before, in ju-jitsu. It'll be ok," Erin brushed off

Anna's concerns, even as her eyes were watering from the pain. Two students came running to carry Erin back to the campsite, keeping all the weight off the hurt leg.

Anna brought over the first aid kit and a couple of ice packs from the chest. "I recommend taking an anti-inflammatory to keep the swelling down and also icing it. You get the last day off. We'll wrap your knee in an ace bandage to immobilize it, and I want you to lie down with your leg elevated."

Sandy, the assistant team leader, came over to make sure Erin was comfortable and brought her some cold water to drink and a couple of ibuprofen for pain. Erin tried to wave her away. "I don't really like to take pills or anything."

"Trust me, you're still in shock, and you're going to need these regularly until we get back to campus tonight. Do you have something to read? It might help to take your mind off the pain." Erin was so grateful for her kindness and impressed with the first aid skills of both the team leaders. She pointed to her backpack, where Sandy found a copy of a required text for one of Erin's classes. "Just a little light reading, right?" Sandy commented with a grin.

Erin took Sandy's advice, accepted the pills, and lay back with elevated knee on a rolled up sleeping bag. "I'm going to take a rest day myself," she said. I'll be nearby if you need anything."

"I hate for you to have to miss all the fun," Erin sighed. Sandy gave her a pat and said, "Trust me, I've been leading trips all summer as a camp counselor. I could really use a little down time. You're doing me a huge favor."

Once the adventurers returned from their hike, everyone loaded up the van, and a couple of the students carried Erin. They headed back to campus, and the student leaders took Erin to the health center to make sure everything was ok. X-rays showed nothing was broken; they lent Erin some crutches, an ice pack, and some more ibuprofen. "Ice and time off your feet are your best friends," the health center doctor said. "No more rock climbing for you for the foreseeable future."

Anna and Sandy made sure Erin was settled in her dorm room and unpacked her belongings. "You've got a couple of days to rest before classes start, so give yourself a break—take it easy!" Erin thanked the girls.

Ellen was reading when Erin and the leaders arrived and gasped when she saw Erin's crutches. "What on earth happened?" she exclaimed.

"Nothing much, really. I have this problem with my ACL, and I managed to turn my knee on one of the hikes. Nothing serious, but it's not the way I wanted to start my college career!" sighed Erin.

Anna and Sandy said good-bye and made Ellen promise to make sure Erin took it easy for a couple of days. Up early the next day, Erin hobbled on her crutches to appointments with her advisor, the financial aid office, the bookstore for textbooks, and she started to explore her extra-curricular interests: tennis, ju-jitsu, the Emerson Literary Society (a social group), and the Shenandoah-Kirkland Initiative, just to name a few. In Erin's typical fashion, she immersed herself in every possible activity in hopes of finding where she might fit.

CHAPTER 24

BRIAN

"Being Irish, he had an abiding sense of tragedy, which sustained him through temporary periods of joy."
—William Butler Yeats

After years of not caring about the arrival of the post, Brian found himself impatiently looking down the lane multiple times, glancing at his watch, shaking his head with impatience. He was aware that his newfound daughter was much more accustomed to communicating by text, email, and something called Facebook, things that he'd never seen the need for and probably would never use.

But his horizons had broadened with the discovery that he *had* a daughter and they had met. He had taken some financial responsibility for her, and she had accepted; they seemed to be in the beginning stages of a relationship. What it all meant, he wasn't quite sure. He'd gone over and over in his mind the brief, uncomfortable, stressful meeting he'd had with Erin and Tracey in Cork.

Why hadn't he encouraged them to fly, so that there would be more time? He hadn't even thought of it, and Tracey hadn't suggested it. Having met Tracey in Cork in the first place made it even more uncomfortable for him. Perhaps he should have come to Belfast, but the thought of it gave him the shudders—totally unfamiliar territory, Tracey's territory, and a large bustling city.

Well, enough brooding. What was he going to do to make sure the next visit was more satisfying? How was he going to convince her that she was making a big mistake by focusing her life on America, when Ireland was where her family was?

He could tell he'd gotten off to a bad start when he'd received the letter from her, essentially telling him to give her some space, and even suggesting that maybe she wasn't so sure she wanted a relationship with him after all. Several sleepless nights after getting that mail, he was overjoyed to hear from her again. It seems that she, too, had been reviewing and scrutinizing the visit, and his too-frequent phone calls and letters which followed. He was grateful she wasn't giving up. He'd been such a fool most of his life, wasting his time on pigs and produce when he should have been thinking about people. That was about to change!

He knew the first thing he would do was to propose a trip home for the Hamilton Christmas holiday break, and he'd pay for the ticket. He hoped she would make the arrangements, since he wouldn't have the first idea how to do it himself. He still hadn't worked out exactly how he was going to explain to his family (eight siblings and his ma) who Erin was and how she'd come into his life in the first place. Since they'd been after him to start a family for decades, he hoped they'd just be as pleased as he was. Yes! He'd said it! When he looked at Erin's photos and saw his own features, blended into a beautiful young woman, he felt an indescribable sense of adoration for this charming, brilliant, well-mannered, and hard-working girl who'd crash-landed into his universe and changed him forever for the better.

He picked up the phone and called his mam, who didn't answer. He realized that the conversation that he needed to have must be in person. He called his sister Siobhan, where he imagined his mam would be if she weren't at home. "Siobhan, I need to speak to Mam; is this a good time to catch her?" Brian's mam picked up the phone. "Are you all right, son? You don't usually track me down when I'm not home."

"Mam, I've things we need to talk about, and I've put them off until it's stupidly ridiculous."

"I'm right here, Brian, what's going on?" His mother began to worry, since communication with her son was sporadic at best and often happened only when something had gone wrong. "I'll be home in the morning. Why don't you stop by for a cuppa after you take care of things on the farm. Is that soon enough?"

"I'll see you then, Ma."

Brian put the phone down, drummed his fingers on the table in impatience, and then began to compose a note to Erin, inviting her to come to Ireland for Christmas and proposing a visit, which would include his mam, his sister and her family, and any of his other siblings who might be available and interested. He guessed that once they'd heard the news he planned to share with his mam, the whole family would be there.

After several attempts at the note, he crumpled them all up and threw them in the bin. He shook his head and decided to go to bed, knowing that sleep would be impossible with so much on his mind. He reread the two letters Erin had written him, the first basically asking him to leave her alone until she could figure out if she wanted a relationship with him, and the second, suggesting that perhaps she'd been too hasty the first time. She just wanted to take it slow. "How else could we take it, with her living all the way over in America," he wondered.

He spent the next several hours tossing and turning, wondering what his family would make of his having a daughter, after having goaded him all these years to find a wife and start a family. Finally, he got up, made some coffee, and started again on the note to Erin.

> *"Dear Erin,*
>
> *I was relieved to hear that you are willing to consider a connection to me. I realize that our first visit was a little awkward, and my eagerness to make up for lost time must have made you uncomfortable. I'm sorry for that. I can only imagine that each of us might feel a bit strange with a new family member, and you are right to want to take it slowly. I'll do my best.*

I'd like to pay for an air ticket for you to come to Ireland for the Christmas holiday and arrange, with your help, for a visit of at least a couple of days to visit me at the farm and to meet and visit with other members of my family. Of course, your mother is invited to come with you, if you and she feel that's best.

If you are open to this idea, I'll wire a deposit to your bank account to cover the costs, and you can let me know the best dates during your stay for our visit."

Brian debated how to sign the letter. *"Yours truly, Dad,"* sounded both stilted and presumptuous. *"Sincerely yours, Brian"* sounded more like a congenial business transaction than a letter to a daughter. He finally decided to dodge the issue by simply saying *"Thinking of you and wishing you a successful start to your college career, Brian."*

With the note off his mind, he could do a few of his farm chores before setting off to his mam's place in Kildare. Visiting the large, rambling family home always made him wistful—for his childhood, filled with his eight siblings growing up and his parents—and for his own adult life, with no relationships to speak of and no kids. Now his dad was gone, died a few years back from a heart attack (probably from having to work so hard to support that huge family), and his mam's house was just as empty as his own, but for different reasons. How he'd love to be able to bring his own child there and see his mam's eyes light up again, seeing him capable of loving.

He pulled up to his mam's house in his truck, finding her on the front porch watering her plants. She waved at him, put down the watering can, and came out to give him a hug as he got out of the truck.

"I've got the kettle on, son," she said. "Let's sit out here on the porch and have a good catching-up."

Brian followed his mam into the kitchen to bring out the tea tray. She'd made some fresh soda bread and put some homemade jam in a small bowl. He set the tray down on the small table on the front porch, and the two of them sat down, a bit awkwardly at first, each waiting for the other to start the conversation.

"Ma, I've spent a very long part of my life keeping a very big secret from you and all the rest of the family. I know I've done many things in my life I'm not proud of and plenty of things shameful to the family. What I'm about to tell you is one of those things. But the good part of my story is that I think I have a chance to turn this story into one with a happy ending—for all of us. And I hope you will agree."

Brian's mam sat quietly, dreading what he was about to tell her, but also curious about where the story might lead. "Who doesn't love a happy ending?" she thought to herself.

"A very long time ago, eighteen years I spent a weekend in Cork, celebrating the harvest with some friends in some bars and enjoying being a man about town. I caught the eye of a beautiful young American girl who was as carefree as I was, and we had a few beers together. As you know, I've rarely been at ease with women, but this was different. For a couple of days, we barely came up for air; it was like nothing I'd experienced before...or since. And I stupidly let her go. She didn't know where she was going, and I thought it was nothing more than a weekend fling."

Brian paused, and his mam continued to listen, fearing if she interrupted with questions or comments, he might clam up, as he often did when talking about anything emotional or difficult.

"A couple of months later, she wrote me to let me know she was going to have a baby, and she needed my help. I ignored the letter."

His mam sighed. She knew what it was like when Brian felt defensive. She braced herself for what was to come next.

"A few weeks later, she called me on the phone, telling me she was sure I was the father of the baby and asking for support. This time I lied to her. I told her I was married and had a family, and that what she was saying would ruin my life. I refused to get a paternity test, and I asked her to leave me alone."

"Oh, Brian, you must have been so afraid. And you never said a word to any of us." Brian's mam could imagine how he felt, backed against the wall, embarrassed and ashamed.

"You have no idea. I didn't know what to do. I started drinking. I think I went a little crazy."

"I remember that part of your life. I was so afraid for you. And your dad...he was going out of his mind with worry."

"I just felt it was better for all of you for me to keep as far away as possible. I was nothing but trouble for everyone. Anyway, the best thing that came from all of that mess was getting stopped for drinking and driving, losing my driver's license, and getting sent to that Anger Management class and therapist. If that hadn't happened, I'd probably be dead by now, or worse still, I might have killed someone.

"Right about that time, I heard from the court with a request for child support for the baby I fathered many years previously," Brian continued. "Thanks to the therapy, I found a different way to respond than I did seventeen years ago. And thanks to that, I now have a daughter, a beautiful daughter, and I've started to mend things with her and her mother. We've met just once. I'm providing some of the support I should have offered years ago. Ma, I want her to be a part of our family. I want you to meet her, and I want her to meet all her cousins, aunts, and uncles. I'm begging you, for all our sakes, to welcome her when she comes to visit over the Christmas holidays."

Brian's mother took her son into her arms as he sobbed inconsolably with longing, regret, and the torment of so many lost opportunities in his life. She patted and soothed as she had when he was a little boy. She gave him a handkerchief and another hug.

"This will be the best Christmas ever, Brian! Now tell me about this young daughter of yours. What is she like? What does she think of having a father after all these years?" Brian's mam didn't want to drown Brian in questions, but her heart was bursting with his news. She could hardly wait to tell all the other family members; she was sure they would be as amazed and delighted at this turn of events in Brian's life as she had been.

Brian pulled a photo out of his wallet to show his mother. "Why, she looks just like you—just as Irish as can be! What's her name?" his mam wondered.

"Her name's Erin. She's got her mother's wit, brains and heart. She loves animals, she's a hard worker with straight A's in school, and she's headed to a first-rate college in America on a full scholarship. I wish she were going to school in Ireland, of course, but I'm sure she'll come back once she's had her fill of American culture and nonsense. Besides, I've bought her a calf! When she comes at Christmas, you can all see for yourselves what she's like." Brian's mind was spinning with possibilities.

"We met this summer, before she headed off to that fancy American college. She and Tracey, her mam, came to Cork by bus. We had dinner together, and they stayed overnight in a hotel before heading back to Belfast, where they live. I'm guessing the two of them will come together at Christmas, too, but I don't know that. The truth is, I don't even know for sure if she'll come. I've just written to invite them. To be honest, there have been a few ups and downs, as I came on too strong at first, and she stepped back. The first visit was fairly stiff and awkward."

"Hardly surprising, I'd say. Put yourself in their shoes, after all. I can't say I'm proud at all of the way you handled yourself all those years ago, but I'm over the moon with how things seem to be going now."

Brian left it to his mom to communicate the developments in his life to his siblings and other relatives, and he headed back to the farm. He had chores to do, of course, but even more important, he wanted to get that note to Erin in the post.

Erin had settled in at Hamilton when Brian's note arrived in her mailbox. She smiled, thinking of the effort that must have gone into writing that note, when writing was clearly not one of his gifts. And this note was written five days ago; an email would have taken a nanosecond to arrive, but he was in the Stone Age technologically, and she couldn't realistically imagine that changing, even though he'd said he would get a computer if she would teach him to use it.

She let the note rest for a few days before responding, wanting to see how her heart felt about a multi-day visit, and how her mother would feel about another trip. She could imagine that spending time with Brian and his family would feel awkward for

Tracey, who didn't even like traveling under the best of circumstances, and this was far from that. Stressful!

> "Hi, Brian,
>
> *Thanks for your note offering to pay for my travel home at Christmas and inviting my mother and me for a visit. I know she'd just as soon stay home, but I feel more comfortable bringing her with me, since that's ok with you.*
>
> *Here are the dates that we could come, arriving mid-day on Dec 19 and returning home in the afternoon of Dec 21. We'll take the train this time; it's faster and easier.*
>
> *If that sounds all right with you, I'll make my plane reservations and get train tickets for my mom and me. Please let me know.*
>
> *As ever,*
>
> *Erin"*

Brian opened the note, delighted that the plans seemed to be working on both sides of the pond. He transferred money to her bank account to cover all the travel expenses with a little extra for Christmas cash. His heart swelled with happiness, such a different feeling from all those years before.

Erin was thrilled to have the means to make the trip home for the long holiday break, a reunion with her beloved pets and the few friends from ju-jitsu. She alternately dreaded and welcomed the visit with Brian and his family. Traveling with her mum was stressful for both of them, and Erin felt a tremendous sense of responsibility on all sides, feeling caught in the middle.

Erin emailed Mimi after the trip knowing she'd be dying of curiosity to hear about the trip.

> "On this trip with my mother 'down south', I visited three different counties. And I had never been to any of them before. Our first stop was Kildare, which is where we met up with Brian (my second time meeting him; I met him for the

first time in the summer) We visited his family home in Kildare, where his mother lives alone, now that all her children are grown up. His father died of a heart attack. Brian is one of nine siblings, most of whom had kids of their own etc. During the holidays, the house is packed with people for family get-togethers, so I'm told, and the walls were adorned with wedding pictures for various people's weddings. I met his mother Bridgette, and we talked and had tea.

The photos I have attached are from County Carlow. This is where Brian drove us next and we spent a night there and most of the next day. This is where his sister Rose lives with her husband and her children, who were home from university over Christmas break.

Next we went to county Cork (the largest county in Ireland), and Ballinora, where Brian's farm is. There is a photo of me and a baby calf somewhere, but not easily accessible right now. I visited his cows and we walked in a park and then had lunch in the town before my mother and I got a train back to Belfast.

Erin"

Mimi was so pleased that Erin seemed open about sharing about her visit, and no emotional mine fields seemed to have opened up as a result. Some of Erin's hesitation about visiting her father seemed to be dissipating, and Erin began to think about her next visit to Ireland in the summer, although she planned to spend most of her summer at Hamilton, because she was applying to do some research related to her work with the Shenandoah-Kirkland project on representation of Native Americans in the history curriculum. She imagined visiting her father on her own this time. Wasn't it strange that calling Brian her father seemed more natural now.

CHAPTER 25

ERIN

"I am no bird; and no net ensnares me: I am a free human being with an independent will."
—Charlotte Brontë

Imagine yourself growing up as I did, with only one family member, and that family member had no close or intimate relationships with anyone besides you. One thing I can say is that the more time you spend alone, the more comfortable it gets," Erin shared with Mimi, during the year Erin spent with Mimi and Matthew and the extended family. Mimi had challenged Erin to reach out to make some friends, to try out being with both girls and boys, just as an experiment, and for heaven's sake, since she was living in California now, she *had* to learn how to hug.

Mimi had to give her credit; during that year, Erin had fulfilled every promise to reach out, through her connections with her circle of girlfriends in Mr. Griswold's class, the tennis team, the mock trial team, at Kai-Jin ju jitsu dojo, and in her brief date with the younger high school student. She had dutifully practiced her hug, but it never felt natural to her; she attributed that as much to Irish culture as to her own personal comfort zone.

Now she was at Hamilton, and her communication with Mimi continued, as she pondered the "stuck" place she was in. After her first year with three roommates yielded no sense of connection or fitting in, her second year was no better, and no worse. She'd hoped for a single room, but instead was paired with a student who had also been looking for a single.

She extended herself by asking to sit at dinner with people she didn't know. But sitting with people you don't know, when you don't feel comfortable in that situation and when you'd rather die than share any part of your personal story, is a sort of self-defeating and self-fulfilling prophesy of isolation and disappointment. Opening with the fact that she hadn't made a single real friend since she arrived at Hamilton verges on the desperate, which neither Erin nor Mimi thought was a great strategy. Because of Erin's action-packed agenda of classes, extra-curriculars, and work-study in an elementary school in Clinton, she was surrounded by acquaintances and participated in the occasional social activity (although frequently she demurred in favor of studying). But she felt she was making no headway in her own personal growth and in learning the skills of building relationships. It made learning Japanese, her most difficult class, seem simple by comparison!

Aside from the cursory kiss that was not returned on the date at Santa Cruz High, Erin had never kissed a guy. Even so, she was not ruling out "falling for a man one day." Mimi was baffled by how a person could determine status as gay, straight, or non-binary based on such limited experience. In her mind, "youth" was a license to explore, experiment, and make mistakes, and Erin was wasting it!

A breakthrough occurred in spring break of her sophomore year when she traveled with a group of Hamilton students and a charismatic lesbian, multi-racial professor and activist, whose provocative writing assignments inspired Erin to think differently about herself and her relationship to her church. In her journal, which she shared with Mimi, she wrote "So, 'love' is actually something that we all gathered around and talked about at ten pm, after our 'Cultural Night.' The cultural night involved sharing a lot of things that were personal to us, which included poems we had written (a lot of beautiful writers in our group), which touched on mental health struggles and struggles with racial identity. There were some other more light-hearted things, including a beautiful performance on a fiddle by one of the two guys in our group of about twenty-five.

"This impromptu late-night talk about love was with our professor, Margaret, who's a bit of a legend, both in California, where she lives, and in the colleges and centers where she's taught, including the Highlander Research and Education Center, where Rosa Parks and Martin Luther King, Jr, had studied."

"The talk wasn't so much about the sentimental kind of love, although of course that can be part of it. Margaret very much believes that love is central to activism, but it's a kind of radical love that blurs the lines between her personal life and her activist work. She really emphasized the importance of being vulnerable."

"Her talking about love in the way that she did - as this radical act that connects us to each other - reminded me of the part of my religion that meant so much to me, that was so central to my faith. The problem for me is that I am unable to separate that deep, pure, love that she speaks of, that I came to know as 'God,' from Catholic doctrine because I associated them with each other from such a young age. Anyone who didn't latch on to religion the way I did will find that very difficult/impossible to understand."

"People will say 'just choose a different religion or denomination,' 'just be spiritual,' or 'just keep that relationship to God and selectively remove the Church teachings that are too difficult.' Church teaching has never been something I chose to believe so much as it became known to me as an objective truth from my childhood, and my understanding became more nuanced and deeper over time. That's the thing about the Catholic Church - she doesn't change her mind about certain things. Many people see that as a problem —but for others, they see this as a huge appeal to Catholicism —its truth lies in its unwavering stability. Although we ourselves will grow and change, it does not. That is the nature of objective truth. For people whofind/get indoctrinated with that truth at a young age, this leaves very little room for radically changing in your beliefs."

"The problem is that I believe in the teachings— despite all my deep love for my LGBTQ brothers and sisters and my immense connection to them— somehow I can hate myself, while not holding them to the same standard as myself. There is an immense schism and disconnect in the way I've been living my life since my 'separation' from religion, because in some ways I am totally separated from it and in other ways I can't get it out of the core being of who I am. Margaret talks about how important integrity is and I used to say that all the time as a young, fervently religious person.

"There shouldn't be disconnect between your actions and your beliefs. That's why, after falling in love with a girl and losing God, I always framed it as: I must 'go back' to who I used to be. But that feels like going backwards. My unique relationship to religion, makes it incredibly difficult for me to choose to believe that certain Catholic doctrine related to sexuality is wrong, despite the fact that it would be so much easier if I could."

"Whether intentionally or not, the Catholic dogma went against its own aims of being pro-love by unintentionally punishing me for getting too close to someone. They claim that you should be able to separate the sin of 'sex' from the love that the Church and Margaret talk about, but that's where I clash with the Church, because while the theory may be sound, it just didn't add up in practice in my case. The deeply beautiful part of the love would have had to have been 'taken' from me in order to not sin.

Much as Mimi would have liked to weigh in with her own numerous opinions, she felt safer asking questions. After all, Mimi had not been raised in the Catholic faith as Erin had, and her own experience in growing up was also different. In Norman, Oklahoma in the 50s, your sexual identity was your biological identity, and if it wasn't, you were in for a rough ride. She was grateful, in a way, for that clarity, but not when she considered the extent of the misery inflicted on those who lived closeted lives, married for all the wrong reasons, or worst of all, committed suicide. As she considered the options that Erin might use to describe herself: gay, straight, gender-fluid or non-binary, asexual, celibate— that was part of the problem for a person with almost no sexual experience at all.

Mimi studied Erin's next email closely, wanting so badly to support her young cousin's growth and not knowing how. "Maybe it's time I practice messily and imperfectly, without so much fear. I am not healed, but I cannot remain static. They say you must love yourself before you love others and so I feel like I've been using that as an excuse for never being in a relationship again because 'oh, I don't love myself, so it wouldn't be healthy.'"

"But Margaret said something today that really relates to this: 'I love myself because other people love me. Love yourself by yourself is a false paradigm. It's also a rather Western one. This is not the same as compulsively seeking approval. It relates to being around people I share values with. Unconditional love. We shouldn't have to earn our love. Earning our love is different from being loved for who we are.'"

"I may still have an identity conflict, but I think I know my values. I hope that, even if I may fail in making deep relationships, and therefore fail in being a teacher (ouch), and even if I fail in all aspects of being a 'successful' human, that you might still love me. I don't know if I believe that, if I'm being brutally honest, given the foundations of our relationship and given the American notion of valuing success and achievement by one's own merit."

Mimi wanted to weep when she read the part about Erin's hoping that Mimi might still love her, even if she were to fail in making deep relationships, just as she wanted to scream as she watched Erin grapple with her perception of the irresolvable conflict of her faith with her sexual identity. When Erin had complained about the intrusiveness of the journal prompts in her education classes, Mimi had countered with how important it was for a teacher to 'love' her students, and being willing for them to love her, too.

In Mimi's view, Erin needed to know herself well and to dig deeply to know her students well, which required being vulnerable (including difficult, intrusive writing assignments for education classes, designed to provoke that inner examination crucial to teacher development). Mimi struggled with how much to push Erin or engage in interventions to promote Erin's personal growth. She was encouraged to hear Erin say "You are important to me, Mimi. I wouldn't be here if it weren't for you and I think about that frequently. I am sure you are well aware of the amount of influence you have had over my life."

Mimi was not really aware of having much influence over Erin's life. She finally decided to create profiles for Erin on Match.com and OkCupid, just to see what the universe had to offer—guys and girls, using two different accounts. Mimi went so far as to create a profile for Erin using Mimi's email address but no photos, all in the spirit of research. She knew their middle son had used those apps and probably more to find women to date. He had been completely unwilling to commit, but he was also really lonely, and the dating apps filled that need for him. Why wouldn't it work for Erin?

Even without photos, people began responding to "Erin's" profile, and Mimi answered, channeling what she felt Erin's responses would be. Eventually, the candidates began pressing for a meeting, which made logical sense, of course—what good is a dating app without actual *dates*?

Matthew was horrified when he learned what Mimi was doing…and how much she enjoyed doing it. "Mimi, tell me this: no matter what path Erin follows, from straight, to lesbian, to gender-fluid/non binary, or asexual, would you still love her just the same?"

"Of course I would. What a silly question!" Mimi replied.

"And what if she never dated, formed deep relationships, or experimented with sex? What if she turned out to be like your great-aunt Ella, forming relationships with three generations of second graders and their families, as well as close connections to her own extended family, and she had nothing to do with sex? Would that seem ok to you?"

"Of course it would," Mimi responded.

"What makes you think you need to be a deus ex machina, manipulating things behind the scene? How would you feel if you were in her shoes? Would you want some elderly cousin messing with your life? You've already given her the gift of a world of cousins, a life in the United States, and an education that has been her childhood dream. Isn't that enough? What's going to be *enough* for you? How can I get you to stop?" Matthew was deadly serious, Mimi could tell, and she was forced to admit that he was exactly right.

Erin was going to be perfectly fine, and even if she wasn't, she was going to have to learn to ask for help if she wanted it. Mimi heaved a big sigh and clicked "delete profile" on the dating sites.

CHAPTER 26

TRACEY

"...there was a new voice
which you slowly
recognized as your own,
that kept you company
as you strode deeper and deeper
into the world,
determined to do
the only thing you could do —
determined to save
the only life you could save."
—Mary Oliver

Tracey read and re-read Erin's emails from Hamilton about her classes, her professors, and the ideas that she was pondering. After years of worrying about Erin's mental health (was it genetics, the environment, or something else?), the existential crisis that Erin faced as she confronted her lesbian sexuality growing up and her relationship with a religion that declared that sexuality ungodly, unholy, and unacceptable, Tracey searched for signs that Erin was coming to terms with herself in a new environment with new people.

Erin had shared with Mimi about her mom. "Growing up, I didn't really think about my mother's relationships (or lack thereof) with other people. And she has had friendships with people as I grew up. But her current friendships are not particularly *intimate*. Opening up to my mother about what I'm going through lately has sort of triggered some of her own deeply held issues about being alone and lacking human connection to anyone other than me. In talking to her this past weekend, I was struck by the similarities between our situations. She has sort of closed herself off from hoping for deeply intimate friendships or dating and has seemed very comfortable for a long time in her self-imposed isolation. I have encouraged her and that's all I can do."

Tracey was facing her own existential challenges: her relationship with her daughter was unconditional and complete. When faced with the conflict of her daughter's sexuality with the edict from her church that homosexuality was a mortal sin, what was she to do? How was she to help her daughter find her way?

She had grown up with no one to offer her unconditional love and stability; her experience of an abortion at a young age and her isolation from anything close to a normal family life had called into question whether she could ever attach to a child. She'd more or less raised herself; then she'd had to prove to the world and to herself that she was more than capable of being a mom. A single mom, with no support system aside from the Catholic Church, she'd lived with the cloud of deportation hanging over her head during most of Erin's childhood. Her career possibilities had been limited by her immigration status. Still, she had been as devoted a mother as humanly possible.

Tracey had searched for resources for Erin. She had found a therapist through the Church, and that person had recommended Prozac for depression and had offered only the standard prescriptions: confess her sins, forswear all future lesbian relationships, and hew to the dogma of the church. Erin dutifully went to therapy for a year, becoming increasingly depressed and withdrawn, with no impact whatsoever from the prescribed antidepressant.

According to Erin, the therapist offered her two options: to live a chaste life, without acting on her homosexuality, or to undergo further counseling which would help Erin find a way to accept her biological gender as her sexual identity. The result of that therapy was a young girl on the verge of suicide, despondent, depressed, isolated, and miserable. Tracey finally realized that the therapy was only making matters worse. Through it all, Erin continued to excel at school, working towards her goal of leaving Ireland and moving to the US for college. She said she saw no future for herself in Ireland.

In desperation, Tracey had reached out to Mimi for support with Erin. Mimi had insisted that Erin be at the center of the communication, which was hard for Tracey, often in the advocacy role for Erin, but that left Erin behind in learning to advocate for herself, struggling to make even the simplest decisions on her own. Imagine Tracey's surprise when Erin had decided, on her own, to accept Mimi's invitation to move to the States to complete her high school diploma in California! Tracey had to revise her emotional timetable about saying goodbye to her beloved daughter. Though she knew it was best for Erin, it was not an easy decision for Tracey.

Tracey knew Mimi was encouraging Erin to break free of the constraints she'd imposed on herself and to do some personal growth work, risk-taking, being vulnerable—all necessary to make friends and experience healthy relationships with both men and women. Erin shared a little of that work with Tracey, and a little more with Mimi…but was still remarkably self-contained.

"If Erin is going to break out of her bubble, then I'm going to do the same," Tracey said to herself, knowing that would be a big challenge. She emailed Mimi that "my group therapy and self-work seems to be bearing a bit of fruit. Major big, long-term job, though, of course. I am trying to not block things out —not distract myself. I am working on my openness and loving skills, in particular! I want to increase the number and quality of my relationships, and I am glad you are here for me to try to do that!"

Mimi swallowed, took a breath and broached the question of where Tracey thought Erin might live after graduation. Tracey responded, "I'd always imagined that we'd live together." Knowing that Erin had no plans to return to Ireland after her education, Mimi inquired gently, "Does that mean you'll plan to move back to the States?"

CHAPTER 27

ERIN

"When you trip over love, it is easy to get up. But when you fall in love, it is impossible to stand again."
—Albert Einstein

Erin had dreamed for years of her graduation from the small, coed, liberal arts college on the east coast, but she never imagined that it would include having her father and mother in the audience, along with Mimi and Matthew and two of their three sons and other assorted relatives and friends. She wasn't sure what was the bigger surprise—her dream of a diploma or her dream of a family. She was valedictorian of her class, with a double major in psychology and feminist studies, and a minor in education.

She had decided to move to the west coast, with Mimi's urging, completed her teacher training at UCSC, and she was beginning her first job as a new teacher in the urban school district of San Francisco. Young, bursting with idealism and energy, intrigued with what seemed to her the glamorous life in the City, Erin wanted to try her wings. She also was intrigued by the gay and lesbian culture and vibe of the city, longing to find at last a group of friends with whom she felt totally at ease with her sexual identity. She had miraculously found a small studio, thanks to connections with a faculty member at UCSC who'd been a mentor, coach, confidante, and now that she'd graduated with her teaching credential, a friend.

As usual in a new situation, Erin looked to ju-jitsu to start her social network and stay healthy at the same time. She found a kendo that suited her and began working out with her usual enthusiasm and vigor. She felt strong and capable and was delighted to have a few weeks to get established before school started. The sensei was impressed with her dedication and quickly began using her as an example to motivate the other students.

One sudden move, however, found her troublesome knee twisted behind her, and she knew this time, she wouldn't be able to suffice with rest, ice, and wrapping. The sensei heard the crack and knew immediately what had to be done. He called 911, and the ambulance came and took Erin to the emergency room of SF General Hospital, where she was processed and placed on a gurney, waiting to be seen by a doctor.

The emergency room at San Francisco General was always bursting with drama—results of gunshots, brain injuries, suspected strokes and heart attacks, bad reactions to chemo, acute symptoms of AIDS and so much more. Erin had had to wait for what seemed like days before she received the attention she so badly needed. She took her mind off the pain by looking at all that was going on around her. So many people were in much worse shape than she was, so she didn't feel she was being neglected. Clearly, the triage put her in a lower category of need than the woman who came in hemorrhaging from a knife wound from a jealous lover, or the man whose arm was dangling loose from the shoulder.

Her first contact was with Jennifer James, a resident in orthopedics, who'd interned at a hospital in Los Angeles. As an intern, she'd done rotations throughout the hospital after she finished medical school. Every department was trial by fire, and the 80-hour weeks took their toll. She'd already decided on the specialty she wanted to pursue, orthopedics and surgery, so she found plenty of action in the emergency room. She was used to hard work, and the fitness from all her years as an athlete enabled her to stay on her feet longer than most of her colleagues.

Erin, writhing in pain on a gurney, caught Jennifer's attention, and Jennifer glanced at the chart with its information about the patient before approaching her. "Looks like you've done a number on that knee and ACL," she said. "How bad does it hurt?"

Erin did her best not to cry out with the pain, but her face was ashen, and she was gritting her teeth. "You've got that right. And it's not the first time, unfortunately. I just can't seem to get jujitsu out of my system. Just when I think everything is healed and going to be ok, I wrench the crap out of it."

Jennifer responded, "I want to make sure you haven't broken anything, and I'd like to take a look at the damage here. We'll start with x-rays, and then you'll probably need an MRI. I don't want to guess at the treatment until we get the tests back, but if you've done this more than once, I wouldn't be surprised if you end up in surgery. I'm a martial arts fan myself, so I'm pretty familiar with what can go wrong. We're going to get you something for the pain, so just sit tight."

Erin smiled wanly, "Well, it's not like I'm going to go anywhere…" She appreciated knowing something personal about this young doctor and the interest she showed in her situation. "I was at a ju-jitsu competition all day, and my knee felt fine, until something snapped on a move, and then it didn't." She started to relax. Jennifer had put her at ease by sharing a little about herself and assuring Erin that she was going to be just fine.

A nurse took her blood pressure and temperature, and she was giving her an IV for the pain, which was excruciating. The next thing she knew, she was being whisked off to x-ray. Jennifer passed her in the hallway as she was being transported. "You're going to be fine; I'll check on you after the x-rays."

Erin noticed Jennifer looking at her as she was wheeled away on the gurney. She couldn't put her finger on what it was; perhaps it was the shared experience of martial arts and orthopedic injuries, but it felt like something intangible, ephemeral, significant, improbable. She felt attracted to her; it was as simple and as complicated as that.

The x-ray technician was very gentle with her and in a little while, an orderly came to roll Erin back from the x-ray department and into an examination room, where Jennifer was waiting. The pain medicine was starting to work, and Erin could feel the throbbing waves of pain easing just a bit.

Erin sighed in relief as she saw Jennifer's warm smile, not feeling quite as alone and with the easing of the pain, not quite so desperate. Jennifer put the x-rays up on the screen and pointed out the areas of damage to the ACL and the shredding of the meniscus around the knee.

"It's clear you've given this knee a workout over all these years. How many times have you gotten banged up?" Jennifer wanted to get as complete a picture as possible to formulate her recommendations for treatment.

"Quite a few, I'm afraid. I grew up in Northern Ireland where I learned to just work through the pain, take it easy, and eventually, the pain would go away. Until the next time. I was never willing to give up ju-jitsu. I loved it so much! It was the one place I could release all my frustrations and energy. The National Health Service was not eager to rush into surgery, and neither was I. Something tells me this time may be different, though," Erin conceded.

"For now, I'm going to wrap and brace your knee and send you on your way with some painkillers, and some crutches. I'm also going to refer you to an orthopedic surgeon I've worked with who really knows what he's doing and has loads of experience. He'll recommend an MRI and get authorization from your medical insurance. You've got health insurance, right?" Jennifer prayed that that was the case and was relieved to hear that it was.

"I've just started my first teaching job here with San Francisco Unified. I looked over the benefits and insurance really carefully, and it looks like the union has done a good job for us teachers. I can't imagine what people do in the States without it," Erin noted. "I'm lucky to have dual citizenship, so I seem to have the best of both worlds!"

"You'll love Dr. Dennison. I've worked closely with him, and his patients think he's the best. Set up a consultation; I'll send over the x-rays and he'll take it from there. I'm going to follow up with you in a week, so don't think you can just blow this off. You really need to get this done NOW."

"Not the best way to start a new teaching career, but I think you're right!" Erin conceded.

After having her knee stabilized and braced carefully, Erin went off with crutches, her x-rays, and Jennifer's business card, promising to follow through with the referral to the orthopedic surgeon. After multiple episodes with her knee, she was accustomed to using the crutches, but she swore this time, she would follow through with the needed surgical repair. She used the Lyft app to get a ride back to her little apartment, mercifully below ground level, with only a few steps to navigate. She emptied the ice container into the ice bag she'd brought from the hospital, and made the two critical calls—one to Dr. Dennison to set up a consultation and one to her school principal, letting her know what had happened. She figured the sooner she made the calls she dreaded, the sooner she'd get on the path to her healthy future.

The receptionist who answered in Dr. Dennison's office couldn't have been any nicer. "Dr. James has already called about you, Erin, so we'll do our best to get you in as soon as possible for a consultation. Dr. Dennison will arrange for an MRI, but he'll want to talk to you first about treatment options and scheduling. ACL surgery is not to be taken lightly, and I understand that you have a new job that's important to you."

Erin was taken aback. She was so used to having to take care of almost everything in her life herself. She was pleasantly surprised how nice it felt to be looked after. "Yes, it would be great if the appointment could be after school hours," she said.

Next she called her principal, Mrs. Johnson, with the bad news about her knee. "I feel so terrible that I've only been on staff for a few weeks, and now I've blown out my knee. The doctor who saw me in the emergency room thinks I've used up all my options except for ACL surgery, but I'm going to get a second opinion from an orthopedic surgeon. I know that one of the reasons I wanted to come to your school in the first place was the terrific job you and the faculty do with mainstreaming students with disabilities. I had no idea that I'd need to be asking for accommodations for myself until I get over this rough spot," Erin said, near tears, as she wondered what Mrs. Johnson would do.

"Don't you worry about a thing. We've seen it all before! We are so thrilled to have you with us, and you'll find that our faculty and the students will spoil you rotten. Are you on crutches?"

"Yes, and I'm making sure to keep it iced. I'll be able to gimp my way through for a while, but I imagine surgery is a real possibility, so I might be out for a few days when that happens."

As Mrs. Johnson predicted, Erin went back to school (ever so grateful for Lyft and her first floor classroom), and each day a different teacher brought a covered dish for Erin to take home for dinner. The room mother for her classroom organized a parent volunteer to help out in class each day, and before she knew it, Erin's appointment with Dr. Dennison and the MRI were completed, and surgery scheduled in two weeks. Erin, who had kept Jennifer's business card tucked in her wallet for safe-keeping, decided to text her, to thank her for her helpfulness in getting her in to see Dr. Dennison and to let her know when and where the surgery was scheduled. Knowing how busy Jennifer was, Erin wouldn't have been surprised not to receive an answer. How many patients did she see every day, anyway? Did she keep up with all of them? she wondered.

In about twenty seconds, Erin heard the ping, and was surprised how eager she was to hear from Jennifer. "So glad you're going ahead with the surgery—you won't be sorry. Let me know how it goes! Who's caring for you afterward?"

Erin stopped short. She hadn't thought about that part. Dr. Dennison had said she needed someone to bring her home from surgery, but Erin figured that she could take care of herself after that. She emailed Mimi, feeling abashed that she was still so reluctant to ask anyone for help, even after all those times that having a family member had come in handy.

At least this time, she'd thought of it first, without Mimi having to suggest it! As she expected, as soon as Mimi knew what was going on, she made plans to do the transportation to and from surgery and to stay over a few days to make sure the post-op directions were followed, ice, food, company, errands, prescriptions, job concerns, and physical therapy coordinated. She let herself nod off to sleep, realizing how stressful the whole two weeks had been and how nice it was to feel cared for, really truly cared for, by colleagues, new friends, and familiar family.

~~~

Months later, Erin and Jennifer were at a café, laughing about how their paths had crossed in the emergency room. After the physical therapist had cleared Erin for gentle ju-jitsu warm ups, they had bumped into each other in the same kendo. They had corresponded by text and WhatsApp after the surgery, but life had gotten busy for both of them as they continued with their lives.

Mimi had helped Erin get on her feet after the surgery, but she knew how badly Erin wanted to do things on her own and to get back to her full life with her students and teachers…and her first love, ju-jitsu.

Erin felt at ease with Jennifer in a way she hadn't with any of her roommates at Hamilton, or her friends at Santa Cruz High, or maybe anywhere. She'd tried so hard to make friends without sharing her innermost self. She was a good listener, she made herself invite people to do things with her, and she tried hard to feel comfortable to extend herself in new situations with new people. But it never had felt comfortable.

She carried around her lesbian identity and her renunciation of her Catholic faith so deep inside that she was not sure how, or whether, she'd ever be able to share it with anyone. Even group therapy at Hamilton had not been able to unlock this psychological iron box, and certainly the therapy she'd had as an adolescent in Ireland, designed to maintain her faith, not her sexual identify, had only made matters worse.

Her colleagues at work were friendly, helpful, and supportive, and they'd been so generous with cards and food when she'd so needed it after her surgery. She didn't know how she could ever repay what she'd been given. But it still wasn't like having a soulmate, who really knew her inside and out. Jennifer, on the other hand, was completely at ease with herself. She made fun of herself; she made Erin laugh about the silliest things, and the time with her just flew by.

They'd started meeting for coffee on Saturday mornings at a little café close to the kendo. Erin was doing stretches and warm up exercises, following her physical therapists' instructions to the letter, not ever wanting to have to relive more injuries, but still dedicated to her sport. She wandered around the beginner classes, just to feel a part of things, and the sensei had seen how badly she wanted to continue with her new kendo, as part of her rehabilitation. When she saw Jennifer there, her heart leaped, because she now knew they had a keen connection beyond the hospital. Jennifer's warm smile made her glow from inside out.

Jennifer encouraged her not to limit herself to ju-jitsu, but to try some other things to stay fit and active, without endangering her newly restored knee. Long walks across the Golden Gate Bridge, through Chinatown, in the Presidio—there was so much to see in her new hometown. Jennifer helped Erin feel she belonged in San Francisco, and she had friends, wonderful friends, who cooked together, hiked together, went to the movies together, and…wonder of wonders, were in relationships. Without coming out directly to Jennifer, Erin sensed that Jennifer knew somehow about Erin's real self and that there was no reason to hide.

On one of their walks, Jennifer asked "So…what's your Wikipedia page, Erin?"

Erin, puzzled, replied, "What do you mean?"

"I mean, what's your back story? I know a little about you, but I want to hear your story the long way. How did you grow up? What's your family like? How'd you decide to move to San Francisco? You know, the story of your life, your narrative, like you'd read in Wikipedia."

"Oh, I get it. Well, I'll tell you mine, if you'll tell me yours, how's that? Just so you know, I have a hard time sharing really personal stuff," Erin confided.

"OK, I know your type. You'll make me drag it out of you, one chapter at a time. Well, that's fine with me. Would you feel more comfortable if I started first?" Jennifer was not in a hurry, and she didn't want to scare Erin away by pressing her too far, too fast.

Jennifer started slowly, beginning with her family, her two younger brothers, her parents, growing up in Pasadena, a Los Angeles suburb. She'd always known she wanted to be a doctor, like her father, and she'd started by doing surgery on her dolls. Then she went through a phase of wanting to be a vet and having all kinds of pets, which drove her mother crazy.

"I can't believe you knew what you wanted to be when you grew up from when you were little—so did I!" exclaimed Erin. "The dolls, the pets—I always wanted to be a teacher. I was always teaching my dolls, lining them up and making worksheets for them. We had lots of pets, too. I wish I could have pets in my little studio, but it's not realistic right now. Too much work, too little time, and too many rules."

Jennifer continued. "My family was Catholic, and we kids all went to Catholic school, at least through elementary. I couldn't stand it, though. I wanted to be with all kinds of kids; I hated all the rules, and gradually, I just didn't believe all that mumbo-jumbo anymore," Jennifer continued her story. "And then there was my little brother Tim, who was always a goodie-goodie. He became a choirboy, and he hung out way too much at church. The priest was always giving him special attention and awards for being perfect, and it was sickening. Years later, after he ran away from home, we finally found out what was going on. The priest was molesting him, and none of us had a clue. I still haven't forgiven myself for not knowing. If I could kill that man, I would. But he took care of it for me—he killed himself after the word got around." Jennifer's voice began to choke, and she stopped. "You know, I've never told anyone that story until today. It's just too painful."

Erin sat like a statue, while Jennifer regained her composure. She desperately wanted to take her friend's hands or give her a hug, but as always, she was afraid it would open the door to that scariest of places in her past.

Jennifer looked at Erin quizzically, waiting for her to respond, or to share a little bit about her growing up, but nothing was forthcoming. She felt she had nothing to lose, so she kept going.

"Tim disappeared. He took a backpack and a sleeping bag, told no one, and was gone for a month. My parents called the police, all of his friends, all of our relatives, and they began looking for him themselves, figuring he'd headed into the woods—he was always a hiker and backpacker, and he knew the back country near where we lived well enough to stay out of sight. Of course, my folks worried that he'd be eaten by bears, or would get hurt and not be able to call for help, or killed by some weirdo. Finally, he just got lonely, tired, and desperate for home. He went to a ranger station, and they called us. It was one of the happiest days of our lives."

"He'd had a long time to think about what had happened to him. He decided that instead of hiding out, he was going to make sure what happened to him never happened to anyone else. So he came home, told all of us about Father Gatlin, how ashamed he'd been and how Father Gatlin made him promise not to tell anyone because he wouldn't be believed, and it would ruin his life."

"To their credit, my parents stood up immediately for my brother, began reaching out to other families, using information provided by my brother, and poured all their rage into action against what they learned was a widespread and systematic system of pedophilia, hidden for decades by the local parish and diocese. I think it saved my brother's life, when he realized that it was not his fault. We left the Catholic Church and found another spiritual community whose ministry was about as far from dogma, judgment, patriarchy, and hypocrisy as you could get."

"I was in college by then, but I went to Pasadena City College, and then on to UCLA, not that far from home. I must say that as awful as that whole chapter was, when my family left the Catholic Church, it opened the door for me to come out as gay and stop pretending that I was a tomboy who loved sports and hiking girls! I'd hung out with guy friends, as well as girls, in high to "pass"—I was so shaken by what had happened to my brother and so confused by all the feelings I was having that I didn't know what was what. But I *did* know that kissing a guy did nothing for me, and kissing a girl was amazing."

Again, Jennifer stopped and looked at Erin carefully, waiting for a reaction and then opting to push even further. "I bet kissing YOU would be amazing!"

Erin thought about all those years of pushing her feelings aside, the shame attached to her middle school love affair, and the emptiness as she gave up her deeply held Catholic faith with nothing to replace it. She considered Jennifer's willingness to be vulnerable in deepening their relationship and her own reticence to reciprocate. She remembered Rule #2 in Mimi's guidebook to life: "If not now, when?" She took a deep breath, and replied shyly, "I think I'd like that."

Now it was Jennifer's turn to be quiet. She still knew almost nothing about Erin's back story, and somehow that seemed an important part of building a strong relationship, which was what Jennifer wanted. But maybe she should just be grateful that Erin had sort of come out to her, and she should go with the flow and see what happened? Maybe she was overthinking?

"Erin, let's get away for a weekend, can we? I think you can tell I want to get to know you better, and right now I'm blown away by what you just said. I don't want to say one other thing that might mess things up. What do you think?" Jennifer wanted more time, more privacy, and a setting in nature that would lend itself to the kind of sharing, both emotional and physical, that would lead them to the deeper intimacy she craved.

"I know just the place! It's called Sea Mist Cottage, up in Marshall on Tomales Bay. It's a cozy little place right on the water, with a hot tub and a fireplace, a little kitchen, and the wildlife is spectacular. You can see otters, and egrets, herons, and cormorants right out the window. We can take my kayak, or go for a walk, or whatever we want to do. It's a little more than an hour away, near Pt Reyes National Seashore. I bet you've never been there."

Erin felt her face flush as she considered this unexpected development. She liked it! She wanted it! It felt like everything she'd been waiting for, and she couldn't believe it was happening—all because she'd torn her ACL to shreds. Maybe it was all worth it!

Jennifer pulled out her phone and went to the Sea Mist Cottage website, looking for the earliest possible weekend. "You're going to love this place." Erin looked over her shoulder at the photos. "I love the photos, but it looks expensive," she noted.

"It's a bargain. Besides, it's my idea, so it's my treat. You can come up with the *next* getaway."

Erin's heart raced at the very possibility that this might not be a one-off weekend, but something longer term. She couldn't believe what was happening and how badly she wanted it to happen.

Jennifer clicked on the "Book now" button, entered her credit card information, and texted Erin the dates. "Put it on your calendar, and we'll work on the details. It's three weeks away, so forget about making up any excuses."

Erin got out her phone, entered the dates, and shook her head. "What does that mean, Erin? Are we on, or not?" Jennifer gave Erin a hard look. Erin replied "Oh, we're on, all right. I just can't believe what's happening, and I want to so badly. You have no idea how badly."

"I *do* know just how badly, because that's exactly the way I feel, too. Now I've got to get to work, and you're headed back to prepare for your students. Let's talk on the phone tonight and plan to meet here on Saturday, as always."

They both stood up, hugged each other, and said good-bye. That hug carried more meaning than it ever had before, Erin's feet flew as she pedaled home on her bicycle; once at home, she threw herself into lesson preparation and grading papers with new energy and motivation. Life had changed, and she could feel herself changing with it.

~~~

The day for the Tomales Bay trip finally arrived. Erin had packed and repacked, with all the items Jennifer had suggested—warm layers for the unpredictable climate, rain jacket, and breakfast items. She'd asked about a bathing suit for the hot tub, but Jennifer laughed. "No one's going to see you but me, so get used to it!"

Jennifer was bringing some homemade chili, cornbread, and salad for their evening meal, and they'd have seafood at Nick's Cove for lunch the next day, with leftover chili in the evening. The weather looked perfect for kayaking, and Jennifer had her kayak on the roof rack of her Subaru Forester. She'd brought extra firewood, kindling, and matches for the fireplace, and blankets to sit on the deck to stay warm. She brought a bottle of Schramsberg champagne and an ice bucket, to add to the feeling of celebrating something special.

They arrived at the cottage after a nerve-wracking drive through traffic over the Golden Gate Bridge in the dark. Erin and Jennifer appreciated the quiet sounds of the water lapping up under the cottage. They put away all their belongings and headed for the hot tub on the deck, with a full moon overhead illuminating beautiful Tomales Bay. Jennifer grabbed the champagne and two chilled glasses, and they eased into the hot water, letting all the cares of work, traffic, and the rest of the world drift away. They stayed there for a long time, watching the stars and the moon reflected on the water and listening to the sounds of the bay on the sides of the dock. A last toast with the remaining champagne, and they said good night to the owl, who'd been hooting in the huge redwood tree on the hillside nearby.

Once inside, Jennifer added some logs to the fire and put some quilts and pillows on the floor in front of the fireplace. Erin could not remember a time when she'd ever felt so relaxed and at ease. "Thank you so much for making this happen, Jennifer. I haven't been to very many places like this before." Jennifer gave her a look, and then they both laughed. "You haven't *ever* been to a place like this before, Erin, and you know it!" Jennifer had gotten used to Erin's customary response to a new situation and could tease her affectionately about it.

"I've been thinking a lot about your family and the things you shared with me in the coffee shop. I know you were probably disappointed that I wasn't more forthcoming. It meant a lot that you trusted me with your story. You know that sharing these personal things is not easy for me, but I'd like to try." Jennifer nodded but said nothing.

With those few words, all of a sudden, Erin found herself talking about her childhood in Belfast, her mother's childhood in Texas and her ensuing mental health issues, the poverty and the fear that was so pervasive—not enough money, not enough food, so much moving around, the Catholic faith that was woven throughout their daily lives, her missing father, the stigma of growing up a bastard child. Erin paused, waiting for Jennifer to ask questions, change the subject, or beg her to stop. But Jennifer just nodded, sometimes adding "I'd like to know more about that…"

"But none of that seems important compared to what happened to me in middle school. I fell in love with my best friend, Deirdre, and we had a love affair. I don't know how to describe it any other way. I only know that we had feelings for each other and expressed those feelings in ways that were abhorrent to the Catholic church, and we were caught kissing in a classroom at school."

"We were forbidden to see or communicate with each other. Deirdre tried to kill herself several times, and it was awful, the end of the world, really. I had been such a devoted Catholic schoolgirl, and my faith was shattered because of what I had done. And I abandoned my friend. I was left with absolutely nothing. Therapy, anti-depressants, and solitude were the solutions prescribed to me, and they left me suicidal. My mom knew, of course, but refused to believe that I could give up my faith, and she refused to believe that I was a lesbian, even though she never stopped loving me. She just thought I'd get over it."

"Does anyone know you are a lesbian? This was back in middle school, right? Have you had any relationships with a woman since then? Have you come out to your mother, your friends, your employer…anyone?"

"A few people—my mom, my cousin Mimi, my biological dad. But I've been unable to form real friendships because of everything I felt I had to hide. While I've always been in situations where gay people were fine, including with my mom, we've never discussed it, and I've just been celibate, hedging my bets with my strong Catholic faith, waiting for some sort of lightning bolt from the sky that told me what to do and how to do it. I'm really a mess."

Jennifer could only imagine how hard it must have been for Erin to tell this part of her story. "So you've been living between a rock and a hard place for all these years, right?"

"I'm so sick of it. So terribly sick of being so careful, working so hard to do the supposedly 'right' thing. I was in group therapy at Hamilton for months, and in all that time, I never came out. The only things I would share were not really things at all, they were just noise. I'm really good at listening, but I suck at being able to make myself vulnerable."

"My mom knows I'm gay but still doesn't really accept it, and my cousin Mimi is fine with it and just wants me to find a gay-friendly church and get on with my life. But it isn't that simple!"

Jennifer nodded. "I've seen it both ways. Sometimes what's most important is super simple and right in front of your very eyes. And sometimes it's not. What works best for me is to go deep into my heart, and then my gut. The answers are usually in one place or the other. And both my heart and my gut are telling me that what we have with each other is so right and so perfect!

"Now the last time I saw you, I told you it would be amazing to kiss you. And you told me you thought it would be amazing to kiss me, too. Did I get that right? Shall we give that a try and see what happens?" Jennifer cupped Erin's face in her hands and pulled her close, kissing her very gently at first, and then, with Erin's eager response, began kissing more deeply until finally, the two of them were wrapped up in blankets together, kissing, touching, caressing, with an intensity surprising to both of them.

When the embers in the fireplace began to die down, the two young women picked up the blankets and moved to the bedroom, where their love continued to unfold. Jennifer nodded approvingly to Erin, "I think you're making some real progress with that vulnerability issue." Erin smiled back. "I think you're right."

They'd intended to be up for the sunrise, but when they finally opened their eyes it was almost noon. "Damn!" said Jennifer, "I'd thought we'd go to Nick's Cove for lunch, but the weather's perfect for kayaking, and the tide table says we should grab a picnic and paddle across the bay. I already know what you're going to say 'I haven't been kayaking very often.'"

Erin threw her arms around Jennifer and said with a laugh, "There's where you're wrong! I've been kayaking a bunch of times! My cousin Mimi took me kayaking in Baja California, and there were all kinds of kayaking trips at Hamilton on the lakes and ponds in the Adirondacks. Don't press your luck—you don't know everything about me yet!"

Jennifer loved how easy it was to tease Erin, and the teasing went back and forth. In fact, everything about being with Erin felt easy, from making the trip plans, to coordinating their paddling in the kayak, to expressions of their physical love. Erin, the less experienced of the two, felt her doubts and confusion melt away in the comfort of Jennifer's skillful touch.

Erin's mind flashed back to her time with Deirdre, and she remembered how earnest and innocent it had felt, child-like in a way, and grown-up in others. Being with Jennifer was completely different. She felt like an adult; she felt fearless, and Jennifer's confidence infused Erin with a sense of her own power and value, as if Jennifer's comfort in her own skin was transferable somehow.

As they paddled across Tomales Bay, sunshine beamed down, otters swam around the boat and pelicans flew overhead to check out the two kayakers, and Erin and Jennifer continued their conversations of the night before, sharing stories of growing up, college, friendships and relationships, dreams of the future. They also talked about all the things friends share as their relationship deepens – their favorite foods, favorite things to do when they had some spare time, and favorite authors. They pulled the kayak up on the other shore and shared their picnic of vegetables, hummus, fruit, and granola bars. They posted selfies on Facebook, and Erin was surprised not to feel self-conscious.

As the sun started to go down, Jennifer and Erin began their paddle back, with the wind behind them and the tide pushing them back towards their cottage on the bay. Windblown, a little sunburned, tired, and joyful, they reached the dock and pulled the kayak out of the water. "I'd suggest going to Nick's for dinner, but I'm sore and tired, ready for a hot tub and a quiet evening. What about you, Erin?"

Erin appreciated how solicitous Jennifer was about her preferences and feelings, and she was delighted to spend their last night taking advantage of all their little cottage had to offer. Jennifer pulled some marinated garlic shrimp out of the cooler and made a delicious salad; she produced another bottle of champagne to keep up the festive spirit of the weekend.

Erin was pensive as they eased into the hot tub. "I get the feeling that being in a relationship is not something new for you, as it is for me. I'm feeling a little apprehensive about what happens when we go back to reality. This whole weekend I've felt like it was too good to be true and would just go 'poof' as soon as we hit the city limits."

Jennifer was careful with her words. "I'm older than you are, Erin. I have had a few relationships, but I promise you, I've never met anyone who blew me away like you do. I've never felt so safe, so trusted, and so at ease with any other woman. I appreciate your lack of pretense, your dedication to your students and your career, and your all-encompassing goodness that just shines through. I don't know what will happen when we get back to reality, but Erin, what if what we've found here *is* reality? What if we can take everything we've learned about each other and just keep growing and knowing each other better? Until a few of weeks ago, we were just acquaintances who were becoming friends. Now we're friends who've become lovers. Who knows what else is possible? Why don't we just keep going and see what happens? Is there something wrong with that?"

"I guess I was feeling the way I do when I have a nice time with a friend and I wonder if the friend will ever call me again. I was just feeling unsure."

"What if *I* was wondering if *you'd* ever call *me* again? It works both ways, you know. And let me tell you, girlfriend, I *will* be calling you, and you better call *me*, too! We've established something very special here, and we're just going to keep going. Sound all right to you?" Jennifer's reassurance about calling was music to Erin's ears, and she beamed. Hearing herself called "girlfriend" made her heart pound in a way it hadn't since middle school, which seemed like a very long time ago.

"Way better than 'all right,' I think," Erin replied with a grin.

CHAPTER 28

JENNIFER

"Hello, sun in my face. Hello you who made the morning and spread it over the fields...Watch, now, how I start the day in happiness, in kindness."
—Mary Oliver

An ordinary friendship forged over shared interests and dedication to career blossomed into an extraordinary relationship. Jennifer and Erin returned from their Sea Mist Cottage vacation and returned to their professions and all the demands that came with them. Jennifer completed her residency in orthopedics and joined a small, bustling sports medicine practice near the UCSF medical complex, making sure that her contract included a month of vacation in between the residency and joining the practice.

Erin finished her first year of teaching, following the trauma of her knee surgery, honored by her school district's Teacher of the Year award. She had considered teaching summer school but decided to take the whole summer off.

Jennifer and Erin had decided together that although they were as committed as ever to their professions, they were also devoted to each other. That required time away from work to have fun and build a life as a couple, one day at a time, week in and week out.

They launched their summer with a trip to Hawaii where they could swim, hike, relax on the beach, snorkel and enjoy the beauty of the sea life. They reminisced about their first trip away together to Sea Mist Cottage and all that had happened since then. Now it was time to start thinking about shaping the next chapter of their future together.

They had spent the school year moving back and forth between their two apartments—Erin's tiny studio in the Mission and Jennifer's small flat near UCSF. They enjoyed the different neighborhoods and different personalities of each place. Now they were starting to talk about moving in together, but neither of their places were big enough for two people...or for the pets they planned to get.

Jennifer knew that Erin was self-conscious about the difference between their two salaries and didn't want to feel beholden. Jennifer, who'd never grown up knowing poverty and financial insecurity, waved off the difference. "We're in this together. It's not your fault that teachers don't get paid much, and it's not my fault that orthopedic surgery is a lucrative field. We put our money together, and we have what we need. Neither of us cares much about material things, so what's the big deal? The important thing is we have a place we've picked out together, and it suits the way we want to live. Are you ok with that?"

Jennifer took her time with the issue of income disparity and its impact on their relationship. Jennifer was careful to listen to Erin's concerns, but she hoped having a joint checking account would equalize the power dynamic. She knew it would take time.

"How about we start looking at some places with an eye to finding a place before school starts for you? If we find a place we love sooner than that, great, but at least we have a sort of plan in mind. I can't imagine moving once we're both back at work, can you?" Jennifer's practical way of looking at things, not impulsive or rushed, but not content with the status quo when change was needed was reassuring to Erin.

The housing market being what it is in San Francisco, Jennifer and Erin decided to pursue multiple fronts. They considered creating a post on Facebook that outlined what they were looking for, but then they weighed that against their desire for privacy and opted against it. The wife of one of the doctors in Jennifer's practice was a realtor, and she offered to help them find a place. She thought they should buy a place, of course, and Jennifer thought that was a great idea.

Erin gasped at the very thought, since even a fixer-upper would cost at least twenty times her annual salary, and she knew how tenuous a beginning teacher's status was. They each checked Craigslist separately every day, looking for listings that were on both their lists.

At least both of them had managed to get through school without college loans; Jennifer's family had underwritten her college and medical school, and Erin had had a full ride scholarship at Hamilton, with a special program through UCSC for her combined teaching credential and master's degree. They started by researching neighborhoods close to Erin's school and Jennifer's medical practice.

Their summer days were spent walking around Bayview, close to Erin's school, Malcolm X Elementary, and around the area near the UCSF medical complex. They liked Bernal Heights, with its lovely park ("great for walking our future dogs," thought Erin), and midway between both of their jobs. As luck would have it, a large two-bedroom apartment next to Erin's studio opened up, and they decided that the simplicity of that situation suited them best.

Jennifer liked the new landlord and her neighbors; the move would be easy, and the location was perfect for Erin's work. With that decision made and a moving date well before school started, they still had time left for traveling.

"I'd like to go to Ireland," Jennifer said, out of the blue, at breakfast on their first Saturday morning in their new place. "I want to see where you grew up and meet your mother and your father. I've never been to Ireland, and I think it's time you came out about us."

"And I'd like to go to LA," countered Erin. You could show me where you grew up and went to school. I want to meet your family, see the Huntington Gardens, Hollywood, and go to Disneyland."

They laughed at each other, recognizing the sensitivity of bringing a partner home to meet the family. Both of them were testing the waters of being more public about their commitment to each other with their family and friends, and they recognized the need to make sure they were in tune with each other's comfort level.

"I'll tell you what," said Jennifer with a grin. "*I'll* go to Belfast, and *you* can go to LA."

"Things are so perfect right now; I'm just reluctant to take a chance on a disaster, just after we're settling into our new home together. But if it's important to you, we could do a quick trip to both places, and then leave some time for damage control when we get back," Erin mused.

"You're such an optimist, Erin. If that's the way you feel, I think we shouldn't go to either place. As you say, don't mess with success!"

"OK, here's the plan: we'll go to LA for Thanksgiving, because it's close and that's easy. We'll go to Ireland for Christmas, both Belfast and Ballinora. We can enjoy the rest of our summer here in our new home, and we'll look forward to our first holidays as official partners with our respective families," Erin proposed.

Jennifer was impressed that Erin had skillfully woven together a plan that moved their relationship along, and preserved some time for them to just enjoy being together and furnishing their new home.

"Done. I'll book the flights, and we'll each communicate the plan to our fams," Jennifer took over the logistics once the decision had been made.

They had a wonderful time deciding which of their most cherished individual items they wanted to bring to their new shared apartment and shopping together for items for their new shared life together. The first priority was a king-size bed (plenty of room for pets they planned to adopt) and a dining table and chairs so they could have friends over for potlucks. They gave away their duplicate kitchen items (blender, toaster, microwave, etc.) and combined the rest.

Erin preferred more traditional furnishings, and Jennifer a more modern, sleek look, but they were pleased at how the blend of styles made their home seem authentically "theirs." It felt warm, welcoming, and comfortable, and thanks to Erin's skill at finding bargains online and at estate sales, gracious.

As people grew accustomed to seeing the young couple together, the idea of "coming out" formally seemed artificial and unnecessary. After all, heterosexual couples didn't do that, so why would it be different for lesbian and gay couples? they figured. In vibrant San Francisco, dominated by millennials, the whole gay/straight divide seemed irrelevant and odd.

They saw couples like themselves everywhere they went; it felt natural to hold hands or not, and they could relax. Erin felt herself shedding the heavy burden of her conflict between her religion and her sexual identity. Erin could feel the waning influence of growing up Catholic in a culture where few friends and acquaintances went to church or expressed an interest in religion of any kind. "Spiritual but not religious" described most everyone they met.

By the time school started, Jennifer had already gone to work in her new orthopedic surgery practice. She'd bought a new electric-assisted e-bike and could get to her office, just 4 miles way, in about fifteen minutes.

Erin enjoyed the freedom of driving to her school in Jennifer's Subaru so she could carry the armloads of books, papers, and projects for her classroom. In her previous life, she'd have to stay late at school to finish everything, and then take the bus home at whatever hour, day or night, with whatever she could easily carry. Life was easier now, and way more fun!

The vacation visits to both families, deferred in the summer, went off without a hitch. Jennifer's family welcomed Erin with open arms, and she responded accordingly. She appreciated the snapshot of Jennifer's growing up, so different from hers in Belfast, and she was fascinated by Los Angeles. She and Jennifer took time away from the family to do some sight-seeing, and they loved spending a child-like Thanksgiving Day at Disneyland, while most of the hordes were at home eating their turkey. They were at the gates of the Magic Kingdom when it opened and returned to Jennifer's parents for a traditional family dinner that evening. She was curious what it was like for a previously devoutly Catholic family to live a religion-free life, but that former part of life was just not even visible.

Jennifer was fascinated to meet Tracey in Belfast and Erin's dad Brian and his family in Ballinora, much more of a culture shock than she had expected. They had flown into Belfast on Christmas Eve, and snow was falling lightly on the city, all decorated for the holidays.

Tracey welcomed them to her home, introduced Jennifer to Jazzbo and Comet, while Erin hung back, trying desperately to be at ease, feeling more aware than ever of the disparity of income and lifestyle of their two families. Tracey had prepared a Christmas Eve feast, and they ate dinner while admiring the decorated Christmas tree with presents for the two young women, and presents brought by Erin and Jennifer for Tracey, Comet, and Jazzbo.

No mention had been made of Christmas Eve midnight mass, to Erin's relief. She'd told Tracey they would not be attending, sure that Tracey would be relieved about not having to explain who Jennifer was to any busybody who might have the nerve to ask.

They spent the next two days exploring Belfast, the neighborhoods where Erin had grown up, St. Patrick's, where she'd attended primary school, as well as the tourist destinations of the Titanic museum and the historic harbor area. Jennifer was intrigued with the leftover signs of The Troubles—neighborhoods with orange Protestant flags, graffiti, and bullet-pocked walls and memorials to those who died in the struggle on either side. Jennifer seemed quite at ease with Tracey, and she asked lots of questions about the Troubles and Irish history, having immersed herself in it in preparation for the trip.

Erin wasn't sure her mum knew quite what to make of Jennifer; Tracey could be quite direct in her communication, and Erin was relieved that Tracey didn't ask probing questions about their relationship or Jennifer's family. It was only a two-bedroom house, so Tracey couldn't exactly offer them separate rooms, and Erin was relieved that she didn't try!

They planned just a day trip to Ballinora, a low-key lunch, Erin hoped, at a restaurant near the train station in Cork. Erin knew that Brian didn't care who she loved, but she knew his sisters were quite religious and while they would be pleasant to Jennifer to her face, they would likely be appalled in the post-visit analysis. She hoped that the day trip would give Brian a chance to get to know Jennifer a little and to help him realize that her sexual identity had not and would not change.

Fortunately, it seemed that Brian was more concerned about his relationship with Erin than about Church teachings on same sex marriage. Brian was fascinated that Jennifer had considered becoming a vet instead of a doctor, so he was quite interested in sharing his experience with taking care of the animals on his farm.

On the long train ride back to Belfast from Cork, Jennifer and Erin, exhausted but satisfied, compared notes and experiences of the three very different family visits. "I can't imagine anything more important than bringing our families into our relationship," Jennifer observed, "and we did it on our terms, not theirs. I think it was a huge step forward. What did you think, Erin?"

"I'm too tired to think, but you're right. It was time to bring our whole selves into our families, and now we've cleared the way for us to *be* a family ourselves."

"What did you have in mind?" Jennifer wanted to hear the words from Erin, who rarely took the lead in the relationship department.

CHAPTER 29

ERIN

"The family is one of nature's masterpieces."
—George Santayana

"I want us to set a date to get married and start thinking about having kids. HAH! I beat you to it, didn't I?!" Erin gloated, pleased that she felt confident in herself, her relationship, and in presenting themselves to the world as partners, and soon, hopefully, spouses, and then parents.

Jennifer stopped short in her tracks, not believing what she'd just heard. "I want some time to just let those words settle into my mind. And we're still in Ireland. I want to hear them again when we're back on our home turf, into our usual routines. But I'm so very happy we're headed in the same direction!"

They took a taxi from the train station to Tracey's Belfast home, where they'd spend one more night before Tracey returned to work. Erin held her breath, hoping for no editorial comments or critical questions about their time with Brian, and they went off to bed. As they got ready for bed, Tracey tapped on their door. "I just wanted to thank you for coming all this way to visit me. I can imagine you worried about how I'd react to you being a couple. I love you both, and that's all that matters. I'll see you in the morning and wish you sweet dreams."

Erin's eyes filled with tears. "Mummy, you have no idea how much your welcome has meant to me — to both of us. Thank you for the most beautiful Christmas ever!"

Jennifer gave Tracey a hug. "Erin's right—it has been an amazing Christmas, and I'm feeling so lucky to be part of such a very special family now."

The next day, as the plane lifted off over the layer of fog and drizzle that covered Belfast, Jennifer and Erin looked at each other and said, "Let's go home!"

The adrenaline from a fall filled with furnishing their first home and meeting each other's families on their home turf was gone, and they tumbled into their own bed, sleeping deeply until mid-afternoon the next day. They still had a few days until New Year's, and their first party in their new home, as a couple. They'd invited Erin's friends from Malcolm X Elementary, Jennifer's friends from the practice, and friends from the kendo. They couldn't wait to share about their trip to Ireland and see how the new apartment was taking shape.

They scoured Chinatown for fortune cookies, favors, and decorations, and then headed over to the Embarcadero for cheeses, marinated mushrooms, salamis, and anything else that looked interesting and appetizing. As they were buying champagne to ring in the new year, Erin reached out shyly and took Jennifer's hand. "I was thinking...as long as we're having this party, and buying champagne and all...what would you think about announcing our...engagement?"

Jennifer looked deep into Erin's eyes. "So this means you weren't kidding when we were in Ireland? Does this mean what I think it does—are you proposing to me?! I guess I always thought I'd have to be the one to pop the question. You never cease to surprise me, Erin, and I love it when you do! If you're sure you're ready, I think it's an inspired idea! As long as we're shopping, let's go look at rings, too!"

"I want some time to pick out something really special for you, Jennifer, and I'd like it to be a surprise. What would you think of that idea?"

"It's so like you, Erin, to be thoughtful and patient in picking out something that means so much. I'll do the same for you! We'll both be surprised on our wedding day!"

276

"I'm going to ask Mimi to suggest some ice-breakers for our New Year's party—she and Matthew always give parties that help people from different groups get acquainted. I want people to really feel at home at our first party, don't you?"

"Absolutely! By the way, had you thought of inviting Mimi and Matthew, and your other SF cousins I've heard so much about but haven't met? Given what we're going to announce, I think it would be important for them to be there. And why don't we have it on New Year's Day afternoon, so we don't compete with all the other stuff going on New Year's Eve?" They quickly texted their friends and the cousins, and the party was ON!

They spent the next day working on not only the party details, but the beginning plans for their wedding, making sure to check in carefully with each other about what their dreams were for this event. Small, casual and simple, something outdoors, in nature, if possible, and not religious. Lots of food. An indoor Plan B for cold, drizzly weather. In the summer, with time for a honeymoon. Blair, their San Francisco Lockhart cousin, just happened to be an event planner, and immediately stepped forward to help the couple with the arrangements.

The party went off better than Jennifer and Erin ever dreamed, with Mimi and the Lockhart cousins taking care of the logistics and the mixing and mingling of guests, who brought piles of food and good cheer. As just the right moment, Erin and Jennifer rang a small brass bell to get everyone's attention, and they each held up a glass of champagne for a toast: "To our friends and families, a joyous new year! And to each other—a happy engagement!" A cheer erupted and everyone clapped and hollered. Mimi played a song that had been written by her high school actor/composer friend in honor of her own wedding to Matthew:

"As we nestle down in some strange town to ring the new year in,
Let us all take stock and face the clock and think of where we've been.

Of the friends we've lost and the friends we've made and the friends we've never met,

And the one or two who decades thru, our hearts will not forget.

We could drink a toast to the ones with most of the things that life can give.

But I lift my glass to the lad or lass who has found a way to live

With a smile for tears and a laugh at years and a heart that's filled with light.

And the memory that what could be is never far from sight."

For a few moments, the room was quiet. A few tears were shed, as people shared their own new year's memories before bidding the newly engaged couple the happiest of new years and congratulations on the wedding to come.

CHAPTER 30

JENNIFER

"Love recognizes no barriers. It jumps hurdles, leaps fences, penetrates walls to arrive at its destination full of hope."
—Maya Angelou

The new year brought the usual breath-taking pace of events at school, leading up to the end of the year. Jennifer's practice also was busier with skiing accidents and sports injuries picking up as the school year went on, not to mention the growing number of hip, knee, and shoulder replacements among her beloved senior patients.

They'd chosen the Conservatory of Flowers in Golden Gate Park for their wedding. Jennifer remonstrated, "Erin, don't worry about the money. You know the father of the bride pays for the wedding, and that would be my dad!"

"What makes you think *you're* the bride?" queried Erin.

"Ok, you're right. Let's flip a coin. Heads, I'm the bride, tails, you're the bride and get to pick the venue. I'll flip." Jennifer tossed a quarter in the air, and it came down heads. She had always loved Golden Gate Park and especially the beautiful Victorian glass house filled with flowering plants.

Erin remembered it from that first San Francisco family reunion when she was twelve, a dozen cousins from all over the country, ages 2 to 72. Her cousin Blair the event planner had created a week of memories for the cousins' reunion, and she was in charge of the wedding, too.

Once they had the venue lined up, they talked to Jennifer's parents about their wedding plans. Her family was thrilled with the news and laughed at how the women had decided who would be the bride. "That's as good a way as any, I suppose," Jennifer's father commented. "You just be sure you throw the best party San Francisco has ever seen and don't worry about money. Is that clear?"

"Yes, Daddy, I already cleared that with Erin. It will be wonderful."

Next, Erin wrote her mum and Brian, with some trepidation. She thought she would call, but she just couldn't seem to do it. It was one thing to visit them in Ireland, but it was another to challenge the ironclad Catholic dogma about same-sex marriage, even though it was legal in California.

Several weeks went by, and she'd received no response from either Tracey or Brian. Finally, she had no choice but to call and check in, to find out if they were going to come to the wedding, if they would bless the new couple, if they would accept them as they had over the holiday.

Erin called Tracey first. "Mummy, just tell me. Will you come to my wedding?"

Tracey responded slowly, choosing her words carefully. "Erin, I love you and Jennifer dearly, and you'll always be welcome in my home. But a wedding! That's a step beyond what I can take, there's my faith to consider, number one. And there's the travel, number two. You know I just about unraveled when I came for your Hamilton graduation. I'm just not meant to leave home. I can't do it."

Erin had fully expected this response, and at some level, she was relieved, since she wouldn't have to worry about taking care of her mother as well as her responsibilities as a bride.

Then she called Brian. "You know, I've talked to your mum," he said, "and I've talked to my family about what you and Jennifer are about to do. We all love the both of you and will always keep you in our hearts and treasure you when you come to visit. But there's the Church, not too important to me, but very important to my sisters and my mam. I don't want to stir up trouble in the family. Besides that, it's so hard to leave the farm, you know that. I hope you understand. I can't come."

"I'll miss you and my mum, Brian. I do understand. It hurts me deeply, but the Church has always been a burden on my heart, and I think I'm finally ready to put that burden aside. This wedding symbolizes that split for me, just as it does for the family. I'm relieved to know you'll still love me."

Now they were free of family and religious pressure and could plan the ceremony they wanted. They imagined not being given away by their parents, but giving themselves, as grown up independent women, to each other. They imagined writing their own vows, drawing from spiritual traditions that had been meaningful to them, and not limited to their Catholic past.

The sun shone brightly for their wedding day, as the group of friends and family assembled at the Conservatory of Flowers, outdoors as planned, with a picnic afterward. Erin read a favorite poem for Jennifer by Mary Oliver:

> "So every day
> I was surrounded by the beautiful crying forth
> of the ideas of God,
> one of which was you."

Jennifer read from Winnie the Pooh:

"Some people care too much. I think it's called **love**." "If there ever comes a day when we can't be together, keep me in your heart, I'll stay there forever."**Pooh**: "You don't spell it, you feel it."

Their best friend became a Universal Life Minister to marry them, and the afternoon turned into evening as everyone enjoyed being in the park. Each child received a kite to fly; everyone had an envelope with a monarch butterfly to release to the sky.

Mimi and Matthew gave them a week on the Uncruise in Alaska for their honeymoon, and as the sun went down, the happy pair bid farewell and headed to the Hyatt Regency at the San Francisco airport to recover overnight before catching a plane to Sitka to board the boat—a week of hiking, kayaking, snorkeling, bird-watching—all the things they loved to do.

When they returned, they'd be ready to rejoin their demanding professional lives again, but this time, as the start of a new family. That announcement hadn't been made at the wedding, but Erin and Jennifer had not only been planning a wedding all these months, they had also been busy researching how to start a family.

Erin was strongly in favor of becoming fost-adopt parents in hopes of adopting an infant, especially considering her mum's bumpy past and the number of kids she'd seen in her classrooms whose paths through the social service system had been anything but smooth. Jennifer wanted Erin to get pregnant and to have that experience of birth as a couple.

In the end, they decided to compromise. They'd take the training to become foster parents and wait to see if a fost-adopt infant became available, and they also consulted with a fertility specialist about their options. Since they both wanted the maximum involvement possible, Dr. Adamson suggested the possibility of doing an egg transfer from Jennifer to Erin and then doing artificial insemination with a sperm donor. Both women thought that was a terrific idea!

They'd let the universe decide: either way was fine with each of them. Neither of them had any idea, nor could anyone tell them, how long either approach might take so they figured they'd best get started. If they both happened at once, they'd have two kids!

They reviewed profiles of sperm donors and went to foster parent trainings, fascinated and horrified by the stories of the children in the system. They settled on a particular donor, and Erin received her first donation in the doctor's office, settling back for a few weeks to see what would happen. They completed all the paperwork to become foster parents, background checks, references, applications. It was clear that would take a while, too.

In the end, after the second cycle of sperm infusion, Erin got pregnant, just a couple of weeks before the wedding. They waited until they were sure the pregnancy was viable and after the wedding and honeymoon were safely behind them before they told anyone.

CHAPTER 31

KATIE

"A baby is God's opinion that the world should go on."
—Carl Sandburg

What'll we name the baby, Erin? I bet you've thought about it! I'm pretty sure you'll want an Irish name for this little girl, won't you?" Jennifer had her own names she wanted to try out, but since Erin was the one who was pregnant, it seemed fair that she would get first dibs.

"I want to name her Katie, after my Irish ancestor. If it hadn't been for her, I wouldn't be here. And from everything I know, she was fiercely independent, just like me. Imagine raising nine kids!"

"I love that name. How about Rose for her middle name, after my grandmother? Katherine Rose Tompkins-James. What a beautiful name! But don't get any ideas about having nine kids, that's for sure!"

Both moms were so busy at work that the days of the pregnancy flew by. Erin was fortunate not to be plagued by morning sickness, and her checkups showed that everything was proceeding beautifully. Erin had shared with her principal that she'd be having a baby a couple of months before school was out and wanted to make sure the district would provide a well-qualified long-term sub for the beloved classroom of students she'd come to love. "Congratulations to you and Jennifer," Mrs. Johnson beamed. "We'll want to have a baby shower for you, of course, and I'll do whatever I can to make sure you won't have a thing to worry about when you're on maternity leave. We *do* hope you'll plan to come back to us, though. We've come to rely on your leadership in our school, along with being a star in the classroom."

"Of course, I'll be back! We need to start making plans for her care, of course, but you can count on me to return in the fall. It will be a busy summer, for sure!" Erin was reminded that she'd been so busy planning for the birth that she hadn't really thought that far ahead. Who *would* look after the baby? What if she didn't really want to leave, once she had a little one at home? Even though she couldn't imagine giving up her classroom, she also couldn't imagine leaving her baby with a stranger, either, no matter how qualified. She had been lucky enough to have her mum when she was little, as the government in Northern Ireland was quite liberal with support for new mothers. Not so much in the US.

She and Jennifer talked over the conversation with Mrs. Johnson, and they considered what they might do. Jennifer was more and more engaged with not only her own medical practice, but also providing leadership to young residents in orthopedics at UCSF.

"Most of my doctor friends get a nanny or an au pair. We could look even look for someone from Ireland—wouldn't that be a trip?" Jennifer was always quick with ideas, and they were usually expensive, since money had never been a problem in her life experience.

"That would cost a fortune! Besides, it isn't just the money, it's turning over our precious little one to a stranger. I'm having a hard time imagining that. I know this is a crazy idea, but I'm wondering if my mum might consider coming to the States to help us out for a while. She's not a stranger, and she's got proven experience. I would be way less expensive than a nanny or an au pair, although of course we'd want to pay her fairly."

Although Erin's mom had not come to the wedding, their warm relationship had continued. Tracey seemed over the moon about the upcoming birth, as Erin had hoped, realizing that her own daughter's out-of-wedlock birth was not exactly what the Church had in mind, either. Tracey had been able to compartmentalize the conflict between her Catholic faith and her love for her daughter and her partner.

Jennifer nodded "I think it would be lovely to ask her, Erin. I know she hates to travel and she's not likely to give Ireland up, but she might like to be a part of our little family until we get things figured out. She might even be hurt if we didn't ask, so let's not risk that."

They initiated their regular WhatsApp call on Saturday morning, letting Tracey know about the progress of Erin's pregnancy and their thoughts about what they might name the little girl. "Mummy, we are starting to think about what happens after the baby is born and how we're going to look after her. One of our ideas was the possibility of your coming to the States and helping us out while the baby is young. I'm not really a fan of day care, but neither of us wants to give up our careers, either. What do you think we should do?"

Erin did her best not to pressure her mum into coming, but she hoped she would, feeling grateful for her mum's dedication to her when she was little, in spite of all the predictions to the contrary by the social services people in Ireland. Her mind drifted back to the past, trying to imagine what their lives might have been if someone had tried to take her away from her mother, or if they had been deported back to the States. She shook off the scary daydream/nightmare.

"Now that's an interesting idea you're posing to me. I know you must have felt I let you down by not coming to your wedding..." Tracey began, before Erin interrupted.

"I wished you could have been here, Mummy, but I understood. The weight of that conflict between the Church and my identity was a burden my whole growing up. I've put that aside. Where it's just between you and us, we agree that love and family is all that matters. So that's why I'm asking—might you consider helping us out?"

"You're right. You are the heart of my heart, and if you and Jennifer find love, happiness, and family together, I'm at peace with that. What other options are you considering for the baby-to-be?"

"Either Jennifer or I can take a leave from work, or do a job-share, cutting back our careers, we can hire a nanny, or we can put Katie Rose in day care," Erin explained. "We're not crazy about any of those choices. We'd much rather she be with a family member."

"I am pleased that you thought of me. I *do* have a bit of experience," Tracey laughed. "I'm not sure what I'd do with the animals, my job, and my house, though. It might take me a bit of time to think it over."

After a few sleepless nights, Tracey decided that she'd at least do the research to see if coming to the States for an undetermined period of time was even possible. Could she get a leave from her job? How would leaving the country for an extended period of time affect her immigration status? Could she rent out her home? Could she take her pets with her (both Comet and Jazzbo had passed away by now, but she had become quite fond of the rescue terrier mix dog called Patsy and her new best friend, a calico cat called Beatrix).

Her employer was surprisingly amenable to a leave of absence for up to two years. Her dearest friend's daughter and her family were looking for a reasonably priced rental in the area, wanting to live closer to their mum, and the dog and cat could travel to the US (much easier for them to go to the States than the other way around). She also researched her immigration status, which was "indefinite leave to remain." She learned that that status would be revoked if she were to leave the UK for a period of longer than two years, which matched the limitation on her employment status.

She would miss her friends, of course, and her Church, but there were churches in San Francisco, and she could find her way. The idea of being close to Erin again, after all these years, and Erin's new baby, was worth the turmoil and effort involved in the move, it seemed to her. She had months to prepare. Jennifer and Erin hadn't gotten any pets of their own, because they'd always been too busy to feel like they could be responsible pet owners, so Patsy and Beatrix would be welcome additions to the family.

She responded to Erin and Jennifer that she'd be up to the challenge, assuming they were okay with the pet issue, which they were. She would only be able to stay for two years. She asked if they'd thought about what it might be like to live all together, which they had.

Jennifer and Erin were elated that Tracey was planning to come. Jennifer was optimistic they'd be able to find a house to own in the meantime, with a place for Tracey as long as she wanted. Jennifer's dad, as always, was eager to help as an investor in the project.

Erin, whose teacher salary had no prospect of home ownership, didn't even pretend to protest. Everything had worked out so far, and she had too many other things to worry about. She was happy to delegate the whole endeavor to Jennifer, and Jennifer was thrilled to accept the job.

Within a week, Jennifer had three houses for her to look at, having scoured research on Zillow and MLS. She used a realtor's help. She kept her favorite to herself, knowing that Erin would want her preferences considered. Her favorite house, with three bedrooms and two baths upstairs, a mother-in-law unit downstairs, a yard, a parking space, and a modern, completely updated and restored interior, was outside the Mission where they'd been living and in nearby Portola, not far from Maclaren Park, with its trails, playgrounds, duck pond, and more. The prices were more reasonable, which Erin would appreciate. "Fifteen Dartmouth Street" had a nice ring to it, and Jennifer thought the location was excellent, in a neighborhood that was becoming trendier.

Jennifer made sure to schedule the viewing of her favorite house last, but she'd done her best to make sure that all three were solid alternatives. Any of the three homes would be fine with Jennifer, and her dad had helped her line up the financing, to keep the monthly payments as low as possible. They'd be on the title as joint tenants, just like most married couples, and Erin could relax. Maybe this would be their "forever" house!

As they entered the third house in their tour, Erin's mouth dropped open. Truly a "turn-key" house, they could move in without doing any fixer-upper chores. Jennifer sat on the couch in the living room, staged to the max, while Erin walked around with the realtor, noting all the features they'd talked about wanting—the fireplace, two bathrooms instead of the one they'd been sharing in their current apartment, and best of all, a lovely, private place for Tracey.

They'd have a bedroom for the nursery and a guest room/study where Erin could do her grading and classroom projects. Erin climbed the stairs from the mother-in-law unit, rolled her eyes, and said, "Well, I guess it's ok, but…" then burst into a fit of giggles as she saw Jennifer's dismay. "It's absolutely perfect! I don't know how in the world we could ever afford it, but you made me promise not to worry about that. So I won't! Let's do this!" Jennifer and Erin grabbed each other and jumped around the room, before they stopped, looked at the realtor, and said, "I think we're not supposed to show how badly we want this place."

The realtor smiled and said, "I'm *your* agent, not the listing agent, and I completely understand. When a house really says to you, 'This is *home…*', you really need to listen to your heart. I love this house, too, and it seems so perfect for you. I'll do whatever I can to make sure you get it."

The realtor was as good as her word, and with Jennifer's dad's help on the financing, the house purchase went smoothly, unlike the horror stories of so many of their friends who'd been priced out of the SF housing market. They gave notice to their landlord, sharing with their friends the opportunity to get in early on the rental vacancy. By the time the Christmas holiday rolled around, escrow had closed, and they were ready to make the move.

On the other side of the pond, Tracey was making her own arrangements. She knew she'd stay at least two years. Of course, depending on how things worked out, she might stay forever, although she seriously doubted it. At least she had choices, and that was somehow reassuring.

She was not comfortable with change generally, and now that she was a homeowner, she was even less inclined to change than she was as a renter. She had been so much happier since she had the stability of owning her own home in Belfast and feeling at ease about decorating it and making improvements. She'd find the right person to rent it while she was gone and someone to manage it for her.

Some nights she found herself tossing and turning from worries about all the decisions that needed to be made; other nights she tossed and turned with excitement about being part of granddaughter's life. Her mind drifted back to Erin's infancy and all the joys and challenges that had come with having her own baby, the baby she was allowed to keep, against all odds. She was so grateful to her beautiful daughter for healing so many of her childhood wounds and giving her a chance to believe in herself as a mother. Here was her chance to return that favor!

Erin sent her photos of the new house, and that clinched the decision for Tracey. She loved the idea of having her own space, some yard for her dog and cat, yet close enough for easy contact between her and the little family upstairs. She rented her house furnished, so she didn't have to make big decisions about what to take with her and what to give away. Making decisions, big or small, was not one of the things that Tracey enjoyed about life.

One of Jennifer and Erin's closest friends suggested a combination house-warming and baby shower. While they didn't really need any items for their new home, they were eager to welcome their friends to see where they would be living. The baby shower was most appreciated, because they were less sure of what they would need in the baby department. They planned the event for shortly after Tracey arrived, dog and cat safely transported on her plane in cargo, just weeks before their baby was due. Mimi came up from Santa Cruz, having wrapped up Erin's seriously well-loved Eeyore, which she'd saved from the items Erin had set aside for Goodwill when she went off to college. Mimi had rescued him from the donation pile, not willing to part with him, because he reminded her of Erin and that special year they'd shared, not to mention Eeyore's long history with Erin growing up. Tracey and Erin both teared up when they saw him, reminding both of them of their Pooh days and the special moments of Erin's early childhood.

As they awaited Katie Rose's arrival, Jennifer and Erin took advantage of time to explore the City with Tracey—the usual tourist spots, of course—Golden Gate Park and its Conservatory of Flowers where they had said their wedding vows, Chinatown, the

Golden Gate Bridge, the Embarcadero, Erin's school and Jennifer's medical practice. They also took her to Holy Redeemer Catholic Church, where they felt welcome (although they didn't belong to any church) and they were sure that Tracey would be surprised by its gay-friendly vibe.

Katie Rose arrived on schedule, without much fanfare. Two moms and a grandmom were in the room, and the little one gave a hearty cry as she announced her presence. Erin and Jennifer started their maternity leaves until fall. Three generations of women took opportunity each day as it came, developing routines that emerged from Katie's sleep and awake times. Erin and Tracey explored Maclaren Park with the baby in a stroller or front-carrier, and Jennifer often accompanied them before heading off on her own for a jog.

Tracey and Jennifer usually went to Whole Foods, where Jennifer found the variety and quality to her liking. Tracey thought it hard not to look at the prices and found the array of choices disorienting. But they enjoyed cooking together and family meals, trying new things and learning old favorites from Jennifer's childhood and the Irish cookbook that Tracey had brought with her.

Tracey walked on her own to the public library nearby, and she enjoyed chatting with the moms and nannies by the duck pond in Maclaren Park when she took Katie for walks on her own. She was so much healthier without the stresses of her life in Belfast. She'd been beset with worries about whether she'd be able to keep up with her busy job, making sure she had enough money to pay her bills and taxes, and so much more.

But her Belfast home generated rent, and together with the funds that Jennifer and Erin provided for looking after Katie, she felt freer than she ever had in her life. She was surrounded by her daughter, daughter-in-law, and granddaughter and three other Lockhart cousins in the Bay area. From a life devoid of roots beyond her own daughter, at last she had more family than she'd believed possible.

As the summer drew to a close, they took some time to reflect on all that had happened in the last year. Erin readied herself for a new school, just a few blocks from her home, where she'd been asked to be a mentor to new teachers at schools in the surrounding area. She'd been given a day of release time each week to do planning meetings, observe in classrooms, and reflect with teachers after their lessons. Erin loved this new responsibility, in a new school and with a new group of colleagues.

Jennifer's practice continued to grow, but like Erin, the favorite part of her job these days was guiding the new orthopedic residents at UCSF. Both women had gifts in becoming mentors, encouraging and supporting others in honing their craft.

~~~

What about Katie? Katie grew up, as infants do, by first turning into a toddler, then a preschooler and so on through the grades and stages of development. She'd considered herself lucky from a very early age, with moms who loved her beyond reason, and a grandma, Mamoo, who absolutely hung the moon for Katie.

Tracey treasured her granddaughter as only a grandparent can. Katie had a dog and cat who tolerated her at first, then fiercely protected her from any potential source of harm, then taught her how to play with them for hours on end.

Katie saw her southern California grandparents from time to time. Katie's childhood of full of enough love, pets, money, a comfortable home, neighborhood friends, and a city of incomparable variety and diversity of all kinds provided her with everything she needed and most everything she wanted.

~~~

Before Katie turned two, it was time to plan for the transition. Tracey would be returning to her life in Belfast.

Jennifer and Erin decided to find a nanny, although no nanny would be able to replace what Tracey had contributed to the little family. They found Olga, who was appropriately vetted and recommended by other families, pleased that she supported the idea of speaking Spanish only to their little girl, so that Katie could grow up bilingual.

Jennifer and Erin surprised Tracey with a Winnie-the-Pooh going away party. Tracey said goodbye not only to her San Francisco family and life but also to Beatrix and Patsy, who were Katie's pets now.

~~~

Before long, Katie was ready for preschool, and off to the Crayon Box, a small private school that offered art, French, music, lots of time outdoors, and new friends beyond their neighborhood. Olga was no longer needed full-time, but Jennifer and Erin felt that she needed the continuity of her care (and her language skills) until Katie was ready for kindergarten.

Katie was a little unsure at first about going to preschool, as most preschoolers are. She was fiercely independent, the "me do it" type, which came as no surprise to her family, but was occasionally a difficulty at school. She hated naps and naptime with a passion, which was ok at home, where there was always someone around. At school, naptime was torture, and she squirmed, sang, and asked constantly, "When's nap over?"

She was curious about why she was lucky enough to have two moms, but no dad. In the world she inhabited, though, plenty of her friends had no dads, and some of them also had two moms. Some of them had two dads, and she wasn't sure exactly how that worked, but it seemed to work pretty well, at least from her limited experience. She was full of questions, not just about families, but about everything. She was good-natured, opinionated, energetic, and compassionate.

~~~

Katie was thrilled with the transition to kindergarten. since kindergarten did not include naps. She was delighted to be at the same school as her mom, at least for now.

Erin made sure her daughter got into classes with teachers best suited for her "spirited" daughter. One day, Erin came into Katie's room and spotted a line-up of stuffed animals, with various limbs removed.

Aghast, she asked Katie what was going on. "These animals had injuries and needed surgery—fast! I'm making sure they're going to be ok." Erin remembered all those days of dolls lined up for class in her bedroom. She bet it was the same in Jennifer's house growing up, too.

~~~

As middle school approached, a new set of decisions emerged. Erin didn't want to leave her school and her mentor teaching position.

Katie was weary of running into her mom in the halls and feeling like she was being watched too closely.

Jennifer wanted to leave her private practice and focus on teaching at the medical school, which she had loved all these years. She would have more time and a more flexible schedule to be with Katie, who might need closer scrutiny. She knew that it was likely to be a roller coaster ride with Katie, and she wanted to be ready.

CHAPTER 32

MIMI

"Life is no brief candle to me. It is a sort of splendid torch which I have got a hold of for the moment, and I want to make it burn as brightly as possible before handing it on to future generations."
—Oscar Wilde

I worried that if I wasn't careful, I was going to get old. As a child, my own small family had been enriched by visits with all my great-aunts and uncles and all the stories they had to tell, or others told about them. Since I'd never had grandparents of my own, I was determined to connect with the children and grandchildren of my cousins. I worried that my younger cousins would go off with their own lives, and the Lockhart legends and history would be lost.

I hadn't heard from Erin and her San Francisco family in a while. As with most young families, "busy" didn't begin to describe what life was like for all of them. I could count on my fingers the number of times we'd been together since that day we'd met in Belfast so long ago.

What better way to build the sense of connection with them that I craved than by traveling together? I called it the "Finding Jamie" tour, which would include, of course, Rathmullan, but a number of other important Irish destinations, including Belfast and Ballinora, along with Derry, Donegal, Doolin, and Dublin. Reciting the destination list out loud reminded me of my childhood recitations of the list of nine great aunts and great uncles, sons and daughters of Katie Lockhart, my great-grandmother, daughter of James Lockhart!

I knew the hardest sell would be Tracey, whose first concern would be looking after her pets, followed by her now-expected reluctance to leave home or change any of her comfortable routines in the safety zone where she could keep her anxiety and depression at bay. I was delighted to get an email from her almost immediately.

"Erin and I are both working on ourselves and it's definitely good for us. I am working on my openness and loving skills, in particular! I really like the idea of us all taking a genealogical-inspired trip to Donegal. I have absolutely no idea when, though."

First hurdle conquered, I reached out to Erin. Almost immediately (unusual for Erin), she responded "I'm looking forward to whatever the adventure brings! Let me know how I can help!

As I began to design the itinerary, looking for things that would appeal to a wide age group and interests, I began to realize that my real goal was not the itinerary. My real intention was to create situations that would lead to discussions and quiet time in pairs, or all together, reflecting on what all this travel between continents over generations meant for each of us.

I considered sharing a list of questions we might think about before going on the trip, but then I realized that might scare them away! I started to look for non-touristy, comfortable places to stay, where we could hang out together in front of a fireplace or in the kitchen, but also withdraw to our own space when some alone time felt appropriate. We were a family of introverts, I realized, including myself.

I decided to book the lodging and share it with my fellow travelers, to lock the arrangements in as much as possible before Tracey or Erin went sideways, which I had to acknowledge, was a very real possibility. Tracey's next email confirmed that concern. "I don't do well away from home or my routine, and I have to be careful to take very good care of myself, but I think I can manage a week, but I wouldn't want to spend much - keeping frugal with it, therefore I might need to cut that a bit short. I'm just thinking it through and communicating. Just to say off the bat, you are a very generous person, and I can imagine you will want to help out, but I want to pay my own way as much as possible! I hope I am not assuming anything, but you have been so generous to me already! Practically speaking, this means I would want to stay in the cheapest possible places, etc.! So hopefully we can manage something like that! I'm really starting to look forward to it! I'm sorry if I've just jumped in and started planning this, but just thinking how I prefer things, and it's good to say."

I read and re-read the email, surprised and delighted that Tracey hadn't changed her mind. I focused on the "I'm really starting to look forward to it" line but also to appreciate her willingness to communicate her considerations up front, rather than having them be a surprise. *Airbnbs* would offer more space and central cooking and living areas with the cost relatively opaque, I hoped, for Tracey and Erin. Time to book the flights and the lodging, one step at a time. I devoted special care to considering not just the destination, lodging, and activities, but also the dynamics and closeness I hoped would develop. I signed up for *23 and Me*, like so many of my friends, to see what technology might add to the genealogical history she'd been doing at the library to prepare for the trip.

Months later, Erin, Katie, and I flew together from San Francisco to Belfast, rented a car at the airport and drove to Tracey's home in West Belfast. Tracey was rightly proud of the improvements she'd added and all the personal touches she was able to do, not possible in all those rental flats she and Erin had inhabited for so many years.

Tracey gave us a tour and introduced us to her new family, two small poodle mixes named Buddy and Pepper. Her friend Molly would be caring for them and would come over after work to take them for their usual walk. We shared a simple breakfast in her garden. Tracey had felt tremendous anxiety about leaving them and her home for the week-long expedition, but that was quickly overcome with her delight in being with her daughter, grand-daughter, and cousin.

The four of us piled in the rental car, along with the luggage, and we set off for Derry. I told them a little about my previous trip to Derry, when Matthew and I had walked the old walls and looked out over the city. On that trip, I had mostly been eager to get to Belfast, to look for Tracey and Erin. I loved telling that story, and Erin and Tracey chimed in, reminding Katie of how she came to have so many cousins and why cousins are important. We stopped for a lunch of fish and chips before heading on to Donegal and Rathmullan, where we'd spend three nights exploring the place where our family story had begun.

I was the only one of the four who had visited Rathmullan and the little village of Ramelton where years before in my search for Tracey and Erin I'd found some Lockhart "cousins." As we drove along the narrow, tree-shaded road with its emerald green grasses alongside, Katie exclaimed, "I feel like I'm in Oz! We're coming in to the Emerald City!"

All of us were struck by the beautiful country scenery, made even more striking by the sunlight shining down through the dappled leaves of the tree tunnels. When we finally reached our destination, the harbor at Rathmullan, Tracey said, "Stop the car! I want a picture of four generations of Lockharts on the very spot where our ancestor James set off for America." I pulled over into a parking space near the water, and we all hopped out. I went over to a woman walking her dog and asked if she'd take our picture for this very special occasion, explaining why we were there. "By the way," I asked, "do you know any Lockharts who live around here? We hope to find some of our cousins!"

I felt a little like I was re-living the movie "Groundhog Day," since I'd already had this experience once before. But I loved seeing the trip through the eyes of my cousins, and they were my gambit of reaching out to people wherever we went, sharing why we were in Ireland, our shared Irish roots, and how lucky we felt to be cousins. The results of my genealogical research confirmed that indeed there were ancestral connections between the Lockharts of

Ramelton and the Lockharts of Rathmullan, and I was eager to revisit the lovely Lockharts I'd met years ago and show them what I'd found.

The dairy farm in Ramelton was unchanged; I had been in touch this time, rather than just popping in on them by surprise as in my previous visit. They were touched that I wanted to reconnect, and the tea and biscuits were every bit as delicious as I remembered. I shared what I'd learned from *23 and Me* about where our ancestry lines crossed. Katie talked about how happy she was to see Ireland for the first time and to learn about family connections. My heart swelled with my young cousin's growing appreciation of her family.

We took long walks along the Rathmullan coastline. We were delighted to find a private guide, Fiona, who led us from the shoreline sculpture commemorating the Flight of the Earls crucial to Irish history, and on through Rathmullan's castle, the ruins of the Carmelite friary and later a Protestant church, and graveyards. Continuing to Ramelton, situated on a picturesque river with a great blue heron posing for our photos we learned about the Scottish settlers (and the Lockharts were among them), the Georgian architecture, and more churches and buildings important to the town's history. Our Airbnb came with a view of Lough Swilly, horses, donkeys and sheep. Katie found watercolors and art paper hidden away in a drawer; she and Tracey sat at a picnic table under sunny blue skies dotted with clouds and painted the views. Tracey and I looked at family photos I had brought, and we compared memories of family members. We cooked a communal dinner of fresh fish and vegetables.

Katie was enthusiastic about the next destination—Doolin, known for traditional Irish music and the Cliffs of Moher. We checked into our cottage, the Cuckoo's Nest, and walked around the tiny town. I arranged a five-mile hike for the next day from a pub downtown with a famous local guide, Seamus McSweeney, over fields and up steep hills to get to the famous Cliffs, instead of being herded along in traffic with tour buses. We cheered each other on the trail and stopped to rest and listen to Seamus' stories of the local area. Katie loved being the cheerleader for the group and was enchanted by the tales and "craic" of our local tour guide. Arriving at the Cliffs, we marveled at their steepness and beauty, wreathed in fog at first, then opening up vistas as the sun burned off the mists. Afterwards, we returned to the cottage, tired but exhilarated by our day of hiking together. We visited all three famous pubs, with local food for our ravenous appetites after the hike, and enjoyed a sampling of music and dancing. Katie was *so* ready for dancing!

The next day, we went down to the little Doolin Pier and set out by a small ferry to Inisheer, the smallest Aran Island, for a day on rented bicycles, miles of ancient stone walls, a shipwreck, and a whole different way of life. On the way back, the sun danced over the Cliffs of Moher from the water. The wind and water were chilly, but all of us had come prepared for weather. "Just like San Francisco in the summer," Katie noted, as she added one more layer. The views were spectacular, a completely different experience than seeing them from the land. The ride was bumpy, bouncing over the waves in the small boat and looking for puffins, my favorite bird, elusive and too tiny to see. By the time we got back, we were ready for warm soup, Irish soda bread, and hot tea, feeling a little beat up by the wind and waves.

Over dinner, Erin suggested an addition to the itinerary—a visit to her father's farm in Ballinora. Both Erin and Brian were most eager for this unplanned detour, even though she had a restless night, wondering what the visit with Katie's grandfather and his family would be like. We were anxious as we set off for the fourth, and most emotionally demanding, stage of our trip. We stayed in an adorable B & B in Cork, balancing our tourist exploration with the deeper dive into family dynamics.

Tracey, who had avoided visiting Brian after the first couple of introductory trips with Erin, had to consciously put aside the memories of all those difficult years as a single mom, struggling to find her way and deal with every challenge on her own. On the outside, she showed no signs of bitterness for those years of hardship and lack of financial or emotional support from Brian --

but on the inside? Who would know how she really felt, because she did not share that part of herself.

Caught in the middle, Erin often felt conflicted. She'd lived half her life wishing desperately she had a father and a larger family. Then she'd found out she had both, and she didn't know exactly what to do with them. She knew they didn't approve of Jennifer, although she also knew they would fall in love with Katie, just as she had been welcomed into their family. They would never understand why Erin had left Ireland or why she hadn't moved back, and Erin found that pressure sometimes suffocating.

Katie's lack of sleep did not come from anxiety over meeting her grandfather for the first time. She was simply drowning in excitement from the Irish scenery, the people she'd met, the intense experiences. She was most excited about getting to Brian's farm, where she was hoping Brian would give her a calf, as he had her mom. She couldn't wait for hands-on experience with all the animals, in a farm setting. Some of her friends loved roller coasters and the experience of arriving at an amusement park; for Katie, the best fun she had was visiting a petting zoo or the SPCA, to hang out with the animals.

As the organizer of the family tour, I felt the anxiety and excitement for all the cousins. I wanted everything to go smoothly, and I wanted unforgettable memories and a newfound sense of closeness. Of course, I knew that most memorable trips involved trip adventures and disasters. What would happen here?

We got an early start from Doolin, passing straight on through Limerick, entertaining each other by making up limericks about our trip as the miles passed quickly. We got settled in our B & B at lunch time and let Brian know we'd arrived. Katie was vibrating with excitement about getting to the farm; she grabbed the phone out of her mom's hand and blurted, "Would now be too soon to come, Brian? I can hardly wait!"

Brian was touched by Katie's excitement, knowing it had been fed by Erin's stories of her visits and close encounters with the animals. He shook his head, finding it a little hard to believe that his farm could hold such attractions for his young granddaughter, but of course, she was a city girl, like her mam. "Of course, come ahead, the sheep, goats, pigs, chickens, cows, and all the rest are eager to meet you! We'll have tea with my family and show you the lay of the land. I'll meet you in Ballinora and then lead you to the farm, to make sure you don't get lost."

Knowing how easy it was to get lost on the tiny Irish farm roads, I was grateful for Brian's offer. We piled back in the car for the short ride to Ballinora and found Brian, waiting for us in his old farm truck. Irrepressible Katie jumped out of the car and ran to the truck, opened the door, and introduced herself to her grandfather. "Just so you know, I'm going to be a vet, and I've been looking forward to today for the entire trip!"

Brian nodded and smiled. "I've been looking forward to today myself, young lady, and I'm eager to see what you think of my little farm. Your mam had told me you had an interest in becoming a vet, and there's a sore need for those, for sure."

Brian pulled out, making sure I was close behind as we made several turns onto smaller and smaller roads. I was sure we were going to end up on goat tracks before we finally arrived at the farm. Brian came over to the car, and Tracey and Erin introduced him to me. "Welcome to my farm, Mimi" Brian said. Or I thought that's what he said. With his very thick Irish accent, I couldn't understand a word. I hoped it would be like Shakespeare, where the more you got into the dialogue, the easier it would be to understand. Apparently, Erin and Tracey had gotten the hang of it, although Erin had said that had happened to her when they first met, too.

The front door of the farmhouse opened, and Brian's mother and sisters and their families came out to welcome them. More introductions followed along with an invitation to come in for tea. Knowing that Katie was eager to get to the animals, Brian said "Katie and I'll be along in a few minutes. She's wanting to say hello to the sheep."

Erin, Tracey and I went into the farmhouse, where Brian's mother and older sister had laid out a feast of tea, pastries, cheese, and sausages! The farmhouse was small, furnished simply but comfortably, with plenty of room to gather around the kitchen table. Large windows looking out on the pastures. A warm fire burning in the fireplace added a sense of Brian's life, focused on the farm he loved and a comfort in being alone. Brian's family was eager to learn about our trip and what life was like in the States; I was interested to find out about life in Ballinora and Cork, comparing it to what Erin had reported from her first visit and the others that had followed.

Brian and Katie joined the family after her introduction to the animals. Flushed and animated, Katie burbled over with excitement about what she'd seen. "I got to feed the baby sheep, look for eggs in the chicken house, and pet the horses. Brian says I can have a ride on his new pony during our visit." Just as Erin had been overwhelmed with Brian's attention when they'd first met, she was now feeling protective of Katie, worried that things were moving a little faster than she was prepared for. She was happy, of course, that Katie was becoming acquainted with her Irish grandfather.

"So how long is your stay in Cork, Mimi?" Brian's mother inquired. "I'm hoping to host you at my house for lunch one day so you get to see a bit more than just the farm," she laughed.

"We're staying three nights in Cork. I've found that it's hard to get a real sense of a place without staying at least that long. I know we'd all like to find some more Irish music and dancing, and I've heard there's night-time kayaking on Lough Hyne, where the bioluminescence in the water is magical!"

"Mimi always makes sure we do things that most people would never think of doing," explained Erin. "I've learned to just enjoy the adventures, since it takes me out of my comfort zone, and that's important."

Brian and Tracey responded, almost in unison "Well, I don't know about that..." and everyone laughed.

"Brian says I can just stay here on the farm if I'd like to, Mom. I bet you're going to say no, but I just wanted to put it out there..."

"You're so right, Katie, you'll not be spending the nights on the farm, but I'm fine if you'd like to spend a day here, if you'd like. I hope you thanked him for the invitation," Erin responded, feeling at ease with putting the brakes on.

We made tentative plans for the lunch party at Brian's mother's house on the last day of our visit and plans for Katie to return to the farm the next day. Music in Cork and the kayaking experience would happen somewhere in between. As they got ready to leave, Brian offered to guide us back to Cork, but I felt sure we could reverse our steps and find our way. Besides, how were we ever going to have a trip adventure if we didn't take any chances?

A couple of hours later, we arrived at our lodging, quite a bit longer than the route we took from Cork on the way to Brian's, which had been about fifteen minutes. We laughed as we wound our way around the single lane farm roads, at times in circles. We finally met a farmer who took pity on us and led us to Cork behind his tractor.

The next day, Brian picked Katie up at the B & B for her day at the farm. The rest of us explored Cork by bicycle. The dedicated bike lanes, sights of the Lee River and impressive architecture, as well as the thousand years of history presented by the bike tour leader, made it a wonderful outing. Since the terrain was relatively flat, we could enjoy the pedaling and not feel used up at the end. Brian brought Katie back in time for dinner and music at a local pub, and we enjoyed swapping stories of our day's adventures. We fell into bed after their busy day, Irish tunes in our dreams and anticipating more adventures.

Brian's mum lived in Kildare, and she was delighted to have us for lunch in the family home where Brian grew up. With eight siblings, many with children of their own, it was to be quite a lively affair. The cousins got up early and talked about what these new family relationships might mean. Jennifer was not on the trip, of course, but Erin wondered whether Katie might mention her other mom, or if one of the siblings might bring her up. Even though Brian described his family as "quite religious," they had certainly welcomed these visitors from the land beyond the rain.

We arrived in Kildare mid-morning and did a little exploring before finding Brian's mom's house (we'd left plenty of time to get lost). When we arrived, we were greeted by cousins of all ages. Katie was quickly surrounded by teenage counterparts, who were fascinated by her stories of the US. Tracey and I talked with Brian's siblings about their lives in Ireland; we shared stories of our "Finding Jamie" tour and what we'd learned about our ancestor, James Lockhart. After a bit of mingling and getting acquainted, Brian's mother announced that lunch was ready, served buffet style. Everyone continued their conversations while enjoying a traditional Irish meal.

Afterwards, we all pitched in to help Brian's mum clear up the dishes. Brian took Tracey aside and asked if she might be willing to walk outside with him for a few minutes. Tracey's anxiety level hit the stratosphere, wondering what he planned to say and how she might respond, since they'd had no conversation beyond social niceties in their very few meetings together and their phone calls to arrange Erin's visits when she was in college.

Brian pointed to a chair on the porch for her to sit down, and he sat down across from her. "I've been wanting to say these words for a long time, so please don't interrupt me or put me off. Expressing my feelings, or even just knowing what my feelings are, has never come easy to me. I just want you to know that I'm so very sorry I let you down all those years ago when you asked for help with Erin. I'm even sorrier that I continued to be an eejit for years afterward. I can't explain it, and I can't make up for it, but I wanted to just say these words and have you see that I mean them. I'm sorry."

Tracey was quiet as she tried to figure out what to say. "Brian, I don't think there's much point in raking over the past. What's done is done. I appreciate the apology, and I forgive you. I was pretty desperate back then, but I learned that I could make it on my own, and I could raise my little girl. That was a big lesson for me, and you're not being there helped me learn it. Let's not do the Irish thing with grudges; let's do something different: let's celebrate Erin and her beautiful daughter Katie. Now they both know they have families both in the States and in Ireland. In spite of all the odds, we've come to a different place, you and I, and I'm grateful for the change. Now let's go back inside before I do something stupid like bawl my head off."

As they walked back inside, all the conversation stopped, and everyone looked at Brian and Tracey. Brian broke the ice by laughing, "Now what are you looking at? You've all been after me all these years to make a family, and now I've brought you one, so give me a break, why don't you?"

Tracey thanked Brian and all the family for the warm welcome and bounteous lunch, as they gathered themselves together for the ride back to Cork, to get ready for the night-time kayaking on Lough Hyne, with its magical luminescence. Tracey wasn't sure the night-time magic could be any more impressive than the magic she'd just experienced, and never expected, in Kildare.

Erin knew better than to press her mum for details of the conversation with Brian on the porch, but of course, the three cousins were curious. The car ride back to Cork was unusually quiet at first, then Katie piped up with her summary of the trip so far: "I LOVE Ireland. I love my new cousins, I love the farm, I love the beautiful sights we've seen and the people we've met. I loved getting lost and being rescued by a farmer on a tractor! Now *that* would never happen in San Francisco! I know we're going to have fun kayaking tonight, but then tomorrow, we're heading for Dublin, and that means the end of the trip is coming. I don't want it to end—ever!"

Tracey laughed. "You sound just like I did when I came to Ireland for the first time! Of course, *you* have to go back to finish high school, but *I* was able to stay. And you'll be able to come back! I hope you'll come back often, and I know your grandfather and his family want that, too."

CHAPTER 33

KATIE

"We discovered that education is not something which the teacher does, but that it is a natural process which develops spontaneously in the human being."
—Maria Montessori

Katie returned with her mom to San Francisco after the "Finding Jamie" tour, surprised by how clearly she saw her future. She had had no desire whatsoever to return to the United States, her birthplace. As soon as her feet had touched the beautiful green grasses of Ireland, she felt at home. She had cherished her time in her mom's birthplace and found it easy to understand why her Mamoo had resisted returning to the United States when Erin was growing up.

Her grandma had told her the story of arriving in Ireland, falling in love with the landscape, the history and culture, and the people, having no family to call her own back in the States. She'd even heard the infamous story of the weekend romance with her biological grandfather, and now she'd met the man who had finally emerged when his biological daughter had tested his will by pushing her mom to make one last attempt to establish his paternity and the responsibilities that went along with it.

She couldn't see herself living on a farm in an isolated village in the Irish republic, but she was intrigued with the idea of getting acquainted with her grandfather, her Irish history, and her grandmother's story. What better way than to move to Ireland and dive deep into the history that had shaped the Irish immigrant family she'd just learned about?

Katie was fully engaged in her junior year learning about universities. She was curious about Erin's memories of her time-warped senior year in California, and she grilled her mom about her experiences. Katie was grateful that they would have two whole years to do the search, instead of compacted into the two months that Erin had described.

Curious about all possible options, Katie was willing to consider her mom's suggestions of west coast colleges that Erin had suggested — Reed, Pitzer, Occidental, UCSC, Stanford, Lewis & Clark, and UC-Davis. Katie wanted to see UC-Davis because of her interest in veterinary school and to get a sense of what a large state school might be like. She also lobbied effectively for a tour of UK colleges as well, with full support from Mamoo: Oxford, Cambridge, Queens in Belfast, and Trinity College in Dublin. Katie knew that Erin would favor a small, co-ed, liberal arts college, as she had, but would prefer a college on the west coast, close to home — at least in the same time zone.

Katie's grades and test scores were in the spectacular range, and she, too, had a story to tell in her admissions essay. She resisted the idea of considering schools on the east coast, even though her mom encouraged her to at least give Hamilton, Erin's alma mater, a try.

"You know me, ma, I want to see it all. What about Mamoo? What do you think she'd want me to see? Does she have a list, too? And what about Mimi? Didn't she help you with your list?"

"Let's ask them, and let's figure out how we're going to cram all this travel into your very busy school and social life. When I did my college search, Mimi hired a private college counselor to help sort things out, and it made all the difference. Would you like to invest some time in doing that?"

"How did it work?" Katie was always interested in the details, wanting to do her own research whenever possible.

"I remember an enormous deck of cards with what seemed like a million different characteristics important to students and families trying to make this choice. Things like location, size, subject matter specialty, cost, and so much more. Since I've never been great at making choices or decisions, it took me several sessions just to work through the cards, but I'm so glad we did. It really helped narrow down the list of places I wanted to visit and the type of college I wanted."

"I knew from the start that I wanted a small, east coast, liberal arts co-ed college, but it was really helpful to think through all the choices there were. Of course, for me, it not only had to have all the characteristics I dreamed about, the college had to offer me a full ride scholarship. You know that my mum had no money to send me to college, no matter where I went or what my preferences were. You are privileged to have more choices," Erin emphasized.

"Believe me, I know a lot more about privilege than I did before we went on the Finding Jamie tour, and I'm a lot more grateful than I used to be," Katie confided. "Maybe you've noticed."

"Oh, sweetheart, you bet I've noticed. We all learned a lot about ourselves and each other on that trip, not to mention how lucky we are."

After multiple sessions with the counselor, conversations with Tracey and Mimi, and research Katie did on her own, the list of colleges to visit was much shorter than expected, and the most important characteristic turned out to be "best veterinary school."

Katie found only one east coast school on that list, Cornell, and she thought the east coast was the worst geographic choice—not close to California and not close to Ireland. So the east coast tour went away. Katie knew that Erin felt a little sad that Hamilton didn't make the cut.

In the US schools, UC-Davis and Texas A & M were at the top. Mimi and Tracey ruled out Texas A & M immediately, thanks to their strong UT-Austin ties. "No child of mine will ever be an Aggie," Tracey swore. Katie had no desire whatsoever to trade California for Texas, which she considered to be troglodytic politically.

Katie's first choice was an excellent veterinary school in Ireland, close to her Irish roots, beloved grandmother, and her grandfather's farm. But the best veterinary schools in the UK were the Royal Veterinary College at the University of London; Cambridge University (where Mimi and Matthew's son had done a post-doc), University of Liverpool, and the Universities of Edinburgh and Glasgow in Scotland.

The college exploration trip became ten days in the UK, starting in London, then Cambridge, Edinburgh and Glasgow, ending up in Dublin, which Katie felt sure would be her top choice, if she could get in. She'd been there, after all, and she felt a strong connection. UC Davis in California was an easy day trip.

Katie was thrilled that Jennifer decided to take the trip with her. Katie had been disappointed that Jennifer had sat out the Finding Jamie tour, but she knew Jennifer felt the trip was really most special for "the cousins." Katie was excited that now Jennifer would have her turn, and she could share her love for science and all things related to the medical field with her other mom.

Each school and location had something special and different to offer: Davis was close and had a superb program. Katie considered it too close and ruled it out on that basis. London was amazing, and the program absolutely first rate, but Katie was afraid she'd be too distracted by everything else going on. She crossed it off her list. Then they arrived in Cambridge, and Katie gasped, eyes opened wide, absolutely swept off her feet. "It's like wandering onto a set for Harry Potter," she exclaimed to Jennifer.

They joined throngs of other students from all over the world, most of them on bicycles. They sat in on a couple of classes in the vet program, viewed the labs, and met students and faculty. They observed a giraffe lowered onto an operating table in a surgical suite for life-saving surgery.

One student invited them to "high table" for dinner at Kings College for the "insider" view of campus life. They looked around at the paintings of historic alumni and the head table, with professors in gowns. Katie had big eyes as she wandered around the grounds, imagining herself there as a student. She loved the smaller size and scale of the University and surrounding town, the quality of the program, the people she met, the beauty of the setting. "Honestly, Mom, I don't think I need to see any more! I can *feel* myself being here!" Katie gushed.

"Don't forget, you have to get accepted, and that isn't going to be easy! Besides, we have three more schools to visit, and we don't want to miss out on a chance to see Scotland!" They compromised by adding an additional day to their visit to Cambridge, and then set off for Edinburgh and Glasgow, close to each other in distance but quite different in atmosphere. The academic programs were similar and excellent, but Katie found that they weren't Cambridge. She'd apply to them, of course, along with the University of London, but the list was taking shape.

Last stop was Dublin. Tracey came down to join them for a day, as they explored Trinity College for the second time. The first time was on the Finding Jamie tour) but this time, their focus was on the Veterinary School, which they found perfectly fine, but without the distinction and reputation of the programs in London and Scotland. By the end of their time at Trinity, Katie began to wonder if maybe Dublin was a little too close to her other relatives, a little like Davis in the US. She wanted more independence and didn't want to be tempted to rely on family, when she needed to make new friends and have new experiences on her own.

By the time she and Jennifer arrived back in San Francisco, Katie had her application list completed. She'd decided to apply to all the schools she'd visited, and she prayed she'd be accepted by Cambridge, specifically Girton College, known to have a higher percentage of acceptance, increasing her chances of admission.

CHAPTER 34

ERIN

"The dialectic between change and continuity is a painful but deeply instructive one, in personal life as in the life of a people."
—Adrienne Rich

Spring sunshine beamed in the kitchen window, as Erin and Jennifer enjoyed the more relaxed pace of a weekend. Erin enjoyed watching Jennifer savor her French press Peet's coffee while Erin sipped her Irish breakfast tea, loaded up with cream and sugar. The centerpiece on the table was Katie's acceptance letter from Cambridge.

Katie was clattering around upstairs, Irish singer Lisa Hannigan's tunes wafting down the stairs. From time to time, she bounded down to ask a question or move a load of her belongings into the storage closet, humming Irish folk tunes as she moved about the house. All this energy was a little unnerving for the parents of this usually late-sleeping adolescent.

"I guess I might have known this was going to happen. After all, I did the same thing, but in reverse. Why would I think Katie would be satisfied living in the US, where I could try to get her do what I wanted her to do?" Erin hadn't worried too much about the Cambridge college application, figuring the chances of Katie's getting in were small. As it turned out, UC Davis waitlisted her, wrecking Erin's plans of having their daughter nearby. Erin sighed when she learned that Katie had decided to do her undergraduate veterinary degree at Cambridge University, and stay on for the two years of veterinary school afterwards.

Jennifer raised her eyebrows and snorted. "We raised her to be independent-minded like we were, to value her Irish roots, and to learn how to find her own way in a very confusing world. That sounds like success to me," Jennifer said, trying to comfort Erin. "Imagine how your mom must have felt when you left her, the Church, and Ireland for the US when you were still in high school. You never looked back!"

Katie poked her head in, arms full of stuffed animals. "You can never throw any of these away, ok? I just don't want them to be lonely in my room while I'm gone," she explained. Erin burst into tears. "*I'm* the one who's going to be lonely," she whimpered.

Katie put the animals down and gave Erin a hug. "I want you to be excited for me! I get to do exactly what I've wanted to do for my whole life, in the place that has become more special than I can even explain. You, of all people must understand that, right?"

"Understanding it is one thing, but *feeling* it is quite another," Jennifer explained.

Katie dragged up a chair, poured herself a cup of tea, and made breakfast seem like a party. During the week, all three of them were on the run to school or work, and on the weekends, Katie rarely emerged from her cozy bedroom until mid-day. Today was special!

"Let's have a Pooh day," Katie said with a smile, holding Eeyore, reminding Erin of their shared past. Both shed a few tears. "You know I'll miss you both madly, but I know you'll come see me, right?"

Erin's mobile phone played Tracey's special ringtone, and Erin picked up, putting her on speaker. "How did you know we were just talking about you?"

"Just psychic, I guess..."

Katie was bursting with her news. "Mamoo, I got into Cambridge! I'm coming to the UK! We'll practically be neighbors!"

Tracey flashed back to her decision to come to California when she'd heard Jennifer and Erin were considering daycare for her precious granddaughter. "Not while there is breath in my body! I know what it's like to be raised by strangers, and I'm not having it, do you understand?!"

She gave a celebratory hoot, which set off her dogs in the background—a symphony of congratulations to the soon-to-be vet. Secretly, she'd been hoping UC Davis would not come through and a UK school would be the winner. Now she was over the moon at the prospect of having her granddaughter nearby.

"I bet your mom is not quite as thrilled as I am with the news, Katie," Tracey wondered.

Erin got caught between a giggle and a sob, which made all of them laugh. "My head is over the moon, and my heart is in shreds."

Katie's phone, never out of her sight, began to ring in the middle of the conversation with Tracey. It was Mimi. Katie put her on speaker, too.

"It sounds like a family reunion! What's the latest?" Mimi inquired.

"I did it, Mimi! I'm going to Cambridge!" Katie blurted, with cheers from her moms in the background.

"You're carrying on the Lockhart family tradition, Katie. Well done! I guess we know where the next family reunion will be. How many of your American cousins do you think we can round up for a trip from the land beyond the rain to the other side of the pond?"

Tracey chimed in. "I think it's my turn to host. Whoever thought that I, the person who'd given up on having a family, would be the host of a reunion in my own home at last!" Now that she'd become closer to her American cousins and their daughters, on the cusp of growing up themselves, she felt confident that the Lockhart family traditions and legends might live on, through their own visits to Ireland.

Mimi was silent for a few moments, as she looked back with pride at what she'd nurtured, one cousin at a time. She loved telling the stories, over and over, of the daring James Lockhart who'd ventured out to the land beyond the rain and everything that had happened since.

AUTHOR'S NOTE

Most of this story is true. James Lockhart was my great-great-grandfather, and he crossed the sea to America from Rathmullan, Ireland in 1840 during the Great Hunger/Potato Famine. He married my great-grandmother, Julia Emma Abbott in Brushy Creek, Alabama. They ended up in Montgomery County Texas, and had nine children. Key events in their history are documented in public records; everything else is my own imagined story. Many of the stories of the other characters, still living, given different names in the novel, are based on actual conversations, communications, letters, legal documents and press accounts, and have been expanded and supplemented by my own creation of the backstory, to add depth and continuity to the narrative. Some characters are fictional, imagining the future for the next generation of cousins to come.

ABOUT THE AUTHOR

Mary Male is a first-time novelist who lives in Santa Cruz, California, with her husband and two dogs. She graduated from the University of Texas with a BA in French and English and an MA in special education. She earned her Ph.D. from the University of Southern California. A former educator, she has written several textbooks and curriculum guides. She loves learning new things and considers the novel-writing experience among the most exhilarating and challenging things she's ever done. Her favorite activities are traveling and being with family and friends.

ACKNOWLEDGMENTS

I am so grateful for my family, who have supported me every step of the way in writing this family saga. My husband, David Brick, listened to me read every word of it, read and re-read it multiple times, edited it, and encouraged me every step of the way. My son, Jonathan Barclay, listened to the stories and came on his first trip to Ireland this summer to learn about his roots. My step-son, Cameron Brick, has always taken an interest in and supported my attempts to try new things. My interest in family history and genealogy was stimulated from a young age by my great-aunts and uncles on both sides of my family, and I was able to build on their letters, memories, and stories.

Turning the novel and into a published book was boosted immeasurably by my friends at the Todos Santos International Writers' Workshop, including my workshop leader, novelist Gordon Chaplin, my dear friend Margreet Fledderus, and new workshop friends Kegan Doyle, Joy Abbott, Ivonne Benitez, Anja Boersma, and Elisa Shevitz.

My Santa Cruz Book Club led by Edna Elkins and participants Phyllis Alturias, Caroline Curry, Toni Danzig, Gail Evans, Peg Lacey, Sue Lawson, Lillian Miranda Cookie, Francine Raphael, and Cookie Sherman, gave me the courage to keep on writing; they served as the first reviewers. My best friends Susan Hollon and Susan Luttrell Burns, who are characters in the book, have traveled with me through life from early days in Norman, Oklahoma, and have supported me in all my endeavors. Rue Turner (who introduced me to my husband long ago) provided helpful early feedback and continuing support.

Sylvia Lockhart and her sons Alastair and Trevor of Ramelton, Ireland, welcomed us in as Lockhart cousins on two trips to Ireland, providing us with countless genealogical documents and cups of tea and biscuits as we searched for our relational roots together.

Ed Dixon, my dear high school friend now celebrated composer, playwright and actor wrote the wedding song in the book.

Damien Peters, my Irish editor, helped my understanding of Irish history and culture, as well as proofreading and editing for flow. Ahmed Moghazy created the cover design.

I have dedicated the book to my cousins Tina and Aoífe, who are central to the story, but my other cousins have been a part of this journey for a very long time, too, as has my brother Frank, who was there when the story began.

Made in the USA
San Bernardino, CA
11 July 2019